Someone
To Watch
Over Me

LISA KLEYPAS

SOMEONE TO WATCH OVER ME

AVON BOOKS ◆ NEW YORK

AVON BOOKS, INC.
1350 Avenue of the Americas
New York, New York 10019

Back flap author photo by Larry Sengbush
Published by arrangement with the author

ISBN: 0-7394-0266-8

www.avonbooks.com/romance

To my mother, who made this book possible by taking care of my son Griffin every day while I wrote.

This labor of love included making at least two hundred peanut butter sandwiches cut into squares, changing approximately four hundred diapers, and watching untold hours of "Thomas the Tank Engine."

Thank you, Mimi, from Griffin and me.

One

From the moment Grant Morgan saw the woman, he knew that—despite her beauty—she would never be any man's bride.

He followed the waterman through the swirls of fog, cold mist clinging to his skin and forming beads on his wool coat. He kept both hands shoved deep in his pockets, while his gaze chased restlessly around the scene. The river looked oily in the dull glow of lamps hung on the massive blocks of granite near the landing. Two or three tiny boats ferried passengers across the Thames, bobbing like toys on the water. Chilly waves lapped against the steps and face of an embankment wall. A wintry March breeze curled around Grant's face and ears and slipped persistently beneath the edge of his cravat. He suppressed a shiver as he stared at the sloshing black river. No one could survive much longer than twenty minutes in water that cold.

"Where is the body?" An impatient frown tugged at Grant's brow. He reached inside his coat, fingering the case of his pocket watch. "I don't have all night."

The Thames waterman stumbled as he twisted his head to glance at the man following him. The drifting mist surrounded them in a yellow-gray haze, causing him to squint in the effort to see better. "Ye're Morgan, aren't ye? Mr. Morgan hisself . . . Why, no one will believe it when I tell 'em. A man who guards the king . . . I would ha' thought you above such dirty business as this."

"Unfortunately not," Grant muttered.

"This way, sir . . . and mind yer step. The stairs is awful slick by the water, specially on a damp night like this."

Stiffening his jaw, Grant made his way down to the small, soaked form that had been hauled onto the landing stairs. In the course of his detective work he often saw dead bodies, but drowning victims were surely among the most unpleasant. The body had been left facedown, but it was clearly female. She was spread akimbo like a rag doll abandoned by a careless child, the skirts of her dress heaped in a dripping mass around her legs.

Crouching beside her, Grant clasped the woman's shoulder with a leather-gloved hand and began to turn her over. He recoiled instantly, startled, as she began to cough and retch salt water, her body spasming.

The waterman yelped in terror behind him, then drew nearer. "I thought she was dead." His voice shook with amazement. "She was cold meat, I swear it!"

"Idiot," Grant muttered. How long had this poor woman been left in the bitter cold while the waterman had sent for a Bow Street Runner to investigate? Her chances of survival would have been far greater had she been taken care of immediately. As it was, her odds weren't good. He flipped the woman over and lifted her head to his knee, her long hair soaking his trousers. Her skin was ashen in the murky light, and there was a swelling lump on the side of her head. Even so, the delicate, distinctive features were recognizable. He knew her.

"My God," Grant breathed. He made a point of never being surprised by anything . . . but to find Vivien Rose Duvall here, like this . . . It was inconceivable.

Her eyes half opened, dull with the knowledge of her imminent death. But Vivien was not the kind of woman to slip away without a struggle. She whimpered and reached upward, her hand brushing the front of his waistcoat in a feeble attempt to save herself. Spurred into action, Grant locked his arms around her and hauled her upward. She was small and compact, but the skirts of her waterlogged gown nearly doubled her weight. Grant held her high against his chest, giving a grunt of discomfort as the icy salt water soaked through his own clothes.

"Will you take 'er to Bow Street, Mr. Morgan?" the waterman chattered, hastening to follow Grant as he took the steps two at a time. "I 'spect I should go too, an' give my name to Sir Ross. I done someone a favor, didn't I, finding the lady afore she croaked. I wouldn't take no thanks, o' course . . . just to do the right thing is enough . . . but there might be a reward, mightn't there?"

"Find Dr. Jacob Linley," Grant said harshly, interrupting the man's eager speculation. "He's usually at Tom's coffeehouse this time of night. Tell him to come to my residence at King Street."

"I can't," the waterman protested. "I 'as to work, ye know . . . Why, I could earn five shillings yet tonight."

"You'll be paid when you bring Linley to King Street."

"But what if I can't find 'im?"

"You'll bring him there within a half hour," Grant said curtly, "or I'll have your boat confiscated—and I'll arrange a three-day stay for you in a prison hulk. Is that motivation enough?"

"I always thought you was a fine fellow," the waterman said sourly, "until I met you. You're not a-tall like they write you in the papers. Hours I've spent in the taverns whilst they read aloud about yer doings . . ." He trotted away, disappointment evident in every line of his squatty form.

Grant's mouth curved in grim amusement. He was well aware of the way his exploits were described in the papers. Editors and writers had exaggerated his accomplishments until he was made to seem superhuman. People regarded him as a legend, not as a normal man with flaws.

He had made the job of Bow Street Runner into a highly profitable one, earning a fortune from recovering stolen property for banks. He had, on occasion, taken other kinds of cases—locating an abducted heiress, serving as a personal guard to a visiting monarch, tracking down murderers—but banks were always his preferred clients. With each case solved, his name had garnered more celebrity, until he was discussed in every coffee shop and tavern in London.

To Grant's amusement, the *ton* had taken him to its bejeweled bosom, clamoring for his presence at their social functions. It was said that a ball's success was assured if the hostess was able to write "Mr. Morgan will attend" at the bottom of the invitation. Yet for all his apparent popularity with the nobility, it was clear to all that he was not one of them. He was more a figure of entertainment than an accepted member of the high social circles he frequented. Women were excited by the notion that he was a potentially dangerous character, and men wanted his friendship in order to appear more brave and worldly themselves. Grant was aware that he would never be accepted except in the most superficial way. And he would never be trusted by the *ton* . . . He knew too many of their dirty secrets, their vulnerabilities, their fears and desires.

A gust of frosty air whirled around him, making the woman in his arms moan and tremble. Clutching his unwieldy burden more tightly, he left the embankment and crossed a cobblestoned street coated with mud and manure. He strode through a small, square court filled with stagnant water barrels, a fetid pigsty, and a cart with broken wheels. Covent Garden was littered with courts like these, from which dark, winding rookeries spread out in disease-ridden webs. Any gentleman in his right mind would be terrified to venture in this area of the city, rife with thieves' kitchens, whores, bullies, and criminals who would kill for a few shillings. But Grant was hardly a gentleman, and the London underworld held no terrors for him.

The woman's head lolled on his shoulder, her weak, cool breath hitting his chin. "Well, Vivien," he murmured, "there was a time I wanted you in my arms ... but this wasn't exactly what I had planned."

He found it hard to believe he was carrying London's most desirable female past Covent Garden's tumbledown booths and open stalls. Butchers and peddlers paused to stare curiously as he passed, while prostitutes ventured from the shadows. "Here, laddie," a sunken-cheeked scarecrow of a woman called, "got a nice fresh cream pot for ye!"

"Some other time," Grant said sarcastically, ignoring the whore's eager cawing.

He crossed the northwest corner of the square and reached King Street, where the decaying buildings turned abruptly into a row of tidy town houses, coffeehouses, and a publisher or two. It was a clean, prosperous street with bow-fronted houses inhabited by the upper class. Grant had purchased an elegant, airy three-story air town house there. The busy headquarters at Bow Street was only a short step away, but it seemed far removed from this serene location.

Swiftly Grant mounted the steps of his town house and gave the mahogany door a resounding kick. When there was no response from within, he drew back and kicked again. Suddenly the door opened and his housekeeper appeared, spluttering with protests at his cavalier treatment of the polished wood paneling.

Mrs. Buttons was a pleasant-faced woman in her fifties, kind of heart but bottled-up, steel-spined, and possessed of stern religious convictions. It was no secret that she disapproved of Grant's chosen profession, abhorring the physical violence and corruption he dealt with as a matter of course. Yet she tirelessly received the wide assortment of underworld callers who came to the town house, treating all with equal parts of politeness and reserve.

Like the other Bow Street Runners who worked under the direction of Sir Ross Cannon, Grant had become so immersed in the world of darkness that he sometimes questioned how much difference there was between himself and the criminals he pursued. Mrs. Buttons had once told Grant of her hopes that he would someday step into the light of Christian truth. "I'm beyond saving," he had replied cheerfully. "You'd better direct your ambitions toward an attainable goal, Mrs. Buttons."

As she beheld the dripping burden in her employer's arms, the housekeeper's normally unflappable face went slack with amazement. "Good Lord!" Mrs. Buttons exclaimed. "What happened?"

Grant's muscles were beginning to tire from the strain of carrying the woman's limp weight so far. "A near drowning," he said curtly, pushing past the housekeeper as he headed for the stairs. "I'm taking her to my room."

"But how? Who?" Mrs. Buttons gasped, making a visible effort to recover herself. "Shouldn't she be brought to a hospital?"

"She's an acquaintance of mine," he said. "I want her seen by a private doctor. God knows what they would do to her at a hospital."

"An acquaintance," the housekeeper repeated, hurrying to keep pace with his rapid strides. It was clear she was burning to know more, but wouldn't presume to ask.

"A lady of the evening, actually," Grant said dryly.

"A lady of the ... and you've brought her here ..." Her voice reeked with disapproval. "Sir, once again you have outdone yourself."

A brief grin crossed his face. "Thank you."

"It was not a compliment," the housekeeper informed him. "Mr. Morgan, wouldn't you prefer to have one of the guest rooms prepared?"

"She'll stay in mine," he said in a tone that quashed further argument.

Frowning, Mrs. Buttons directed a housemaid to wipe up the puddles they had left on the inlaid floors of the amber marble entranceway.

The town house, with its long windows, Sheraton furniture, and English hand-knotted carpets, was the kind of place Grant had once never dared to dream of living in. It was a far cry from the crowded flat he had occupied as a small child, three rooms crammed with the eight offspring of a middle-class bookseller and his wife. Or the succession of orphanages and workhouses that had come later, when his father had been thrown into debtor's prison and the family had fallen to pieces.

Grant had eventually found himself on the streets, until a Covent Garden fishmonger had taken pity and given him steady work and a pallet to sleep on at night. Snuggled up against the heat of the kitchen stove, Grant had dreamed of something better, something more, though his dreams had never taken precise shape until the day he met a Bow Street Runner.

The Runner had been patrolling the jostling market square and had caught a thief who had snatched a fish from the fishmonger's stall. Grant had stared wide-eyed at the Runner in his smart red waistcoat, armed with cutlass and pistols. He had seemed larger, finer, more powerful than ordinary men. Grant had immediately known that his only hope of escaping the life he had been consigned to was to become a Runner. He had enlisted in the Foot Patrol at age eighteen, was promoted to the Day Patrol within a year, and a few months later was chosen by Sir Ross Cannon to complete the elite force of a half dozen Bow Street Runners.

To prove his worthiness, Grant had hurled himself into his work with unflagging zeal, treating each case as if it required a personal sense of vengeance. He went to any lengths to catch a culprit, once following a murderer across the Channel to apprehend him in France. As success mounted on success, Grant had begun to charge exorbitant fees for his private services, which had only made him more sought-after.

Acting on advice from a wealthy client who owed him a favor, Grant had invested in shipping and textile companies, purchased a half interest in a hotel, and bought several choice pieces of property on the west side of London. With some luck and determination, he had climbed far higher than God or man had intended. At age thirty, he could retire with a comfortable fortune. But he couldn't bring himself to resign from the Bow Street force. The thrill of the chase, the lure of danger, were strong, almost physical needs he could never seem to satisfy. He didn't care to dwell on exactly why he couldn't settle down and lead a normal life, but he was certain it didn't speak well of his character.

Reaching his bedroom, Grant brought Vivien to the massive mahogany tester bed with draped swags carved at the headboards and foot. Much of his furniture, including the bed, had been specially made to suit his proportions. He was a tall, big-framed man, for whom the tops of doorframes and ceiling beams posed a frequent hazard.

"Oh, the counterpane!" Mrs. Buttons exclaimed as Vivien's clothes saturated the heavy velvet embroidered with gold and blue silk. "It will be ruined beyond repair!"

"Then I'll buy another," Grant said, flexing his sore arms and stripping off his drenched coat. He dropped his coat to the floor and bent over Vivien's still form. Intent on removing her clothes as quickly as possible, he tugged at the front of her gown. A curse escaped his lips as the buttons and hooks remained obstinately entrenched in the shrunken wet wool.

Grumbling about the damage that was being done to the velvet counterpane, Mrs. Buttons endeavored to assist him, then pulled back with a frustrated sigh. "They'll have to be cut off her, I suppose. Shall I fetch the scissors?"

Grant shook his head and reached for his right boot. In a smooth move born of long habit, he extracted an ivory-handled knife with a six-inch spearpoint blade.

The housekeeper gaped as he began to cut through the gown's thick woven bodice as if it were butter. "Oh, my," she faltered.

Grant focused intently on the work at hand. "No one can wield a knife like a former Covent Garden fishmonger," he remarked dryly, spreading the sides of the gown wide to reveal a wealth of white linen undergarments. Vivien's chemise was soaked and plastered to her snowy skin, revealing the rose-colored points of her nipples beneath. Although Grant had seen countless female bodies, something about Vivien's barely clad form made him hesitate. He struggled with the unaccountable feeling that he was violating something—someone—tender and virginal. Ludicrous, considering the fact that Vivien Duvall was an accomplished courtesan.

"Mr. Morgan," the housekeeper said, fidgeting with the edges of her large white apron, "if you would prefer, I can have one of the housemaids assist me in removing Miss . . ."

"Duvall," Grant supplied softly.

"Miss Duvall's garments."

"I'll see to our guest," Grant murmured. "I'll wager at least a regiment's worth of men have had the privilege of seeing Miss Duvall naked. She'd be the first to say, 'Get the job done and modesty be

damned.' '' Besides, after the trouble he'd gone to
tonight, he was entitled to this one small pleasure.

"Yes, sir." She gave him an odd, considering
look, as if he weren't quite behaving like himself.
And perhaps he wasn't. A strange feeling suffused
him, the chill from the outside mingling with a heat
that burned at his core.

Stone-faced, Grant continued to cut away the wet
clothes, slicing through one sleeve and then the
other. As he lifted Vivien's slim upper torso and
yanked the sodden wool from beneath her, someone walked through the half-open door and gasped
loudly.

It was Kellow, his valet, a dignified young man
with a prematurely balding head and a pair of
round spectacles settled firmly on his nose. His
eyes seemed to fill the spectacle lenses as he beheld
his employer standing with a knife over the half-
clad body of the unconscious woman. "Oh, dear
God!"

Grant turned to fix him with a ferocious scowl.
"Try to be of some use, will you? Get one of my
shirts. And some towels. And now that I think of
it, some tea and brandy. Now, *hurry*."

Kellow started to reply, appeared to think better
of it, and proceeded to fetch the required articles.
Carefully averting his eyes from the woman on the
bed, he handed a fresh shirt to Mrs. Buttons and
fled the room.

Grant's growing need to have Vivien clothed and
warm overrode any desire to see her naked. He
caught only a brief glimpse of her body as he and
the housekeeper worked to pull Vivien's arms

through the long linen sleeves . . . but his brain gathered the image greedily and kept it to savor later.

Vivien wasn't perfect, but the promise of delight was captured in her imperfections. She was charmingly short-waisted, as so many petite women were, with gorgeous round breasts and softly dimpled knees. Her smooth abdomen was crowned with a triangle of spicy red hair just a few shades darker than the sunset locks on her head. No wonder she was the most highly paid prostitute in England. She was lush, pretty, dainty . . . the kind of woman any man would want to keep in bed for days.

They weighted Vivien with linens and heavy blankets, and Mrs. Buttons wrapped her stiff, salt-tainted hair in one of the towels Kellow had brought. "She's a lovely woman," the housekeeper said, her face softening with reluctant pity. "And young enough to change her life for the better. I hope the Lord will choose to spare her."

"She won't die," Grant said shortly. "I won't allow it." He touched the pure ivory curve of Vivien's forehead, using his thumb to brush a tendril of hair beneath the towel. Carefully he laid a cold cloth over a bruise at her temple. "Though it seems someone will be disappointed by her survival."

"Pardon, sir, but I don't follow . . . oh." Her eyes widened as Grant's fingertips swept gently over Vivien's throat, indicating the shadowy bruises that encircled her slim neck. "It looks as if someone tried to . . . to . . ."

"Strangle her," he said matter-of-factly.

"Who would do such a thing?" Mrs. Buttons wondered aloud, her forehead creased with horror.

"Most often in the case of a murdered woman, it's a husband or lover." His lips twitched with a humorless smile. "Females always seem to fear strangers, when it's usually the men they know who do them harm."

Shaking her head at the ugly thought, Mrs. Buttons stood and smoothed her apron. "If it pleases you, sir, I'll send up some salve for Miss Duvall's bruises and scrapes, and wait downstairs for the doctor's arrival."

Grant nodded, barely aware of the housekeeper leaving the room as he stared at Vivien's expressionless face. Gently he rearranged the cloth on her forehead. He stroked the curve of her pale cheek with a single fingertip, and made a sound of grim amusement in his throat. "I swore you would rue the day you made a fool of me, Vivien," he murmured. "But the opportunity has come a hell of lot sooner than I expected."

Two

*S*he found herself in a waking nightmare of cold and pain. The act of breathing was an unwelcome burden on her lungs. Her throat and chest were on fire, as if she had been scoured on the inside. Trying to speak, she emitted a rough, bleating sound, and flinched in agony. "Oh . . ."

Strong hands adjusted her position, wedging a pillow beneath her head and neck . . . brushing a straggling lock of hair away from her forehead. A growl of a voice fell on her ears. "Don't try to talk. Here, this will help." She felt the edge of a warm spoon against her lips and recoiled slightly. But the man beside her persisted, cupping a huge hand around the back of her head and bringing the spoon to her mouth once more. Her teeth clattered against the metal, her body seized by trembling she couldn't control. She swallowed a spoonful of hot sugared tea, though the movement of her throat muscles was pure agony.

"Good girl. Take another."

She forced herself to swallow a second spoonful, and a third. Her head was eased back to the pillow, and a sheaf of blankets was pulled snugly over her shoulders. Only then did she try to open her eyes, wincing as they smarted from the glow of a nearby lamp. A stranger was leaning over her, his face painted half in shadow, half in light. He was dark-haired and attractive, with no trace of boyishness in his features. His complexion was tanned and slightly weathered, the grain of black shaven whiskers lending a dark cast to his jaw. The hard planes of his face were complemented by a long nose and a generous mouth, and vivid green eyes. Strange, cynical, perceptive eyes, that seemed to look right through her.

"Die . . . ?" she asked in a hoarse croak. It hurt to talk, to move, to breathe. Icy needles stung her inside and out, and a great vise around her lungs made it nearly impossible to draw in air. Worst of all was the violent shaking in every muscle, shudders that racked her bones and joints until she feared she would come apart. If only she could make herself be still for a moment. When she tried to hold herself rigid, the shaking only intensified. She was breaking to pieces, sinking, drowning.

"No, you're not going to die," he said quietly. "And the shaking will stop eventually. It often happens in cases like yours."

Cases like hers? What had happened? Why was she here? Her swollen eyes flooded with tears of confusion, and she bit her lip to keep from crying. "Thank you," she gasped, though she had no precise idea of what to thank him for. She groped for his hand, needing the reassurance of a human touch. He moved, sitting on the side of the bed, his weight depressing the mattress, and she felt him take her fingers in his large hand. The heat of his skin, the burning vitality of his grip, shocked her.

"Please don't let go," she whispered, clinging to him as if to a lifeline. "Please."

His formidable masculine face softened in the lamplight. A strange self-mockery gleamed in his fathomless green eyes. "I can't stand a woman's tears. Keep crying and I'll leave."

"Yes," she said, chewing harder on her lip. But the tears kept leaking out, and the stranger swore beneath his breath.

He gathered her in the mass of bedclothes and carefully pulled her into his arms, compressing her trembling limbs. She gasped at the relief of it. He was so infinitely strong, holding her hard against him. Resting her head on his shoulder, she crushed her cheek against the linen of his shirt. Her vision was filled with details of him: the smooth tanned skin, the neat question-mark shape of his ear, the silky-rough locks of dark brown hair cropped unfashionably close to his head.

"I'm s-so cold . . ." she said, her mouth close to his ear.

"Well, a swim in the Thames will do that to you," he said dryly. "Especially this time of year." She felt him breathe against her forehead, a rush of heat, and she was flooded with desperate gratitude. She never wanted to leave his arms.

Her tongue felt thick as she tried to moisten her cracked lips. "Who are you?"

"Don't you remember?"

"No, I . . ." Thoughts and images eluded her efforts to capture them. She couldn't remember anything. There was blankness in every direction, a great confounding void.

He eased her head back, his warm fingers cupping around the back of her neck. A slight smile tipped the corners of his mouth. "Grant Morgan."

"What h-happened to me?" She struggled to think past the pain and the distracting tremors. "I-I was in the water . . ." She remembered the salty coldness burning her eyes and throat, blocking her ears, paralyzing her thrashing limbs. She had lost the battle for air, felt her lungs exploding, felt herself descending as if invisible hands pulled her from below. "S-someone pulled me out. Was it you?"

"No. A waterman found you and sent for a Runner. I happened to be the only one available tonight." His hand moved over her back in slow strokes. "How did you end up in the river, Vivien?"

"Vivien?" she repeated in desperate confusion. "Why did you call me that?"

There was a moment of silence that terrified her. He expected her to recognize the name . . . *Vivien* . . . She struggled to think of some meaning or image to attach to the name. There was only blankness.

"Who is Vivien?" Her sore throat clenched until

she could barely produce a sound. "What's happening to me?"

"Calm down," he said. "Don't you know your own name?"

"No . . . I don't know, I . . . can't remember *anything* . . ." She shuddered with frightened sobs. "Oh . . . I'm going to be sick."

Morgan moved with remarkable quickness, snatching up a creamware bowl from the bedside table and lowering her head over it. Dry heaves racked her body. When the convulsion passed, she hung limply over his arm and shivered miserably. He lowered her onto his lap and rested her head against his hard thigh.

"Help me," she moaned.

Long fingers slid gently over the side of her face. "It's all right. Don't be afraid."

Incredibly, though it was clear that nothing was right and there was a great deal to fear, she took comfort in his voice, his touch, his presence. His hands moved tenderly over her body, soothing her shaking limbs. "Breathe," he said, his palm moving in circles on the middle of her chest, and somehow she drew in a gulp of air. Hazily she wondered if this was what it felt like when heavenly spirits visited to minister to the suffering . . . Yes, an angel's touch must be like this.

"My head hurts," she croaked. "I feel so strange . . . Have I gone mad? Where am I?"

"Rest," he said. "We'll sort everything out later. Just rest."

"Tell me your name again," she begged in a hoarse whisper.

"My name is Grant. You're in my home . . . and you're safe."

Somehow through her misery, she sensed his ambivalence toward her, his wish to remain remote and unfeeling. He hadn't wanted to be kind to her, but he couldn't help himself. "Grant," she repeated, catching at the warm hand on her chest, feebly pressing it against her heart. "Thank you." She felt him go very still, his thigh tautening under the weight of her head. Exhausted, she closed her eyes and went to sleep in his lap.

Grant eased Vivien onto the pillows and tucked her neatly beneath the covers. He struggled to make sense of what was happening. He had helped women in trouble too many times to count. By now he was no longer capable of being moved by the sight of a damsel in distress. It was better for the people he served, not to mention himself, to remain efficiently impassive and get the job done. He hadn't wept in years. Nothing could break through the protective shell that had formed around his heart.

But Vivien, in all her damaged beauty and unexpected sweetness, had affected him more than he would have believed possible. He couldn't ignore a chord of elemental pleasure at seeing her in his home . . . in his bed.

His palm tingled at the feel of her heartbeat, as if the rhythm of her life force were captured beneath his hand. He wanted very much to stay with her, to hold her, not out of passion but from a desire to give her the warmth and protection of his own body.

Grant scrubbed his hands roughly over his face, through his short hair, and stood with a growl. What the hell was the matter with him?

The memory of the one time he and Vivien had met, two months ago, was still fresh in his mind. He had seen Vivien at a birthday ball given by Lord Wentworth for his mistress. The ball had been attended by members of the demimonde, the half-world of high-living prostitutes, gamblers, and dandies who were not fit for the *ton* but considered themselves far above the working classes. Since Grant's position in society was well nigh impossible for anyone to define, he was invited to gatherings of every stratum of society, from the highest to the lowest. He associated with the morally righteous, the ethically questionable, and the overtly corrupt, belonging nowhere and everywhere.

The private ballroom, with its elaborate plasterwork scenes of Neptune, mermaids, porpoises, and fish, was a perfect backdrop for Vivien. She resembled a mermaid herself, wearing a green silk gown that clung to every curve of her body. The deep neckline and hem of the gown were trimmed with ruchings of white satin and dark green gauze, and the sleeves were mere wisps of gauze at the shoulders. It did not escape Grant's or any other man's attention that Vivien had dampened her skirts to cling more closely to her legs and hips, heedless of the bitter clime outside.

That first sight of her was like a blow to the stomach. She wasn't classically beautiful, but she was as vibrant as a flame, with an intriguing combination of sweetness and witchery in her face. Her mouth was a fantasy come true, tender, full, and unmistakably carnal. The mass of her sunset-red curls had been pinned at the crown of her head, exposing a vulnerable neck and the most beautiful ivory shoulders Grant had ever seen.

Becoming aware of his intent stare, Vivien looked back at him, her red lips curved in a smile that invited and taunted at the same time.

"Ah, you've noticed Miss Duvall, I see." Lord Wentworth appeared at Grant's side, a wry expression settling on his wrinkle-scored face. "I warn you, my friend, Vivien Duvall has left a trail of broken hearts in her wake."

"Whom does she belong to?" Grant murmured, knowing that a woman of her beauty would not be unattached.

"Lord Gerard, until quite recently. He was invited to attend the ball, but declined without giving an explanation. It is my belief that he's licking his wounds in private while Vivien searches for a new protector." Wentworth chuckled at Grant's speculative expression. "Don't even consider it, man."

"Why not?"

"To begin with, she'll demand a fortune."

"And if I can afford her?" Grant asked.

Wentworth tugged idly at a lock of his gray hair. "She likes her men titled and married, and . . . well, a trifle more refined than you, my friend. No offense intended, of course."

"None taken," Grant murmured automatically. He had never tried to conceal his rough background, had even made use of it on occasion. Many women were actually excited by his occupation and his lack of pedigree. It was possible that Vivien Duvall would enjoy a change from her aristocratic protectors with their manicured hands and self-important demeanors.

"She's dangerous, you know," Wentworth persisted. "They say she drove one poor forlorn bastard to suicide just a fortnight ago."

Grant smiled cynically. "I'm hardly the kind to expire for the love of a woman, my lord."

He continued to watch Vivien, who had extracted a jeweled patch box from her beaded reticule. Flipping the box open, she beheld her reflection in a tiny looking glass fitted behind the lid. Carefully she touched the tip of a gloved finger to the heart-shaped patch that had been strategically glued near the corner of her delectable mouth. It was clear she only half heard the nearby gentleman who was trying earnestly to engage her in conversation. Seeming annoyed by his attentions, she gestured toward the long refreshment tables. He left at once to fetch her a plate, and she continued to study her reflection intently.

Seeing his opportunity, Grant snatched a glass of wine from a tray carried by a passing waiter. He approached Vivien, who closed the patch box with a snap and slipped it back into her reticule.

"Back so soon?" she asked without looking at him, her tone languid and bored.

"Your companion should know better than to leave a beautiful woman unattended."

Surprise flickered in Vivien's midnight-blue

eyes. Her gaze dropped to the proferred glass in his hand. She took the artfully twisted stem of the trumpet-shaped glass and sipped delicately. "He's not my companion." Her voice fell on his ears like a stroke of velvet. "Thank you. I am parched." She drank again, her gaze lifting to his. Like most successful courtesans, she had a flattering way of looking at a man as if he were the only one in the room.

"You were staring at me earlier," she remarked.

"I didn't mean to be rude."

"Oh, I'm accustomed to such stares," she said.

"I'm sure you are."

She smiled, revealing a flash of pearly white teeth. "We haven't been introduced."

Grant smiled back at her. "Shall I go find someone to do the honors?"

"No need." Her soft pink mouth pressed against the rim of the wineglass. "You're Mr. Morgan, the Bow Street Runner. That's only a guess, but I'm sure I'm right."

"Why do you think so?"

"You fit the description. Your height and your green eyes are quite distinctive." She pursed her lips thoughtfully. "But there's something else about you . . . a sense that you're not quite comfortable in these surroundings. I suspect you would rather be doing anything but stand here in a stuffy room making small talk. And your cravat is too tight."

Grant smiled as he tugged at the white starched linen that bound his neck with an artful knot. The civilized confinement of high collars and stiff cravats was more than he could bear at times. "You're wrong about one thing, Miss Duvall—there's nothing I'd rather be doing than talking with you."

"How do you know my name, sir? Has someone told you about me? I insist on knowing what was said."

"I was told that you've broken many hearts."

She laughed, clearly entertained by the notion, and her blue eyes sparkled wickedly. "True. But I suspect you've broken your share of female hearts."

"It's fairly easy to break hearts, Miss Duvall. The more interesting challenge is how to keep someone's love, not to lose it."

"You speak of love too seriously," Vivien said. "It's only a game, after all."

"Is it? Tell me your rules."

"It's rather like chess. I plan my strategy carefully. I sacrifice a pawn when it's no longer useful. And I never reveal my true thoughts to my opponent."

"Very pragmatic."

"One has to be, in my position." Her provocative smile dimmed slightly as she stared at him. "I don't quite like your expression, Mr. Morgan."

Grant's initial attraction to her had begun to fade as he reflected that any involvement with her would ultimately lead to nothing. She was manipulative, hard-edged, offering sex without real companionship. He wanted more than that, no matter how prettily packaged she was.

Her gaze searched his impassive features, and she affected a small, delicious pout. "Tell me *your* rules, Mr. Morgan."

"I only have one," he replied. "Complete honesty between myself and my partner."

A bright peal of laughter escaped her. "That can be quite inconvenient, you know."

"Yes, I know."

Obviously confident in her own attractiveness, Vivien preened and posed before him, angling her breasts outward, resting a graceful hand on the elegant curve of her hip. Grant knew that he was supposed to be admiring her, but instead he couldn't help wondering why it was that so many strikingly lovely women were self-absorbed.

Out of the corner of his eye he saw Vivien's former companion bearing down on them with quick, anxious strides, a plate of tidbits clutched in his hands. Clearly the man was determined to defend his territory, and Grant was hardly inclined to argue with him. Vivien Duvall wasn't worth a public dispute.

Vivien followed his glance, and sighed shortly. "Ask me to dance before that bore returns," she said in a low voice.

"Forgive me, Miss Duvall," Grant murmured, "but I would hate to deprive him of your company. Especially after the trouble he's taken to fetch you refreshments."

Vivien's eyes widened as she realized she had been rejected. A mottled pink flush covered her cheeks and forehead, clashing with the cinnamon tones of her hair. When she managed to reply, her tone dripped with disdain. "Perhaps we'll meet again, Mr. Morgan. I'll send for you if I'm ever bothered by a pickpocket or footpad."

"Please do," he replied, utterly polite, and took his leave with a brief bow.

Grant had thought the matter was over, but unfortunately their brief encounter had not gone unnoticed by others at the ball. And Vivien, taking a petty stab at revenge, had explained the situation in a way that had the gossips snickering behind their palms. Delicately Vivien had insinuated to a host of wagging tongues that the redoubtable Mr. Morgan had made an offer for her, which she had summarily rejected. The idea of the celebrated Bow Street Runner trying and failing to win the favor of Vivien Duvall was greeted everywhere with amusement. "He's not so dangerous as they claim," someone had slyly remarked within Grant's hearing, "if he can so easily be set back on his heels by a woman."

Grant's pride had smarted at the spread of deliberate lies . . . but he had managed to hold his silence on the matter. He'd known that, like all rumors, it would fade more quickly if nothing was said to add fuel to the fire. Still, the mention of Vivien's name never failed to annoy him, especially when people watched so carefully for his reaction. He had done everything possible to make his indifference clear, while inwardly promising himself that Vivien would come to regret the lies she had spread. It was a promise he was still bound and determined to make good on.

Wandering to the window, Grant pushed aside the dark blue damask curtain and stared through the long panes of glass. Impatiently his gaze hunted the quiet shadowed street for a glimpse of

Dr. Linley. In less than a minute, a hired hack stopped in front of the town house. Linley emerged from the vehicle, hatless as usual, his shock of dark blond hair gleaming in the light of the streetlamps. He gave no appearance of great haste, but his legs moved in long, ground-covering strides. Hefting his heavy leather doctor's case as if it weighed next to nothing, he approached the front entrance.

Grant waited at the bedroom door, giving the doctor a nod of greeting as he ascended the main staircase with the housekeeper. Linley's progressiveness and intelligence had made him one of the most sought-after doctors in London. And it hardly hurt his popularity to be a handsome bachelor in his late twenties. Wealthy society ladies clamored mightily for his services, claiming that only Dr. Linley could cure their headaches and female ailments. Grant was frequently amused by Linley's disgruntlement at being monopolized by the fashionable women of the *ton* instead of being allowed the time he desired to take on more serious cases.

The two men shook hands briefly. They had a genuine liking for each other, both of them professional men who regularly saw the best and worst that people were capable of.

"Well, Morgan," Linley said pleasantly, "this had better be worth dragging me away from a mug of brandied coffee at Tom's. What is the matter? You seem well enough to me."

"I have a guest who requires your attention," Grant replied, opening the door and showing him into the bedroom. "She was pulled from the Thames about an hour ago. I brought her here, and she regained consciousness for a period of almost ten minutes. The odd thing is, she claims to have no memory. She couldn't tell me her own name. Is such a thing possible?"

Linley's gray eyes narrowed thoughtfully. "Yes, of course. Memory loss is more common than you think. It's often caused by aging, or excessive amounts of alcohol—"

"What about a blow to the head and a near drowning?"

The doctor's lips puckered in a silent whistle. "Poor lady," he murmured. "Yes, I once saw a case of amnesia that was caused by a head injury. The man had been wounded in a shipyard accident—a falling beam struck him on the crown, and he was unconscious for three days. When he awoke, he was beset by extreme confusion. The habits of walking, writing, and reading were easy for him, but he didn't recognize a single member of his family, and could recall nothing of his past."

"Did his memory return?"

"In five or six months. But I've heard of another case in which the memory came back in a matter of days. There's no way of predicting how long it might take. Or if it will happen at all." Brushing past Grant, Linley approached the bed and set his doctor's case on the chair. As he bent over the sleeping patient, the doctor gave a startled murmur that barely reached Grant's ears. "Miss Duvall!"

"You've attended her before?"

Linley nodded, looking troubled. Something about the doctor's expression alerted Grant to the fact that Vivien's visit had been for an ailment far more serious than a headache.

"What for?" Grant asked.

"You know I can't divulge that."

"She can't remember anything—it won't make a damned bit of difference to her if you tell me or not."

Linley wasn't swayed by the argument. "Would you care to leave the room, Morgan, while I examine my patient?"

Before Grant could reply, Vivien stirred and moaned. She rubbed her eyes, squinting at the doctor's unfamiliar face. Strangely attuned to her moods, Grant sensed the exact moment she began to panic. He reached the bedside in three strides and took her trembling hand. The strength of his grip seemed to calm her. "Grant," she croaked, her gaze lifting to his face.

"The doctor's here," he murmured. "I'm going to wait outside the door while he has a look at you. Is that all right?"

A long moment passed before she gave a tiny nod and released his hand.

"Good girl." Grant gently tucked a lock of her hair behind her small ear.

"You two seem to have become fast friends," Linley remarked.

"It's my way with women," Grant said. "They can't resist my charm."

Linley's mouth quirked. "Charm? I've never suspected you of having any."

They were both surprised to hear Vivien's feeble

scratch of voice join in the conversation. "That's because . . . you're not a woman."

Grant stared at her with an unwilling smile. Half dead, she might be, but the instinct to flirt had not left her. And God help him, he was far from immune. "Rallying to my defense, are you?" He reached down to stroke the curve of her cheek with his fingertip. "I'll have to thank you later." A slow tide of pink crept over Vivien's face. Grant didn't realize his tone was unconsciously seductive until the doctor shot him a speculative glance.

Abruptly Grant left the room. Scowling, he wedged his back against the papered wall of the hallway. "Damn you, Vivien," he muttered beneath his breath.

He had found it so easy to reject Vivien before, when he'd viewed her as shallow, vain, manipulative. And he wouldn't have spared her a thought since then had it not been for the pride-stinging lies she had sprinkled all over London. Grant would have hated her if she had been worth such expenditure of emotion.

But there were times in every man or woman's life when circumstances made one vulnerable, and Vivien's time had come. Could she really have lost her memory, or was she shamming? And if her memory really was gone . . . then she had been stripped of all defenses, all the grievances and pretensions that kept adult human beings from revealing their true selves to each other. How many men had been given the chance to know the real Vivien? Not one. He would bet his life on it.

A gentleman would not take advantage of the situation. But he was no gentleman.

He had once promised himself that Vivien would pay for her petty little game—and she would, with interest. Now that she was in his possession, she wasn't going to leave until his pride had been assuaged. He was going to amuse himself with her for as long as he wanted, or until her memory had returned. Whichever came first.

He smiled in satisfaction, the hot wistful ache in his chest seeming to ease.

After what seemed an unaccountably long time, Linley opened the door and welcomed him into the room. Vivien appeared calm but exhausted, her face as pale as the white linen pillow behind her head. An uncertain smile touched her lips as she saw Grant.

"Well?" Grant asked, while Linley bent over his medical case and latched it shut.

Linley glanced up from his task. "It appears Miss Duvall has suffered a concussion, though not a severe one."

Grant's eyes narrowed at the unfamiliar term.

"A blow to the cranium," Linley proceeded to explain, "resulting in distress to the brain. The aftereffects usually last for a few weeks, perhaps a month, and may include confusion, nausea, and physical weakness. And also, in this particular case, amnesia."

"How will you treat it?" Grant asked tersely.

"Unfortunately, the symptoms of concussion, including amnesia, must run their course. There's nothing I can do except prescribe rest. I don't think

Miss Duvall will have any lasting problems from her experience tonight, although the next few days will be uncomfortable. I've left a few digestive powders to counteract the effects of the salt water she ingested, and a salve for the bruises and abrasions. I can't find evidence of fractured bones or internal injuries, just a mild sprain in one ankle." He went to Vivien's side and patted her hand. "Sleep," he advised kindly. "That's the best advice I can give."

The doctor picked up his bag and crossed the room, stopping near the doorway to confer with Grant. His serious gray eyes met Grant's, and he spoke in a tone too low for Vivien to overhear. "There are finger marks around her throat, and signs of a struggle. I assume you're going to investigate?"

"Of course."

"Obviously Miss Duvall's amnesia will make your job more difficult. I don't have great experience in these matters, but I do know that the mind is a fragile instrument." A warning note laced the doctor's matter-of-fact voice. "I strongly suggest that Miss Duvall remain in a calm environment. When she feels better, perhaps she can visit some familiar places and people in an effort to aid her memory. However, you could possibly injure her by making her remember something she's not ready for."

"I'm not going to harm her." Grant's brows lowered in a scowl.

"Well, your skills at inquisition are well known. I've heard that you can obtain a confession from the most hardened criminals ... and in case you were thinking of somehow forcing Miss Duvall's memory to return—"

"Point taken," Grant muttered, offended. "Christ. One would think I went about kicking dogs and frightening small children."

Linley chuckled in the face of his annoyance. "I only know your reputation, man. Good evening— I'll be sending you a bill soon."

"Do that," Grant said, making no secret of his impatience for the sawbones to leave.

"One more thing ... a patient with a concussion is quite vulnerable. A second trauma to the head, perhaps caused by a fall, could prove harmful or even fatal."

"I'll take care of her."

"All right, Morgan." The doctor sent a warm smile toward Vivien. "*Au revoir*, Miss Duvall. I'll visit again in a few days."

Mrs. Buttons popped her head around the door, her gaze fixed on Grant. "Sir? Is there anything you require?"

"Nothing right now," Grant murmured, and watched as the housekeeper accompanied the doctor to the main staircase.

"What is your reputation?" Vivien asked feebly, apparently having caught the last of the doctor's comments.

Grant went to her and sat in the bedside chair. He wove his fingers together and extended his long legs, crossing them at the ankles. "Damned if I know." He shrugged irritably. "I'm a Bow Street Runner. In the course of my work people are always lying, hiding things, evading questions. I just have a way of cutting to the truth, and that makes them uncomfortable."

Despite her weariness, a spark of amusement appeared in Vivien's blue eyes. "You 'have a way,' " she repeated drowsily. "What does that mean?"

He grinned suddenly, unable to keep from leaning forward and smoothing a straggling tendril away from her face. "It means I do whatever's necessary to find out the truth."

"Oh." She yawned, fighting to stay awake, but her exhaustion was clearly overwhelming. "Grant," she whispered, "what is *my* reputation?"

She fell asleep before he could reply.

Three

*G*rant awoke as the weak morning sunlight began to filter through the windowpanes. Perplexed, he stared at the ice-blue ceiling of the guest
room, expecting to see the wine-colored canopy
over his own bed. Suddenly he recalled the events
of the previous evening. There had been no sound
from Vivien's room. He wondered how she had
fared the night. After all she had been through, she
would likely sleep for most of the day.

Fitting his hands behind his head, Grant lay
there for another minute, pondering the knowledge
that Vivien was here, in his house, only a few
rooms away from him. It had been a long time
since a woman had slept beneath his roof. Vivien
Duvall, at his mercy . . . The thought entertained
him prodigiously. The fact that she didn't remem-

ber what had happened between them only heightened his enjoyment of the situation.

Yawning, Grant sat up and scratched his fingers
through the pelt of dark hair on his chest. He rang
for his valet, padded to a nearby chair, and dressed
in the linens and pale gray trousers that had been
laid out for him. His morning routine had been es-
tablished by years of habit. He was always out of
bed at sunrise, had finished his personal ablutions
and dressed within twenty minutes, spent the next
half hour devouring a huge breakfast and scanning
the *Times,* and left on foot for Bow Street. Sir Ross
Cannon required all Runners who weren't on duty
to report by no later than nine.

In fewer than five minutes, his valet, Kellow, appeared with a ewer of hot shaving water and all
the necessary implements. At the same time, a
housemaid quickly laid the fire and tidied the
grate.

Grant poured steaming water into a washbowl
and sluiced handfuls of it onto his face, trying to
soften what had to be the most obstinate beard in
London. When his shaving was concluded, Grant
put on a white shirt, a patterned gray waistcoat,
and a black silk cravat. The official uniform of the
Bow Street Runners included a red waistcoat, blue
coat and navy trousers, and tall black boots polished to an immaculate shine. Grant detested the
garb. On an average-sized man the brightly colored
clothes—which had inspired the public to nick-
name the Runners "Robin Redbreasts"—were

somewhat foppish. On a man of his height, the effect was startling.

Grant's personal taste favored dark, well-tailored clothes in shades of gray, beige, and black, with no personal adornment save his pocket watch. He kept his hair conveniently short and was sometimes compelled to shave twice a day when a formal occasion called for him to remove another layer of his encroaching beard. He bathed every evening, as he was unable to sleep well otherwise. The physical exertion of his job, not to mention the foul characters he often associated with, often made him feel unclean within and without.

Although many valets were called upon to assist their masters with their clothes, Grant preferred to dress himself. He found the notion of standing still while some other fellow dressed him as more than a little ridiculous. He was an able-bodied man, not some tot who needed help with his skeleton suit. When he'd expressed this view to one of his socially elevated friends, the friend had told him with amusement that this was one of the essential differences between the lower classes and the aristocracy.

"You mean only the lower classes know how to fasten their buttons?" Grant had asked wryly.

"No," the friend had replied with a laugh, "it's just that they have no choice in the matter. The aristocracy, on the other hand, can get someone else to do it for them."

After tying his black silk cravat in a simple knot, Grant jerked the tips of his collar to neat standing points. He dragged a comb through his ruffled dark hair and gave a cursory glance in the looking glass. Just as he reached for his charcoal-gray coat, he heard a muffled sound from a few rooms away.

"Vivien," he murmured, dropping the coat at once. He reached the master bedroom in a few strides, entering without bothering to knock. The housemaid had already visited and had stoked a small fire in the grate.

Vivien was attempting to get out of bed by herself, the linen shirt twisted around the middle of her thighs. Her long hair fell in wild straggles down her back. She was standing on one foot, maintaining a precarious balance. Her sprained ankle was bound and swollen, and the pain it caused was obvious as she took one limping step away from the bed.

"What do you need?" Grant asked, and she started at the sound of his voice. She didn't look much better than she had the previous night, her face ghastly pale, her eyes still swollen, her throat bruised. "Do you want the privy?"

The blunt question clearly caused Vivien no end of mortification. A scarlet flush cascaded over her skin. The sight of a redhead blushing was not something to miss, Grant thought with a sudden flicker of amusement.

"Yes, thank you," she murmured, her voice hoarse and strained. She took another cautious hobbling step. "If you could just tell me where—"

"I'll help you."

"Oh, no, really—" She gasped as he scooped her into his arms, her body small and light against his chest. Grant carried her the short distance to the privy, two doors down the hall, while Vivien tried in agonized modesty to pull the thin linen shirt farther over her thighs. The gesture struck him as odd for a courtesan. Vivien was known for her lack of sexual inhibition, not to mention her elegantly provocative style of dressing. Modesty had not been in her repertoire. Why did she seem so distressed now?

"You'll be stronger soon," he said. "In the meantime, stay in bed and keep off that ankle. If you want anything at all, ring for one of the maids."

"Yes. Thank you." Her small hands crept around his neck. "I'm sorry to trouble you, Mr. . . ." She hesitated, and he knew that she had forgotten his last name.

"Call me Grant," he replied, setting her gently on the floor. "It's no trouble."

Vivien emerged from the privy a few minutes later, clearly surprised to find him still there. She seemed no bigger than a child, dressed in his shirt with the sleeves rolled back several times and the tail reaching below her knees. Her gaze lifted to his, and she returned his friendly smile with an abashed one of her own.

"Better?" he asked.

"Yes, thank you."

He extended a hand to her. "Let me help you back to bed."

She hesitated before hobbling forward. Carefully Grant reached around her slender body, hooking one arm behind her back and the other beneath her knees. Although he lifted her with extreme gentleness, mindful of her injuries, Vivien gasped as he brought her against his chest. Of all the women he had held in his arms, none had ever possessed such lush, exquisite delicacy. Her bones were slender, but her flesh was pliant, voluptuous, utterly desirable.

Returning to the bedroom, Grant eased Vivien onto the mattress, fumbling to arrange a stack of pillows behind her. She tugged the blankets upward, bringing them high over her chest. In spite of her bedraggled condition, or perhaps because of it, he was struck again with the disconcerting urge to cuddle and caress her. He, who was known for possessing a heart of granite, or some similarly impermeable substance. "Are you hungry?" he asked gruffly.

"Not really."

"When the housekeeper brings a tray, I want you to eat something."

For some reason his tone of command made her smile. "I'll try."

Grant stood frozen in place by her smile . . . lucent and warm, a flash of magic that illuminated her delicate face. It was so unlike the self-absorbed woman he had met at Wentworth's ball that he wondered briefly if she was the same person at all. Yet she was, unmistakably, Vivien.

"Grant," she said hesitantly. "Please, would you bring a looking glass?" She pressed her hands to her cheeks in a self-conscious gesture. "I don't know what I look like."

Somehow managing to tear his gaze away from her, Grant went to the gentleman's cabinet in the corner of the room. He rummaged through the narrow drawers and located a wooden *nécessaire* covered in leather. The case was designed to hold scissors, files, and grooming items, the lid fitted with a rectangular looking glass inside. Returning to the bedside, Grant opened the *nécessaire* and gave it to her.

Vivien tried to hold the case near her face, but her hands still trembled violently from her experience of the previous evening. Grant reached over and steadied the *nécessaire* as she viewed her reflection. Her hands were very cold beneath his, the fingers stiff and bloodless. Her eyes widened, and she barely seemed to breathe.

"How strange," she said, "not to recognize one's own face."

"You have no cause for complaint," Grant said huskily. Even bruised and pale and ravaged, her face was incomparable.

"Do you think so?" She stared into the looking glass without a trace of the self-satisfaction she had displayed at the ball. *That* Vivien had had no doubt of her many attractions. This woman was far less confident.

"Everyone thinks so. You're known as one of the great beauties of London."

"I don't see why." Catching his skeptical expression, she added, "Truly, I'm not fishing for compliments, it just . . . seems a very ordinary face." She produced a comical, clownish expression, like a child experimenting with her reflection. A shaken laugh escaped her. "It doesn't seem to belong to me." Her eyes glittered like sapphires, and he realized with a flare of alarm that she was going to cry.

"Don't," he muttered. "I told you last night how I feel about crying."

"Yes . . . you can't stand a woman's tears." She wiped her wet eyes with her fingers. A wobbly smile touched her lips. "I didn't think a Bow Street Runner would be so sensitive."

"Sensitive," Grant repeated indignantly. "I'm as hard-shelled as they come." He gathered a handful of the linen sheet and swabbed hastily at her face.

"Are you?" She gave a last sniffle and peered at him over the edge of the sheet, and he saw a hint of laughter appearing behind the last glimmering tears. "You seem rather soft-shelled to me."

Grant opened his mouth to argue, but realized suddenly that she was teasing him. With great difficulty, he tamped down an unexpected surge of warmth in his chest. "I'm about as sensitive as a millstone," he informed her.

"I'll reserve opinion on that." She closed the *nécessaire* and shook her head ruefully. "I shouldn't have asked for a looking glass. I look rather the worse for wear."

Grant contemplated her dry, cracked lips with a frown. Reaching for a little glass jar of salve on the night table, he handed it to her. "Try some of this. Linley left a special mixture for bruises, dryness, scrapes, chafing . . ."

"I could use a barrel of it," she said, fumbling with the hinged porcelain lid.

Retrieving the jar, Grant opened it for her. Instead of handing it back, he held it in his palm and let his gaze wander over her. "The shaking is better this morning," he observed quietly.

Vivien colored and nodded, seeming embarrassed by the involuntary tremors. "Yes, but I still can't seem to get warm." She rubbed her palms over the fair, chapped skin of her arms. "I was wondering . . . if it wouldn't be too great an imposition—"

"A hot bath?"

"Oh, yes." The throb of anticipation in her voice made him smile.

"That can be arranged. But you'll have to move carefully, and let the servants help you. Or me, if you'd rather."

Vivien stared at him, openmouthed at the suggestion. "I-I wouldn't care to put you to such trouble—" she stammered.

"No trouble at all," he said mildly. Only the glint in his green eyes betrayed the fact that he was teasing her.

Before she could suppress it, an image appeared in her mind, of herself soaking in a steaming tub while he bathed her naked body.

"What a blush," Grant observed with a sudden smile. "If that doesn't warm you up, nothing will." He drew his fingertip over the velvety anise-scented salve and brought it to her mouth. "Hold still."

Vivien obeyed, her gaze locked on his face as he gently applied the salve to her lips. The sore, dry surface absorbed the preparation at once, and Grant dipped his finger into the jar again. The room was utterly quiet except for the sound of Vivien's deep, trembling breath.

There was a tugging sensation in Grant's chest that bothered him profoundly. He wanted to kiss her, hold her, comfort her as if she were a lost child. He would never have guessed that Vivien Duvall could be so endearing and vulnerable. Damn her, if this was somehow an act on her part, he would probably end up throttling her.

Obviously she had already driven some other poor bastard to it already.

Grant paused at that thought, and grimly warned himself not to be affected by her. Enjoy her, take what he wanted . . . but not for a minute would he allow himself to care for her. That much trouble, he didn't need. He rubbed more of the salve between his fingers, until the cool scent of anise spiced the air. With the lightest possible touch, he spread the salve over her bruised, swollen throat. Vivien was very still beneath his hand, her gaze focused on his hard face.

"We knew each other before last night, didn't we?" she whispered.

His lashes lowered, and he took his time about replying. "You could say that."

Another soft pass of his fingertips over her skin, rubbing the salve deeper into her bruises.

Mired in confusion, she tried to analyze the sensation of his touch, the surprising sense of familiarity and comfort she found in his presence. Nothing in the world was familiar to her, not even her own face . . . but somehow he made her feel safe and reassured. She wouldn't feel this way in the company of a stranger, would she?

"H-how well did we know each other?" Vivien asked unsteadily.

"We'll discuss it later." Exactly what he was going to say to her, and how he would present the situation, would take some consideration. In the meantime she would rest and heal, and remain under his protection. Although Vivien seemed none too pleased with his evasiveness, she refrained from pursuing the matter, and he guessed she was still too exhausted to debate. Reaching into the pocket of his waistcoat, he extracted his watch. The lateness of the hour made him frown. "I have to leave for Bow Street," he said. "I'll visit your town house today and fetch some clothes for you."

She made an effort to smile, but her blue eyes were pleading. "Do I have family or friends to send for?"

"I don't know about your family," Grant admitted. "I'll find out what I can. And yes, you have friends . . . but now isn't the time for visiting. You need to rest." Unable to resist the temptation, he reached out and traced one of the worry lines on her downy forehead. "Don't worry, sweet pea," he murmured.

Vivien settled back against the pillows, her eyelids heavy with exhaustion. "So many questions," she sighed.

"You'll soon have all the answers you desire." He paused, and some of the vibrant tenderness left his voice as he added, "Although you may not like some of them."

She stared at him solemnly, her hand creeping

to her throat. "What happened to me last night?"

"I intend to find out," he replied in a grim tone that left no room for doubt.

The street shaped like a bow had been built in the mid sixteen hundreds. There had been a few famous residents of Bow Street in the last century. But after the turn of the century, there was only one name associated with Bow Street that truly mattered . . . Sir Ross Cannon.

It seemed at times that the attention of the entire world was focused on the narrow, four-story building and its famous inhabitant. Cannon directed his half dozen Runners and eighty other assorted officers like a master conductor. The Runners had gained worldwide fame as they suppressed riots, solved crimes, and protected the royal family.

At the death of one of Fieldings's successors five years ago, many important men had been discussed as candidates for the new chief magistrate. However, a relative unknown was finally appointed to the position . . . Ross Cannon, who had previously served as a magistrate in the Great Marlboro Street office. Cannon had assumed the duties of chief magistrate as if he had been born to it. In no time at all he had left his own distinctive stamp on the Bow Street office, treating detective work as if it were a science, inventing methodology, testing theories, guiding and encouraging his officers with an infectious zeal. He was demanding and driven, and any one of his men would have gladly died for him. Including Grant.

Grant ascended the three front steps and gave a

vigorous knock at the door. It was answered by Cannon's housekeeper, Mrs. Dobson, a fat, motherly woman with a head of bobbing silver curls. Her pudgy face glowed with a smile as she welcomed Grant inside. "You without a hat again, Mr. Morgan . . . You'll catch your death one of these days, with the wind blowing from the north like this."

"I can't wear a hat, Mrs. Dobson," Grant replied, shedding his heavy black greatcoat and giving it to her. She was nearly smothered by the huge mound of wool. "I'm tall enough as it is." The high-crowned hats that were currently fashionable made him look ridiculous, adding needless inches to his towering height until passersby stared openly.

"Well, *not* wearing a hat hardly fools anyone into thinking you're short," she pointed out.

Grant grinned and pinched her cheek, causing the housekeeper to gasp and scold him. Her reprimands, however, contained little heat—they both knew that of all the Runners, he was her favorite. "Where is Cannon?" Grant asked, his green eyes sparkling, and Mrs. Dobson indicated the magistrate's office.

The property at number 4 Bow Street contained a house, a tiny yard, offices, a court, and a strong room to hold prisoners.

Having been born to a family of means, Cannon could have lived an indolent life in a far more luxurious place than this . . . but that was not his nature. He had a passion for justice, and with all that needed to be done, there was no time for laziness or frivolity.

To Cannon, life was serious business, and he lived it accordingly. Rumor had it that his young wife on her deathbed had made him promise never to remarry, and Cannon had been faithful to his word. His tremendous energy was expended on his work. Even the closest and dearest of his friends would readily swear that nothing could break the iron control Cannon held over his own secretive heart.

Striding down the narrow hallway that led to Cannon's private office, Grant nearly collided with two Runners who were leaving . . . Flagstad and Keyes, the two oldest Runners, both of them fast approaching forty. "Off to guard the royal hind-quarters again," Keyes remarked cheerfully, while Flagstad revealed that he had been given the more lucrative assignment of attending the Bank of England, as quarterly dividends were being paid.

"And what are you about this morning?" Flagstad asked Grant. His weathered face creased with good humor. "No, don't tell me . . . another bank robbery, or a burglary on the west side that you'll charge a fortune to solve."

Grant responded with an answering grin, having endured much ribbing from his colleagues on his hefty commissions. He forbore to point out that in the last year he had literally caught more thieves than the other five Runners put together. "I only take what they're willing to pay," he said mildly.

"The only reason the nobs demand your services is because you're a bloody swell," Keyes said with a chuckle. "Just the other day a lady said to me, 'Of all the Runners, only Mr. Morgan looks the way one ought to look.' " He snorted at the statement. "As if a man's appearance has a damned thing to do with how he does the job!"

"*I'm* a swell?" Grant asked incredulously, glancing at his own conservative attire, and then at Keyes's dandified appearance . . . the carefully arranged "windswept" style of his hair, the gold pin in his elaborate cravat, the tiny silk flowers and fleurs-de-lis embroidered over his waistcoat. Not to mention the wide-brimmed, cream-colored hat worn carefully angled over one eye.

"I have to dress this way at court," Keyes said defensively.

Chuckling, Flagstad began to guide Keyes away before an argument could brew.

"Wait," Keyes said, an urgent note of interest entering his voice. "Morgan, I heard you were sent out last night to investigate a bloat found in the river."

"Yes."

Keyes seemed impatient at his terseness. "Talkative as a clam, aren't you? Well, what can you tell us about it? Was the victim male or female?"

"What does it matter to you?" Grant asked, perplexed by the Runner's interest in the matter.

"Are you going to take the case?" Keyes persisted.

"Probably."

"I'll take it for you if you like," Keyes offered. "God knows you haven't much interest in investigating a dead woman. I hear bloats aren't paying much these days."

Flagstad snickered at the lame jest.

Grant stared at Keyes with new alertness. "Why do you think it's a woman?" he asked idly.

Keyes blinked, and took a moment to answer. "Merely a guess, lad. Am I right?"

Giving him a last questioning glance, Grant refused comment and entered Cannon's office.

Sir Ross sat with his back to the door, at a massive oak pedestal desk arranged to face the long rectangular window overlooking the street. A massive brown-and-gray-striped cat occupied a corner of the desk, glancing lazily at the newcomer. The reticent feline had been discovered on the front steps of the Bow Street office a few years earlier. She was missing a tail, either by accident or some act of mischief, and had promptly been dubbed "Chopper." Strictly a one-person cat, Chopper reserved all her affection for Cannon, and barely tolerated anyone else.

Cannon's dark head turned, and he regarded Grant with a pleasant but unsmiling expression. "Good morning," he murmured. "There's a jug of coffee on the side table."

Grant never refused an offer of coffee. His passion for the bitter brew was rivaled only by Cannon's. They both drank it black and scalding hot whenever possible. Pouring a liberal amount into an empty creamware mug, Grant sat in the nearby chair Cannon indicated. The magistrate bent his attention to some documents on his desk once more, signing one with a deft flourish.

While he waited, Grant let his gaze roam over the comfortably familiar room. One wall was covered with maps of the city and surrounding coun-

ties, as well as floor plans of Westminster Hall, the
Bank of England, and other buildings of significance. Another wall was covered with bookshelves,
containing enough volumes to crush an elephant.
The furniture consisted of a few heavy oak pieces,
plain and functional. A library terrestrial globe was
poised on a mahogany stand in the corner. Enough
wall space had been allowed for a single painting,
a landscape of North Wales in which a small
stream rushed over craggy rocks, with dark trees
and gray hills looming in the distance. The landscape was jarringly pristine in comparison with the
bustling artifice of London.

Finally Cannon turned toward him, black brows
arched in a request for information. With its sharp
features and wintry gray eyes, his face possessed a
wolfish cast. Were he to allow any warmth in his
expression, he would have been considered handsome.

"Well?" he murmured. "What of the bloat you
investigated last night? Is there a need for a coro-
ner's inquest?"

"No bloat," Grant replied briskly. "The victim—
a woman—was still alive. I brought her to my
home and sent for Dr. Linley."

"Very charitable of you."

Grant responded with a careful shrug. "I know
the lady rather well. Her name is Vivien Duvall."

The name caught Cannon's interest. "The one
who rebuffed you at the Wentworth ball?"

"I gave *her* the shove-along," Grant said with a
quick flare of annoyance. "Somehow in the course
of gossip, the story was twisted around."

Cannon's black brows inched upward, and he made a sardonic "hmm" deep in his throat. "Go on. Tell me about Miss Duvall's condition."

Grant drummed his fingers on the arm of his chair. "Attempted murder, no doubt about it. Heavy bruising and finger marks around the throat, not to mention a blow to the head. According to Linley, she'll be all right . . . but there is one difficulty. She's lost her memory. She can't provide a single detail of what happened, or even recall her own name."

"Did the doctor say when or if her memory might return?"

Grant shook his head. "There's no way of knowing. And until the investigation brings some evidence to light—or she regains her memory—it's safer if everyone thinks she's dead."

Cannon's gray eyes narrowed in fascination. "Shall I assign one of the Runners to investigate, or will you take the case?"

"I want it." Grant drained the last of his coffee and wrapped his long fingers around the cup, absorbing what little warmth remained. "I'm going to begin by questioning her former protector, Lord Gerard. It seems likely that he or some jealous lover may have tried to strangle her. The Devil knows there's probably a long list of them."

Cannon's mouth twitched with suppressed humor. "I'll send a man to question the waterman who found her, as well as the others who were ferrying passengers near Waterloo Bridge last evening. Perhaps one of them may have seen or heard something useful. Let me know how your investigation proceeds. In the meantime, where will Miss Duvall reside?"

Grant studied the sparkling black droplets that clung to the interior of his mug. He made his tone as matter-of-fact as possible. "With me."

"Surely she has friends or relatives who will take her in."

"She'll be safest under my protection."

Grant met Cannon's wintry, piercing gaze without flinching. The magistrate had always declined to comment on his Runners' personal lives, so long as they performed their jobs well. However, Cannon had a soft spot in his heart for women and children, and would do everything in his considerable power to prevent mistreatment of them.

Cannon let the silence linger uncomfortably long before speaking. "I believe I know you, Morgan . . . well enough to be certain that you wouldn't take advantage of this woman, no matter what your personal grievances."

Grant replied coldly. "I would never force myself on an unwilling woman."

"I wasn't referring to 'force,'" Cannon said softly. "I was referring to manipulation . . . opportunism . . . seduction."

Tempted to tell the magistrate to mind his own damned business, Grant stood and set his empty mug on the side table. "I don't need a lecture," he growled. "I won't harm Miss Duvall in any way. You have my word on that. Bear in mind, however, that she is hardly an innocent. She's a courtesan. Manipulation and seduction are tools of the trade.

Her memory loss doesn't change the fact of what she is."

Unruffled, Cannon made a temple of his fingers and stared at Grant contemplatively. "Is Miss Duvall willing to accept this arrangement?"

"If she doesn't like it, she's free to go elsewhere."

"Make certain she understands that."

Biting back several choice comments, Grant inclined his head in agreement. "Anything else?" he inquired in a tone so bland as to be mocking.

Cannon continued to pin him with an assessing stare. "Perhaps you would care to explain why you wish to harbor Miss Duvall under your own roof, after all your avowed dislike of her."

"I never said I disliked her," Grant countered.

"Come now," came the gently chiding reply. "You made no secret of your resentment, after you'd been run through the rumor mill because of her."

"Call this my opportunity to make amends. Besides, it's my duty."

Cannon gave him a speaking glance. "Regardless of the lady's character—or lack thereof—I would prefer that you keep your hands off her until she recovers her memory and the investigation is concluded."

Annoyed almost beyond bearing, Grant smiled thinly. "Don't I always do as you ask?"

Cannon expelled a short, explosive sigh and turned toward his desk. "I wish to hell you would," he muttered, waving him away with a brief gesture.

"Good-bye, Chopper," Grant said lightly, but the

cat turned her head with a disdain that made him grin.

Park Lane, the centerpiece of the prestigious area of Mayfair, was London's most desirable address. Suffused with an air of wealth and authority, the street was fronted with imposing columned mansions designed on a huge scale. The homes were meant to convince passersby that their inhabitants were superior to ordinary humans.

Grant had seen too much of the aristocracy's intimate personal lives to be awed by the grandeur of Park Lane. The nobility had as many flaws and foibles as average men . . . perhaps more. The only difference between an aristocrat and a commoner was that the former was far more resourceful at covering up his wrongdoings. And sometimes the nobility actually believed they were above the laws ordinary men were bound by. It was this kind of man that Grant most enjoyed bringing to justice.

The name of Vivien's most recent protector was William Henry Ellyot, Lord Gerard. As the future Earl of Norbury, his chief occupation was waiting for his father to die so that he could inherit a revered title and a considerable fortune. Unfortunately for Gerard, his father was in excellent health and would likely retain the earldom for many years to come. In the meantime, Gerard searched for ways to amuse himself, indulging his rampant tastes for women, drinking, gambling, and sporting. His "arrangement" with Vivien Duvall had made him the envy of many other men. She had been a lovely and highly visible trophy.

Gerard was known for his bad temper, given to violent tantrums when deprived of something he wanted. Although a gentleman was supposed to take his gambling losses with good grace, Gerard cheated and lied rather than accept defeat. It was rumored that he took out his frustrations on his servants, proving such a poor master that it was difficult to hire domestic help for his various households.

Grant mounted the steps of the classically styled manor with its columned pediment and statue-filled niches. A few strong raps on the door with his gloved fist, and one of the double portals was opened to reveal a butler's dour face.

"Your business, sir?" the butler inquired.

"Inform Lord Gerard that Mr. Morgan is here to see him."

Grant saw the instant of recognition on the butler's face, and a faint wariness threaded through the man's tone. "Sir, I regret to inform you that Lord Gerard is not at home. If you will leave your calling card, I will see that he receives it later."

Grant smiled wryly. "Not at home" was a phrase used by butlers to convey that a particular lord or lady might very well be in the house, but was unwilling to receive visitors. But if Grant wanted to question someone, social niceties were the last things to stand in his way.

"I don't leave cards," he said flatly. "Go tell your master that Mr. Morgan is here. This is not a social call."

The butler's face remained impassive, but he reeked of disapproval. Without offering a response, he left Grant at the doorstep and disappeared into the house. Grant shouldered his way inside and closed the heavy door with a hard nudge of his boot. Rocking back on his heels, he surveyed the entrance hall. It was lined with gleaming marble columns, the walls painted a soft matte shade of a fashionable color called "Parisian gray." Cool white plasterwork covered the upper portion of the walls, rising to a lofty ceiling. Directly opposite the front door was an apse containing a small statue of a winged female figure.

Approaching the statue, Grant touched one of the delicate feathery wings, admiring the elegant work.

The butler reappeared at that moment, frowning in bristling hauteur. "Sir, that is part of Lord Gerard's prized collection of Roman statuary."

Grant drew back and replied matter-of-factly, "Grecian, actually. The original sits in the hand of Athena in the Parthenon."

"Well . . ." The butler was clearly nonplussed. "It's not to be touched. If you would care to follow me, Lord Gerard is at home now."

Grant was shown into a large drawing room with walls covered in creamy white woodwork and octagonal panels of red damask. The ceiling was remarkable, inset with red and gold panels that spread outward from a central golden sun. Between a pair of diamond-paned windows, a series of medallion portraits displayed the fleshy, dignified faces of the past five Earls of Norbury.

"Care for a drink, Morgan?"

Lord Gerard entered the room, clad in an embroidered green velvet dressing gown. His un-
combed hair sprung untidily around his
heavy-cheeked face, and his skin was florid from
strong drink. Holding a snifter of brandy in one
hand, Gerard made his way to a massive wing
chair with ball-and-claw feet, and lowered himself
gingerly. Although Gerard was in his early thirties,
a life dedicated to self-indulgence had made him
look at least ten years older. He was relentlessly
average in appearance, neither fat nor thin, neither
tall nor short, neither handsome nor ugly. His only
distinctive feature was his eyes, dark, small, and
intense.

Gerard gestured with his snifter. "A damn fine
Armagnac," he commented. "Shall you take some?"

"A bit early in the day for me," Grant said with
a slight shake of his head.

"I can think of no better way to begin the day."
Gerard drank deeply of the bloodred liquid.

Grant kept his expression pleasant, but something dark and ugly stirred inside him as he
watched Gerard. The image of Vivien with this
man, servicing him, pleasuring him, passed before
Grant in a disquieting flash. She had been Gerard's
whore, and would undoubtedly sell herself to the
next man who could meet her price. Jealous and
repulsed, Grant sat in the chair adjacent to Gerard's.

"Thank you for agreeing to talk with me," Grant
murmured.

Gerard tore his attention away from the snifter

long enough to manage a sour smile. "As I understood it, I hadn't much choice."

"I don't expect this will take long," Grant said. "I only have a few questions for you."

"Are you conducting an investigation of some sort? What and whom does it concern?"

Grant sat back in his chair, appearing relaxed, but his gaze did not swerve from Gerard's face. "I'd like to know your whereabouts last evening, around midnight."

"I was at my club, Craven's. I have several friends who will verify my presence there."

"When did you leave the club?"

"Four o'clock, perhaps five." Gerard's thick lips curved with a self-satisfied smile. "I had a run of luck at the hazard tables and then took a flier with one of the house wenches. An excellent evening all around."

Grant launched abruptly into the next question. "What was the nature of your relationship with Miss Vivien Duvall?"

The name seemed to puncture Gerard's sense of well-being. The flush on his face deepened, and the dark, narrow eyes resembled chips of obsidian. He leaned forward, holding his snifter in both hands. "This is about Vivien, then? What happened? Has she landed in some kind of trouble? Bloody Christ, I hope it's nasty and unholy expensive, whatever it is. Tell her that I won't lift a finger to help her, even if she comes crawling. I'd sooner kiss the pope's toe."

"Your relationship with her," Grant repeated quietly.

Gerard finished his Armagnac in a slurping swallow and blotted his mouth with his sleeve. The liquor seemed to calm him, and his face split with a crafty smile. "I believe you already know that, Morgan. You once displayed a bit of interest in her yourself, didn't you? And she wouldn't have you." He chortled, tickled by the notion, then sobered quickly. "That hellcat Vivien. Two years I had with her. I paid her bills, gave her the town house, jewelry, a carriage, horses, anything she desired. All for the exclusive right to bed her. At least, it was supposed to be exclusive. I didn't delude myself into thinking she was faithful to me, however. Vivien isn't capable of fidelity."

"Is that why your arrangement ended? Because she was unfaithful?"

"No." Gerard stared moodily at his empty glass. "Before I divulge anything further, *you* can explain something . . . Why the hell are we talking about Vivien? Has something happened to her?"

"You can answer my questions here or at Bow Street," Grant said calmly. "You wouldn't be the first peer I've inquisitioned in the strong room."

A spurt of incredulous rage caused Gerard to rise from his chair. "That you dare to threaten me . . . By God, someone ought to take you down a few buttons!"

Grant stood as well, eclipsing Gerard's height by almost a head. "You're welcome to try," he said softly. He rarely used his size to bully others, preferring to rely on his wits. There were too many men who tried to test their own strength against him, provoking him to fight in the hopes that they might impress their friends with their daring. Grant had long ago tired of thrashing the endless parade of bantam roosters who challenged him. He only fought when strictly necessary—and he always won. He took little pleasure in beating a man senseless. For Gerard, however, he might make an exception.

Gerard's face sagged in dismay as he beheld the giant figure before him. He smoothed the top of his disheveled head in a quick, nervous gesture. "No, I shan't take you on," he mumbled. "I wouldn't lower myself to trade blows with a common bruiser."

Grant gestured toward the wing chair with exaggerated courtesy. "Then have a seat, my lord."

A new thought seemed to occur to Gerard, and he lowered himself heavily into the upholstered cushions. "Good God," he said thickly. "Vivien's dead, isn't she? That's what this is about."

Grant sat and leaned forward, bracing his elbows on his knees. He stared intently at Gerard's flushed face. "Why do you say that?"

Gerard spoke as if in a daze. "She's gone missing for the past month, ever since she broke off our arrangement. Her servants were dismissed and the town house was closed. I went to balls Vivien was supposed to have attended, a soiree, a musical evening . . . No one knew where she was, or why she hadn't come. Everyone assumed she had secluded herself with some new protector. But Vivien wouldn't have stayed away from London that long unless something was drastically wrong."

"Why do you say that?"

"Vivien is easily bored. She has a constant need for stimulation and amusement. A quiet evening at home would drive her mad. She hates to be alone. She insists on going to some soiree or party every night of the week. I could never match her pace." Gerard gave a small, defeated laugh. "She stayed with me longer than with any of her other protectors—I've taken some measure of comfort in that."

"Does she have any enemies that you know of?"

"No one I would label that way . . . but there are many who dislike her."

"What was Miss Duvall's financial situation at the time she parted from you?"

"Money pours through Vivien's fingers like water. She didn't have sufficient funds to last long. She had to find a new paramour without delay."

"Any notion of whom the next candidate might have been?"

"No."

"What do you know of her family?"

"She has none that I am aware of. As you might guess, our conversations rarely turned in that direction." Gerard sighed and nibbled at a rough spot on one of his manicured cuticles. "Will this take much longer, Morgan? I have a thirst for more Armagnac."

"What direction did your conversations turn to?" Grant asked. "Does Miss Duvall have any particular hobbies or pursuits? Any new interests she has developed of late?"

"None that exist outside of bed. Why, I doubt she's ever even read a book."

"Any new acquaintances you were aware of? Male in particular?"

Gerard rolled his eyes. "God Himself couldn't account for all of Vivien's male acquaintances."

"Tell me about the day she broke off your arrangement. Did you argue?"

"Naturally. I had invested quite heavily in her, and I saw no reason things could not continue indefinitely. I've closed my eyes whenever she cared to have a dallaince. I became quite heated—I even threatened her—but she laughed in my face. I demanded to know the name of the man who would be my replacement, as I was certain that she wouldn't leave me without first securing another arrangement. She was quite smug, and would say nothing except that she expected soon to marry into a great fortune." He snorted with bitter amusement. "The idea! One doesn't marry soiled goods like Vivien Duvall, unless he wants to be the laughingstock of England. Of course, I would put nothing past her. I suppose it's possible she could have enticed some decrepit widower to make an offer for her."

"Were there witnesses to the argument?"

"Vivien's servants were aware of it, I'm certain. No doubt I raised the roof a time or two."

"Did you strike her?"

"Never," Gerard said instantly, seeming offended. "I'll admit, I was tempted to choke the life out of her. But I would never do harm to a woman. And in spite of my anger, I would have taken Vivien back if she had desired it, my pride be damned."

Grant's brows pulled together at the statement. In his opinion, no woman was worth the sacrifice of a man's pride, no matter how attractive she might have been. There was always another pretty face, another well-shaped body, another display of feminine charms that would soon blot out the memories.

"I can see what you're thinking," Gerard said. "But there's something you don't understand ... Vivien is one of a kind. The smell, the taste, the feel of her ... No one could compare. There was nothing she wouldn't do in bed. Have you ever slept with a woman who has no shame? If I could have just one more night with her ... even one hour ..." He shook his head with a mumbled curse.

"All right, my lord," Grant said tersely. "We're finished for now. As my investigation proceeds, I may have more questions for you." He stood and headed for the door, but paused as he heard Gerard's pleading voice.

"Morgan, you must tell me ... What has happened to her?"

Grant turned to glance at him curiously. "If she were dead," he said slowly, "would you mourn her?" He waited a long time for the other man to reply, but Gerard apparently found it difficult to answer.

Grant smiled cynically. Gerard was like a child deprived of his favorite toy—he would miss the sexual pleasure Vivien had given him, but he felt no genuine caring or concern. Some courtesans and their protectors genuinely loved each other, had relationships that lasted for decades. Grant knew

more than one man who had escaped the bitter disappointment of his arranged marriage by taking a
mistress who would bear him children and serve
him as the loving companion his wife should have
been. For Vivien, however, the role of courtesan
was played purely for reasons of business and
profit.

"Do you have a set of keys to her town house?"
Grant asked Gerard.

The question clearly nonplussed him. "I suppose
I might. Do you intend to search her possessions?
What do you expect to find?"

"Where Miss Duvall is concerned, I'm learning
not to expect anything," Grant replied dourly,
while curiosity and an odd touch of dread tangled
inside him at the prospect of visiting her town
house. The more he discovered about Vivien and
her sordid past, the darker his mood became.

Four

*G*rant deftly unlocked the bronzed door of Vivien's town house, one of many located behind the palace front of east Grosvenor Square. The prestigious address, with its spectacular row of columns and arched doorways, must have cost a pretty penny. A further testament to Vivien's skill at her profession, he thought darkly.

The interior was dim and quiet, with a faint mustiness in the air from being closed up for weeks. Grant lit a lamp and a pair of wall sconces, which shed a bright glow on walls covered in hand-painted wallpaper. Taking the lamp in hand, he wandered through the first-floor rooms. The house was elegant and decidedly feminine, with abundant frescoes of pastel flowers, walls covered in French paper, delicate furniture with spindly legs, and large framed looking glasses over every fireplace.

He ascended the stairs, noting the costly twisted balusters with carved tread ends, and the lamps housed in crystal cases. It seemed no expense had been spared in decorating the place to Vivien's satisfaction. Upstairs, the air seemed to hold a hint of stale perfume. He followed the scent to the main bedroom, lit more lamps, and surveyed his surroundings intently.

The walls were covered in emerald-green silk, a jewel tone that was echoed in the rich Brussels floral-patterned carpet underfoot. Although the current fashion for ladies' bedrooms was to half conceal the bed in an alcove, Vivien had made hers the central attraction, placing it on a carpeted platform to increase its visibility. What drew Grant's attention most strongly, however, was a portrait of Vivien hung on the wall facing the bed. She had been painted in the nude, half turned away from the viewer to expose her pale back and buttocks. She glanced artfully over her shoulder, her torso angled to reveal the profile of one round, lovely breast.

The artist had idealized Vivien, making her form a little fleshier than in reality, the legs and waist slightly elongated, the unswept hair so red that it contained tongues of purple flame. Had the artist bedded Vivien during one of the many sittings it had taken to paint her? It seemed likely. Nothing but lovemaking could have given her face that flushed, replete look, the mouth soft with satisfaction, the blue eyes heavy-lidded and catlike.

Staring at the painting, Grant experienced what was fast becoming a familiar reaction to Vivien . . . a mingling of fire and ice . . . a flare of intense desire balanced by cold deliberation. He wanted her, and more than that, he wanted to humble and chasten her. He was going to use her, the way she had used so many men. It was time for Vivien Duvall to receive her reckoning.

He wandered to a Louis XV dressing table with an inlaid tulipwood top, and picked up a large crystal flacon of perfume. The scent was heavy with roses and tempered by the crispness of sandalwood. Instantly it brought back the memory of Vivien at the Wentworth ball. She had smelled exactly this way, her warm skin emanating the sweet fragrance.

Setting aside the perfume, Grant opened the shallow drawers of the dressing table, finding a jumble of brushes, jars filled with pastel-colored creams, hair ornaments of tortoiseshell, ivory, and silver. Beneath the clutter, there was a small book bound in red moroccon leather.

Grant extricated the volume and leafed through it quickly, finding lists of gentlemen's names, detailed descriptions of sexual activities, times and dates of romantic assignations. It would serve as an excellent tool for blackmail. He recognized some of the names in the book, a few belonging to gentlemen who prided themselves on their solid marriages and sterling reputations. None of them would care to have his infidelities exposed, and would doubtless pay dearly to ensure Vivien's silence. Or perhaps even resort to murder to make her silence permanent.

"What a busy girl you've been," Grant muttered, slipping the book into his pocket. He closed the drawer with unnecessary force.

His jaw was clenched as he searched the room methodically, locating a leather valise. He stuffed the first decent clothes he could find into the valise . . . a few richly colored gowns, linen undergarments, stockings and shoes, and a box containing lace handkerchiefs and three pairs of cream-colored gloves. With the valise filled to overflowing, he picked up the lamp and left the bedroom. Tomorrow he would return to search the terrace in earnest, but for now he wanted to pay a visit to his new guest and see how she was faring.

Hiring a hackney to convey him to King Street, Grant returned to his house. Mrs. Buttons greeted him at the door, shivering a little as a blast of wintry wind slipped inside the house. She took his coat and folded it over her arm. "Good afternoon, sir. Will you be taking a midday meal today?"

"I'm not hungry," he replied, glancing in the direction of the staircase. "How is she?"

Unperturbed by his abruptness, the housekeeper replied calmly. "Very well, sir. Miss Duvall had a nice soak in the bath, and one of the maids— Mary—helped me to wash her hair. I believe her condition is much improved."

"Good." He studied the housekeeper closely, having the feeling there was more she could tell him. "You strike me as an apt judge of character, Mrs. Buttons."

She took visible pride at the compliment. "I believe I might be, sir."

"Tell me, then . . . what do you make of Miss Duvall?"

Mrs. Buttons seemed eager to answer the question, her usual reticence giving way to animated interest. She lowered her voice to keep from being overheard by passing servants. "Her behavior has been rather perplexing, sir. After I brought Miss Duvall a plate of toast this morning, and left to oversee the preparation of her bath, she arose by herself and tidied the room. She even made the bed, despite the pain it must have caused her. I can't think why she would have gone to such effort, especially considering her state of health. And then in the bathing room, she tried to lift one of the buckets the maid had brought, to help fill her own bath. We took it from her immediately, of course, but she apologized for the extra work we had done on her behalf. She seems anxious not to cause trouble for anyone and grateful for any assistance we render, as if she is unused to having anyone serve her."

"I see." Grant's face was wiped clean of expression, as it always was when he puzzled over contradictory facts.

Mrs. Buttons warmed to the subject. "She seems to be one of the most considerate and gentle-spirited young women I have ever encountered. With all due respect, sir, I can scarcely believe that what you told me about her last evening is true."

"It's true," Grant said curtly.

Could it be that Vivien's memory loss had altered her character as well? Had she forgotten how to behave with her usual smug superiority . . . or was she merely playing some game with them all? Impatiently Grant handed the valise to Mrs. Buttons. "Have one of the maids put Miss Duvall's clothes away."

"Yes, Mr. Morgan." The housekeeper set the valise on the floor and regarded him with calm brown eyes. "Sir, Mary offered her best night rail for Miss Duvall's use, as we had nothing else to clothe her in."

"Thank you. I consider any kindness done for Miss Duvall as a direct favor to me. Tell Mary to have a new gown and matching pelisse made for herself, and charge it to the household account. A nice gown—she needn't skimp on the trimmings."

Mrs. Buttons turned an approving smile on him. "You're a kind master, if I may say so."

He responded with a scowl. "I'm a reprobate, and we both know it."

"Yes, sir," the housekeeper replied demurely.

Grant headed for the stairs. Some unidentifiable feeling knotted and tightened inside him. Vivien Duvall playing the sweet damsel in distress . . . he wouldn't tolerate it. In the space of a few minutes, he was going to expose her for the fraud she was. If she didn't remember that she was an unprincipled whore, he would damn well remind her. He would reveal every cunning, shameless facet of her dissolute character, and let her ponder *that* for a while. Then let her try to play the innocent.

Reaching his bedroom, he opened the door without knocking, halfway expecting to find Vivien laughing privately about how she was deceiving everyone with her pretense of virtue. He entered the room . . . and stopped dead in his tracks. She was sitting in an armchair by the grate, her small bare feet drawn up and to the side, an open book in her lap. Golden shards of firelight played over her vulnerable face as she glanced up at him. She was dressed in a high-necked white nightgown that was a little too big for her, with a blue cashmere lap robe draped over her waist and thighs.

After setting the book on the floor, she pulled the lap robe up to her chest. The tension inside Grant rose to an excruciating pitch. She had the face of an angel, and the hair of the Devil's handmaiden. The freshly washed locks flowed around her in a waist-length curtain, waves and curls of molten red that contained every shade from cinnamon to strawberry-gold. It was the kind of hair that nature usually bestowed on homely women to atone for their lack of physical beauty.

But Vivien had a face and form that belonged in a Renaissance painting, except that the reality of her was more delicate and fresh than any painted image could convey. Now that her eyes were no longer swollen, the pure blue intensity of her gaze shone full and direct on him. Her mouth, tender and rose-tinted, was a marvel of nature.

Something was wrong with his breathing. His lungs weren't working properly, his heartbeat was too fast, and he clenched his teeth. If he weren't a civilized man, if he didn't pride himself on his renowned self-possession, he would take her here, now, with no regard for the consequences. He wanted her that badly.

Seeming not to understand his silent, ferocious struggle, Vivien gave him a hesitant smile of welcome. He almost hated her for that smile, so soft and warm that it pulled at something deep in his chest.

He returned the smile with a confident one of his own. "Good afternoon, Miss Duvall. It's time for us to talk."

Vivien kept the lap robe pulled high around herself as she stared at the man before her. Emotions tumbled inside her, not the least of which was curiosity. The servants had told her Grant Morgan was a Bow Street Runner, the most famous of the pack. The most fearless man in England, one of them had added, and now Vivien understood why.

He was a giant. Somehow in the fear and discomfort of the last twenty-four hours, she hadn't really noticed that the gruff, deep voice and brooding green eyes belonged to a man who was so . . . well, large. Not merely tall, but large in every way. Now that she had recovered somewhat from her dunking in the Thames, she was able to take a good, clear look at him. His shoulders were as broad as cathedral doors, and his rangy body was impressively developed, with long muscled thighs, and upper arms that bulged against the constraints of his coat sleeves.

He wasn't handsome in the conventional sense. This man's face was as expressive as a block of granite. Her gaze fell to his hands, and she felt a wash of fire cover her face as she remembered the gentle touch of them.

"Yes, I would like to talk," she murmured.

Morgan picked up a heavy armchair and moved it close to hers, hefting its weight with astonishing ease. Watching him, Vivien wondered how it might feel to possess such boundless strength. The sheer physical presence of him, his raw masculinity and vitality, seemed to fill the room. He sat and studied her with those perceptive green eyes . . . long-lashed eyes that weren't quite emerald. The shade was deeper than that, a color that reminded her of beech leaves, or the smoky green of an antique wine bottle.

"Mr. Morgan," she said, helpless to look away from those riveting eyes, "I can never thank you enough for all you done . . . your kindness and generosity, and . . ." She felt the color on her face condense into two bright spots on her cheeks. "I owe you my life."

"I didn't pull you from the river," Morgan said, not seeming particularly pleased by her gratitude. "The waterman did."

Vivien was unable to let the matter drop without making certain he understood how she felt. "Even then, I would have died. I remember lying on the steps, and I was so cold and wretched that I didn't particularly care if I lived or not. And then you came."

"Do you remember anything else? Anything about yourself, or your past? Do you have impressions of struggling with someone, or arguing—"

"No." Both of her hands went up to her throat,

investigating the soreness, and she stared at him wonderingly. "Mr. Morgan . . . who did this to me?"

"I don't know yet. It would be a damned sight more convenient if you hadn't lost your memory."

"I'm sorry."

He shrugged. "It's hardly your fault."

Where was the tender stranger who had taken care of her last night and this morning? She found it hard to believe that this was the man who had held and comforted her, rubbed salve on her bruises, and tucked her in bed as a parent would a beloved child. Now he seemed forbidding and utterly unapproachable. He was angry with her but she didn't know why. The realization made her feel more lost and confused than before, if that was possible. He was all she had—she couldn't bear for him to be cold to her.

"You're displeased," she said. "What has happened? Have I done something wrong?"

The questions seemed to soften him a little. Although he didn't quite meet her eyes, he exhaled deeply, as if releasing some unpleasant pent-up emotion. "No," he muttered with a quick shake of his head. "It's nothing."

Perhaps he had learned something about her that he didn't like, Vivien thought, and anxiety made her entire body tauten until all her muscles quivered.

"I'm frightened," she said, and brought her clenched hands down to her lap. "I keep trying to remember something, anything about myself. Nothing is familiar. Nothing makes sense. And knowing that someone hates me enough to want me dead—"

"For all he knows, you are dead."

"He?"

"No woman could have possessed the strength to strangle you with her bare hands. Moreover, your personal history includes very few women. The great majority of your associates have been men."

"Oh." Why wouldn't he just tell her what needed to be said, instead of making her ask him questions? It was a form of torture, having to stare at his stony face and wonder what secrets of her past had brought her to this incredible situation. "You said . . . I might not like some of the things you would tell me about myself," she prompted unsteadily.

Reaching into his coat pocket, he extracted a small book bound in dark red leather. "Have a look at this," he said curtly, placing the volume in her hands.

"What is it?" she asked warily.

He didn't reply, only stared at her with a restless gaze that conveyed his impatience.

Carefully she opened the book, discovering page after page of neat feminine script. There were lists, names, dates . . . It took a half minute of reading before she encountered a passage so explicit that she snapped the volume shut with a mortified gasp. Her shocked gaze lifted to his. "Why in heaven's name would you show me such a thing?" She tried to hand the book back, but he did not move to take it. Casting the object to the floor, she regarded it as if it were a coiled snake. "Whom does it belong to, and how does it pertain to me?"

"It's yours."

"*Mine?*" An icy feeling crept over her, and she pulled the length of cashmere more closely around herself. "You're mistaken, Mr. Morgan." Her voice was clipped and cool with outrage. "I didn't write those things. I couldn't have."

"How do you know that?"

"Because I couldn't!" Startled and offended, she gave him a look of rebuke.

When he spoke, his voice was flat and quiet. "You're a courtesan, Vivien. The most notorious one in London. You've garnered a fortune from your talent."

She felt her face turn stark white. Her heart pounded frantically in her chest. "It isn't true," she cried. "The book must belong to someone else."

"I found it in your terrace house, in your bedroom."

"Why would I . . . that is, why would any woman write such things?"

"A tool for blackmail," he suggested gently. "Or perhaps it was just the only way you could keep track."

Vivien left her chair as if she had been jolted out of it, letting the cashmere lap robe drop to the floor. Wincing as pain shot through her bound ankle, she hobbled backward a few steps, needing to put some distance between them. "I didn't do any of the things in that book!"

To her chagrin, Morgan's gaze swept over her, and she realized that the firelight shone through the muslin, illuminating every detail of her body. Hastily she pulled handfuls of the loose gown in front of herself, clutching the folds to her midriff. "I'm not a prostitute," she said vehemently. "If I were, I'm certain I would know it in some part of myself, but I don't because *it's not there*. You're absolutely wrong about me. If this is an example of your investigative abilities, I am not impressed! Now . . . now go out and ask more questions and do what is necessary to find out who I really am."

Morgan rose from his own chair to follow her. "I can't change the truth just because you don't like it."

"Not only do I not like it," Vivien said, breathing hard, "I reject it entirely. You are *wrong*, do you understand?" To her humiliation, she wobbled off balance, her weak ankle refusing to support her.

"Would you like me to parade you in front of witnesses who will swear on the Bible that you are Vivien Duvall?" Morgan asked harshly. "Would you like to go to your house and see the nude painting of yourself on the bedroom wall? I brought back some of your clothes—would you care to try them on and see how they fit? I can dig up mountains of proof for you." He caught her as she tried to stumble away from him, his arm locked firmly behind her back.

Vivien whimpered as he brought her against his massive body. She wedged her arms between them, her head falling back as she stared into the face so high above hers. His ribs were as sturdy as frigate timbers beneath her cold hands. He imprisoned her between his powerful thighs, holding her steady.

"Even if I am Vivien Duvall," she said stubbornly, "you can't prove that I did all the things in that book. They are made-up stories."

"It's all true, Vivien. You sell your body for profit." He didn't seem any more pleased about the idea than she. "You go from one man to another, taking what you want from each of them."

"Oh, really? Then who, exactly, is supposed to be my latest protector? Where is he, and why haven't you sent for him?"

"Who do you think he is?" Morgan asked softly.

The words sent Vivien reeling. She was openmouthed, dazed, suddenly limp in his grasp. "No."

"We've been lovers ever since you left Lord Gerard. I've visited you in your town house on several occasions. We've kept things discreet, but we were on the verge of drawing up a proper contract." Grant told the lies without a shred of guilt. The deceit would hardly hurt her, after the sordid life she had led, and it served his purpose. He wanted her, and this was the most expedient way to have her.

"Then you and I are . . ." She choked on the words.

"Yes."

"You're lying!" Vivien strained against him, pushing, twisting, but his arms were like steel bands. Soon she was exhausted by the fruitless struggle. She couldn't help but be aware that her movements had aroused him. The hard protrusion of his masculinity pressed high against her stomach, branding her with its aggressive heat. How in God's name could she have been intimate with this man and not remember?

Trembling, she collapsed against him, leaning full into the long, muscled length of him. She was too exhausted to move. A pleasant mixture of linen and spicy shaving soap clung to him, and she breathed deeply of the fragrance. Her head fell to his chest, her ear pressed to the resounding beat of his heart. "You're wrong," she said, too bewildered to cry. "I'm not that kind of woman. I just can't be."

He did not reply, and she realized that he was so convinced on the matter that it didn't merit arguing. A flicker of fury intruded on her confusion. Very well. She would not further exhaust herself by denying the accusation . . . Time would certainly prove him wrong.

"What do you want from me now?" she asked in a thick voice. A shiver chased down her body as she felt his hand move over her back, the heat of his palm sinking through the muslin.

"I'm going to keep you here," he replied, "for your protection and my convenience."

His convenience? That could only mean that he intended to continue their previous arrangement, regardless of her memory loss. She glanced over her shoulder at the oversized bed that had seemed such a haven until now. If he planned to take her tonight, she wouldn't be able to stand it. She would flee the house and run screaming through the streets in her nightgown. "I can't oblige you tonight, if that's what you're planning," she said rebelliously. "And not tomorrow night, either. And not—"

"Hush." For the first time a note of amusement entered his voice. "I'm not such a bastard that I would inflict myself on you while you're ill. We'll wait until you're well enough."

"I won't want to ever again! I'm not a prostitute."

"You'll want to. It's in your nature, Vivien. You can't change what you are."

His matter-of-fact statements infuriated her. "I won't want any man from now on. Especially not you."

Her defiance seemed to trigger something inside him, unleashing a grim determination to prove something to her . . . and to himself. Swiftly he pulled her into his arms, before she had time to think or react. He carried her to the bed and deposited her on the neatly folded-back covers. His dark face obliterated the glow of the fire as he leaned over her.

"No," Vivien gasped.

There was a cruel edge to his mouth, but when he fitted his lips over hers, the kiss was soft, slow, utterly consuming. He placed his hands flat on the mattress on either side of her head, not touching her with any part of his body except his mouth. Had she wanted, she could have rolled away from him easily. But she stayed beneath him, transfixed by the sweet, hot flowering of sensation that spread rapidly and made the downy hairs all over her body rise.

She lifted her hands to his face in a halfhearted

gesture to push him away, but he angled his head and kissed her harder, and any thought of resisting him disappeared. His tongue ventured inside her mouth, teasing, stroking. He tasted of coffee, and some pleasant masculine essence that lured her own tongue to respond timidly. The feathery touch seemed to excite him. Breathing deeply, he twisted his mouth over hers in long, searching kisses, each one more tender and intimate than the last. Vivien relaxed helplessly beneath him while a heavy, delicious ache formed in her breasts and low in her stomach and between her thighs. Her dazed mind no longer comprehended what was happening, or even cared. All that existed was sensation, every part of her focused on the consuming heat of his mouth.

With a suddenness that stunned her, Morgan tore his lips away and pinned her with a simmering gaze. "You see?" he said hoarsely. "Now tell me what kind of woman you are."

It took a moment for Vivien to understand what he had said. Ashamed and furious, she rolled to her side. "Go away," she gasped, pressing her hand over her exposed ear, blocking out any words he might utter. "Leave me alone."

He obliged at once, leaving her curled on the bed in a silent huddle.

Barely aware of where he was going, Grant made his way downstairs, his mind overtaken by questions, sensations . . . "Vivien," he muttered more than once, the name alternately a curse and a prayer.

He found himself in the library, a haven of leather and oak, fitted with comfortably worn chairs and specially designed bookcases. The cases were fronted with beveled glass, and brass grill-work on the bottom shelves. He collected books ob-sessively—anything between two covers would do. The stacks of newspapers piled on desks and tables often moved Mrs. Buttons to complain that the house was the greatest fire hazard in London.

Grant never sat for a quiet moment without a book or paper close at hand. When he wasn't work-ing or sleeping, he read. Anything to keep himself from thinking about the past. On the nights when regrets lingered in his head like ghosts, driving out all possibility of sleep, he came to the library and drank brandy and read until the words blurred be-fore his eyes.

Prowling past the shelves of leather-bound tal-ismans, Grant sought something to divert his at-tention. His fingers trailed lightly over the cool, shining glass doors, opened one, brushed over a row of books. But for once, the touch of leather repelled him ... His hand ached for soft female skin, for silken hair, for round breasts and hips ...

He caught sight of his reflection in the glass, his face set and miserable.

Turning away with a groan, Grant went to the sideboard fitted between a pair of small matching cupboards. One of the cupboards was used as a cellarette for wines. He rummaged in the cabinet until his hand closed around the flattened lozenge-shaped body of a brandy bottle, sloshing with dark liquid. Uncorking it, he drank directly from the bottle, the fullness of expensive French brandy roll-ing down his throat. Waiting for a familiar warmth to spread in his chest, he felt only emptiness.

His mind returned to the image of Vivien, the sweetness of her mouth, the innocence of her re-sponse. As if she weren't used to kissing, as if she were an awkward but willing pupil in the hands of an experienced teacher. All an illusion.

"Innocence," he muttered with an ugly laugh, and poured more brandy down his throat. Vivien was prime quality goods to be sure, but she was a whore nonetheless. And he was a fool for feeling protective of her, wanting her, and worst of all, *lik-ing* her.

He sat in an armchair and braced his feet on the edge of his desk, and silently acknowledged the mortifying truth. If he didn't know who and what Vivien was, he would be mad for her. What man wouldn't? She was lovely, intelligent, and seem-ingly vulnerable. Her response to the news that she was a courtesan had been a perfect blend of anger and bewilderment. The way an innocent woman would react. His instincts and his brain had rarely given him such opposing messages, and the few times they had, he had been inclined to trust his instincts. But not in this case. He knew all about Vivien's unique brand of faux innocence. It didn't matter how she behaved at present, she would sooner or later revert to character.

Therefore, he couldn't let himself be taken in by her.

But hell and damnation . . . it wasn't going to be easy.

Five

Vivien curled up in one corner of the acre-wide bed, fuming and worrying until she finally drifted into a fog of oblivion. But there was no peace to be found in sleep, only a bizzare dream that became increasingly sinister.

She hurried through a shadowed street, pursued by faceless strangers. Occasionally she paused to laugh and taunt them, then turned and ran just before they reached her. Approaching a bridge, she climbed onto the embankment wall, surmounting a pier topped with a bronze statue of a river deity. The men below her clamored to reach her, climbing after her, but she laughed throatily and kicked them away. Suddenly, to her horror, the massive bronze statue beside her began to move. Huge metal arms wrapped around her, imprisoning her in a cold merciless embrace.

Crying out in terror, she fought the statue, but it clutched her, turned toward the river . . . and plunged into the black, bitterly cold depths. Its weight pulled her down quickly, the surface receding far above her. She screamed beneath the water, but no one could hear her, and the choking liquid filled her mouth and throat—

"Vivien. Dammit, Vivien, wake up."

She started awake, still fighting the arms around her . . . then saw Morgan's face above hers. He wore an anxious scowl as he hauled her into his lap, one hand smoothing the damp hair back from her face. His upper torso was covered only by a thin linen shirt, open at the neck to reveal the hollow at the base of his throat.

Disoriented, Vivien fought to catch her breath. She glanced at their surroundings, realizing they were on the floor.

"You fell off the bed," Morgan said.

"I-I had a nightmare."

"Tell me," he said softly. As she remained silent, he stroked the ruffled arc of her eyebrow with the pad of his thumb. The intimate gesture somehow moved her to speak when words would have failed.

Vivien gnawed her lower lip nervously. "I dreamed I was drowning. It was so real . . . I couldn't breathe."

A gentle, sandpapery sound came from his throat. He patted her back in a soothing rhythm, rocking her as if she were a child. The heat of his body permeated the layers of clothing between them, warming her. For a moment she was tempted to push him away, the memory of his distasteful accusations still fresh in her ears.

But she stayed motionless against him. Although he was hateful and arrogant, he was also large and safe. At the moment there was no more appealing place in the world than his arms. A delicious scent clung to him, a blend of brandy and salt and linen . . . smells that reminded her of something . . . someone . . . whose comforting image was locked deep in her memory. A father or brother, perhaps? A lover she had held dear?

Confused and frustrated, she chewed harder at her lip as she strained to remember.

"Don't do that," Morgan said, touching her mouth with gentle fingers. "Try to relax. Would you like a drink?"

"I don't know."

He held her for a moment longer, cradling her in his lap, until the frantic jerking of her heart slowed to a normal pace. His hand slid over her leg and hip and settled at the curve of her waist, and in a despairing flash, Vivien sensed that his touch was somehow familiar and natural. As if she belonged in his arms, against his body . . . as if they had indeed been lovers. She moved her face, blotting her tear-dampened cheek against his shirt, and she felt his mouth brush over her hair.

Carefully Morgan lifted her from the floor and placed her on the bed, and busied himself with straightening the tangled mass of sheets and blankets. Going to the bedside table, he poured a small quantity of liquor into a verriere glass etched with leaves. "I had a feeling you might need some of this during the night," he said. "You'll have dreams about it from time to time. Occasionally one of them will be so damned vivid you'll wake with a scream in your throat. It happens after one comes close to dying."

He sounded quite knowledgeable on the subject, Vivien thought, accepting the verriere. She sipped the rich, slightly fruity beverage. "Have you come close to death before?"

"Once or twice."

"What happened?" she asked.

"I never discuss my exploits." A self-mocking smile touched his lips, softening the angles of his face. "It's tempting for a Runner to develop a habit of boasting, and then we tend to spend all our time spinning elaborate tales . . . so it's better not to talk of work at all, or nothing gets done."

"I'll find out anyway," Vivien said. She took a larger swallow of the brandy, the pleasant fire spreading through her veins and restoring her shattered nerves. "Mrs. Buttons told me there have been a few ha'penny novels published about your adventures."

"Trash only fit to use as kindling," he said with a snort. "You won't find those in my house."

"Yes, I will. Some of your servants collect them."

"The devil they do," he muttered, clearly surprised at the information. "Crackbrains. Don't believe a word any of them tells you."

"I've embarrassed you," she said with a trace of satisfaction, and buried a fleeting smile in the verriere glass.

"Whom have you been talking to? Mrs. Buttons?

One of the maids? I'll have someone's head if they've been gossiping."

"The servants are all quite proud of you," Vivien said, delighted at having found a way to needle him. "It seems you're a legend. Rescuing heiresses, tracking murderers, solving impossible cases—"

"Legend, my arse." Morgan looked as though she had mocked him instead of complimenting his reputation. "Mostly I recover stolen property for banks. I have a great fondness for banks and the reward money they offer. Sir Ross and any of the Runners can tell you there's a cash box where my heart should be."

"You're trying to tell me that you're not a hero," Vivien said with a questioning lilt.

"Based on your acquaintance with me during the last twenty-four hours, wouldn't you agree?"

She considered the question and answered thoughtfully. "Obviously you are not a perfect man—as if there could be such a thing—but you have done good for many people, sometimes at the risk of your own life. That makes you heroic, even if I don't approve of you."

"*You* don't approve of *me*," he repeated blankly.

"No. I think it very wrong of you to pay for the services of a woman like me."

The comment seemed to simultaneously amuse and puzzle him. "Why, Vivien," he mocked, "you don't sound like yourself."

"Don't I?" She fiddled awkwardly with the edges of the bed linens. "I have no idea what I'm supposed to sound like, or what I should say. All I know is that the more you tell me about myself, the more I wonder why you or anyone else should desire my company. I'm not a very nice woman, am I?"

A stiff silence descended on them. Morgan's stare was searching, critical, like that of a scientist examining the unexpected results of an experiment. Wordlessly he turned and headed toward the door, and Vivien thought he was leaving. However, he picked up a tray that had been set on a side table, and returned to the bed with it.

"Your supper," he said, setting the tray on her lap, straightening a piece of silverware that had slid to the edge. "I was carrying this upstairs when I heard you fall."

"You were bringing a supper tray to me?" Vivien asked, wondering why he had not had one of the servants do it.

Morgan read the unspoken question in her expression. "I intended to offer it with an apology." His voice turned brusque as he added, "My manner with you earlier this evening was uncalled-for."

Vivien was rather taken by his charming gruffness. Her instincts told her that he was sincere. Although he surely did not respect or esteem her, he was willing to apologize when he believed himself to be in the wrong. Perhaps he wasn't quite the ogre she had thought him.

She tried to meet his honesty in equal measure. "You were only relating the truth."

"I should have been far more gentle in the telling of it. I'm not what anyone would call a diplomat."

"I shouldn't have blamed you for what you said.

After all, it's not your fault that I'm a—"

"A beautiful and fascinating woman," he finished for her.

Flushing, Vivien fumbled with the napkin and laid it over her midriff. She didn't feel beautiful and fascinating, and she certainly didn't feel like a worldly-wise courtesan. "Thank you," she said with difficulty. "But I'm not the woman you think I am . . . at least, for the present I'm not. I don't remember anything about myself. And I don't know how to behave with you."

"That's all right," Morgan interrupted, sitting in the bedside chair. He seemed relaxed and casual, but his gaze didn't leave her for a moment. "Behave however you wish. No one is going to force you to do something you don't want, least of all me."

Difficult as it was, she took a deep breath and returned his gaze. "Then you won't want me to—"

"No," he said quietly. "I've already told you that I won't bother you that way. Not until you desire it."

"And if I never desire it?" she forced herself to ask in a mortified scrape of a whisper.

"The choice is entirely yours," he assured her. A crooked smile tugged at his mouth. "But be forewarned. My attractions may grow on you."

Abashed, Vivien swiftly dropped her gaze to the dainty meal before her. The plate contained slivers of chicken, a dab of pudding, a spoonful of vegetables in cream. She picked up a bread roll and bit into it. It seemed to take an unusual amount of effort to chew and swallow the morsel. "This is your room, isn't it? I would like to move to the guest room as soon as it's convenient. I don't wish to deprive you of your own bed."

"Stay here. I want you to be comfortable."

"It's very grand, but the bed is too large for me, and . . ." Vivien hesitated, unable to tell him that she felt surrounded by him in this room, even when he wasn't here. His smell and his distinctly masculine aura seemed to linger in the air. "Have I been here before?" she asked suddenly. "In your house . . . in this room?"

"No. This is the first time you've been a guest in my home."

On the occasions when they had been intimate, she guessed they had trysted in her bed, or some other place. She was too embarrassed to ask for details. "Mr. Morgan—Grant—there is something I want to ask . . ."

"Yes?"

"Promise you won't laugh at me. Please."

"All right."

She picked up a silver fork and toyed with the prongs, focusing all her attention on the utensil. "Was there any love between us? Any affection? Or was it merely a sort of business arrangement?" She could hardly bear the thought that she might have sold her body only for money. Her face burned hot with shame as she waited for the answer. To her relief, he didn't jeer or laugh.

"It wasn't all business," he said carefully. "I thought you would offer some ease and enjoyment I needed badly."

"Then one could say we're friends?" Vivien asked, grasping the fork so hard that the prongs left scarlet marks on the flesh of her palm.

"Yes, we're—" Breaking off, Morgan took the fork from her and rubbed the sore spot on her palm with his thumb. He cradled her hand in his large one, frowning at the little red marks. "We're friends, Vivien," he muttered. "Don't distress yourself. You're hardly a cheap wh . . . prostitute. You're an exclusive courtesan, and few people think the worse of you for it."

"I do," Vivien said painfully. "I think very much the worse of me for it. I wish I were anything else."

"You'll get used to the idea."

"That's what I'm afraid of," she whispered.

Something in her woeful gaze seemed to bother him. Letting go of her hand, he muttered an imprecation and left the room, while she stared morosely at the cooling food on her plate.

"Oh, I couldn't wear that," Vivien said, staring at the gown that had been laid out for her. It was one of four that Mr. Morgan had brought from her town house, and while she had no doubt that the gown was hers, she very much doubted its tastefulness. Although the garment was beautifully designed and well made, the color, a dark velvet that captured the intense tones of a ripe plum or black cherries, would prove a jarring clash with her hair. She added ruefully, "Not with this carrot top. I'll look a fright."

Mrs. Buttons surveyed her critically as Mary helped her from the bath and began to dry her off with a thick length of white toweling. "I think you might be pleasantly surprised, Miss Duvall. Won't you try it on and see?"

"Yes, I'll try," Vivien said, shivering as the cool air chased over her exposed skin, raising gooseflesh from head to toe. "But there's every chance I'll look ridiculous."

"I assure you, such a thing isn't possible," Mrs. Buttons replied. Over the last three days, the housekeeper's manner with Vivien had changed from distant politeness to warm kindness, and the rest of the household staff had promptly followed suit. Sincerely grateful for the help they offered her, Vivien praised and thanked the servants whenever the opportunity presented itself.

Had Vivien been a high-ranking noblewoman, she supposed she would have accepted their service as her due, and taken care not to become familiar with them. However, she was far from an aristocrat, and in light of what she knew about her own dissolute past, she thought the servants of the Morgan household were more than kind. There was no doubt they all knew what she was, and what she had been, and still they treated her with the deference they would have accorded a duchess. When she remarked on this fact to Mrs. Buttons, the housekeeper had explained with a wry smile.

"For one thing, Mr. Morgan has made it clear that he values you, and wishes you to be treated as a respected guest. But more than that, Miss Duvall, your character speaks for itself. No matter what is said about you, the servants can see that you are a kind and decent young woman."

"But I'm not," Vivien said. Unable to look into the housekeeper's face, she bent her head. There had been a long silence, and then she had felt Mrs. Button's gentle hand on her shoulder.

"We all have mistakes to overcome," the house-keeper said quietly. "And yours aren't the worst I've heard of. Thanks to Mr. Morgan's profession, I have seen and known some of the more wretched characters imaginable, who have no bit of goodness or hope left in them. You are far from that desper-ate state."

"Thank you," Vivien had whispered, utterly humble. "I'll try to justify your kindness to me." Ever since that moment, Mrs. Buttons had assumed an almost motherly protectiveness toward her.

As for Grant, Vivien had seen little of him, as he occupied himself with investigating her case and one or two others. He checked on her in the morn-ings, talked for five minutes or so, and then was gone for the rest of the day. In the evenings he returned for a spartan and solitary supper and read books in the library.

Morgan was a mysterious figure to Vivien. The ha-penny novels that the maid, Mary, had loaned to her had shed little light on his character. The novels emphasized the adventurous side of Mor-gan's nature, detailing the crimes he had solved and his famous pursuit of a murderer across two continents. However, it was clear the author knew nothing of him personally. Vivien suspected that few people desired to know the real nature of the man, preferring the outsized tales of a legend. It was usually that way with famous men—people wanted to know about their accomplishments and strengths, not their vulnerabilities.

But it was precisely Morgan's weaknesses that interested Vivien. He appeared to have so few of them. He was a private, seemingly invulnerable man who did not like to talk about his past. Vivien couldn't help wondering what secrets and memories were contained in his carefully guarded heart. One thing was certain ... Morgan would never trust *her* in that way.

Vivien was well aware of Morgan's contempt for the life she had led before her "accident." It was obvious that he did not like or approve of the woman she had been, and she could hardly blame him, as she felt exactly the same. Unfortunately, in the course of his investigation, Morgan seemed to be uncovering more unsavory facts about her. He had admitted that he had been questioning the people who knew her. It appeared that whatever they had told him had been neither especially helpful nor particularly pleasant.

Frowning, Vivien tried to push the depressing thoughts to the back of her mind. She held on to the back of a nearby chair to preserve her balance as Mary fastened the velvet gown. Her ankle had healed rapidly, until it was almost as good as new, except for an ache that occurred when she stood on it for too long.

"There," Mrs. Buttons said in satisfaction, standing back to view Vivien with a smile. "The gown is lovely, and the color couldn't be more perfect."

Carefully Vivien made her way to the dressing table mirror, which afforded a three-quarters view.

To her surprise, the housekeeper was right. The deep black-cherry velvet made her skin look like porcelain, and brought out the ruby fire of her hair. Black silk braiding trimmed the modestly high neckline. More lengths of silk braiding defined the vertical slash that went from neck to collarbone, affording a subtle glimpse of white skin. No other adornment marred the simple lines of the gown, except for the puffs of black silk that edged the hem of the flowing skirt. It was an elegant garment, suitable for any lady of quality. Vivien was relieved to discover that she owned some clothes that did not proclaim "courtesan" to everyone who saw her.

"Thank goodness," she murmured, giving Mary and Mrs. Buttons a self-deprecating smile. "I feel nearly respectable."

"If you please, Miss Duvall," Mary said, "I should like to brush out your hair and pin it up proper. You'll look every inch the fine lady then— and won't Mr. Morgan be pleased to see you turned out so well!"

"Thank you, Mary." Vivien made her way to the dressing table, pausing to pick up the length of damp toweling discarded from her bath.

"No, no," the maid scolded, rushing forward at the same time that Mrs. Buttons did. "I've told you, Miss Duvall, you're not to help me with such things!"

Vivien surrendered the towel with a sheepish smile. "I can pick up the linens just as easily as you can."

"But it's not your place," Mary said, ushering her toward the dressing-table chair.

Mrs. Buttons stood close to Vivien, meeting her gaze in the mirror. The housekeeper smiled pleasantly, but her eyes were speculative. "I don't believe you're accustomed to being waited on," she remarked.

Vivien sighed. "I don't remember what I'm accustomed to."

"A lady with servants would never think to straighten a room or pour her own bath, even if she forgot every blessed fact in her head."

"But I know I had servants." Vivien picked up a stray hairpin from the little box Mary had brought, and traced the crimped edge. "At least, I did according to Mr. Morgan. I was a spoiled creature who did nothing except . . ." She stopped and frowned in confusion.

Mrs. Buttons watched as Mary brushed out the shining length of Vivien's rich red hair. "You certainly don't behave like a 'spoiled creature,'" the housekeeper said. "And in my opinion some things about you would not change no matter what has happened to your memory." She shrugged philosophically and smiled. "But then, I'm hardly a doctor. And I can scarcely keep order of what's in my own head, much less divine what's in someone else's."

Mary dressed Vivien's hair in a simple style, pinning a braided knot atop her head and allowing a few sunset wisps to curl around her neck and ears. Enjoying the feeling of being properly clothed and turned out, Vivien decided she would like to visit some other part of the house. "It would be a treat just to sit for a while in a room different from this one," she said. "Is there a small parlor or perhaps even a library downstairs? Does Mr. Morgan have a few books I might be able to look at?"

For some reason the question caused the house-keeper and the maid to exchange a smile. "Just a few," Mrs. Buttons replied. "I'll show you to the library, Miss Duvall. But you must take care not to injure your ankle again, and you mustn't tire your-self."

Eagerly Vivien took the woman's arm, and they made their way downstairs step by careful step. The town house was exceptionally handsome, filled with dark panels of mahogany, thick English carpets underfoot, clean-lined Sheraton furniture, and fireplaces fitted with generous slabs of marble. As they approached the library, the air was rich with the smells of beeswax, leather, and vellum. Sniffing appreciatively, Vivien entered the room. She wandered to the center and turned a slow cir-cle, her eyes wide with wonder.

"One of the largest rooms in the house," Mrs. Buttons said proudly. "Mr. Morgan spared no ex-pense in housing his precious books in first-rate style."

Vivien stared reverently at the towering glass-fronted bookcases, the map cabinets embossed with gold letters, the marble busts positioned at each corner of the room. Her gaze fell to the tables loaded with books, many of them left open and piled atop each other, as if the reader had been called away hastily in the middle of an intriguing passage. "It's not merely a vanity collection, is it?" she asked aloud.

"No, the master is quite devoted to his books."
Mrs. Buttons repositioned a comfortable chair by
the cheerful fire and drew back a curtain to admit
plenty of daylight. "I'll leave you to explore, Miss
Duvall. Shall I send a tea tray for you?"

Vivien shook her head and wandered from one
bookcase to another, her gaze rapidly scanning the
enticing rows. The housekeeper laughed suddenly.
"Until now, I've never seen anyone look at books
the way Mr. Morgan does," she remarked.

Barely aware of the housekeeper's departure, Vivien opened a glass door and examined a row of
poetry. Something strange happened as she read
one title after another . . . Many of them seemed
startlingly familiar, the words connecting in a way
that made her quiver with surprise. Mesmerized,
she reached for one of the books. She opened it, the
textured leather binding soft beneath her fingers,
and found a poem by John Keats entitled "Ode to
a Grecian Urn." *Thou still unravished bride of quiet-
ness* . . . It seemed as if she had read the words a
thousand times before. A door opened in her mind,
illuminating knowledge that had been stored away
until this moment. Thoroughly unnerved, Vivien
clutched the open volume against her chest and
grabbed another off the shelf, and another . . .
Shakespeare, Keats, Donne, Blake. There were
many other instantly recognizable poems, frag-
ments of which she could even recite by memory.

The relief of remembering *something* made her
almost dizzy with excitement. She picked up and
held as many books as possible, crowding them
against her body, dropping a few in her haste. She

wanted to carry them all to a quiet corner, and read and read.

On a lower shelf she discovered well-worn volumes of philosophy. Snatching up Descartes's *Meditations*, she flipped it open and feverishly read a passage aloud. "There is nothing, among the things I once believed to be true, which it is not permissible to doubt . . ."

Vivien hugged the open book to her chest, mind swimming with chaotic impressions. She was positive she had once studied this book, these words, with someone she had cared for very much. The familiarity of the words gave her a sense of safety and comfort she needed desperately. She closed her eyes and clutched the book harder, straining to capture some elusive memory.

"Well." A sardonic rumble broke the silence. "I wouldn't have expected to find you in the library. What have you found that interests you?"

Six

$\mathcal{V}$ivien whirled to see Morgan filling the door-way, the corner of his mouth tightened in a jaded quirk that passed for a smile. The somber gray of his trousers and waistcoat was balanced by a moss-colored coat that brightened the antique green of his eyes. She stumbled forward in her excitement, anxious to share her discovery.

"Grant," she said breathlessly, while her heart raced in an uneven canter. A few books cascaded from her overburdened arms. "I-I found these . . . I *remember* reading some of them . . . You can't imagine how it feels." A wild, frustrated laugh escaped her. "Oh, why can't I remember more? If only—"

"Vivien," he said quietly, his smile fading. He reached her in three strides, helping to steady the jostling pile in her overburdened arms. As Vivien read the frown of concern on his face, she knew that she must appear half mad. More words bubbled to her lips, but he hushed her gently.

"Let me," he said, taking the mass of heavy volumes out of her unsteady grip. He set them on a nearby table and turned to her. Clasping her shoulders in his large hands, he eased her against his body. He held her in a reassuring embrace, his hand smoothing over the back of the velvet gown and lightly rubbing the lowest point of her spine. As he spoke, his breath stirred the fine hairs at her temple. "Tell me what you remember."

Vivien shivered at the pleasure of being in his arms. "I know I've read some of these books before, with someone I was very fond of. I can't see his face, or hear his voice . . . It seems the harder I try, the farther it slips away."

"You've read *these* books?" Grant asked dubiously, glancing at the ungainly pile beside them.

Vivien nodded against his chest. "I can even recite a passage or two."

"Hmm."

Perplexed by his noncommittal grunt, she glanced at his skeptical face. "Why do you say 'hmm' like that? Don't you believe me?"

She was encompassed in his vivid, considering stare. "It's not in character for you," he finally said.

"I'm telling you the truth," she said defensively.

"You've read Descartes," he remarked, every syllable edged with disbelief. "I should like to hear your opinion on Cartesian dualism, then."

Vivien thought for a long moment, inwardly relieved to discover that she understood the question. "I suppose you're referring to Mr. Descartes's theory that spirit and matter are separate entities? That we cannot rely on our senses as the basis of knowledge? I believe he is correct, and I think . . ." She paused and continued more slowly. "I think the truth is something you recognize with your heart, even when the evidence seems to prove otherwise."

Though Morgan's expression gave little away, Vivien sensed that she had surprised him. "It seems I'm harboring a philosopher," he said, his eyes suddenly glinting with humor. He set the book on the library table and reached for another on the shelf. "Tell me what you make of Locke, then, and his differences with Descartes."

Vivien took the book from him and spread her small hand on the morocco leather binding. "Mr. Locke argues that the human mind is a blank tablet at birth . . . doesn't he?" She glanced at Morgan and received an encouraging nod. "And he claims that knowledge is founded in experience. Thought can only come after we learn through our senses. But I don't think I agree with him entirely. We are not born blank slates, are we? I think some things must exist in us at birth, before experience begins to work upon us."

Morgan took the book from her and replaced it on the shelf, and turned back to her. Unaccountably gentle, he tucked a stray wisp of red hair behind her ear. "Can you tell me what other books are familiar to you?"

Vivien went to another set of shelves and began pulling titles from the tidy rows . . . history, novels, theology, and drama. She began to stack them in a

second heap on the table. "I'm positive I've read
this one, and this, and these . . . Oh, and this was
one of my favorites."

He smiled at her enthusiasm. "You're remarkably well read for a woman who never reads."

"Why would you say such a thing?" she asked
in surprise.

"Lord Gerard assured me that you dislike reading."

"But that can't be true."

"You're a chameleon, Vivien," he said quietly.
"You adapt to the taste of whatever company you
find yourself in."

"Then you're suggesting that I concealed my enjoyment of reading and pretended to be stupid in
order to attract Lord Gerard," she said.

"You wouldn't be the first woman to use that
ploy. Many men are made uneasy by an intelligent
female."

"Is Lord Gerard that kind of gentleman?" Read-
ing the answer in his face, she sighed heavily.
"Every day I learn something new about myself.
None of it pleasant."

As Grant regarded her downcast head, he was
assailed by a strange yearning he had never experienced before. He had been so certain of who and
what Vivien Rose Duvall was . . . and she kept confounding him.

His gaze skimmed over her in a thorough survey. The sight of her in the velvet gown, a red so
dark it approached black, caused a response that
was alarming in its intensity. He had never once
allowed himself to imagine that somewhere in the

world there might be a woman who was not only beautiful but intelligent, kind, and unaffected. The fact that he seemed to have found her in Vivien was astonishing. He was again uncomfortably aware that if she had not been a courtesan, had he not possessed his prior knowledge of her true character, he would be mad for her.

The neat auburn upsweep of her hair revealed the daintiest pair of ears he had ever seen, a vulnerable neck, a delicate jaw that made his fingers itch to investigate the soft curve. He murmured her name, and she looked up at him with clear, deep blue eyes that contained no hint of guile. Remembering how wickedly seductive her gaze had once been, Grant shook his head.

"What is it?" she asked.

"You have the eyes of an angel." His gaze searched her face until a tide of pink crept over it.

"Thank you," she said uncertainly.

Grant took her arm in a gentle grasp. "Come with me."

As he drew her to a chair by the fire and urged her to sit, Vivien glanced at him warily. "Are you going to question me further?"

"No," he said, a reluctant smile tugging at his lips. For now, he was going to ignore all the contradictions about Vivien and allow himself to simply enjoy being with her. A beautiful woman, a fire on the hearth, a roomful of books, and a bottle of wine . . . It might not have been every man's idea of heaven, but God knew it was his.

Carrying an armload of books to Vivien, he deposited the stack on the floor near her feet. Seeming to understand that he merely wanted to spend some time with her, Vivien began to sort through the pile, while he pulled a bottle of bordeaux from the sideboard and opened it expertly. After filling two glasses, he sat in a chair beside Vivien and handed one to her. He noted that she sipped the wine immediately, without the usual ritual of those accustomed to sampling fine vintages . . . no swirling of the glass to test the aroma, or the rivulets that the English called "legs" and the French more poetically referred to as "tears." As a member of the beau monde, Vivien should have been experienced at such a ritual. However, she did not look like a worldly courtesan accustomed to the finer things in life . . . she looked like a sheltered, naive young woman.

"This gives me hope," she remarked, picking up the volume at the top of the pile and holding it in her lap. "I know it's a small thing, to remember reading some of these books . . . but if this little bit of my memory has come back, then perhaps other things will follow."

"You said you remembered reading with someone." Grant drank from his own glass, his gaze remaining on her lovely firelit face. "You referred to that person as a 'he.' Any impression of him? Any detail of his appearance or the sound of his voice? Or a place you might have been with him?"

"No." The soft curves of her mouth became enticingly wistful. "But trying to remember makes me feel . . ." She paused and stared into the ruby depths of the wine. "Lonely," she continued with visible effort. "As if I've lost something, or some-one, that was very dear."

A lost love, Grant speculated, and experienced a sudden wash of jealousy. Concealing the unwel-come emotion, he stared hard into his own glass.

"Here," Vivien murmured, handing him the book of Keats. "Won't you tell me which is your favorite passage?"

Vivien watched Morgan's bent head as he thumbed through the worn pages. The firelight flickered over his dark hair, making it gleam like ebony. The thick locks were cropped too short, but even so, they contained a hint of curl and wave that intrigued her. He should let them grow longer, she thought, to add a touch of softness around the un-compromising angles of his face.

Her gaze moved to the volume that was nearly engulfed by his long-fingered hand. No sculptor would ever desire to capture the shape of those brutally strong hands in marble . . . and that was a pity. Vivien thought them a hundred times more attractive than the slender, fine hands of a gentle-man. Besides, it wouldn't seem right for a man built on his impressive scale to have delicate little hands. The thought brought a smile to her face.

Glancing upward, Morgan caught sight of her expression and arched his brow quizzically. "What's so amusing?"

She pushed herself out of the chair and knelt be-side him, her skirts billowing briefly and settling in velvety wine-colored puddles on the floor. For answer, she took one of his hands and measured her own against it, flattening their palms together.

His fingers extended well beyond her own meager reach.

"I don't remember the other gentlemen of my acquaintance," she said, "but I have no doubt you must be the largest man I have ever met." Heat collected between their clasped palms, and Vivien snatched her hand away, blotting a faint sheen of moisture on the skirt of her gown. "What is it like to be so tall?" she asked.

"It's a constant headache," Morgan answered dryly, setting the book aside. "My head is well acquainted with the top of every doorframe in London."

Vivien's smile turned sympathetic. "You must have been a long-legged, gangly child."

"Like a monkey on stilts," he agreed, making her laugh.

"Poor Mr. Morgan. Did the other boys tease you?"

"Endlessly. And when I wasn't trading insults, I was busy fighting. They each wanted to be the one to thrash the largest boy at Lady of Pity."

"Lady of Pity," Vivien repeated, the name unfamiliar to her. "Is that a school?"

"Orphanage." Morgan seemed to regret the revelation as soon as it left his lips. At Vivien's silence, he threw her an unfathomable glance. For one electric moment, she saw a flash of defiance—or perhaps it was bitterness—smoldering in the depths of smoky green. "I wasn't always an orphan," he muttered. "My father was a bookseller, a good man, though damned poor at making business decisions. A few bad loans to friends followed by a year of poor sales landed the entire family in debtor's prison. And of course, once you go in, you never come out. There is no way for a man to make money to pay his debts once he's in prison."

"How old were you?" Vivien asked.

"Nine . . . ten, perhaps. I don't remember exactly."

"What happened?"

"Disease went through the prison. My parents and two sisters died. My younger brother and I lived through it, and were sent to Lady of Pity. After a year I was thrown out to the streets for 'disrupting internal order.' "

The recitation was matter-of-fact, emotionless, but Vivien sensed the pain and hostility banked beneath his calm facade. "Why?" she murmured.

"My brother, Jack, was small for his age, and somewhat sensitive by nature. The other boys were apt to bully him."

"And you fought to defend him," she said.

He nodded briefly. "After a particularly nasty fight, the director of the orphanage reviewed my record, which was filled with words like 'violent' and 'incorrigible.' It was decided that I posed a hazard to the other children. I found myself outside the orphanage walls with no food or possessions save the clothes on my back. I stayed by the gate for two days and nights, shouting to get back in. I knew what was going to happen to Jack if I weren't there to protect him. Finally one of the teachers came out and promised me that he would do what was in his power to look after my brother. He advised me to leave and try to make some kind of life for myself. And so I did."

Vivien tried to imagine him as a boy, young and frightened, torn away from the last living link with his family . . . forced to make his own way in the world. It would have been so terribly easy for him to turn to crime and violence as a way of life. Instead he had come to serve the society that had victimized him. He made no effort to pose as a hero, however. In fact, he had deliberately painted himself as a self-serving scoundrel who upheld the law only for the profits he made from it. What kind of man would commit himself to helping others while at the same time disclaiming his own good motives?

"Why this?" she asked. "Why become a Bow Street Runner?"

Morgan shrugged, and his mouth twisted cynically. "It comes naturally to me. Who better to understand the criminal element than someone who comes from the streets? I'm a mere step away from being one of them."

"That's not true," she said earnestly.

"It is," he muttered. "I'm just the other side of the same bad coin."

In the ensuing silence, Vivien made a project of straightening a stack of books on the floor. She pondered his bleak words, the stillness of his large body, the tension that shredded the air. He seemed as unfeeling and immovable as a block of granite. However, she suspected that his invulnerability was an illusion. He had known so little softness in his life, so little comfort. A powerful urge took hold of her, to reach out and hug him, and pull his dark head to her shoulder. Common sense prevailed, however. He would not want or welcome comfort from her, and she would probably earn a humiliating jeer for her pains. If she was wise, she would let the subject drop for now.

But another question slipped out before she could prevent it. "Where is your brother now?"

Morgan seemed not to hear.

"Where is Jack?" she asked again, kneeling before him, staring into his averted face.

The green eyes shifted, his gaze meeting hers with searing impact.

"Please," she said softly. "You know the worst about me. Surely you can trust me this far. Tell me."

Dark color crept over his face. It seemed as if some terrible secret were leaking poison inside him. Just as she thought he would not answer, he spoke in a rusted, halting ramble, so softly that she could not hear some of the words. "I went back for Jack when I was able . . . had secured a promise of work for him at a fishmonger's stall where I cleaned and wrapped fish. I knew they would let him leave the orphanage if . . . some relative were to speak for him. I was nearly fourteen, a man by most standards, ready to take care of him. But when I went to Lady of Pity and asked for Jack . . . they told me he was gone."

"Gone?" Vivien repeated. "Had he run away?"

"Smallpox. Half the children in the orphanage had it. Jack died without me there . . . without anyone who loved him."

Words failed her. She regarded him sorrowfully, pressing her hand hard against her thigh to keep from touching him.

"And I knew," he said quietly, "that if I had come sooner . . . I could have saved him."

"No," Vivien replied, shocked. "You mustn't think of it that way."

"It's a fact. There's no other way to think of it."

"You're not being fair to yourself."

"I failed him," he said flatly. "That's all that matters." He stood in one fluid movement and turned to the fire, staring into the sputtering coals. Snatching up a poker, he jabbed at a log until it erupted into fiery life.

Vivien stood as well, her hands clenched into fists as she stared at his broad, hard back, his dark head silhouetted in fire-glow. Her compassion for him overrode any concerns about her own problems. Morgan had devoted his life to saving others because he hadn't been able to save his brother. Yet no matter how many times he rescued and helped and served others, he would never be able to absolve himself of his one great failure. He would be haunted by guilt for the rest of his life. Her entire being was filled with one aching wish . . . that she could find some way to help him. But there was nothing she could do.

Her hand touched his shoulder, lingered, then slid to the hot nape of his neck. His entire body seemed to stiffen at her touch, and she felt the ripple of nerves in his neck. He jerked away with a muffled curse, looking as if she had stabbed him. "No," he said savagely. "I don't need pity from a—"

He stopped, choking off the rest of the sentence.

The unspoken word floated in the air between them.

Vivien knew perfectly well what he had been about to say, and the hurt of it jolted through her. But why hadn't he completed the sentence? Why had he reined in his temper in a last-second attempt to spare her feelings? She stared at him curiously, while a feeling of artificial calmness descended on her. "Thank you," she said with only a slight tremor in her voice. "Thank you for not saying it."

"Vivien," he said gruffly, "I—"

"I shouldn't have asked such personal questions," she said, clinging to her meager supply of dignity as she began to retreat from the room. "I am very tired, Mr. Morgan. Perhaps I'll go upstairs and rest."

She heard him begin to say something else, but she fled the library as quickly as possible, leaving him to his brooding contemplation of the fire.

Morgan left the town house well before supper, while Vivien dined in solitude. She wondered what companions he would seek tonight, if he would lounge in a coffeehouse and take part in some political discussion, or visit his club and play cards while a saucy wench perched on his knee. There would be no shortage of available women for such a man. Morgan had the appearance of a gentleman, but he possessed a hint of street swagger, a combination irresistible to any female. No doubt he had inspired countless fantasies among the women of London, both high and low.

A cold heaviness settled in her chest, making it difficult to eat more than a few bites of supper. Taking several books with her, Vivien retired to bed and read until midnight. However, the books failed to work their magic. She couldn't lose herself in the written word when an array of problems seemed to hover over the bed like malevolent spirits.

Someone had tried to murder her, and would possibly try again when it was discovered that she was alive. Although she had faith in Morgan's ability to protect her and uncover the identity of her assailant, she also knew that he was not infallible. And instead of being a help to him and supplying the information that would solve everything, she sat here like a dunce, all relevant facts locked away in some impenetrable vault in her mind. It was maddening.

Setting the book aside, Vivien rolled to her stomach and contemplated the shadows cast by the bedside lamp. What would become of her? She had ruined herself by choosing a path that no decent woman would venture along. There were few options left, other than to return to prostitution, to find some man who might condescend to marry her, or to try her hand at some kind of respectable work that might yield enough to support her. Only the third choice held any appeal. But who would employ her when she had a publicly ruined character?

Morosely Vivien stared at a lock of her own

flamboyant red hair as it curled across the mattress. Without vanity, she understood that her looks were sufficient to attract men, whether or not she desired their attentions. And she would never be able to hide the fact that she had once been a prostitute. The truth would always come out. No matter what position she held, there would be men, insulting and propositioning, offering sexual bargains if she wished to retain her job.

Vivien wrestled with the increasingly unpleasant thoughts before falling into an uneasy sleep. More nightmares awaited her, dreams of water and drowning and choking. She twisted against the sheets, kicked and struggled until the bed was a shambles. Finally she awakened with a low cry and sat bolt upright, breathing hard, eyes staring blankly in the darkness.

"Vivien."

The quiet voice made her quiver in startled reaction. "What—"

"I heard you cry out. I came to see if you were all right."

Morgan, she thought, but his familiar presence did not make her relax. For a split second she feared that he had come to demand that she take him into her bed. Or his bed, as the case was. "It was only a nightmare," she said shakily. "I'm all right now. I'm sorry if I bothered you."

Vivien saw Morgan's outline in the darkness, a huge shadowy figure that approached the side of the bed. Her heartbeat fluttered and faltered in alarm. Shrinking to the center of the mattress, she went rigid as he reached for the covers. In a few quick, deft motions he straightened the linens and folded the top of the sheet over the edge of the blankets. "Would you like a glass of water?" he asked matter-of-factly.

The question was reassuringly innocuous. Although Vivien didn't remember any of her previous knowledge about men and sexual matters, it didn't seem likely that a seducer would offer a woman a glass of water before ravishing her. "No, thank you," she murmured, reshaping a pillow behind her. A shaky laugh escaped her. "Perhaps you could light the lamp? The nightmares are so vivid, I'm afraid to fall asleep again. Silly, isn't it? I'm no better than a child afraid of the dark."

"No, it's not silly." His voice changed, becoming very gentle. "Let me stay with you tonight, Vivien. It's only a few hours until morning."

She was silent with confusion.

"I'll hold you as a friend," he said quietly. "As a brother. All I want is to keep the nightmares away." He paused, and a subtle trace of laughter wound its way through his next words. "Well, that's not *all* I want . . . but the rest will keep for later. Shall I stay, or would you prefer me to light the lamp?"

With more than a little surprise, Vivien realized that she did indeed wish him to stay. It wasn't the wisest of decisions. She was certainly inviting trouble. But the comfort of another human being would indeed keep the nightmares at bay . . . and it hardly hurt that he was a large, strong male who feared nothing.

"First let me ask something," she said cautiously. "What are you wearing?"

"What do you mean, what am I wearing?" he asked blankly.

She decided to be blunt. "You aren't naked, are you?"

"I put on a robe before I came in here," he replied flatly. "Disappointed?"

"No," she said, so quickly that it drew a catch of laughter from him.

"I'm a fairly impressive sight without my clothes."

"I'll take your word for it."

"Let's have it, Miss Duvall ... Shall I stay or leave?"

Vivien hesitated a long time before replying. "Stay," she said softly.

Seven

The mattress depressed beneath Morgan's considerable weight. Vivien sucked in a deep breath and pressed her fists hard in the lee of her stomach to calm the nervous flurry inside. The covers were lifted and his long, large body slid beside hers. Immediately she was suffused with warmth as they were coccooned beneath the layer of linen and wool.

With extreme care, Morgan curved his arm around her waist and pulled her back against him, so they were pressed together spoon fashion. Vivien couldn't prevent a small gasp at the animal heat and hardness of his body, evident through the nightclothes that separated them.

"You're not afraid, are you?" he murmured at the soft sound.

"No," she replied breathlessly. "But . . . I'm

having a difficult time thinking of you as a friend."

The arm at her waist tightened a minute degree. "Good," he said thickly.

Vivien was quiet for a time, absorbing the sensation of being held by him. She was surrounded by the scents of soap and clean male skin, and the heat that warded off the night-chilled air. Her limbs turned heavy and relaxed, and she felt her spine conform to the shape of his body. She inched backward, seeking more of the delicious contact with him. Gently his hand fell to her hip, keeping her still.

"Don't wiggle about." He sounded a bit gruff. "I'm not a eunuch."

A wave of mortification engulfed her as she became aware of the burning shape of his arousal, wedged high against her buttocks and the small of her back. "I don't think this is a good idea," she managed. "I'll never fall asleep this way."

"Do you want me to leave?"

Considering the question in confounded silence, Vivien struggled with the heedings of her conscience and the pure physical pleasure of being in his arms. Her conscience was soon to be disappointed. "Well . . ." she said uncertainly. "I'm not sleeping, but at least I won't have nightmares."

He chuckled. "I'm glad you trust me. I expected you to turn down my offer."

"I almost did," she replied. "But it occurred to me that if you were going to ravish me, you had a few opportunities before tonight."

"I would never force myself on an unwilling woman."

"I should imagine you rarely encounter one of those."

"Oh, there have been a few," he said dryly.

Resting quietly against him, Vivien felt his breath stir the downy fuzz on the nape of her neck. One of her bare feet touched his ankle, the brush of wiry masculine hair tickling her skin pleasantly. He was an excessively masculine creature, and the knowledge that all his strength and virility were held in check but for one word from her should have frightened her. Instead she was fascinated. Flirting with danger was an undeniably heady feeling.

"Grant?" she said softly. "Why have you never married?"

He laughed softly. "I'm not the marrying kind." He picked up the braided rope of her hair and played with the feathery ends.

"You never intend to have a wife and children?"

"What reason is there? I feel no overwhelming need to continue a damned undistinguished family line. Neither do I have great confidence in my ability to stay faithful to one woman for a lifetime. When I want female companionship, I can get it. My servants look after the household and see to my meals and my comfort. What use would I have for a wife?"

"You've never met a woman you couldn't live without?"

She felt him smile against the back of her head. "You've read too many novels."

"I'm sure you're right," she said ruefully. "Nevertheless . . . won't you regret it when you're old and gray, and you have no life's companion to reminisce with—"

"And no grandchildren to dandle on my knee," he finished. "Thank you, but I have no ambitions to produce offspring who will yank my whiskers and hide my walking stick behind the settee. I'd rather enjoy some peace in my old age . . . if I live that long."

"How cynical you are."

"I am," he acknowledged evenly. "The strange part is, you are too. But to listen to you, one would think you're an idealistic innocent."

"I don't feel cynical," she remarked after a moment. "I don't feel like anything you've told me I am."

A contemplative silence followed, while the warm pressure of his hand settled at her shoulder.

"Grant," she said with a stifled yawn, "how long before I'm allowed to visit my town house?"

"When Dr. Linley says you're fit to be up and about."

"Good. He's coming to see me tomorrow. I'm sure he won't have any objections to my going."

"Why the hurry?" Morgan asked softly. "What do you hope to find at the town house?"

"My memory." She pressed her head deeper into the welcoming softness of the pillow. "When I see my familiar possessions and all my own books, I'm positive that everything will come back to me. I'm so weary of feeling so . . . so *blank*."

"You don't have many books," he said. "I don't recall seeing more than a handful."

"Oh." She twisted to face him, their noses nearly

touching in the darkness. "Why do I like things now that I didn't like before?"

"I don't know." His breath, scented with cinnamon and the slightest hint of coffee, puffed against her chin. "Perhaps Linley will have an answer for that."

"What do you think will happen when I regain my memory? Will I change back to the way I was before?"

"I hope so," he muttered.

"Why?" she asked, hurt by the blunt statement. "You don't like me the way I am now?"

"I like you too damned much," he said brusquely. "And you're going to make it bloody inconvenient for me to . . ."

"To what?"

He didn't reply, only growled a curse that set her ears on fire. "I warn you, Vivien, if you're playing some kind of game with me, I'll probably end up killing you myself."

"I'm not playing a game," she replied with injured dignity. "Why would I? If I had anything to tell regarding the person who tried to drown me, believe me, I would come out with it right away. I won't be safe until he's caught, will I?"

"No, you won't. Which leads to one last point . . . You're not to go anywhere without me."

"Of course. I'm not stupid."

His large hands turned her over to face away from him and urged her to the center of the bed, until they were at least an arm's length apart. "Now, stay there," he said. "And mind you don't roll against me in the night, or you won't like what happens."

"There's no danger of that," she responded pertly. "This bed is so large, we may as well be in separate counties."

Somehow, against Vivien's expectations, she did fall asleep that night, and she wasn't troubled by a single dream. Once or twice she awoke and saw the dark outline of Morgan's body. There was a novel comfort in sleeping with a man, a sense of being utterly protected. Perhaps they did have their uses, she reflected drowsily, before sinking into a satisfying slumber.

It was one of the worst nights of Grant's life. Offering to stay with Vivien had been pure madness, and he had paid for it dearly. He had tried to be kind—a mistake he wouldn't soon repeat.

No, he amended sourly, trying to be honest with himself . . . kindness had nothing to do with his offer. He had simply wanted to hold her. His reluctant liking for Vivien, combined with a powerful physical attraction, made it impossible to stay away from her. He wanted to become the one person she would turn to, to fulfill all her needs. And that was wrong.

Why was his simple plan of revenge becoming such a muddle?

Because Vivien was warm, spirited, and unexpectedly intelligent, everything he admired in a woman. He hadn't made love to her even once, and already he knew a night, a week, a month with her wouldn't be enough. He wanted her for a long time. And he wanted her like this, without her memory, without the sophistication and vanity that had made her so repellent before.

Damn Vivien, it would be so much easier if she had stayed that way. Then he could have cheerfully used and discarded her, and laughed in the face of her annoyance, telling her she deserved her come-uppance. But that wasn't possible now. He couldn't hurt Vivien, and he would probably kill anyone else who tried.

Opening his sore, scratchy eyes, Grant stared broodingly at the slender form cuddled so trust-ingly against his. She had moved up against him at least an hour ago, causing his every nerve to screech in protest. His hands actually trembled with the urge to pull up her nightgown. He thought of taking her now, before she had even awakened, thrusting inside her sweet feminine warmth until he had brought them both to ecstasy. But he wouldn't abuse her trust . . . and he couldn't make himself push her away. So he had stayed like this, suffering and waiting, his groin hot with car-nal needs he could hardly control.

Grimly he reviewed the past few hours, each one more exquisitely torturous than the last. Every movement of Vivien's body, every shift of her head on the pillow and sigh that escaped her lips, had teased and titillated him beyond bearing. He, who had always prided himself on being the master of his own passions, had been reduced to a mindless fool. All because of one small female who had al-ready slept with half the men in London anyway. He was beginning not to care about that now, he was even making excuses for the legion of lovers she had taken. Damn them all, he just wanted to be one of them.

Her quiescent body fit perfectly against his, the hem of her nightgown twisted around her knees. Her trim ankles and calves were tucked neatly beside his own legs. She was as petite and dainty as a doll. The smell of her warm, unperfumed skin was making his blood race until he was light-headed. He pressed his scratchy jaw into the red silk of her hair, longing to unbraid the rippling locks and spread them over his own chest and throat.

As if the intensity of his thoughts had somehow been communicated to her, she sighed in her sleep, one small foot insinuating itself between his.

That was his undoing. Grant couldn't keep from touching her any more than he could stop his lungs from taking in air or his heart from beating. He settled his hand over the indentation of her waist, his thumb brushing the low edge of her rib cage. Her body was resilient and soft beneath his hand. Inflamed, he moved higher, his fingers exploring the sweet undercurve of her breast, cupping gently beneath the plump rise. Filling his palm with the soft roundness, he wondered what it was about Vivien that made her so different from any other woman he had known. It seemed as if she had been made for him alone. How many other men had felt that way about Vivien? he thought bleakly, struggling with the primitive need to put his own stamp on her, erase every kiss and caress that had not come from him.

He drew his thumb in a slow circle over the tip of her breast, and again, repeating the gentle stimulation until he felt the gathering response of her nipple. It was not enough to feel her through the fabric of her high-necked gown. He was dying to stroke her bare skin, taste it, press his mouth to every part of her. As he caught the sensitive point of her nipple between his thumb and forefinger, he heard Vivien's breathing change, the relaxed rhythm turning shallow and rapid.

There was a barely detectable motion beneath her stillness, a deep trembling that betrayed her. She was awake . . . she knew he was touching her . . . and she wasn't trying to escape him. That meant something, though whether she was holding still from shock, willingness, or just plain curiosity was difficult to ascertain. Cautiously he released her breast and slid his hand down her midriff . . . slowly, slowly, reaching the low plane of her abdomen and the soft springiness where fragile cotton concealed a thatch of cinnamon curls. He felt her body quiver, and her weight shifted in preparation to escape.

Lowering his mouth to the side of her throat, he worked his way up to the tiny hollow beneath her ear, whispering reassurances, telling her that he wanted her, needed her, that he would be gentle and patient. He slid his hand further between her thighs, cupping lightly, while the pressure of his erection rose hard against her hip. He allowed her every chance of moving away, if that was what she desired. But Vivien stayed with him, responding with a strange awkwardness, like an ardent, overwhelmed virgin. Breathing jerkily, she twisted in an effort to face him, her eyes tightly closed as she brought her hands to his shoulders. He kissed her, his mouth slow and searching, his tongue engaging hers with teasing strokes. She moaned and slid her hands further around his back, holding him close as he rose above her—

The door vibrated with a perfunctory knock. It was pushed open before a reply was given, the usual routine of a housemaid come to clean the grate and light the morning fire. The maid entered the room and saw instantly that the bed was occupied by two people instead of one. She stopped with a sound of dismay.

Becoming aware of the intrusion, Vivien froze beneath Grant, her blue eyes filled with panic.

Grant raised his head and glared at the housemaid. "Not now," he said curtly.

"Yes, sir," she mumbled, and fled the room, closing the door behind her.

It was not the girl's fault, of course. The servants at the Morgan household were largely unused to goings-on of this sort, as Grant was inclined to visit his occasional bed partners at *their* homes rather than bring them to his. He had never demanded a great degree of privacy in his own bedroom. However, that was about to change. Savagely Grant made a mental note to tell the housekeeper that a new system was to be instituted right away.

It was clear from Vivien's stricken expression that any amorous inclinations had fled. Her body was stiff beneath his, and she was scarlet with embarrassment. Scowling, Grant rolled to his side and watched her scramble out of bed. His groin throbbed viciously with an erection that was slow to subside. If he didn't find relief soon, he would likely be crippled.

Pulling on a pelisse to cover her nightgown, Vivien hastily tied the garment closed. She went to the washstand and poured some cold water into a bowl, industriously splashing her pink cheeks. Grant watched her intently, noting her rigid spine and the determined haste of her movements. She patted her face dry with a cloth, squared her shoulders . . . and turned toward him with the expression of someone facing an unpleasant task.

"Do you want me to return to bed?" she asked, staring at the carpeted floor.

The question surprised Grant. As a matter of fact, he did . . . but first he needed to know why she had made the offer. When he asked, she continued to avoid his gaze.

"I owe it to you," she said tonelessly. "You saved my life, offered me your hospitality and protection . . . and on top of all that, there is our prior relationship to consider. It's not as if we haven't done . . . this . . . before. All things considered, it's hypocritical of me to withhold myself. So if you would like, I am willing to return to bed."

She was as resolved as a martyr, her stiff posture and averted face cooling his passion more effectively than a bucket of freezing water.

"No, I would not 'like,' " he muttered, frustrated and surly. "I'll be damned if you'll come to my bed like it's some damn sacrifice." He left the bed and jerked the front of his disheveled robe together, sneering as he saw her blush deepen at the startling flash of nakedness. "The virginal blush doesn't become you, Vivien. You forget, I knew you before you lost your memory."

"What do you want from me? I've offered you the use of my body. If I understand correctly, your complaint is that I don't display a sufficient amount of enthusiasm."

He gave her a speaking glance. "*Sufficient* enthusiasm?" he repeated acidly. "Try all the enthusiasm of Joan of Arc going to the stake."

The room was charged with an intense silence. All at once Vivien's beautiful face looked penitent, and her eyes sparkled with amusement. She turned away swiftly, but not before Grant saw her lips quiver with suppressed laughter.

"I'm sorry," she said in a muffled voice. "That was hardly flattering, was it?"

"No, it wasn't," he growled. He would laugh, too, if he weren't hampered by a painful erection. Getting back into bed, he rolled to his stomach, buried his face in a pillow, and willed his fierce arousal to subside. Sensing that Vivien was approaching him, he lifted his head and gave her a warning stare. "Stay away from me—or I may decide to bed you anyway."

"Yes, sir." She sounded suspiciously meek. "Perhaps I'll just gather my clothes and dress in the adjoining room."

"Do that." He dropped his head back to the pillow with an explosive sigh.

*   *   *

Vivien dressed in a rich blue gown of velvet and Italian corded silk, with long sleeves that were puffed at the top but close-fitting from the elbow to wrist. The ends of the sleeves were finished by a spill of crisp white Brussels lace, as was the high scooped neckline. Twisting awkwardly, Vivien fastened as many of the buttons in the back of the gown as she could reach, and resolved to ask Mary to help with the task later.

She unplaited her hair, combed her fingers through the rippling, braid-crimped locks, and moved to regard her reflection in an oval looking glass affixed to the damask-covered wall. The gown was becoming, enhancing the blue of her eyes and the unruly color that still flooded her cheeks.

As she thought of Grant in the next room, she expelled an unsteady breath. Her body was hot, her hands were cold, and she was glowing all over with a bewildering mixture of agitation and delight. Even now she wanted to go back to him, ask him to touch her again . . . let him take her beneath him.

She understood the mechanics of the act, but she had no memories of performing it and no real idea of what to do. All the unknowns made her distinctly nervous. Just now he had been so incredibly gentle, and she had very nearly surrendered herself to his experienced hands. No one, least of all she, could deny that Grant Morgan had appeal. But she did not love him. And some deep-seated instinct warned that the intimacy of lovemaking must be reserved for a man she loved very much. That feeling was entirely contrary to the way she had lived her life up until her accident.

Frustrated, Vivien pressed her hands to her head and groaned. She couldn't blame Grant for suspecting that she was playing some kind of game. How else could her puzzling behavior be explained? She was a prostitute, and no one could change her nature overnight.

"Oh, why can't I remember?" she said aloud, clenching her fists against her temples, pressing her knuckles hard against the throbbing of her pulse.

Grant dressed and left for Bow Street without eating or reading the *Times,* without saying one word to Vivien. It was obvious that the housemaid had told the other servants about the scene in his bedroom that morning. Every one of them, including Mrs. Buttons, had treated him with a careful politeness that made him want to bite someone's head off.

Entering number 4 Bow Street, he gave his coat to Mrs. Dobson. The atmosphere at headquarters was busy and quiet this morning, as Sir Ross Cannon was finishing the latest edition of *The Hue and Cry.* The weekly report was circulated to magistrates from one end of England to the other, containing details of unapprehended criminals and their foul deeds.

As Grant reached Cannon's office, the magistrate appeared at the doorway and thrust a sheaf of paper and a pencil at him. "Good, you're here," Cannon said briskly. "Have a look at this. It's going to the printers in ten minutes."

Grant wedged his shoulder against the door-frame and rapidly scanned the document, scribbling a minor correction here and there. When the chore was finished, he ventured into Cannon's office and found Keyes leafing through a procedural book. Dandified as usual, Keyes was dressed in moss-green trousers, an embroided cream brocade waistcoat, and a tailored brown coat. His throat was swathed in an intricate waterfall necktie that kept his chin propped high.

"Good morning," Grant said, placing *The Hue and Cry* on Cannon's mahogany desk.

Keyes grunted noncommittally, having found the passage he sought. He read half a page, closed the book, and reinserted it among the others on the shelf.

In the meantime, Grant sat in the chair next to Cannon's desk. Reaching into his coat pocket, he extracted the small leather-bound book he had found at Vivien's town house and regarded it morosely. He had scanned every page repeatedly, searching for information. By now the lurid details should have lost their ability to shock, but the acts conveyed by the lines of delicate feminine script still gave him an uncomfortable crawling sensation. Every inflammatory word was stuck in his memory as if it had been nailed there.

"What are you reading?" Keyes inquired.

Grant responded with a brief, humorless laugh. "It's not suitable for one of your tender years, Keyes."

"I'll be the judge of that." The older man plucked the book from Grant's hand. As he opened the volume and read a page or two, his bushy eyebrows climbed his forehead like a pair of ascending spiders. "Filthy stuff," he remarked, handing back the volume. "May I ask the identity of the author?"

Grant smiled grimly. "You don't want to meet her, Keyes. She's a tormenting witch. One smile from her can twist your insides like a rag mop."

Although Keyes's manner was deliberately causal, his hazel eyes were keen with interest. "This has to do with the bloat from the river, doesn't it? She's still alive—and you're harboring her in your own home. I've heard the rumors."

Grant leaned back in his chair, slanting an impassive stare at the Runner. "You should know better than to listen to rumors, Keyes."

"Who is she?" the other man persisted. "Has she named her assailant?"

"Why such a fascination with my case?" Grant countered.

"I merely wish to offer my assistance if it's needed," Keyes said. "You've helped me a time or two, after all. You seem a touch defensive, lad . . . A simple question or two, and you scowl at me like a baited bear."

"If I need your help, I'll ask for it."

"See that you do," Keyes replied with a neutral smile, and left the office.

Grant sat brooding in silence. Keyes was right— he *was* defensive and ill tempered, as any other man in his position would be. When he was with Vivien, it was easy to forget who she really was and what she was capable of. Only when he was away from her did he see the situation in its true light. She was a courtesan, a woman who had proven herself incapable of love or fidelity. Someone had tried to kill her, most likely one of her legion of past lovers. His job was to find out who had assaulted her, and catch him. And then remove Vivien Duvall from his home and his life for good . . . before she ripped his heart out.

Sir Ross reappeared in the office and headed for the earthenware jug of coffee. At the same time, his cat Chopper leisurely walked through the doorway, jumped up to the unoccupied corner of the oak desk, and reclined on her side, surveying Grant solemnly.

"Good morning, Chopper," Grant murmured, reaching over to pet the broad, furry head. Chopper shrank back disdainfully, her eyes narrowing to slits. She endured the gentle pat with a flinch, and lowered her head to her paws. Grant couldn't help smiling at the long-suffering feline. "Just like a woman," he murmured. "You only give a fellow affection when you want something."

Cannon poured a cup from the meager amount left in the bottom of the vessel. He made a face as he tasted the brew, which was tepid and filled with grounds. "Mrs. Dobson," he called, leaning his dark head outside the door, "my jug is empty."

There was a protesting response from down the hall, containing the admonition ". . . your nerves, sir . . ."

"My nerves are fine," he replied, a thread of annoyance working through his tone. "I have a great deal of work, Mrs. Dobson. I require another jug to see me through the morning." Cannon went to his chair and smiled briefly as he seated himself. The flash of amusement temporarily lightened the dark cast of his face. "May God spare us from women who think they know better."

"Amen," Grant muttered in brief affirmation of the prayer.

Cannon leaned back in his chair, his wintry gray eyes narrowing as he surveyed Grant. "You look like hell. Are you ill?"

Such an unusual question from Cannon would be enough to send any of the Runners into a state of alarm. Cannon never took an interest in the personal lives of his men, as long as their jobs were being done. Grant frowned at the magistrate, resenting the personal inquiry.

"I haven't been sleeping," he said curtly.

"Trouble with Miss Duvall?"

"Nothing of significance," he muttered.

"How is her health?" Cannon inquired.

"I believe she's almost fully recovered. But there's been no progress on recovering her memory."

Cannon nodded, reaching out for the book that Grant extended to him. "What's this?"

"It's a diary and appointment book. I found it in Miss Duvall's town house. I believe it might contain the name of whoever tried to kill her."

As Grant watched him leaf through the small volume, he wondered what Cannon, who had taken what amounted to a vow of celibacy, would think of such sexually explicit material. It would be only natural for the magistrate to exhibit some sign of emotion but there was no telltale color, no tension, no mist of sweat. The man had astonishing mastery over himself.

"Miss Duvall appears to have led a colorful life," the magistrate remarked blandly. "Why do you assume her assailant is listed in the journal?"

"The attempted murder was a crime of passion," Grant said matter-of-factly. "Miss Duvall has no history of criminal dealings with anyone, no nefarious associates, no significant debts—she has always been well cared for. Only a long list of lovers, most of whom she was unfaithful to. She kept scrupulous track of them, however . . . and their particular tastes. It was a business to her, and as you can see, she was damned organized about it. Whenever a better opportunity presented itself, she left her current lover without a backward glance."

"And you believe one of them became so incensed by her desertion that he tried to kill her?"

"Yes."

Cannon handed the journal back to him. "You'd best narrow down this list quickly, Morgan. In matters of this sort, one can't allow a suspect too much time to collect himself or the case is lost."

Staring at the small book in his hands, Grant passed his thumbs over the smooth leather binding. "What I'd like to do," he said slowly, "is find a way of letting the public know that Vivien is still alive. Then whoever tried to kill her would know that he had failed."

"And come after her again," Cannon murmured. "That would be putting Miss Duvall at great risk."

"No," Grant said immediately. "She's under my

protection now—and I'll be waiting for the bastard when he tries again."

"Very well. Let's reveal Miss Duvall to London, then. Have you already decided on a place and time?"

"Not yet."

"Then allow me to make a suggestion. I have a friend, Lady Lichfield, who is giving a ball this very Saturday evening. Invitations to any event she hosts are greatly sought after, and a detailed account is always published in the *Times* afterward. I'll prevail on her to send you an invitation, and include anyone you choose in her guest list."

Grant grinned suddenly. "Bring Vivien to Lady Lichfield's estate?"

"Why not?"

"Vivien isn't readily accepted by so-called decent society. At least not the female half. She's slept with quite a few of their husbands."

"So much the better, if any of her former lovers are attending," Cannon replied.

Their conversation was interrupted as Mrs. Dobson appeared with a tray bearing a steaming jug of coffee and clean mugs. "You drink far too much of this brew," she said disapprovingly. "Both of you."

"It stimulates the senses and promotes clear thinking," Cannon informed her, while she poured a large does of the black liquid for him. Eagerly he accepted the mug and wrapped his long hands around it.

"And keeps you awake half the night," Mrs. Dobson scolded, shaking her head until her silver curls danced. She turned toward Grant as if he were an ally in her cause. "Sir Ross never sleeps more than four hours a night, never has time for a hot meal . . . and what for? The more work he does, the more it piles up around him."

Ross gave her a swift scowl. "If Mrs. Dobson had her way," he remarked to Grant, "I'd soon become as fat and lazy as Chopper."

The maligned cat resettled her stocky body on the corner of the desk and sent her master an insolent glance.

Continuing to shake her head, Mrs. Dobson left the office.

Cannon blew gently into his mug, causing steam to swirl up from the coffee. "Very well," he said, his gaze arrowing to Grant. "With your permission, I'll approach Lady Lichfield and ask to expand her guest list."

"Thank you." Grant paused before adding thoughtfully, "There is one bit of news I haven't yet mentioned . . . something Lord Gerard said when I questioned him. I'm not certain whether to give it any credence, as it wasn't confirmed by Miss Duvall's diary or anyone else I've interviewed."

"Well?" Cannon prompted.

"Gerard said that he believed Miss Duvall was expecting to marry soon. Someone with a large fortune."

"Hmm. What man of means would choose to 'buy old boots'?" Cannon mused aloud, using the popular phrase to describe someone marrying another man's mistress.

"Exactly," Grant said. "As Lord Gerard pointed out, 'one doesn't marry soiled goods like Vivien

Duvall unless he wants to be the laughingstock of England.' But it's possible she found someone in his dotage, willing to take her on."

Despite Grant's effort to sound dispassionate, his tone was infected with a trace of bitterness that Cannon could hardly miss. Silently Grant cursed himself as he was subjected to Cannon's discomfiting scrutiny.

"Tell me your opinion of Miss Duvall, Morgan," the magistrate said quietly.

"My opinion has no relevance." Grant stood to brush imaginary dust from the legs of his trousers. "If you're referring to evidence—"

"I asked for your opinion," Cannon said inflexibly. "Sit, please."

Abruptly the office became stifling. Grant longed to ignore the request. Cannon's cool, perceptive gaze was a jabbing annoyance. He thought of putting off the question with an insolent reply or a convenient lie . . . but he would be damned if he would ever fear the truth, no matter what it was. Glowering, he eased back into his chair.

"There are two women inside Miss Duvall," he said stonily. "There's the one you find in that book, experienced, jaded, greedy . . . a perverse bitch. And then there's the one who is currently residing in my house."

"And what is she like?"

"Intelligent . . . sweet . . . gentle. Most men's fantasy."

"And yours?" Cannon murmured.

Grant gripped the arms of his chair as if he were

manacled to it. "And mine," he finally admitted gruffly.

Cannon contemplated him with a hint of sympathy that was well nigh unendurable. "Take care, Morgan," was all he said.

Grant thought of assuring him he would in his usual cocky manner . . . but somehow the words wouldn't come.

"All right," Cannon murmured in dismissal, and Grant took his leave with ill-concealed relief.

Eight

"*A* ball?" Vivien stared at Grant as if he had gone mad. They sat in the downstairs parlor, where he had told her of the plan he had devised with Sir Ross. Although Grant appeared sympathetic to her distress, he was obviously not giving her a choice in the matter.

"You're asking me to appear in public," Vivien continued uneasily, "not merely in public, but at a large formal *ball*, to let everyone in London know that I am alive. And then I'll be in danger at least ten times worse than now."

"You'll be under my protection," Grant replied quietly, coming to sit beside her on the gold damask-upholstered settee. He took her small, knotted fist in his hand and chafed it gently until her fingers relaxed in his. "Trust me," he said, smiling faintly as he stared into her worried face. "I would never let anyone harm you."

"I won't know anyone there," she said, clinging tightly to his hand. "I won't know what to do or say."

"You don't have to do or say anything. All you have to do is make an appearance."

"I don't want to," she pleaded, rubbing her forehead with her free hand to ease a throbbing ache.

"I understand," he replied softly. "But it has to be done, Vivien. Now . . . I want to take you to your town house and find something for you to wear. You have at least two dozen ball gowns, and I would have the devil of a time picking one out for you. You've said you want to visit your home, and this is the perfect time to do it."

Vivien frowned at their entwined fingers and took a deep breath, trying to settle her agitated nerves. Everyone would stare at her. How could she make small talk and smile and dance when she didn't remember a single person from her former life? She didn't want to mill among strangers who would undoubtedly think of her as odd or fraudulent, or something equally disagreeable. Most of all, she dreaded making herself a highly visible target. What if the man who had attacked her came back to finish the job he had started? And what if Morgan was hurt or even killed in the process?

"It doesn't make sense," she said. "Why must I go to a ball and reveal myself in such a dramatic fashion? Why can't you leak the information in some other way? You have no idea who wants me dead, do you? This is a desperate attempt to draw him out because you can't decide on a suspect."

"I want the bastard caught," Morgan said evenly. "This is the fastest way of accomplishing it."

Drawing her from the settee, he guided her to the entrance hall and signaled the housekeeper to bring their coats. After fastening a cloak around Vivien's shoulders, he settled a velvet bonnet on her head. A veil of lilac gauze hung from the front brim, concealing her face behind a pastel haze.

Vivien sent him a simmering glare from behind the veil. "This looks like a mourning bonnet," she said. "As if I'm going to attend a funeral. I only hope it won't be my own."

He laughed softly. "It was the most concealing hat I could find. And I'm not going to let anything happen to you. The world would be a dull—albeit more peaceful—place without you."

After Morgan donned his own coat, a footman accompanied them to a carriage waiting outside. Having expected that they would use a hired vehicle, Vivien was surprised to discover that the carriage was a handsome private curricle, painted with gleaming black lacquer and touches of matte gold, and pulled by two perfectly matched chestnuts. Vivien couldn't help but be impressed by the elegance of the vehicle. "I wouldn't have thought you possessed a carriage like this," she remarked. "I thought the Runners went everywhere on foot."

His green eyes danced with amusement. "We can, if you'd rather."

Responding to the gentle teasing, she gave him a small smile. "No, thank you," she said with an effort at lightness. "I'll make do with this."

The footman helped her into the curricle and tucked a thick, cushiony cashmere robe around her. Vivien thanked him and snuggled back into the soft leather seat with an exclamation of pleasure. The wind was pleasantly crisp and biting, refreshing on her face after the past days of confinement. Climbing into the space beside her, Morgan took the ribbons in an expert grip. He waited until the footman ascended to the seat behind the vehicle, then snapped the ribbons and clicked to the horses. They started with a smooth, synchronous gait, the well-sprung carriage moving easily over the cobblestoned street.

Vivien stared blankly at the array of sights spread before them, her gaze searching for any small detail that might strike her as familiar.

Each street possessed its own character, one populated by printers and writers, another occupied by butchers and bakers, another featuring a stately row of churches. Gentlefolk cut through the meandering paths of prostitutes and beggars. Wealth and poverty were wedged together in sharp juxtaposition. The air was thick with the scents of animals, food, the brine of the river, sewage, dust . . . She soon lost the ability to distinguish smells as her nostrils were overwhelmed. They passed a group of urchins who were harassing a satin-clad fop . . . a libertine lurching drunkenly from a tavern with a trollop on each arm . . . peddlers carrying wooden boxes strapped around their necks and shoulders.

Soon Vivien's attention transferred to Morgan,

who deftly navigated the carriage among the carts, cattle, and pedestrians that clogged a section of the street. He was completely at ease amid the bustle of town life, familiar with every alley and corner. It occurred to her that Morgan was one of the few men in London who mingled with everyone from royalty down to the meanest pickpocket.

They reached a row of elegant town houses, and stopped before one with a large bronzed door. "Is that mine?" Vivien asked hesitantly, staring at the grand arched doorway bordered with columns.

Morgan gave her an inscrutable glance. "That is yours."

The footman hurried to take charge of the horses, while Morgan helped Vivien from the carriage. He lowered her gently to the ground, bearing her weight until she gained her footing. Giving her his arm, he escorted her to the door and unlocked it.

Vivien entered the town house cautiously, standing still in the entrance hall while Morgan proceeded to light lamps and wall sconces. The place, with its flowered French fabric panels and dainty Louis XIV furniture, was beautiful, feminine . . . and crushingly unfamiliar. She removed her hat and placed it on the end of a stairway banister.

Light flooded the entrance hall. Slowly Vivien moved from a framed pier glass to a marble-topped giltwood table. Picking up a delicate piece of Staffordshire porcelain from the table, Vivien regarded it closely. Two figures, a gentleman and lady, were conversing while the lady reached forward to pluck wildflowers for a basket nestled in her lap. The scene was charming in its innocence.

When Vivien turned the porcelain over, however, it showed the gentleman's hand intruding far beneath the lady's skirts. Frowning at the crude joke, Vivien set the figures down and glanced at Morgan. He was watching her with a strange mixture of amusement and resignation.

"Remember anything yet?" he asked.

She shook her head and went to the staircase. Morgan followed at once, his measured tread matched to hers as she made her way to the second floor. The lamp he carried threw misshapen shadows in their wake. Pausing at the top landing, Vivien wondered where to go.

"The bedroom is this way," Morgan said. He took her elbow in a light grasp and led her to the last room on the right. They entered a room lined in dark green silk, with a richly carved bed set on top of a pavilion. It reminded her of a small stage, all prepared for a performance. Frowning in discomfort, Vivien stared at the bed while Morgan lit more lamps. Then she turned and saw the painting.

For a moment all she saw was a startling expanse of skin, the artful display of female flesh . . . and then she realized just who was depicted.

"It's me," she said in a strangled whisper. Hectic color surged in her face. She whirled around with a gasp, unable to look any longer.

"I gather you don't recall posing for it." There was a suspicious quiver of amusement in Morgan's voice. However, Vivien couldn't share his humor, or even berate him for it. She was too overcome with shame, and anger that was directed solely at herself. Until now there had always been some tiny corner of her mind in which she believed that she had not done the things he accused her of. But now the truth was there in a heavy gold frame, her past exposed and flaunted in florid detail.

"How could I . . . how could anyone pose for that?" she asked, covering her face with her hands.

"Artists frequently use nude models. You know that."

"Obviously that painting was not intended as any sort of artistic statement," she said scornfully. "Its only purpose is to . . ."

"Arouse," he suggested softly.

She lowered her hands and clenched them at her sides, still facing away from him. It seemed almost impossible that she could feel such humiliation . . . It scorched the very insides of her veins. "Take it down, or cover it," she said desperately.

The amusement left his voice, and he sounded faintly puzzled as he replied. "I've seen it before, Vivien."

It made no sense, but she couldn't bear the painting hanging there before them both—it was like being naked in front of him in person. "I don't like it," she said sharply. "I can't stay in this room with that hanging there. Do something with it, *please.*"

She stiffened as he approached her from behind, his hands closing over her narrow shoulders. "You're trembling," he murmured in surprise. "There's no reason to be upset."

"You wouldn't say that if it were a nude painting of *you* hanging up there."

He snickered suddenly. "I doubt there's an artist alive who would agree to paint me in the nude, sweetheart. I'm not exactly the right material."

An arguable point, she thought privately. From what she had seen of him, Morgan was as attractive as any masculine form ever committed to canvas . . . but she was hardly going to tell him that.

Gently he tried to turn her to face him. "Come, it's not so bad. Take a deep breath."

She resisted, stubbornly ducking her head and fixing her gaze on the floor. "I'm not going to move until you take away that painting."

A brief, warm huff of laughter fanned her ear. "All right, blast you." Releasing her, he crossed the room to the painting. A scraping noise, a faint creak of the heavy frame, and then Morgan's dry voice cut the tense silence. "You can open your eyes now."

Vivien turned to see that he had taken the painting down and propped it against the wall, back facing outward. "Thank you," she said, heaving a sigh. "I want to have that dreadful object burned."

"You may change your mind, once you recover your memory."

"I don't care what happens after my memory returns," she retorted sharply. "As I've told you before, I won't be a courtesan any longer."

Morgan regarded her with a frank skepticism that annoyed her beyond reason. "We'll see," he muttered.

Another painting caught her eye, a small oil with a delicate gilded frame. It was hung on the wall next to the dressing table, as if she had wanted to look at it while applying perfumes and powders and brushing her hair. Moving closer, she stared at

the painting with growing curiosity. It didn't seem
at all in keeping with the rest of the house. Obviously done by an amateur, the picture had been
painted in bright, cheerful colors. The scene was of
a little country cottage, timber-framed and painted
white, with a carpet of lavender heather all around,
and silver birch trees behind it. A profusion of rosebushes bearing dainty white blossoms covered the
front of the cottage.

Vivien couldn't seem to take her eyes from the
painting. She felt certain it was a place she had
once visited, a place where she had been happy.
"How strange," she murmured. "I think . . . I think
this picture was given to me by someone who . . ."
She stopped in confusion. "Oh, if only we knew
where this cottage was!"

"It could be practically anyplace in England,"
Grant said sardonically.

Vivien touched the signature in the corner of the
canvas. "Devane," she read aloud. "How familiar
that sounds. Devane. I wonder if he is a friend or
perhaps even a . . ."

"Lover?" Grant suggested quietly.

She drew her hand back and frowned. "I suppose he might be." Memories strained behind the
impenetrable wall in her mind. Frustrated, Vivien
went to a massive breakfront wardrobe, fitted with
huge pieces of silvered glass and flanked with cabinets of linen trays on either side. Opening one of
the two sets of doors, she beheld a long row of
gowns in every imaginable shade of silk, velvet,
and satin, the skirts fluttering like butterfly wings.
Many of the garments held a faint note of perfume,

a combination of roses and spicy wood that mingled with sweet crispness in her nostrils.

"There seems to be a range of styles," she remarked, conscious of Morgan's gaze on her. "Everything from sedate to shocking. What effect are we hoping to achieve?"

"Vivien Duvall in all her glory," he said.

She looked back over her shoulder at him. "What was I wearing when we first met?"

"A mermaid gown. Green silk with little gauze sleeves."

Busily she combed through the collection until she found a gown that matched the description. "This one?" she asked, holding it up for his inspection.

He nodded, looking unaccountably grim.

Vivien held the gown up against her front and glanced down at it. The garment was beautifully made, shimmering green with little ruches of white satin at the neckline that reminded her of foam on the waves. A mermaid gown indeed. She had excellent taste in clothes, evidently . . . and why not? A courtesan's primary concern would be the art of displaying herself to the best advantage.

"I could wear this one to the ball," she said. "What do you think? Shall we give it another outing?"

"No." A shadow flitted across his face, and he regarded the gown with obvious dislike.

Lost in thought, Vivien replaced the gown in the wardrobe. "We didn't get on well that first meeting, did we?" she asked, riffling through the row of clothes.

His voice was subtly serrated with tension. "Do you remember?"

"No . . . but the look on your face . . . Anyone could see that it wasn't a pleasant memory."

"It wasn't," he agreed curtly.

"Was it *I* who disliked *you*, or have I got it backward?"

"The dislike was mutual, I believe."

"Then how did we . . . that is, why did you ever enter into an arrangement with me?"

"You have a way of sticking in a man's craw."

"Like a fish bone," she said ruefully, and laughed. She pulled out a white gown, a bronze, and a lavender, and brought them to the bed in a colorful heap. Carefully she began to fold the delicate garments while Morgan watched her. "One of these will do nicely," she said.

"Aren't you going to try them on?" he asked.

"Why bother? They're all mine. Why shouldn't they fit?"

"You've lost a bit of weight since your dunking in the Thames." He came to measure her waist experimentally, his large hands nearly spanning the neat circumference. Vivien started at his touch, at the solid feel of him behind her back. The dual proximity of Grant Morgan and a silk-covered bed was enough to rattle her nerves. Remembering his hands, so wickedly gentle as they searched her body, and his mouth imprinting warm, delicious kisses on hers, she tried to suppress a hard shiver. He must have felt the involuntary movement, for his hands tightened at her waist, and his lips moved close to her ear until she felt the caress of his breath.

"There's no need for me to try anything on," she managed to say. "Besides, I can't fasten and unfasten rows of buttons all by myself."

"I would be willing to help."

"I'm certain you would," she replied with a smile that turned wobbly. Sensation, or the exquisite promise of it, raced through her body and pooled low in her stomach making her knees weak. For a breathless moment she thought of leaning back, arching her throat in invitation, pulling his hands up to her breasts.

However, just before her eyes closed, she caught sight of the ostentatious bed reflected in a looking glass . . . this room, where she had entertained so many men . . . The idea suddenly sickened her. It was possible Morgan had a few private fantasies that she would be expected to satisfy. Even if she wanted to sleep with him, how in the world could she live up to her own reputation? She didn't remember a single thing about how to please a man. But shouldn't she? She certainly recalled any number of things she had read in books . . . why had she not retained some of her vast knowledge of the sexual arts? Confused, she jerked away from him.

"Grant," she said, flustered, "there is something I must know. When you and I had . . . that is, when we . . ." She cast a miserable glance at the bed, and then looked back into his alert green eyes. "How did you find the experience? I mean . . . how was I? Did I justify my reputation? Did I . . . oh, you know what I mean!" Face reddening, she kept her gaze trained on his.

Strangely, Morgan seemed as discomfited as she by the questions. "I can't compare you to any other woman I've slept with," he said evasively.

"Yes?" she prompted, wanting him to continue.

Grant was still and tense, feeling cornered, while the memory of Lord Gerard's rapturous descriptions of Vivien's lovemaking skills buzzed in his ears. He heard himself repeating a few of Gerard's words, in a flat tone that betrayed none of his own agitation. "You have no shame in bed. It makes you an entertaining partner, to say the least."

"How strange," she muttered, her face still scarlet. "Because I have more than an ample amount of shame *outside* of bed."

They regarded each other with an almost identical wariness, as if they were each protecting secrets that the other must never discover.

Nine

*a*s the veteran of countless balls and soirees, Grant had come to view such events with a jaded eye. One was the same as any other; the parade of dark formal wear for the gentlemen, revealing gowns for the ladies . . . the elderly guests playing whist in the cardroom while the younger crowd danced in the drawing room and amorous couples gathered in the sitting rooms. The music played by pianist, violinist, and cellist . . . the ladies seated in small chairs at the side of the room, awaiting invitations to dance . . . the busy hum of guests in the refreshments room . . . the large, lukewarm supper.

And the heat, the gossip, the plague of insincere social smiles, the mélange of grease-and-sugar-based pomades and heavily applied perfume.

A monotonous bore, every bit of it.

But tonight would be different. He was appearing with a woman whom most of London assumed to be dead. By tomorrow the news would have spread through every layer of society that Vivien Duvall was alive—and that she had appeared at the Lichfield ball on Grant Morgan's arm. He had no doubt that after the revelations of this evening, the man who had tried to kill her would be flushed out.

Drinking from a snifter of brandy, Grant waited in the entrance hall of his home. His black and gold carriage, attended by outriders and footmen, had been stationed at the front door. It was ten minutes past the time he had bid Vivien to be ready, but he knew from experience that women were always late for such events.

One of the housemaids, Mary, descended the stairs at a rapid pace, her face glowing with excitement. "She's almost ready, sir. Mrs. Buttons is seeing to the last few details."

Grant nodded shortly, glancing around and realizing that the entrance hall was becoming filled with footmen, the butler, the maids, and even his valet, Kellow, all of them staring expectantly at the stairs. It puzzled him, the feeling of pleasure they seemed to share in the proceedings. Vivien's presence had enlivened the house, had subtly altered the starkly masculine atmosphere until it no longer seemed a bachelor's residence. This could have been any ordinary gathering of servants waiting eagerly for the lady of the house to appear in her finery, a ritual that occurred in so many of the elegant residences in London . . . but never his.

Grant scowled at the group of servants, although none of them seemed to notice his simmering disapproval. Vivien was not the lady of the house. No one seemed to want to acknowledge that, however. She had made them like her in spite of themselves, using the power of her charm and sweetness to mesmerize everyone from the housekeeper down to the scullery maid. He had contempt for all of them, including himself, for being taken in by her.

Every thought in his head disappeared the moment Vivien appeared and a collective sigh of admiration escaped the servants. She made her way downstairs unescorted, wearing a glimmering bronze gown that swirled around her hips and legs as if it were liquid metal. No other color could have brought out the richness of her hair or the peaches and cream of her complexion half so well. The low, scooped bodice pushed the mounds of her breasts up and together in a display that literally made Grant's mouth water. Swallowing hard, he stared at her while the brandy snifter wobbled precariously in his fingers. He was hardly aware of Kellow tactfully removing it from his unsteady grasp.

The short, full sleeves exposed the curves of Vivien's shoulders, while her arms were encased in full-length white gloves. A French silk scarf of bronze trimmed in gold was draped loosely around her elbows. The only ornamentation on the gown was a stomacher of woven gold and bronze, cinched just above her small waist.

As he met Vivien's gaze, the smile in her thickly lashed blue eyes made his heart slam against his ribs in a funny little extra thump. Her hair was pinned up in a regal crown of braids and curls, in a style he had never seen before but which would undoubtedly be copied by every woman in London on the morrow. She wore no jewelry—he hadn't given it a thought until now. The old Vivien would have demanded some kind of ornamentation, especially when going to a ball where all the other women would be wearing their most ostentatious jewels.

Instead, it appeared that Vivien and the servants had improvised. A length of sheer bronze gauze had been wrapped around her throat, concealing the last remaining bruises. A tiny gold cravat pin shaped like a crown had been used to secure the gauze in front. The pin was unmistakable, a gift the king had given to each and all of the Runners who had guarded him on special occasions. It was the only bit of personal finery Grant possessed.

Seeing one of the Runners' distinctive crown pins adorning Vivien's pretty throat would arouse a torrent of gossip. Everyone at the ball tonight would have no choice but to assume that Vivien was Grant's mistress.

Half pleased, half annoyed, Grant shot a questioning glance at Kellow. The valet's long, balding forehead turned pink. "Er . . . Mrs. Buttons asked if there were some kind of pin they might use," he said apologetically. "It was the only one I could find, sir."

"In future, don't lend my personal possessions before asking my permission," Grant muttered.

"Yes, sir."

Vivien reached Grant and raised the arc of one

cinnamon-colored eyebrow in silent question.

Grant stared at her without smiling. "You'll do," he said tersely. He was unable to say more without his voice cracking.

There was a moment of silence, and he was aware of the servants' chiding stares. Suddenly, as a group, they broke into effusive compliments in an effort to atone for their master's boorishness.

"You're as lovely as a picture, miss!"

". . . no one there will outshine you . . ."

". . . a queen in that gown . . ."

A hot, troubling feeling expanded in Grant's chest, and he wanted to snap at them for being so ungodly solicitous of the feelings of a professional harlot. But he couldn't . . . because he was as much under her spell as the rest of them.

The desultory conversation in the enclosed carriage faded into silence as they traveled along the entrance avenue of the Lichfields' London estate. Obviously Vivien was nervous, and Grant felt a pang of guilt for not soothing her fears. She was about to face a crowd of strangers. Added to that pressure was the knowledge that after this evening, she would once again be a target for whoever had tried to kill her. Grant admired her bravery, her outward calmness, her willingness to trust him with her own safety.

However, he deliberately withheld the reassurance that she needed. Some obstruction in his throat prevented him from making the situation easier for her. He was angry with her, for being so beautiful, for having led the kind of life that made all this necessary. He wanted to punish her for being spendthrift with her sexual favors . . . for not saving herself for him alone.

The thought shocked him, but he couldn't get it out of his mind. He wanted exclusive rights to Vivien, past, present, and future. Such a thing wasn't possible or reasonable.

It was hypocritical of him to hold Vivien's past against her, he told himself. After all, he had hardly led the life of a monk. And it wasn't in Vivien's power to change what she had done in the past. She claimed to regret her promiscuity, and he believed her. But he couldn't control his own jealousy . . . jealous of a whore . . . Oh, his friends and enemies alike would take malicious pleasure in the situation, if they knew. No one must ever find out, including Vivien, how he cared for her.

"How many people will attend, do you think?" Vivien asked, staring out the window at the huge gabled manor house, its E-shaped design of heavy front porch and two wings contained in a shell of amber-tinted stone. The area at the sides and back of the stately manor was surrounded by high garden walls topped with sculpted lions that seemed to survey the surroundings with regal disdain.

"At least three hundred," Grant replied briefly.

A visible shiver chased across the exposed flesh of Vivien's shoulders as she continued to lean toward the window. "So many people watching me . . . I'm glad I won't be able to dance." She settled back and lifted the hem of her gown to expose a trim silk-stockinged ankle, regarding it idly.

Grant's eyes narrowed as he stared at her prettily

turned ankle. He wanted so badly to touch it, and slide his hand up to her knee, her inner thigh, and beyond, that his fingers twitched. The atmosphere in the carriage turned deadly quiet, and Vivien stared at him in concern.

"Something is wrong," she said frankly. "Your manner is . . . well, you're being distant. Could it be that you're having an attack of nerves just as I am? Or is something else bothering you?"

The fact that she had to ask what was bothering him, when it would have been obvious to any woman of experience, made Grant long to grab her and shake her. "Guess," he said in one sharp, bitten-off word.

Clearly perplexed, Vivien shook her head. "If I've said or done something to offend you . . . *oh.*" She stopped suddenly, her fingers flying up to the cravat pin at her throat. "It's this, isn't it?" she asked remorsefully. "I knew I shouldn't have worn it, but we had nothing else, and I wanted to hide the marks on my neck. I told Mrs. Buttons and Kellow, but they said you never . . ." She tried to remove the little gold pin. "I'm so sorry. Help me take it off before we go inside, and forgive me for borrowing something of yours—"

"Stop," he said harshly. "It's not the damned pin." When she continued to tug at it, he leaned forward in the confined space of the carriage and caught her agitated hands in his. She went motionless, her small face close to his, the luscious display of her breasts right under his nose and chin. With little effort, he could reach down and free those delectable curves, fondle and kiss them, fasten his mouth over the soft pink tips and swirl his tongue over them.

His grip tightened on Vivien's fingers until she winced, but she made no attempt to pull away from him. Grant knew his breathing was betraying him—he was starting to sound like a running footman keeping pace with his master's carriage. With each deep inhalation, he was aware of a sweet, pure fragrance that entered his nostrils and spread through his brain like a drug.

"What is that smell?" he muttered.

Vivien answered in a hushed voice. "Mrs. Buttons distilled some vanilla water for me. Do you like it?"

"We brought your perfume from the town house. Why didn't you use that?"

Her gaze flickered to his mouth and back to his eyes. "It didn't suit me," she whispered. "Too heavy."

Grant drew in another lungful of delicate vanilla-scented air. "You smell like a sugar biscuit," he said gruffly. One he badly wanted to bite into. Her scent was innocent and homey and appetizing, making his blood surge and his muscles harden in acute yearning.

Vivien's hands relaxed in his compelling grip, her body yielding to the proximity of his. Their breath mingled, and Grant saw the soft color rising in her face. Thoughts slid through his mind . . . He considered signaling the driver to move on, and as the carriage rolled and swayed through the streets of London, he would make love to Vivien right here, pulling her to his lap and fitting himself inside her body while she writhed in pleasure—

The footman knocked at the carriage door and opened it perfunctorily. Grant released Vivien with a suddenness that caused her to gasp. Bewildered and lovely, she occupied herself with gathering up a brown silk pelisse and pulling it over her shoulders. The night air flooded the carriage with blessed coolness, helping to restore the function of Grant's brain. He rubbed his eyes hard, as if waking from a deep sleep, and left the carriage. The footman placed a movable step beneath the carriage door and assisted Vivien as she emerged from the vehicle.

Almost immediately Vivien attracted the attention of the groups of gentlemen and ladies who were making their way to the manor's entrance. Her red hair seemed to catch every stray shaft of light from the carriage lanterns and glow with a life of its own. She took Grant's arm in a deceptively light grasp, but he felt her fingers digging into the surface of his coat.

"My God," he heard someone murmur nearby, "can it really be . . ."

"Just look . . ." someone else exclaimed.

"But I had heard . . ."

"Hasn't been seen . . ."

Muffled gossip followed them during the short walk from the carriage to the manor. Vivien's face was devoid of expression, her gaze darting from one side to the other. They merged into the stream of guests entering the house, halting at random intervals as the hostess personally welcomed each party. The interior of Lichfield House was grand

and Italianate, with rich oak paneling, and ceilings and walls that had been liberally covered with gilded plasterwork. As they arrived in the massive great hall, with its pilaster-lined walls and elaborate stone mantelpiece, Vivien tugged at Grant's sleeve. He bent his head to hear her whisper.

"How long must we stay here?"

The question brought a reluctant smile to his lips. "We haven't even met Lady Lichfield, and you want to leave?"

"I don't like the way people are staring at me . . . as if I were a spectacle at the county fair."

Her assessment was absolutely correct. People were indeed staring openly, clearly amazed to learn that the rumors of Vivien's death had been unfounded . . . and at such a time and place! Her appearance at Lady Lichfield's ball—an event she would never have ordinarily been allowed to attend—was a source of shock for the ladies and profound uneasiness for the gentlemen. Many of the fine lords who were present tonight had enjoyed Vivien's favors in the past, but they hardly wanted to be confronted with her while their suspicious wives were at their sides.

Grant touched the small hand clinging to his arm, running his fingers over hers in a quick, reassuring stroke. "Of course they're looking at you," he mumured. "Rumors of your disappearance and death have been flying all over London. They're surprised to see that you're still alive."

"Now that they've seen me, I want to go home."

"Later." Grant suppressed a taut sigh, ignoring his own desire to return home with her at once, rather than put her through the gauntlet of first society. It promised to be a long evening for both of them. "In the meanwhile, try to have some backbone. The old Vivien would have enjoyed all this attention. You would have welcomed any opportunity to flaunt yourself."

"If I didn't have backbone, I wouldn't be here," she retorted beneath her breath.

They reached Lady Lichfield, a plump woman in her forties who had once been considered the greatest beauty in London. Although the years of indulgence had taken a toll on her striking face, she was still remarkably attractive. The thickly lashed blue eyes were still radiant above her heavy cheeks, and her shining black hair was coiled atop her head to reveal a classic profile. She was a queen of London's elite circles, a widow who led an outwardly circumspect life—though it was rumored that she had often taken young men as lovers and rewarded them richly for their services. Indeed, she had flirted with Grant at their last meeting, a soiree at the beginning of the season, and had hinted broadly that she would like to "deepen their acquaintance."

As she caught sight of him, Lady Lichfield proffered both her hands. "How can it be that this is only the second time we have met?" she asked. "I feel as if we are old friends, Mr. Morgan."

"Say 'dear friends,' " Grant suggested, pressing an obligatory kiss to the gloved backs of her hands. "The word 'old' should never be mentioned in the same sentence with you, milady."

She giggled and preened. "I doubt I am the first,

nor the last, to fall prey to your flattery, you charming rake."

He grinned and deliberately held her hands longer than was strictly proper. "Nor am I the last to fall under the spell of an enchantress with the bluest eyes in England."

The flattery obviously pleased her, though she laughed with a touch of irony. "Mr. Morgan, pray stop before you reduce me to a puddle at your feet." She turned to Vivien, subjecting her to a head-to-toe inspection. Her smile cooled considerably. "Welcome, Miss Duvall. I see you're in good health, contrary to the astonishing rumors that have flown about the past month or so."

"Thank you, my lady." Vivien curtsied and regarded her with a hesitant smile. "Please forgive me, but . . . have we met before?"

All traces of good humor left Lady Lichfield's expression. "No," she said softly. "Although I believe you were once quite well acquainted with my late husband."

There was no mistaking her meaning. Faced with yet more evidence of her own scandalous past, Vivien could make no reply. She was grateful when Grant ushered her away speedily, leaving Lady Lichfield to welcome more guests.

"She doesn't like me," Vivien said in a dry tone, pausing as Grant removed her cloak and handed it to a waiting servant.

"Few women do."

"Thank you for that boost to my confidence. I feel so much better after the multitude of compliments you've showered on me."

"You want compliments?" They entered an over-heated drawing room, the buzz of conversation intensifying as soon as they appeared.

"One or two would hardly hurt," Vivien said in a subdued tone, wincing as hundreds of gazes arrowed to her. "Though now you'll make me out to be silly and vain for desiring it."

Seeming entirely comfortable in spite of the public scrutiny, Grant nodded in response to the greeting of a passing acquaintance, and drew Vivien to an unoccupied space at the side of the room. He stared down at her with smoldering green eyes. "You are beautiful," he said. "The most beautiful woman I've ever known, and the most desirable. I've never wanted anyone the way I want you. And I'm afraid to look at you for too long, or I'll end up taking you in the middle of the drawing room floor."

"Oh." Flustered, Vivien toyed with the edge of her stomacher. Byron, he was not. But the blunt statements caused little knots of excitement and pleasure to tighten in her stomach. She returned his gaze with a direct one of her own. "Why were you flirting with Lady Lichfield like that?" she asked. "Were you once lovers?"

"No. It amuses her to banter with younger men, and it's easy enough to indulge her. She's already proven to be a useful acquaintance. Besides, I happen to like her."

Vivien frowned, experiencing a sting of jealousy. "You wouldn't have an affair with a woman her age, would you?"

"She's hardly an ancient relic," he said. Suddenly the shadow of a smile played on his lips. "She's an attractive woman in her forties."

"But she is at least ten years older than yourself. Perhaps even fifteen."

His dark brows lifted expressively. "You don't approve of women having affairs with younger men?"

Vivien made an effort to swallow back the unpleasant tightness in her throat. "I'm hardly in a position to disapprove of anyone."

"The French have a more relaxed attitude toward these matters than we do. They believe a woman's appeal increases with maturity and experience . . . and if she gives her favors to a younger man, he's considered quite fortunate."

"Pray don't let me keep you from Lady Lichfield, then," Vivien said tartly. "Why don't you go to her?"

"I'm not going to have an affair with Lady Lichfield," he murmured, amusement flickering in the depths of his verdant eyes.

"Why are you smiling like that?" She felt sour and uncomfortable, as if she had somehow made a fool of herself.

"Because you're jealous."

"No, I'm not," Vivien countered in rising dismay. "Really, I'm—" She stopped as a dark figure approached them. "Who is that?" she asked warily.

Grant glanced over his shoulder, then turned to face the visitor. Although there was no change in his expression, Vivien sensed that this was a man whom Grant liked and respected very much . . . one of the few people on earth whose good opinion he desired. "Sir Ross," he said easily, bringing Vivien forward a step. "May I introduce Miss Duvall?"

Sir Ross Cannon, the Bow Street magistrate. Vivien curtsied and stared at him intently, finding him to be an extraordinary figure, though she couldn't quite say why. Sir Ross was a tall man, though he did not match Grant's towering height. He possessed a self-contained quality, a sense of tremendous power held in check. He had black hair, a build that was just a bit too lean, and curiously light gray eyes that seemed to have observed too much of everyone else's business. Most striking about his appearance was a distinctly remote air, as if he were not quite part of the gathering even though he was mingling among them. And he seemed comfortable with his quality of aloneness.

A mortifying thought occurred to Vivien... Grant reported to this man, consulted with him. There was no doubt that he knew all about her, including the things she had written in that dreadful book. Instinctively she moved closer to Grant.

Cannon's watchful gaze did not leave her. "Miss Duvall... a great pleasure to make your acquaintance."

"Have we..." Vivien started, then bit her tongue. She could hardly go about asking everyone at the ball if she had met them before.

Cannon understood the unfinished question, and answered gently. "To my regret, no."

She searched his expression for traces of censure or sarcasm, but found none. The cool gray eyes were comfortingly impassive.

Cannon and Grant exchanged a glance that seemed to contain an entire conversation. After bowing once more to Vivien, Cannon left them with a polite murmur.

Grant cupped his hand around Vivien's elbow. "Come, Miss Duvall," he said smoothly. "I think it's time we exchanged pleasantries with the other guests."

"Is it?" she asked, accompanying him reluctantly. She dreaded the prospect of meeting anyone, when there was no way of knowing who was friend or foe. "I was just thinking it's time to have a glass of wine. A large one."

"You'll have all the wine you want later." His hand inexorably urged her forward.

To hide her unease, Vivien made her face still and composed. They approached a group amid the sea of speculative faces, two ladies and three gentlemen, and introductions were made. Lord and Lady Wenman, Lord Fuller, and Mrs. Marshall, all of them curiously stilted and brittle as they regarded Vivien. Mercifully there seemed to be little need for her to speak. Vivien glanced frequently at Grant as he made conversation with the others. His expression was bland, but his eyes were watchful, and she sensed that he was taking measure, testing, waiting.

Vivien's gaze flickered to Lord Wenman, who appeared composed except for the subtly agitated rat-a-tat-tat of his toes on the floor. He returned her glance, his pale blue eyes filled with an insolence that perplexed her. Wenman . . . She did not recognize his face, but the name was oddly familiar.

Where had she seen or heard it before?

Grant guided Vivien to another group, pointedly introducing her to Viscount Hatton. The viscount was an elderly gentleman with yellow-gray hair and skin like crumpled paper. Although his manner was polite, he stared at her with a mixture of accusation and wariness that was impossible to miss. It didn't take long for Vivien to remember that he and Wenman were two of the names mentioned in her diary.

She had had affairs with them. Discomfort fanned over her like an icy breeze. It was bad enough to have read the details of her own affairs in that damned book, but even worse to be forcibly brought face-to-face with the men she had slept with. How many more of her past lovers were here tonight? She turned toward Grant with an accusation leaping from her lips.

Before she could say a word, she was approached by a man with eyes like small chips of coal, set deep in a ruddy face. Unlike the others, he did not pretend to be a stranger. He came up to her immediately, taking her hands in a possessive, familiar grip, seeming unaware of the way Grant stiffened at her side.

"Good God, Vivien," the man said in a strained voice. "I literally thought you were dead. How could you disappear like that? Have you no concern for what you've put me through? I had no way to reach you, no way to assure myself of your well-being." As he spoke, his liquor-soaked breath wafted heavily into her face. "Though knowing you, I shouldn't have wasted a moment of worry."

He paused to give Grant a baleful glance, then returned his attention to Vivien. "You've always landed on your feet like a cat, haven't you?"

Vivien allowed her hands to remain unresisting in his. She was uncomfortably aware that the attention of the entire room was focused on them.

"Good evening, Gerard," Grant said softly.

Of course. Lord Gerard, her former protector. Vivien forced herself to smile, though her lips were trembling. Anger, protest, shame, all shot through her veins in a scorching blast. She felt as if she had been put on display for the amusement of the snobbish members of the *ton* . . . and indeed, she had been.

Seeming too foxed to notice the attention they were attracting, Gerard gripped her gloved hands more tightly. He bent to whisper thickly in her ear. "Promise you'll slip away to meet me later. I must talk with you."

"I promise," she murmured, tugging at her hands until they were free.

Gerard meandered away, and Vivien headed in the opposite direction, hardly noticing where she was going. Grant followed her, seeming no more pleased by the situation than she. Striding through the doorway of the drawing room, Vivien located a long picture gallery lined with upholstered benches. She stopped before a portrait of a haughty-faced Lichfield ancestor, and stood with her arms locked tightly across her chest.

Knowing without turning around that Grant was close by, Vivien spoke through her teeth. Anger made her jaw stiff, but she kept her tone soft, mindful of another couple perusing works of art at the other end of the gallery. "How on earth did you manage it? I've met three of my past lovers before ten minutes have elapsed. Somehow you've managed to have everyone in my diary included in the guest list."

"Lady Lichfield was persuaded to send extra invitations," Grant said tonelessly.

"How helpful of her," Vivien replied bitterly.

"Who the bloody hell did you think would be attending, Vivien? You knew we were using this as an occasion for you to come out in the open."

"But you've done more than that. You've invited anyone and everyone who could possibly wish me harm! I'm being dangled before them like live bait, and you're waiting to see who will snap!"

"There are half a dozen Runners and constables attending tonight, not to mention myself and Sir Ross. We're all keeping our eyes on you. You're in no danger."

His words had the effect of throwing brandy on a fire. She flared in fury, her lips drawn back from her teeth. "You could have told me what you were planning! But you didn't, because you wanted me to be unprepared, and humiliated, and shamed by the sight of the multitude I've slept with."

"So you think this is all some elaborate punishment I've devised for you?" he sneered. "Try again, Vivien. Bow Street has better things to do than support personal vendettas. My job is to catch the man that tried to kill you, and this is the best way of doing it. If you happen to be embarrassed by the evidence of your past, that's no fault of mine."

"You manipulative, arrogant..." She tried to think of the nastiest word possible, while her hand rose to slap him.

"Go on," Grant said softly, "if it makes you feel better."

Vivien stared at him, so handsome in his black evening wear, so strong and invulnerable that one slap would only amuse him. She curled her shaking hand into a fist and clenched it against her middle, using all her will to control her tumult of emotions.

"You can hardly bear to hurt anyone, can you?" Grant murmured. "Even when they deserve it. But that's not like you. You used to rip a man's heart out and crush it beneath your foot with no more concern than you would swat a damned fly. What the hell has happened to you?"

She had never truly felt like a prostitute until this moment. Suddenly she wished—for the first time—that she could instantly change back into that other Vivien, the shameless, uncaring woman who did exactly as she pleased. Perhaps then the ache of betrayal would fade away. Until now she had regarded Grant Morgan as her protector, her friend. She had fallen in love with him, though she would never have expected anything to come of it. But he was not her friend. He was as much her adversary as everyone else here tonight. She felt very much alone, like a woman about to be stoned. Well... damn them all and let them all stare.

Raising her head, she stared at Grant steadily,

the color fading from her face except for two bright arcs high on her cheeks. "All right," she said in a low voice. "Tonight I'll give everyone, including you, what they want."

"What the hell does that mean?"

"Only that I intend to make your job easier for you."

She squared her shoulders and left the gallery with determined strides, plunging back into the drawing room like a gladiator. Grant followed more slowly, his gaze locked on her small, trim form. Any trace of shame or timidity had left her. She moved among the guests with a straight spine and a regal tilt to her head. It seemed as if the Vivien he had remembered was now back, as alluring and coquettish as ever.

Openly flirting and teasing, Vivien began to attract men like flies to a honey pot. Before long a circle of five had gathered around her. Three of them were former paramours, and by all appearances more than willing to renew their previous arrangements with her. Clasping a goblet of wine in her delicate fingers, Vivien finished it far too quickly and accepted another.

Grant moved forward, feeling like a starving man being forced to watch as others feasted at *his* picnic. At that moment he felt Sir Ross's restraining clasp on his shoulder. "Let her be," came Cannon's cool murmur. "She's doing exactly what needs to be done. A clever woman, your friend."

"Vivien is merely reverting to type," Grant said bitterly. "She can't rest until she's made every man in the room want her."

"Really." Cannon's voice turned dry and chiding. "Take a closer look, Morgan, and tell me what you see."

"A courtesan, enjoying the hell out of herself." Grant drank deeply of his brandy.

"Oh? I see a woman with perspiration on her forehead, holding her wineglass in a death grip. I see the tension of a woman attending to an unpleasant duty regardless of the embarrassment it causes her."

Grant snorted. "She isn't capable of embarrassment."

Cannon regarded him speculatively. "If you say so. Though at the moment I haven't much faith in your objectivity."

Grant waited until the magistrate left him before he replied under his breath, "Neither do I."

He continued to watch Vivien while jealousy and anger swirled in a fomenting mass inside him. This was what it would be like for any man fool enough to care about Vivien. He watched her flirting and talking with her former lovers, and he couldn't help recalling the sickening details of what she had done with each and every one of them. He wanted to smash, pummel, skewer, mangle someone . . . anything to release this welling violence. He hadn't known he was capable of such irrational rage, and he was appalled by it.

Until now, Vivien hadn't known it was possible to present a facade of pleasure and gaiety when she was abjectly miserable. It was the worst kind of torture to stand here and pretend sexual interest in any and all the men that surrounded her, when all she wanted was to be alone.

She did not look directly at Grant, but she saw him from the corner of her eye, a grim giant who looked as though he had swallowed a bellyful of wasps. She couldn't help thinking of him as the cause of her problems . . . though that wasn't quite fair. If she hadn't led the kind of life that had resulted in this unholy mess, she wouldn't need his protection. She was to blame for the entire situation. But he, damn his arrogant hide, didn't have to treat her with such ambivalence, being kind and caring one moment and sarcastic and superior the next. It would be easier for them both if he would either like or hate her, instead of tormenting her with his mercurial moods.

Lord Gerard caught her eye from afar. He was standing near the glass-paned doors that led to the outside gardens. Inclining his head questioningly, he gestured to the door.

Realizing that he wanted her to meet him outside, Vivien gave him an agreeable wink, though her heart shriveled in dread at the prospect. No doubt he would attempt to seduce her . . . either that or try to strangle her. As her former protector, and reputedly jealous by nature, he might very well have been the one to throw her into the Thames. She was afraid to be alone with him. But Grant had said that she would be safe, and she believed him.

Recognizing the need to separate herself from the crowd that had accumulated around her, she glanced about for Grant. Her gaze was momentarily caught by a tall, elderly man with a shock of iron-gray hair and a long, angular face. He was staring at her intently. Although he was not handsome, he was undeniably distinguished in appearance. What attracted her notice the most was the hatred in his eyes.

Uncomfortable, she tore her gaze from him and continued to look for Grant. Finding his tall, familiar form in the crowd, she sent him a meaningful glance. The subtle signal was all Grant required. He was at her side in an instant, shouldering through the besotted herd. Ignoring the group's protests, he jerked her out of their midst.

"What is it?" he muttered, bending his head to catch her soft murmur.

"Dance with me."

He scowled at the request. "I don't dance well."

"Lord Gerard has indicated that he would like to meet with me in the garden. I was hoping you would dance with me to the doors at the other side of the room, and help me to slip outside discreetly."

Grant hesitated, his gaze flickering to the outside doors. It was highly likely that a meeting between Gerard and Vivien would yield valuable information. The fact that Vivien was willing to confront the ex-lover who might have killed her, and to face him without the aid of her memory, was proof of her courage. However, he didn't want her to do it. He was jealous, and concerned for her safety, and at the moment there was nothing in the world he wanted more than to be alone with her.

"What about your ankle?" he asked.

"I'll manage," she said immediately. "I only feel a little twinge now and then."

"When you go outside, you'll stay in view of the house," he said quietly. "You won't venture past the doors leading to the lower lawns. Agreed?"

"Yes, of course."

Reluctantly he pulled her into the swirl of dancers as a waltz began. Despite the tension that had gripped each of them, or perhaps because of it, Vivien was tempted to giggle. Grant had not been falsely modest—he was definitely *not* a good dancer. He was proficient but hardly graceful, handling her as if she were a rag doll.

Gamely they struggled on, making slow but steady progress to the other side of the room. Grant stared at the shiny flame-hued curls on the top of Vivien's head, mechanically drawing her through the figures of the waltz. He was terrified of stepping on her. One misplaced foot and he could cripple her for life. Vivien was silent, apparently as uncomfortable as he . . . and then he heard a smothered sound that sounded like weeping. He broke their rhythm long enough to shove his fingers beneath her chin and force her face upward. Her lips quivered violently, and her deep blue eyes glimmered with laughter.

"This is dreadful," Vivien gasped, and bit her lip to control an eruption of amusement.

Grant was offended and relieved at the same time. "I told you," he growled.

"The fault isn't yours. Really. You would do much better with a taller partner. We're so unsuited to each other." She shook her head, and a wistful softness swept through her tone. "We're a mismatch."

"Yes." But Grant didn't agree, or more precisely, didn't care. He loved her short legs and high waist and little hands . . . loved the way she felt in his arms . . . loved every detail of her, perfect and imperfect. The knowledge spread inside him like an opiate, the kind that caused the senses to soar dizzyingly high and then crash with sickening speed. Of all the women he had known . . . why did it have to be her?

The music rose to a crescendo, and as the ballroom spun with color and light, Grant shoved Vivien toward the door that led outside. "Go," he muttered. "Gerard is waiting." And he shielded her with his back while she slipped out to meet her former lover.

Ten

The slope at the back of the manor had been cut in a succession of three terraces. A wide, gently angled flight of steps led to the velvety expanse of lower lawn, bordered by carefully clipped yews. It was an old-fashioned garden, perfectly manicured with geometrically shaped flower beds and box-edged paths. A wrought-iron gate admitted entrance to the lower lawns, its towering stone gate piers topped with bronze urns.

Seeing no trace of Lord Gerard, Vivien descended the stairs. Grant had warned her about not going to the lower lawns, but it appeared she had no choice. Suppressing a tense sigh, she turned full circle. The garden rustled, and a night owl hooted gustily.

"Vivien." She heard Lord Gerard's thick whisper. "This way." A hand wormed between the wrought-iron scrolls of the gate, and his finger waggled at her.

The lower gardens it would be, then. Shivering in the cool darkness, Vivien slipped past the gate and confronted Gerard. In the blue wash of moonlight, his face was as pale and formless as blancmange. He was average in height and build, his hairline beginning an inevitable recession to the top of his head. Vivien studied him, thinking that if she had indeed been lovers with this man, she should remember something, anything about him. However, the sight of his face and the sound of his voice had not summoned any ghosts from the void of her memory.

He made a move to embrace her, and she drew back at once.

Gerard laughed low in his throat and shook his head admiringly. "Vivien, you tease," he murmured. "You're as splendid as ever. God knows my eyes have missed the sight of you."

"I won't stay long," she replied, forcing herself to pout prettily. "I don't want to miss a word of gossip at the ball, as I've been away from town much too long."

"Where have you been the past month? Come, you can confide in your old friend."

"Are you my friend?" she countered softly.

"If I am not, then you have none."

Unfortunately that could very well be true. Tilting her head, Vivien affected a coquettish pose, twirling a stray tendril of hair around a slender finger. "Where I've been is none of your concern, my lord."

He paced in a half circle around her. "I believe there are a few questions I'm entitled to ask, pet."

"You have five minutes. Then I will return to the ball."

"All right, then, let us begin with the subject of our dear friend Morgan. What is he to you? Surely you can't have accepted him as your latest protector—or have your standards fallen so low since last we met? Oh, I suppose he has a primitive appeal for some women . . . but he's a commoner. A thieftaker, for God's sake. What sort of charade are you playing at?"

"No charade," she replied with veiled contempt. How dare this soft-waisted, indolent creature insult Morgan's lack of blue blood? Oh, Morgan had his faults, to be sure . . . but he was a hundred times more of a man than Gerard could ever hope to be. "He's an attractive man."

"An oversized ape," Gerard scoffed.

"He amuses me. And he can afford my tastes. That is enough for now."

"You're much better suited to me," Gerard remarked quietly. "And we both know it." His obsidian gaze swept over her with ill-concealed greed. "Now that the problem that separated us is apparently resolved, I don't see why we can't resume our former relationship."

Problem? What problem? Vivien stifled a leap of curiosity behind a delicate yawn. "You talked to Morgan about me," she said idly.

Apology colored his tone. "I thought you were dead, otherwise I wouldn't have said one word to the bastard."

"Did you confide in him about our 'problem'?"

"Of course not. I wouldn't tell a soul about it, and besides . . . in light of your disappearance, I feared it would cast me in a rather suspicious light." He paused and asked almost sheepishly, "How did it end, by the by?"

"How did what end?"

"Don't be obtuse, darling. The pregnancy, of course. Obviously you've miscarried, or perhaps deliberately . . ." He stopped uncomfortably. "After much reflection, I admit I was wrong to refuse to acknowledge the babe, but you know the relationship between my wife and me. Her health is delicate, and the knowledge of your pregnancy would have distressed her too greatly. And there is no proof that the child was mine."

Vivien turned away, her mind on fire. *Pregnancy.* She had been carrying a child. Slowly her hand crept to her flat abdomen, and trembled as it pressed there. It couldn't be true, she thought frantically. Oh, dear Lord, if she had been pregnant, what had become of the child? A series of hot and cold shivers rippled through her as she mulled the possibilities. It must have resulted in miscarriage, because the alternative was not something she cared to contemplate.

She closed her eyes, squeezed them tight in horror. She wouldn't have aborted the babe . . . would she? The hows and whys of the question flew around her like attacking birds, pecking and shredding until she flinched.

"I see," Gerard said, reading her obvious discomfort and deducing that she had indeed deliberately terminated the pregnancy. "Well, no need to blame yourself, darling. You're hardly the mothering kind. Your talents lie elsewhere."

Her lips parted, but she couldn't produce a sound. In her guilt and pain, she could only focus on one overwhelming fact. Grant must not find out. If he knew what she had likely done, his contempt for her would know no bounds. He would despise her for eternity . . . but no more than she would despise herself.

"Vivien." Gerard's voice penetrated the desperate whirl of her thoughts. He approached her from behind and grasped her gloved arms, his hands sliding in a downward caress. "Vivien, leave Morgan and come back to me. Tonight. He's only flash gentry. He can't do for you what I can. You know that."

Poisonous, angry words flooded her mouth, but somehow she held them back. It would be best not to make an enemy of him . . . He might eventually be of further use to her. She turned a tremulous smile on him. "I'll consider it," she said. "However, don't expect me tonight. Now . . . we'll go back to the drawing room separately. I won't embarrass Morgan by appearing there with you."

"One kiss before we go," Gerard demanded.

Her smile lingered teasingly. "But I couldn't stop at one, darling. Just leave, please."

He caught her hand and squeezed, pressing a kiss to the back of her glove. As soon as he walked away, Vivien's smile disappeared. She passed the backs of her fingers over her cold, sweaty brow and fought the urge to cry. Taking a separate path from

Gerard's, she wandered back to the manor house.

Consumed by regret and bitter fear, Vivien paused by a thick hedge bordering a massive stone statue of Father Time. A welcome breeze fanned over her. She felt feverish, dazed, and she knew she had to compose herself before entering the drawing room. She did not want to face the crowd inside, and she especially did not want to face Grant.

"Harlot." A man's hate-thickened voice darted through the silence, causing her to start. *"I won't rest until you're dead."*

Stunned, Vivien whirled in a circle, searching for the source of the voice. Shadows danced around her. Her heart thudded with sickening speed. The sound of footsteps caused her to bolt like a frightened rabbit. Grabbing handfuls of her skirts, she let out a muffled sob and raced up the stone steps, stumbling, scrambling toward the lights from the manor. Her foot slipped on a patch of moisture, or perhaps a stray leaf, and she fell heavily, banging the front of her shin on the edge of a step. Crying out in pain, she gathered herself to run again, but it was too late—a pair of arms had already begun to close around her.

"No," she whimpered, flailing out in self-defense, but she was firmly restrained in an iron grip.

A harsh voice rumbled in her ear, and it took several seconds for her to recognize the familiar sound. "Vivien, be still. It's me. Look at me, dammit."

Blinking, she stared at him until the panic cleared from her vision. "Grant," she said between hard spurts of breath. He must have seen her from the house, and started for her the instant she panicked. Sitting on the stone steps, he held her, his dark face only inches from her own. The moonlight shimmered over the long plane of his nose and threw shadows from his thick lashes down his cheeks. Vivien clutched at him in shivering relief, her arms wrapped tightly around his neck. "Oh, thank God—"

"What happened?" he demanded curtly. "Why did you run?"

She licked her dry lips and struggled to speak coherently. "Someone spoke to me from behind the statue."

"Was it Gerard?"

"No, I don't th-think so—it didn't sound like him, but I don't—Oh, look!" She pointed as a dark shape moved past the statue and disappeared around the hedges.

"That's Flagstad," Grant muttered. "One of the Runners. If there's a man in the area, he'll find him."

"Shouldn't you be chasing after him, too?"

Grant toyed with one of the pinned curls atop her head that had come loose, and tucked it gently back in place. Suddenly a caressing smile touched his lips. "Are you suggesting I leave you alone?"

"No," she said immediately, her arms tightening around his neck. "Not after what he said to me."

His smile vanished at once. "What did he say, Vivien?"

She hesitated, sharply aware of her own need for caution. Nothing about the pregnancy must be mentioned . . . at least not until she discovered more about it. Settling deeper into his arms, relishing the solid muscularity of his body, she replied cautiously. "That he won't rest until I am dead."

"Did the voice sound familiar?"

"No, not at all."

Gently Grant pulled one of her sagging gloves back in place, his thumb coming to rest against the intimate softness of the hollow beneath her arm. Though his own hand was gloved, the touch was solid and reassuring. "Are you injured?" he asked,

"My leg . . . I hit the front of it, but I think it's only a bruise—" She squeaked in protest as he began to hike the front of her skirt upward. "No, not here! *Wait*—"

"The skin doesn't appear to be broken." Grant inspected the swelling bruise intently, ignoring her determined wriggling. "Hold still."

"I will *not* hold still while you expose my—Oh, do let go!" Mortified, she realized that someone else had joined them on the steps. Grant pulled her skirt back down, concealing the injured leg, but not before Sir Ross Cannon had reached them. Vivien pressed her crimson face against the front of Grant's coat and peered up at Cannon.

"Flagstad couldn't make out the man's face in the darkness," Cannon said without expression. "However, he did say our fellow is tall, gray-haired, and lean of build. And by an interesting coincidence, a carriage belonging to Lord Lane, who matches that description, is departing the estate as we speak."

"Lane," Grant repeated with a quizzical frown. "He's not on the list of suspects."

"Was he mentioned in Miss Duvall's book?"

"No," Grant and Vivien said in unison.

Tentatively Vivien tugged at the front of Grant's coat. "There was an elderly man staring at me in the drawing room . . . He looked as if he hated me. He had a nose like a hawk's beak. Could that have been Lord Lane?"

"It could have been," Grant replied thoughtfully. "But I'll be damned if I can figure out what connection he has to you. No one has mentioned him before."

"Allow me to investigate what relevance he might have to Miss Duvall's case," Cannon said. Although the words were phrased as a question, he was clearly not asking for permission. "Lane happens to have led the opposition to my bill on the expansion of my night-watch patrols." He smiled grimly. "I would like to repay the favor."

"By all means," Grant replied. He moved Vivien from his lap and helped her to stand. She was grateful for the partial concealment of darkness around them, acutely aware of her disheveled condition and the way Grant's hands lingered on the rise of her hips.

"May I go home now?" she asked softly, and Sir Ross answered.

"I don't see why not. You did well tonight, Miss Duvall. In my opinion, it shouldn't be long before the case is concluded. Soon you'll be free to return to your old life."

"Thank you," Vivien said in a hollow voice. Perhaps she was being ungrateful, but the prospect of returning to her former life was hardly something she looked forward to. And what of her lost memory? How and when would it come back? Or would it come back at all? What if she had to flounder through the rest of her days without a past, without any of the secrets and memories that made a person complete? Even if Cannon and Grant solved the mystery of her would-be killer and made her safe from further assault, she would face her own future with dread. She didn't know who she was, who she should be. What a strange punishment, to be robbed of the first half of her life.

Perhaps sensing her inner despair, Grant took her arm in a gentle grip. He guided her toward a path that led around the manor to the row of carriages parked along the circular drive.

"What will Lady Lichfield and the others think if we disappear without saying good-bye?" Vivien asked.

"They'll assume that we left early so I could take you home and bed you."

She blinked at his flat statement, while prickles of heat and cold chased over every inch of her skin. Wondering at his mood, she was tempted to ask if that was indeed what he planned to do. But the words clashed together and clumped in one huge, choking ball . . . because it occurred to her that she wished him to do exactly that. It had something to do with recklessness, and hopelessness, and the simple need for a few moments of pleasurable closeness. Whom would it harm if she gave herself to him? They had already done it before. She just couldn't remember it. Why shouldn't she let it happen again? It wasn't as if she had a reputation to protect. She felt empty, lonely and afraid ... She wanted to please him ... and herself.

She should have recoiled from the direction her thoughts were taking. Instead she felt wild and unpleasantly giddy, as if she had already committed herself to a course from which it was too late to retreat.

The footman saw them approach the carriage and hastened to fetch the movable step for Vivien. He was too well trained to show surprise at their early departure, nor did he ask questions, other than making a brief inquiry about their destination. "Home," Grant said gruffly, handing Vivien into the carriage himself and gesturing for the footman to tell the driver.

Vivien reached beneath her skirts to touch the throbbing bruise on her shin, wincing slightly.

"Are you in pain?" A scowl crept over Grant's face.

"Not really, but ..." She glanced at the fitted compartment that contained various crystal decanters. "Might I have a drink of brandy? I still feel a bit unsteady after what happened."

Wordlessly Grant poured a minute amount of brandy into a small glass and offered it to her. Vivien accepted the glass, raised it to her lips, and downed it in one swallow. The velvety fire spread down her throat and into her chest, bringing a sheen of moisture to her eyes. She suppressed a cough and held out the glass. "More, please," she said hoarsely.

One brow arched as he regarded her intently, and he filled her glass again. The second brandy went down more smoothly than the first, and the satisfying warmth drifted through her body. Sighing a little, Vivien surrendered the glass and snuggled in the corner of her seat. "Oh, that's better," she murmured.

"There's no reason to feel afraid, Vivien," Grant said, evidently deciding that was the reason she'd asked for the brandy. "I won't allow Lane or anyone else to hurt you."

"Yes, I know." She gave him a trusting smile, which he promptly dispelled with his next words.

"What did you and Gerard talk about in the lower garden?"

"Nothing of significance," she said.

"Tell me what was said. I'll decide if it is significant or not."

Since there was nothing on earth that would induce her to confide her secret pregnancy to him, she sought for something to tell him. "Well . . . Lord Gerard asked why I was with you, and he said that you were only flash gentry."

The comment elicited a smile of sardonic amusement. Vivien deduced that Grant had been the target of similar barbs many times in the past. "I'd say he's a fair judge of character," Grant commented dryly. "Go on."

"Then he asked me to leave you and return to him."

"How did you reply?"

"I didn't say yes or no, I only said I would consider it."

"A wise maneuver," he said coolly. "In your position, it's best to keep all options open."

"I'm not going to become his mistress again," she said, insulted that he assumed she might.

"Who knows?" It seemed he was deliberately trying to antagonize her. "When this is all over . . ."

"Is that what you want me to do?" she asked in annoyance. "Go back to Lord Gerard? Or find some other man to keep me?"

"No. That's not what I want."

"Then what *do* you—" She gasped as he reached for her, swift as a striking tiger, snatching her onto his lap. One large hand tangled in her coiffure, ruining the arrangement of curls and scattering a few stray pins to the carriage floor.

Grant's breath came in unsteady bursts, while heat climbed over his face. He was jealous, frustrated, painfully aroused, all because of the provoking creature in his arms. He was tired of wanting what he could not have, of repeatedly stumbling over his own conscience. She was a tumbled heap of flesh and silk in his lap, and he longed to lose himself in her warmth.

"I want you to stay with me," he said hoarsely. "I want you to be mine."

Vivien stared at him with heavy-lidded blue eyes, seeming to understand his torment. Gently she touched his face with a cool gloved hand. "Then I will," she murmured, her sweet brandy-scented breath wafting in his face. "Because I want you too."

The words released the ravening devil inside him. Unable to stop himself, Grant reached for the edge of Vivien's glove and stripped it from her arm. He caught her bare hand and pressed it hard to his mouth and jaw, greedily savoring the tender skin. His mouth delved into her palm, and he closed his eyes in lust and pleasure.

Vivien tugged at her hand, and as soon as it was released, she slid her trembling fingers behind his taut neck. He needed no further urging. Lowering his head, he crushed his mouth over hers, demanding that she open to him. Her lips parted, welcoming him into her sweetness, her own tongue yielding to the aggressive sliding and stroking of his. Groaning, he gathered her more tightly into his lap, twisting his mouth harder over hers. The kiss turned frantic as he searched for a deeper taste of her, but instead of becoming sated, he was increasingly desperate for more.

He ripped his mouth away with a growl, his gaze raking over her flushed face. "I can't get enough of you," he said hoarsely. "You're so beautiful, so sweet . . . Vivien, let me . . ." His hands fumbled with the back of her gown, pulling and tearing at the uppermost fastenings. The bronze fabric gave way with a jagged sound, hooks popping free of their moorings, and the cups of her bodice fell away from her pale flesh. "Let me," he muttered again, one arm locked around her slender back to prevent her from shrinking away. His hand cupped beneath the firm globe of her breast, his thumb drawing over the soft pink nipple until it contracted and darkened to bright rose. Vivien bit her lips and writhed as his dark head bent over her chest. The wet heat of his mouth surrounded the tip of her breast, and he flicked the peak with his tongue.

Lost in a fog of brandy and sensation, Vivien curled both her arms around his head. He tugged at her nipple, gently, skillfully, his large body shaking with the ferocity of his need. Vivien's eyes closed as she surrendered to pure physical feeling. Only a brief flicker of shame intruded on her thoughts, the despairing awareness that only a shameless woman, a courtesan, would allow a man to do this to her in a carriage. But she didn't care. It didn't matter how, when, or where he touched her. She wanted him as badly as he seemed to want her, and nothing in the world would keep them apart now.

He moved to her other breast, his teeth closing on the tender peak, his tongue circling and darting until she arched upward with a groan. With each caress of his tongue, she felt a prickling sensation of delight deep in her stomach, and lower between her thighs. Agitated, she pressed her legs together and drew her knees upward, instinctively seeking to ease the gathering ache.

Grant tore off his glove and grasped her ankle, the calluses on his hand catching on her silk stocking. Spreading his fingers wide, he trailed them up to her knee and beyond, to the place where a garter held the silk against her thigh. He explored the soft skin above the garter and slid his hand beneath her crumpled linen drawers. Reaching higher and higher, he found the patch of curls between her thighs.

Vivien resisted in a reflex of modesty, quivering

in his lap and gasping out a muffled protest. Instantly his mouth took hers in a surging kiss. She moaned and wrapped her arms around his broad shoulders, all thought of refusal melting like ice in the sun. His hand searched the front of her drawers, found the ribbon-edged slit of the garment, and reached right up inside. His fingers slid gently amid the curls, a blunt fingertip drawing along the delicate furrow that protected her private place. Her body shook with confusion, fear, excitement, and her head dropped weakly against his shoulder.

The wicked exploration continued, his teasing fingertip repeating its long, light stroke until the feminine lips became swollen and unbearably sensitive. He touched the tiny, aching center of her desire, circling, shocking her with a visceral pleasure that made her want to scream.

Vivien writhed on his lap, against the protruding bulge that pressed upward into her buttocks. A shaken laugh bubbled up from her throat as she realized that he was more than ready to take her here, in the carriage.

His fingers had located a source of perplexing dampness and probed the soft hollow. Without warning, he slid his middle finger inside her. At first she resisted the gentle intrusion, a slight burn making her jerk and arch in an attempt to push him away. But her inner flesh gripped him tightly, and her thighs closed around his hand, and he pressed soothing words and kisses in the little cove beneath her earlobe.

"You're so tight," he said thickly. "Why? Are you afraid?"

"Yes." she whispered, her senses whirling.

"You have nothing to fear."

"I . . . I don't remember how to do this," she choked out. His finger slid more easily now, a surge of unexpected moisture preparing the way for him. A slow plunge, another, in a seductive rhythm that made her hips arch eagerly. The pleasurable ache grew stronger, sharper, until she quivered and clawed the back of his coat.

The world shifted off its axis, spinning out of control. She needed to touch his skin, but layers of clothes and starch and buttons prevented her. Lowering her to the carriage seat, he crouched over her with one foot braced on the floor. He held her head in the crook of his arm as he kissed her. His mouth was rough, hot, agitated, and they both moaned at the heart-thumping pleasure of the kiss.

The carriage became a lurching, swaying coccoon of shadows and leather, the air fragrant from her own vanilla-perfumed skin. Reaching up for him, Vivien locked her arms around his broad shoulders and nuzzled tightly into his throat.

"I love you," he whispered, pushing her flat against the seat, staring down at her face.

"You don't have to say that," she said unsteadily, though the words sent a rush of intense pleasure through her.

"I love you," he repeated, his green eyes gleaming like a cat's in the darkness.

Wondering if he was truly aware of what he was saying, if he was possibly the kind of man who did not distinguish between love and desire, she stared at him wordlessly.

The carriage stopped, and she realized they were at King Street. Grant's dark head lowered, and his voice was a low scrape of sound in her ear. "Make love with me tonight, Vivien."

Eleven

The hour was late and the servants had retired for the evening, except for a lone footman who opened the door. After a blink of surprise, the footman averted his gaze from the small, disheveled form in Grant's arms.

Carrying his precious burden upstairs, his coat wrapped snugly around her, Grant glanced at Vivien's half-hidden face. She was flushed and silent, her expression conveying uncertainty but not unwillingness. Remembering his words of love to her in the carriage, he felt his own color heighten, though he did not, would not, regret having said it. This was the first time in his adult life that he had ever told a woman he loved her. He had discovered a side of himself that he had never known existed until tonight, and he wanted to show Vivien all the tenderness and passion he was capable of.

They reached his room, and he set Vivien beside the bed. Smoothing his hands over her tousled hair, he kissed her mouth, shaping her lips with his own. He pulled the pins from her fiery locks and loosened her braids, letting her hair flow soft and warm over his hands.

"Tell me what to do," she whispered, her hands slipping beneath his coat, exploring the hard lines of his waist and back. "I don't know how to satisfy you. I don't remember how to do any of this."

"You don't have to remember," he said, his voice soft and fierce. He held her against his tremendously aroused body, his breath catching at the delicious feel of her. Pressing his mouth to the top of her throat, he kissed and tasted the fragile skin, working his way downward until he reached the vanilla-scented valley of her cleavage. Vivien shivered and leaned back against the support of his arm, while her heart beat fast beneath the pressure of his exploring mouth.

He undressed her slowly, pulling at the fastenings of her garments and letting them drop away from her. Her newly revealed skin was white and luminous, her body tender and abundantly curved . . . He closed his eyes briefly, striving to subdue his violent passion. When he opened them again, Vivien had moved away from him and hastily climbed into bed, pulling the linens over her nakedness. Her bashfulness was so genuine, so . . . well, *virginal*, that he wondered if this was what she had been like long ago, before embarking on her career as a courtesan.

"Don't cover yourself," he murmured. "Your body is too beautiful to be concealed."

The bedsheet did not lower an inch. "I'm cold," she said breathlessly, her cheeks flushed.

"I'll warm you," he promised with a quick grin, stripping off his coat.

Vivien watched as his clothes were discarded, uncovering an expanse of skin much tougher and darker than her own, covered with springy hair in some places, scarred in others. She was amazed by the power and grace of his body, which had been honed and punished and exercised until no trace of softness remained. "You were right," she said unsteadily. "You *are* an impressive sight without your clothes."

He smiled and approached her, bracing his hands on either side of her hips as he leaned over her. She felt the gentle brush of his mouth over her hair. "Any second thoughts?" he asked. "Tell me now, before I get into bed with you."

Vivien slid her arms around his neck for answer, and pulled him down to her. The full length of his body pressed against hers, and suddenly she could barely hear above the roaring pulse in her ears. Her thoughts scattered and vanished, and all that remained was sensation . . . the startling heat of his skin, the coarse hair on his chest, the exquisite glide of his mouth over her throat and shoulder and breast. His hands were everywhere, stroking and exploring, sliding between her limbs with no heed to modesty.

Had there been any doubts remaining in the back of her mind, they dissolved immediately. She had not suspected that a man so well acquainted with the harshness of life could be so tender, his hands unimaginably gentle as they searched the intimate places of her body. He breathed so fast, as if from great exertion, each forceful exhalation burning her like steam. Pressing her back to the mattress, he kissed and nuzzled the rise of her breasts, softly biting the stiffened tips.

Gasping, she wrapped her arms around his dark head, while pleasure and a peculiar tension made her writhe beneath him. Suddenly a stray thought appeared in her mind. How could she have done this with many different men? This act required more trust and intimacy than she could have imagined. It was not possible . . . Somehow everyone must be wrong about her . . . But before she could dwell on this thought further, it was whisked away.

She felt his hand close around her wrist, drawing her fingers downward until they brushed against a length of hot, silken skin. With a gravelly murmur of encouragement, Grant pressed her hand against his groin. Curious, excited, she curved her hand around the hard masculine shape, timidly stroking and gripping his arousal. Her touch seemed to impassion him beyond bearing. He kissed her deeply, his tongue stroking inside her as he spread her thighs and lowered his hips between them.

There was pressure against the tender opening of her body, causing a slight burn of discomfort. Stiffening in reaction, Vivien felt the weight of his body settle a little harder over hers, and the blunt force increased. Before she could protest or wriggle away, he made a sound low in his throat and pushed forward in a strong thrust. Vivien's breath stopped as she experienced a kind of pain she had never felt before—she was certain of it. No woman could feel it and not remember. Her hands spasmed against his chest, and she tried to push him away, but he pushed again. Suddenly he was inside her, his massive length buried deep and hard.

Through a shimmer of bewildered tears, she caught a glimpse of his stunned face. "Vivien, be still," he said harshly, but she struggled and twisted, pinned helplessly beneath him.

Astonished by the tightness of the flesh that surrounded him, her obvious pain, and the inevitable conclusion his brain was reaching, Grant moved automatically to subdue her, and prevent her further discomfort.

"You're hurting me," she gasped.

Holding her tightly, he murmured soothing words against her ear, that he loved her, he would take care of her, he would take the pain away if she would let him. Gradually she relaxed and clung to him, her nails digging into the tough muscles of his back. Still joined with her, he slid his hand down her body. His thumb eased into the damp patch of red hair, coming to rest lightly on the sensitive peak hidden amid the fiery curls. He circled it slowly, teasing a response from her trembling body.

Moaning, she lifted her hips into the caress, and he knew that her discomfort was fading. He con-

tinued to tease and stroke her, and at the same
time, he moved inside her with a deep, gentle
nudge. Vivien cried out, her body instinctively tilting to receive him, her hands working restlessly
over his back. He began a slow rhythm, adjusting
himself to please her, his entire being focused on
the delight of thrusting within her. She climaxed
with startling swiftness, her body clenching tight
around him, her limbs quaking with surprise. As
he held himself inside her, Grant experienced a release more powerful than anything he had experienced in his life. He groaned and buried his face
against the curve of her shoulder, his groin pump-
ing, his pulse hammering, his body flooded with
luxury.

In the heavy silence that followed, Grant withdrew from Vivien carefully and found a tell-tale
sign that defied all logic. Perplexed, remorseful, furious at himself, Grant faced a fact he would never
have believed without physical proof.

She was—or had been until this moment—a virgin.

Staring into Vivien's dazed face, Grant shook his
head incredulously. She fumbled for the sheet and
pulled it over herself, returning his gaze with a
mixture of confusion and suspense. He rested his
hand on the shape of her hip, and though she
flinched, she did not push him away.

"Why did it hurt like that?" she asked scratchily.

He did not answer immediately, his mind occupied with a slew of questions. "Because you were
a virgin," he finally said.

"But . . . I couldn't have been. I . . . I'm Vivien

Duvall ... am I not? You told me ..." She stopped speaking, staring up at him with amazement.

"Christ," he muttered to himself, trying to understand how he could have made an error of such magnitude. "You can't be Vivien."

"What if I am? What if you and everyone else was wrong about me? What if—"

"There is no chance in hell that Vivien Duvall could be a virgin," he said, staring at her as if he had never seen her before. "It's impossible. Physically you're an exact match ... but you're not Vivien."

"But how could I could resemble her exactly unless she and I were somehow related ... perhaps even ..." She fell silent as another thought occurred to her.

"A twin?" he finished for her, his face grim. "Given your physical appearance, that's entirely likely. Though no one even hinted at the possibility that Vivien had a sister, much less an identical twin."

"Are you certain I'm not Vivien?" she asked in a stricken whisper. "The things you said about me ... the men I slept with ... the things in that diary ... That wasn't me?"

"That wasn't you," he said quietly.

She shocked him by bursting into tears, her hands jerking up to her face, glittering rivulets leaking out from between her fingers.

Grant hauled her into his arms, crushing her against his bare chest. The feel of her tears on his skin caused him to ache with painful remorse. He cursed and did his best to comfort her.

"I'm sorry for this damned mess," he muttered. "I can't give you back your innocence. I've hurt you unforgivably."

"No, no," she sobbed against his shoulder. "I-I'm not c-crying about that. I'm just s-so relieved that I'm not Vivien, and yet . . ." She tried to hold back another sob, but it broke free with renewed force. "I thought I knew who I was, a-and there was some comfort in that, even if I couldn't remember anything. And now . . ." She sniffled and choked on a fresh onslaught of tears. "Who am I? I can't stand not knowing any longer. I feel so . . ." Her sobs made further speech impossible.

Grant held her as she cried, feeling guiltier and more remorseful with each second that passed. "I'll find out," he said gruffly. "I swear I will. Dammit . . . don't cry anymore. Please."

Stroking the wild mass of her hair, he wondered who the hell she was, and how she had come to be in Vivien's place. And why had no one been searching for her? Somewhere there must be a family, friends, someone who was worried by her absence. It was even possible she had been betrothed. Someone with her youth and beauty would not be unspoken-for. The thought rattled him even more.

She had an entire life that neither of them knew a damned thing about.

And where in the hell was the real Vivien? Had her would-be murderer already found her and accomplished the job he had set out to do?

Confounded by the turn of events, Grant waited until Vivien—he could think of her by no other name—had calmed somewhat, and he laid her gently on the bed. Procuring a striped burgundy dressing robe, he tied the belt around his waist and strode to the bellpull. He rang for Kellow, who appeared in less than five minutes. The valet had dressed hastily, his hair mussed and his eyes sleep-heavy. Grant met him at the door, keeping it partially closed to prevent him from seeing Vivien. "A ewer of hot water and some washcloths," Grant said curtly.

"Yes, sir." The valet vanished, and Grant turned back to the bed. Vivien had not moved. At first he thought she might have fallen asleep, but as he came to her, he saw that her eyes were open. Her gaze was turned inward, her mind dwelling on thoughts she couldn't or didn't want to share with him.

"I'm going to make up to you for what I've done," he said quietly.

She stirred then, turning her head to regard him with a tremulous smile. "You don't have to," she whispered, her eyes sparkling with tears. "It wasn't your fault that you mistook me for Vivien . . . Everyone did. No one questioned my identity. I can't blame you for accepting what seemed to be the obvious." She released a shaky sigh. "And as far as *this* is concerned . . ." She made a quick, embarrassed gesture to the rumpled bedclothes, and her gaze lowered. "I was more than willing," she said in a bashful whisper. "And you couldn't have known I was a virgin."

"That makes me no less responsible." Half sitting beside her on the bed, he took a lock of her hair in his hand, rubbing the silken strands between his fingers. "Vivien—" he said, and stopped as soon as the name left his lips. "Damn. What should I call you now?"

Her lips curved in the faintest of smiles. "You may as well continue to call me Vivien. I'm accustomed to it by now, and besides . . . I don't want to choose yet another wrong name. I just want to find my own."

"I'm glad you're not really Vivien," he murmured, still toying with the lock of hair as he stared at her. "I'm glad that no man has made love to you except me."

She hesitated before replying, her blue eyes questioning as she gazed up at him. "So am I."

They stared at each other for an endless moment, lost in unspoken thoughts of what had just occurred between them, and how it had changed everything.

Reflecting on how he had treated her, Grant was deeply troubled. He was in an impossible position. He, of all men, had managed his own life so efficiently, so carefully. Now he had fallen in love against his will, only to discover that she wasn't the woman he had thought her to be, and then he had unintentionally taken her virginity. He faced a devil of a reckoning on the morrow. His only choice was to tell her the truth and expose his own lies, and hope to hell that she might be able to forgive and trust him again. And even if she did, there was still every chance he would lose her when she regained her memory and returned to her former life.

Grant had never expected to feel such responsibility for a woman, such an emotional and physical connection to her. The act of sex seemed almost new, as if in taking her innocence he had somehow gained back a little of his own. He wanted to make love to her again, teach and explore and share with her. Although he had reluctantly acknowledged his growing love for her before tonight, the feelings were suddenly infused with promise and wonder, and every fragment of bitterness was gone. He felt humbled, almost clumsy, a great moonstruck creature whose every hope of happiness was absurdly precarious.

Impatiently Grant wondered where Kellow was, and why he was taking so long to fulfill a simple request. Opening the door, he stared at the darkened hall. His foot touched the edge of an object on the floor. Glancing down, he saw a tray loaded with hot water, washcloths—and brandy and a glass. Kellow had tactfully left the tray just outside the door.

Grant picked up the tray and closed the door with his foot. Returning to the beside, he set the tray on the night table. "Here," he said, handing a linen cloth to Vivien. She wiped her streaming eyes and blew her nose with a childlike vigor that almost made him smile. He filled a creamware bowl with steaming water, and soaked and wrang out another cloth. Self-consciously Vivien averted her pink and puffy face as he began to wipe it. The warm cloth passed over her fragile skin, erasing the salty tear tracks beneath her eyes and on her cheeks.

Quietly he bid her to lie back against the pillows,

and she obeyed. He dampened the cloth again and began to wash her as if she were a child. He bathed beneath her arms, over the chest, stomach, legs. His dispassionate demeanor seemed to soothe her, and gradually she relaxed, not resisting even when he washed between her thighs. Using another clean, warm cloth, he bathed away every trace of blood and semen. He was as gentle as possible, but even so, she winced as he performed the intimate service.

When the task was done, he covered her with the bedclothes and undressed and washed himself. He blew out the lamp, shrouding the room in darkness, and got into bed beside her. Exhausted but still awake, Vivien went still as his weight depressed the mattress. "What are you doing?" she whispered.

"Holding you." He kissed her temple, the curve of her ear, the side of her neck, taking his time, his mouth moving over her in light, warm brushes. Vivien blinked and gasped, and pushed at his chest. "Not again," she said unsteadily. "I'm very tired." He sensed rather than saw her blush as she added, "And sore."

"I won't hurt you. I promise." He opened his mouth over the tip of her breast, stroking with his tongue until he felt it gather in a sensitive bud. Cupping both breasts in his hands, he lingered first on one, then the other, until Vivien let out a shivering sigh and put her hands to his head. At first he thought she intended to push him away, but her fingers curved to his scalp and urged him closer. He clasped her hips in his hands and kissed a trail down to her navel. Making his tongue into a point, he jabbed it softly into the small hollow, again and again. As his mouth began a hot downward slide toward the triangle of cinnamon curls between her thighs, she gasped and covered it with a protective hand. "Wait," she said, a pleading note entering her voice.

"Take away your hand," he urged.

"I can't." She gasped as he kissed around the barrier of her hand, searching between the crevices of her fingers. His mouth settled over the back of her hand, and he drew small wet circles with the point of his tongue, until her entire body tingled with shocked excitement.

"Take away your hand," he said huskily, pulling gently at her wrist. She continued to cover herself, and he licked each of her taut fingers from base to tip. His tongue was agile, restless, playing over her wrist and hand and fingers until she moaned that she could not bear it any longer.

"Then let me do as I want, dammit," he whispered tenderly. "Take away your hand, darling."

She obeyed, revealing the place she had shielded, and Grant growled in satisfaction. He nuzzled into the soft wealth of red curls, using his fingers to spread her open. One surging lick into the tantalizing salty cove, and he felt her entire body shake. Another lick, and he lingered in hungry exploration, teasing, tasting, his senses spiraling in pleasure.

Grant felt her pushing at his head, but he ignored the feeble gesture and concentrated on the delicate flesh beneath his tongue. Her fingers trembled on his head, and her hips tilted in helpless offering. She was unable to hold back her response now, her body yearning and tensing in an unmistakable rhythm. He knew he could do anything he wanted with her now, and for a moment he was tempted to raise upward and thrust himself inside her throbbing warmth. But equally compelling was the desire to feel her climax against his mouth, and so he stayed where he was, his tongue moving in rapid flicks until she bit back a scream and gave a long, sweet shudder of release.

"Oh . . ." she whispered between uneven breaths. "I didn't know . . . I never thought . . ." Her body trembled violently as he rose upward and folded her against the shelter of his chest.

Grant crushed his mouth into her hair, kissing her damp scalp. "That's just the beginning," he promised. "That's the very least of what you're going to feel with me."

She had thrown herself willingly into the fire. She had only herself to blame if she had gotten burned. That was the first thought that entered Vivien's mind as she awakened by herself, her body spread diagonally across the huge bed. A spark of hope flared inside her, that perhaps she had dreamed an unusually vivid dream. But the pillow beneath her head carried a faint masculine scent, and she was naked beneath the sheet and coverlet. Her bleary eyes cracked open. As she pushed aside the covers, she saw the hints of bruises on her pale legs and hips, as if someone had held her too tightly.

She was sore in places she had never been sore before. There was a sting of discomfort right between her thighs, and strained muscles all down the insides of her legs to her knees. Her shoulders and neck also ached. Just as she thought longingly of a hot bath, someone entered the room.

Instantly Vivien jerked the covers under her chin as Grant approached the bed. He had already bathed and dressed. His face was shaven and his hair damp and neatly combed. It seemed he had taken special pains with his appearance this morning, his black silk cravat tied with crisp precision, his shirt starched and snowy in contrast to his immaculate gray coat and charcoal waistcoat. Pearl-colored trousers had been neatly strapped over black boots polished to a blinding gleam.

As she stared into his alert green eyes, Vivien was filled with conflicting feelings. She could not, would not, blame him for taking her virginity. She had offered herself to him willingly. They had shared the most intimate experience a man and woman could have, and part of her actually gloried in the fact. However, she would not admit her love for him aloud. There were even more pressing matters to deal with . . . as well as a few suspicions that lurked in the back of her mind.

Grant came to her at once, cupping her face in his hands, possessing her mouth with a long, fervent kiss. "Good morning," he murmured with a slight smile. The way he looked at her, his gaze warm with intimate knowledge, made her flush.

"Sh-shouldn't you be at Bow Street?" she asked, her voice sleep-thickened. Judging from the strength of the light pouring into the room, it was a late hour of the morning. Grant was usually gone before the sun had finished its daily ascent.

"I'm not going to Bow Street this morning," he replied, leaning his hip beside her, his weight causing one side of the mattress to depress.

She considered the statement, her small hand twisting in the sheet. "Because of last night?" she asked.

"We're going to pay a visit to Linley."

"I have no need of a doctor," she said, leaning closer to inhale his spicy masculine scent. "Most women survive their first time without requiring medical attention afterward."

"Perhaps I'm the one who needs it," he said sardonically, rubbing his cheek against the silken tangles of her hair. "The Devil knows that last night was as much of a shock to me as it was to you." Drawing back, he stared into her troubled face and added gently, "You may as well be there while I talk to Linley, sweet pea. The good doctor owes us both the answers to a few questions."

He reached across the bed to a pool of burgundy silk and shook it out, holding it up for her. Realizing it was his robe, Vivien attempted to slide her arms in the sleeves without revealing her breasts.

"I've seen a thousand signs of your innocence," he remarked, carefully pulling the mass of her hair free and letting it flow down the back of the robe. His voice was shadowed with regret, and dark color crept across the high edges of his cheeks and the bridge of his nose. "Until last night I thought every one of them was false. I couldn't fathom that

you could be anyone other than Vivien Duvall."
Taking one of her hands, he brought it to his face
and pressed the tender inside of her palm to his
cheek. His mouth touched the delicate crease of her
wrist. "Forgive me," he muttered, with a visible
effort that betrayed how difficult the words were.

"There is nothing to forgive," Vivien said, her
hand tingling from the warmth of his smooth-
shaven cheek. "You've done no harm to me.
You've harbored and protected me, and . . . I will
continue to rely on you. However . . ." She paused,
searching for the appropriate words and not finding them.

Grant lowered her hand and looked at her warily. "However?" he asked, a frown working between his dark brows.

"I don't think there should be further intimacy
between us," she forced herself to say. "At least not
for a while."

Although his face was suddenly expressionless,
she sensed that he was preparing a score of argu-
ments. "Why not?" he asked.

Gathering the robe tightly around herself, she
summoned as much dignity as possible. "I would
rather not explain right now."

To her relief, he did not pursue the matter . . .
though it was clear that he was very far from agreeing with or accepting her statement. Instead, he
gave her a smile brimming with charm. "You're
not getting away from me, you know," he said
softly.

Vivien suppressed a rueful laugh, somehow both
moved and alarmed by the realization that he was

determined to win her. She allowed him to escort her to the bath, where a row of towels had been set on a warmer by the fire, and the enameled hip tub had been liberally filled with steaming water. The burgundy robe was so long on her that it formed a silken train, and she scooped up handfuls in front to keep from tripping on it.

"I'll assist you with your bath," Grant offered.

"No, thank you," she said firmly. "I want a few minutes of privacy. Please."

"I'll be waiting in the next room."

As Vivien soaked in the bath, letting the hot water soothe her minor aches, she wished for a moment's respite from the worries that plagued her. However, nothing would keep them at bay. Questions tormented her repeatedly, as she wondered just who—and what—she really was. Certainly she was not a gently born aristocrat's daughter . . . she didn't feel herself to be a member of the nobility. But she was not a courtesan, either. She had no name, no family, no memory. She was foundering once again, feeling utterly insignificant, frustrated, and helpless. What if she never found out who she really was? Would it be possible to create a new life for herself, never knowing what and whom she might have left behind—friends, family, perhaps a man she had loved?

A maid came to help her from the bath, bringing with her a gown made of rich green cashmere. The simple garment closely followed the lines of her figure and fastened at the left side with a gold clasp. The narrow sleeves were finished with green ribbon, as was the wide shawl collar. The plunging neckline of the gown had been supplemented with a snowy white lace inset that contrasted crisply with the soft jewel-toned cashmere. The maid braided Vivien's still damp hair and pinned it in a heavy coil at the crown of her head.

After thanking the maid, Vivien went to the door of the bedroom where Grant waited. She hesitated before entering, trying to gather the courage to ask him the nagging question that weighed on her mind. She was almost afraid to learn the answer. However, it served no one, least of all herself, to behave in a cowardly manner. The truth must be faced squarely, no matter how unpleasant it might be. Squaring her shoulders, she went into the room.

Grant had been seated in a chair by the window. He stood immediately, his gaze flickering over her. "How do you feel?" he asked quietly.

She tried to smile, but her lips felt too stiff. "I think . . ." she began, and swallowed hard. "I think there are some things you haven't yet told me, aren't there?"

His expression revealed nothing. "Such as?"

"I would like to know about your relationship with the real Vivien."

Twelve

*a*fter seating Vivien in a damask-upholstered chair, Grant sat next to her. He leaned forward, bracing his arms on his knees, and contemplated the coals on the grate for what seemed to be an unduly long time. And when he finally spoke, Vivien did not like the scrupulous way he seemed to be considering his words, as if he were preparing to present a nasty situation in its best possible light.

"All right," Grant finally said, sliding a narrow-eyed glance at her. He sighed and rested his closed fists on his knees. "You have every right to know about my behavior concerning Vivien Duvall . . . but first let me say . . ." He paused as if he found it difficult to speak, and a muttered curse escaped his lips. "Dammit. I've done bad things in my life— I could write a list of sins a mile long. Some of them were done for the sake of survival, and some were out of pure selfish greed. And I have regrets. But of all the sins I've committed, I don't regret anything half as much as the fact that I lied to you. And I swear on my life—no, on my brother's grave—that I never will again."

"What did you lie to me about?" Vivien asked softly, shivering as an icy lump of dread formed in her stomach.

His gaze arrowed to the hearth, and he didn't answer.

As she watched his granite-hard profile, understanding dawned.

"About Vivien Duvall?" she guessed. "She was never your mistress . . . is that it? You never slept with her, as you claimed. But why?" She regarded him with raw bewilderment. "Why would you lie about such a thing?"

It took all of Grant's self-discipline to remain there beneath her steady, clear-eyed scrutiny. It had never been difficult for him to own up to his misdeeds. He had always cheerfully rationalized his mistakes and pointed out to himself and everyone else that he was, after all, only human. However, this was something he couldn't blithely skim over and forget. He had set out to take advantage of someone—a woman—and what was worse, his petty vengeance had been taken out on the wrong person. Guilt thickened his voice as he answered.

"I wanted revenge because of a lie Vivien had spread about me among the London gossip circles. On the night I found you and brought you here, I decided that I would sleep with you—her—as a salve to my pride."

"And then what were you going to do? Use and discard her? Hurt her in return for the embarrassment she caused you?"

He gave a single shamed nod.

Vivien inhaled sharply. Perhaps it should have made her feel better that another woman, and not she, had been Grant's intended target. But it didn't. She didn't want to think him capable of such pettiness, such dishonor. And it hurt dreadfully to realize that what for her had been an act of giving had been for him only an act of revenge. "I see."

"No, you don't."

"The fact that I was injured and helpless didn't matter to you," she murmured. "In fact, it made it easier for you to take advantage."

His eyes gleamed with frustration, and she sensed the sudden boiling of his emotions beneath his controlled surface. "It all went wrong from the beginning. You didn't behave like the woman I thought you were."

Vivien's calmness evaporated as she was filled with a sense of utter betrayal. "You were the one solid thing in the world, the one person I could trust . . . and you've lied from the very beginning."

"Only about our supposed affair."

"Only?" she repeated, angry that he was trying to minimize his actions. "What if I had indeed been the real Vivien, and I were every bit as promiscuous and self-absorbed and unlikable as you expected? That doesn't excuse your behavior at all."

"If I had known who you really were—or

weren't—I would never have hurt you."

"But you have," she said bitterly.

"Yes, the damage is done." His voice was flat and unemotional. "And all I can do now is try to make reparations and ask your forgiveness."

"Not my forgiveness," she corrected. "Vivien's."

Grant stared at her as if she had suddenly gone mad. "I'll be damned if I'll go with my hat in hand to that woman."

"That is the only reparation I'll accept." She stared at him without blinking. "I want you to apologize to Vivien when you find her, for your cruel intentions toward her. And I'll forgive you if *she* does."

"Apologize to Vivien," he repeated, his voice rising to a thunderous pitch. "But I didn't sleep with her. I slept with you."

"What if you had indeed slept with her as you planned? Would you feel sorry then?"

"No," he snapped.

"Then you would not regret manipulating and deceiving someone if you thought he or she deserved it?" Her face was taut with disappointment and censure. "I would not have thought you capable of such ruthlessness and small-mindedness!"

"I said I was sorry, dammit!"

"But you're not," she replied gently. "You don't regret having come up with your horrible plan . . . you only regret that you didn't hurt the person you had intended to. And I could never love a man who behaves in such a manner." It almost gave her satisfaction to watch him struggle to control his spiking temper. Closing his eyes, he somehow managed to stave off an explosion, although his color heightened and his jaw vibrated with a visible tic.

"It's time to leave," he finally said. "I've sent word ahead to Linley."

Although Dr. Linley's fashionable residence was within walking distance, Grant had ordered his carriage to be prepared. The ride was silent, uncomfortable, and mercifully short. Vivien glanced frequently at the huge, aggravated male in the seat opposite hers. Grant seemed to be in a state of battened-down consternation, more than ready to do battle—except there was no one to do battle with.

She suspected that he was considering their argument and silently debating the points she had made. She longed to say something else, to soften him with a few pleading words . . . perhaps even try to coax him into agreeing with her. However, she kept her mouth tightly closed. He must resolve this issue on his own. She knew that he had no liking for the real Vivien Duvall, but that didn't excuse his own actions. A man wasn't entitled to lie or take advantage of others merely because he didn't respect them.

They reached Linley's town home, one of a long row of Grecian-fronted residences adorned with immaculate white plasterwork and columns. Grant helped her from the carriage and escorted her up a small flight of steps, and they were immediately welcomed into the house by the butler. Dr. Linley awaited them in the library, a small but tidy room lined with oak bookcases and furnished with shield-backed Hepplewhite chairs and a matching table.

Greeting them pleasantly, Linley seated Vivien in an armchair by the fire. He smiled and brushed back a swath of blond hair that had fallen over his forehead. "Miss Duvall," he murmured, "you are not feeling unwell, I hope?"

Vivien opened her mouth to reply, then closed it again. She stared at him with hot color climbing up her face as it struck her that the main purpose of this visit was to discuss the unexpected discovery of her virginity, and its bearings on her case. How had she come to be in this ignominious position?

Regarding her with mild perplexity, Linley turned his attention to Grant, who was stone-faced. An inquiring glint shone in the doctor's gray eyes. "I had to cancel two appointments because of the message you sent this morning, Morgan," he remarked. "Would you care to explain the urgency of this visit?"

"There has been a new development in Miss Duvall's case." Grant half sat, half leaned against the edge of a heavy library table. "I assume you keep a file on each of your patients. I want to see Miss Duvall's, with no detail omitted."

"That file is only for my eyes and Miss Duvall's," Linley replied equably.

"It has relevance to my investigation." Grant paused in visible discomfort, his nostrils flaring. "Tell me, Linley, when you examined Miss Duvall . . . was she a virgin?"

The doctor's perplexed gaze flickered from Vivien's downcast face and back to Grant's. "Assuredly not," he replied, tugging at the golden forelock that had slipped over his brow once more.

"Well, she is—or was, until last night."

Silence descended in the room. The doctor's face was carefully composed. "Are you certain of that?" he asked, contemplating them both.

Vivien flushed and refused to meet his gaze.

"I'm not a green lad, Linley," Grant muttered.

Linley strove for a matter-of-fact tone. "Then this is not the woman I examined. Vivien Duvall was in the earliest stage of pregnancy. When I saw her at your house, I assumed she had either had a miscarriage or had rid herself of the baby. I observed that there was no longer any enlargement of the womb and no bleeding. It was not my place to comment on her decision. And I wasn't looking for evidence of virginity."

"Christ." Absorbing the information, Grant glanced at Vivien. Her obvious lack of surprise at the news caused his green eyes to narrow suspiciously. "You knew," he said. "Somehow you knew about the pregnancy."

"It was probably Lord Gerard's baby," she said. "He told me while we were talking in the garden last night."

"Why the bloody hell didn't you tell me?"

"I knew what your reaction would be if you thought I had deliberately ended the pregnancy," she said. "You would have despised me. So I decided to keep it to myself for a little while."

Grant responded with a string of blistering curses and turned a threatening gaze toward the doctor. "The file, Linley. I'd like to see what other minor details you've been keeping from me."

While many men would have been intimidated by the irate giant before him, Linley displayed no unease. "All right, Morgan, you may view the damned file. But not until after I talk to Miss Duvall . . . er, that is, this young woman . . . in private."

"Why in private?" Grant asked.

"Because her welfare is my first concern. I've attended newly married women in hysterics after their wedding nights. I'd like to ascertain for myself if she is well, and it doesn't help her nerves—or mine, for that matter—for you to be charging about like an enraged boar."

"Nerves!" Grant's mouth twisted in a sneer. "Her nerves are fine." He glanced at Vivien's averted face with a sudden flicker of concern. "Aren't they?" he asked her.

She did not reply, only sat with her hands twisting in her lap.

"Out," Linley commanded briskly, seeming to enjoy the rare privilege of telling Grant what to do. "You're familiar with the house, old fellow. Go amuse yourself in the billiards room. Have a drink or a smoke. I'll send for you in a few minutes."

A warning grumble erupted from Grant's throat, and he left reluctantly.

Vivien looked up warily as Linley approached her. She braced herself for censure, but found only kindness and concern in his gray eyes. Asking permission to sit in a nearby chair, Linley regarded her with a faint smile. "Beneath all that snarling and blustering is one of the finest men I have ever known," he remarked. "Morgan is accomplished in many ways, but not where women are concerned. That is, he is not usually a seducer of innocents."

"He wanted revenge for some slight that the real Vivien had done him," she answered dully. "He planned to sleep with her and then cast her aside."

Linley shook his head. "That is not like him," he said thoughtfully.

"Now he intends to make amends, of course," Vivien said. "I believe he is even trying to convince himself that he loves me."

"After what has happened, I would say you deserve whatever compensation Morgan can offer."

"No," she murmured. "I don't want compensation—I just want to know who I am."

"Of course." The doctor regarded her with frank sympathy. "I'm afraid there is not much I can do to help you. However, I would at least like to assure you that the discomfort you undoubtedly experienced is a temporary thing. It all becomes easier on subsequent occasions."

Rather than tell him that there would be no subsequent occasions, Vivien nodded briefly. "I understand," she said quickly. "No more need be said, Dr. Linley."

He gave her a comforting smile. "Bear with me for one moment longer. I merely wish you to understand that in this act between a man and a woman, there should be honesty, affection, and trust. Don't give yourself to a man unless you believe those things are shared between you. And then it is a wondrous experience, and something not to be missed."

Vivien thought of the man pacing around the house as they spoke, and her insides ached with yearning. She wondered if she could somehow summon the courage to trust him again, or if he was even worthy of such trust.

"Morgan is a good fellow," Linley assured her, seeming to read her thoughts. "Arrogant, stubborn . . . but also compassionate and courageous. I hope you won't give up on him too easily, my dear. Especially considering the way he feels about you."

"About me?" Vivien asked, startled. "I don't know what you mean."

The doctor smiled wryly. "In the five years that I've known Grant Morgan, I've never seen him in such a state over a woman. Guilt is the least of the emotions that are working on him."

"If you're trying to imply that he's in love with me . . ." Vivien began warily.

"It doesn't matter what I imply. The fact is, he *is* in love with you." Linley stood and went to the door. Before opening it, he added prosaically, "What comes of that is up to you."

Linley found Grant in the billiards room, seated on a chair at the baize-covered table with his arm and chin resting on the edge. One by one, he rolled a succession of ivory balls in varying patterns across the table, sending them to a corner pocket where a green braided silk bag waited to catch them. He surveyed the clicking orbs as he spoke. "How is she?"

"Considering the whole of what she has been through since the night she was rescued from the river . . . very well indeed. She is a resilent girl."

Grant felt an easing in his throat. He trusted Linley. And in the course of treating the varied physical and emotional complaints of the women of London, the man should be an expert. Grant gripped the last ivory ball, engulfing it completely, then sent it rolling gently to the corner pocket. "I have an issue to take up with you, Linley," he muttered. "Your silence on the matter of the real Vivien's pregnancy—"

"I was obliged to keep silent," Linley said matter-of-factly. "Miss Duvall made it clear on the day of the visit that the babe's future, perhaps even its life, depended on secrecy. And although she seemed to be given to dramatics, I was inclined to believe her. She was none too happy about my confirmation of the pregnancy, and she left with suspicious haste. As if she were afraid of something . . . or someone."

"You should have told me before!" Grant stood and scrubbed his fingers distractedly through his short hair. "For God's sake, someone is trying to kill her. The fact of her pregnancy could be one of the most important clues about what happened to her and why."

"Morgan," the doctor said calmly, "do you know what would happen to my practice if it became known that I divulged private information without a woman's consent? Do you know how many of my patients are obliged to keep the circumstances of their pregnancies secret for one reason or another?"

"I can only guess," Grant said sardonically. The

respectable ladies of London's first society often escaped their loveless arranged marriages by taking lovers. Sometimes they foisted their illegitimate children off as their husbands'. No doubt the popular Dr. Linley was the keeper of many secrets.

"I understand the concept of confidentiality," Grant continued tersely. "However, the real Vivien is probably alive and in hiding somewhere. She is most likely pregnant and definitely in danger . . . and the girl you've seen today is in danger as well. So if there is anything you can remember about what Vivien said to you that day, you'd do well to tell me."

"All right. But before we return to the library to examine my files, I'd like to offer a word of advice. It concerns Vivien . . . that is, the young woman who is awaiting us. She was understandably disinclined to discuss her recent, er . . . experience with you, but she seems a sensible enough creature, and I don't believe she suffered unduly."

"You thought sleeping with me might be enough to frighten her into fits?" Grant inquired acidly.

A humorless smile pulled at Linley's mouth. "You would be surprised at what a physician discovers about women, Morgan. I've attended some who are so refined that they can't say words like 'stomach' or 'breast' aloud. There are women who can't bring themselves to tell me what ails them, and so I keep a stuffed doll in a drawer of my desk, and let them point to the body part that is giving them pain. Fully grown, married women, mind you. At times I'm certain it's mostly a pretense of delicacy, but there are unquestionably those who are acutely uncomfortable with all things pertaining to sex and physicality."

"Vivien's not that rarefied, thank God."

"You're right," the doctor said equably, "but even so, she may have a few private fears and concerns that only you—or her next lover—can assuage."

"There isn't going to be a 'next lover,'" Grant said automatically, outraged by the idea. "I'm the only man she's going to have."

"Well, for most women the second sexual experience is even more important than the first. It either confirms or disproves their worst fears. In my professional opinion, most of the women I see who claim to be inherently cold-natured have in reality been mishandled by husbands or lovers."

Grant sent him a simmering glare. "I know how to please a woman, Linley. Or are you preparing to expound on your own vast experience with females?"

The doctor laughed suddenly. "No, I'll leave the matter in your capable hands."

They returned to the library, discovering Vivien beside a bookcase loaded with ham-sized medical and scientific tomes. Her gaze left the rows of ponderous volumes with Latin and Greek titles, and flew to Grant's face. They exchanged a wary stare, while Vivien wondered what had been said between Grant and Linley. Grant wore a disgruntled expression, his black brows lowered over his eyes.

Busily Dr. Linley hunted through cabinets and drawers until he produced a thin sheaf of documents tied with string. "Ah, here it is," he remarked, spreading a few papers across the library table. Grant was at his side immediately. "You see?" Linley continued, tracing one finger along a page of notes. "Nothing untoward, except . . ." He fumbled a bit with the pages, and suddenly a small square of paper slipped out and fluttered to the floor. Vivien went to retrieve it quickly. It was a letter, sealed with brown wax and addressed to "V. Devane, White Rose Cottage, Forest Crest in Surrey."

"What is that?" Grant asked.

Vivien was silent, staring at the face of the letter. Something about the way the words were formed, the phrase "White Rose Cottage," seemed to reach into her sleeping memories and jostle them. Her lips parted, and she read the address soundlessly, again and again.

"Well, Linley?" Grant demanded, interrupting Vivien's concentration.

The doctor shrugged, actually seeming a touch sheepish. "Good God. I had forgotten about that."

"Where did it come from?" Grant asked impatiently.

"Miss Duvall left it here on the day I confirmed her pregnancy. As I told you, she was quite distressed. In her haste to leave, she dropped her reticule. The contents spilled out, and she scooped them back inside. After she left my house, I discovered that she had overlooked this letter, which obviously she had intended to send to someone. I had intended to return it to her on her next visit. I placed it in the file for safekeeping."

"Didn't it cross your mind that the letter might be important?"

"I'm a busy man, Morgan," the doctor said defensively, folding his lanky arms across his chest. "I have more important things to do than oversee my patients' correspondence. Now, you can continue to berate me for a small oversight, or you can open the blasted thing and read it."

Vivien had already broken the seal. Unfolding the neatly creased paper, she discovered a few lines written in flowery script. Some of the words had been dashed off hastily, a few letters left unfinished.

Dearest,

No, you must not come to town. There is trouble brewing here, but nothing I can't manage. I'm off to settle a few minor matters, and then I'll come to Surrey. Together soon, dear—

Vivien

Barely aware of Grant reading over her shoulder, Vivien continued to stare at the letter. "Did she mean to send this to a lover?" she murmured.

"Probably."

"Do you think she could be there now? At this White Rose Cottage?"

"We'll find out. I'm going there today," Grant said. "Right after I report to Cannon at Bow Street."

"I want to go with you."

"We don't know who will be there, or what to expect. You'll be safer here."

"But that's not fair!" Vivien exclaimed. "If the real Vivien is in Surrey, I want to see her too. She might be able to explain how I came to be in her place. She might even know who I am. I must go with you!"

"No," Grant said. "You're staying in London in the protection of my own home. I'll have one of the Runners assigned to watch you this evening, in the event that I need to stay away longer than expected." Seeing her unhappy expression, he slid an arm around her waist and bent his head to speak softly. "I won't risk a precious hair on your head. I don't know what I might find in Surrey—and I'd prefer you to stay here and be safe and comfortable. Let me take care of this alone."

Vivien nodded, feeling comforted by his concern for her. "You'll hurry back as soon as possible?" she asked.

His lips pressed against her forehead, and she felt him smile against her skin. "Believe me . . . the only place in the world I want to be is wherever you are."

Staring at the letter in her lap during the short ride home, Vivien traced the feminine script with the tip of her finger. V. Devane . . . The name bothered her, tugged at her. Like so many other things, it seemed familiar but evoked no actual memories. V. Devane . . .

"Do you remember the little painting in Vivien's bedroom, by her dressing table?" she asked. "A cottage covered in white roses . . . and it had been signed by Devane. This man must mean a great deal to her, if she keeps his painting in her bedroom and runs to him when she is in trouble." She fidgeted with the letter until Grant finally held his hand out for it.

"Give me that thing before you rip it to shreds," he said.

Vivien surrendered the letter without protest. "Do you really believe that Vivien is still alive?" she asked softly.

His hand slid over her knee, and he squeezed it reassuringly. "I believe she's landed on her feet like a cat."

She was relieved by his answer. "I feel so protective of her. I wonder if I truly am related to her. Do you think she and I might be sisters?"

"You look too much alike not to be."

Closing her eyes, she let out a tense sigh. "I want to know about my family . . . friends . . . I want to know why no one seems to be looking for me. A person can't disappear without *someone* noticing . . . Isn't there anyone who misses me?" Her voice faded to a near whisper. "Anyone who loves me?"

"Yes."

Startled, Vivien looked up into his purposeful face, while her heart pounded hard. He must be referring to himself, she thought in wonder.

"If I find Vivien today," Grant said, his green eyes filled with warmth, "it will change nothing between you and me. And when you recover your memory, I don't give a damn about what or whom you remember. I had no part of your past . . . but I intend to be your future."

"I-if you're talking about somehow making reparations f-for last night," she stammered, "I've already told you it's not necessary—"

"No, I'm not referring to that. I'm talking about my feelings for you."

His words caused equal parts of delight and dismay. Vivien could imagine no greater joy than being loved by a man like Grant Morgan. However, she feared that he still harbored guilt for having taken her virginity, and she did not want him to propose merely because she had been "ruined." Above all else, she must not be an obligation that had been thrust upon him. And she had not forgotten what he had once said on the subject of marriage. He had no use for a wife, he had told her. He hadn't wanted to stay faithful to one woman for a lifetime. Had he sounded less certain, less cynical . . . but he had left no room for doubt. And therefore, if he were saddled with a bride he had never really wanted, he might eventually come to resent her.

"Don't make promises to me," she begged, silencing him with her fingers as he began to say something. "Not yet."

Catching her hand, he kissed her fingers and palm and the fragile veins of her wrist. "We'll talk when I come back."

The carriage stopped, and Vivien realized they were home. "Have a safe journey," she said, her fingers closing tightly around his.

"Don't worry," he said. "I intend to find Vivien

Duvall and solve this infernal mess. And after that . . ." He paused and grimaced. "I'll apologize to her, dammit."

"You will?" She stared at him with patent surprise, her lips parting softly.

"Even if it kills me." A self-mocking grin twisted his lips. "It just may," he added with a short laugh, leaning forward to steal a kiss before helping her from the carriage.

Thirteen

The small village of Forest Crest was located in the heathland of Surrey. Unspoiled and half hidden by surrounding slopes of gorse and heather, Forest Crest possessed two main streets, a church, and a green planted with acacia trees. It seemed that the dragonfly was something of a village symbol, carved into a few shop signs and the front of the village inn. Indeed, there were many dragonflies buzzing in the air around the green. Stopping his curricle on the side of the central street, Grant went into the village bakery. The air was hot and sweet, and he inhaled appreciatively as he ventured further into the shop.

A plump woman with well-muscled arms was pulling a flat of large buns from the depths of an inglenook hearth. "Will ye have some baked goods, sir?"

Grant shook his head. "Thank you, but I'm looking for White Rose Cottage . . . Can you tell me where to find it?"

"Aye. For years it was occupied by the village schoolmaster and his daughter, the Devanes. A lovely pair, they were, always up to their ears in books and surrounded by children. But poor Mr. Devane died two years ago of a weak heart. His daughter still abides there. Follow Cottage Street to the lane that goes past the Church of All Angels. Out in the heathland, ye'll see the cottage. Mind ye don't frighten the girl, she's a timid sort. We've not seen her in town for weeks. Just the maid." She paused and asked with a slight frown, "May I ask what yer business with her is, sir?"

He smiled. "You may ask, but I won't tell."

The baker's wife chuckled. "I would say she's a fortunate girl, to have a big handsome lad appear on her doorstep. Fare-thee-well!"

Returning to his carriage, Grant urged the horses forward with an impatient flick of the ribbons. The light curricle bounced and jostled along the uneven road, until Grant arrived at the thatched and timbered cottage. The little structure stood at the end of the lane in a profusion of rosebushes. It was so quiet that Grant could hear the dragonflies' wings beating the air, and the drone of insects browsing among the flowers. The heavy, powdery scent of roses surrounded him as he approached the arched doorway bordered with thick wooden posts. The cottage looked like an illustration for a fairy tale, with a stone garden shed nearby and a brook trickling amidst a grove of yew and willow.

Unconsciously Grant held his breath as he knocked at the door with two knuckles. He sensed movement within the house, a scrape, a whisper, a sudden awareness that a stranger had come to call. After what seemed an interminably long wait, he knocked again, this time using the side of his fist.

A young cook-maid came to the door, dark hair tucked beneath a blue cap, her face uncertain. "Good day, sir," she murmured.

"I'd like to speak with the lady who lives here."

"She's not at home, sir." The girl didn't lie well. "No one's at home."

Ironically Grant reflected that no one was ever "at home" when a Runner came to call. "Go fetch her," he advised softly. "I have little time, and even less patience."

The cook-maid flushed with obvious distress. "Please, sir, won't you go away?"

Before he could reply, a cool, velvety voice came from inside the cottage. "I'll speak to him, Jane. Perhaps *this* will be suitable inducement for him to leave."

Grant shoved the door open wide. A woman was standing in the central room of the cottage. She wore a gown of sprigged muslin, the dainty fabric draped over the burgeoning swell of her stomach. Rapidly Grant's gaze moved over her pregnant form, and lingered at the pistol held in one small, steady hand.

The weapon wavered slightly as she saw his face. "My God," she gasped. "It's you. Morgan."

"Vivien?" He identified her in a tone loaded with dark irony. "Or are there more than two of you running around England?"

Fourteen

*V*ictoria. Finally he had discovered his beloved's name. Grant had repeated it to himself at frequent intervals during his journey back
to London.

Victoria and Vivien were indeed twins. Vivien
had changed her last name to Duvall when she had
begun her career as a courtesan. Victoria had remained in Forest Crest with her father.

There had been a feeling of warmth and coziness
about White Rose Cottage, though it was clear that
the Devanes had been genteelly poor. The place had
been piled with books in every conceivable corner,
ancient volumes with ragged covers. Small paintings
of village scenes had covered the walls, executed in
an amateurish but cheerful style. They had all been
signed by the same person. Victoria Devane.

After talking with Vivien this afternoon, Grant

still found it impossible to believe that two women who were identical on the outside could be complete opposites in every other way. Victoria was an innocent country gentlewoman who spent her time reading, teaching the local children, painting, gathering armfuls of heather in the meadow. Vivien, by contrast, was pleasure-loving and self-serving . . . with a moral compass that was most definitely skewed. A remnant of their conversation lingered in Grant's mind, the moment when he had accused Vivien of intentionally luring her innocent sister to London in the hopes of deflecting the danger from herself.

"You threw her to the wolves to save yourself," Grant had said with chilling matter-of-factness. "You wanted her to be mistaken for you, and she was. And after conveniently disposing of her, you decided to live here and pretend to be her."

The ugly accusation had caused the muscles of Vivien's face to work angrily. She had sounded like a hissing feline as she replied. "I chose to stay here because I'm hardly in a condition to go search for my missing sister. I've been worried sick about where she has been and what might have happened to her. I thought for certain that if she went to London to discover I wasn't there, she'd come home. And for your information, I sent a message warning her *not* to come to town!"

"This one?" he had sneered, withdrawing the letter from his breast pocket.

Receiving the folded parchment, Vivien had read it quickly. "How did you get this?"

"You left it at Dr. Linley's office."

"I did not!" she had said heatedly. "I posted it as soon as . . ." She had stopped suddenly, her fingers fluttering to her lips, and her voice had dwindled away. "I must have," she had eventually whispered. "I'm almost positive I sent the letter, but . . . there were so many things to worry with . . . Oh, God!" She had dropped the letter as if it were a snake, and stared at it sullenly. "I never wanted Victoria to come to town. It was her own fault for intruding where she wasn't wanted. I refuse to feel guilty for what happened to her, when she should have had the sense to stay here."

"No one's asking you to feel guilty," Grant had returned evenly. "All I'm asking you to do is help me—and your sister—by answering a few questions."

Vivien had complied at once, making it clear that she was more than ready to dispel the threat hanging over her head. "I'll tell you everything you want to know," she had said. "However, after we're finished, there is someone else you will want to talk to. Lord Lane."

Unfortunately Lord Lane was not to be found at his London residence this evening. Having managed to pry his whereabouts from the butler, Grant had learned that Lane spent most of his spare time at his club, Boodles, a haven for titled country gentlemen who preferred to discuss hunting over politics.

With the sky rumbling moodily and darkness descending, Grant drove his carriage to St. James Street. He was impatient and tired of traveling, and more than anything he wanted to return to Victoria.

He was filled with anticipation as he considered the moment when he would finally reach her and explain everything . . . her name, her identity, the hows and whys of all that had happened to her. He wanted to make her feel safe and secure. She had been through so much, and he wanted her to understand that the worst was over. From now on he would make her life comfortable, pleasurable, if only she would allow him.

Grant had never felt like this before, his head filled with plans for the future, his mood damned close to optimistic. He would conclude the mess involving Vivien Duvall, and then he was going to set about making himself happy with Victoria. After years of serving as a Runner, he was getting damned tired of alley fights and subduing riots, and chasing criminals through rookeries and cesstrenches. It was time to let some other poor bastard do the footwork . . . time for him to find some enjoyment and pleasure in life.

Boodle's, named after the club's original headwaiter, was an intentionally dull place where gentlemen could find peace and relaxation. They sat in heavy upholstered chairs, held cigars and brandies, and viewed the paintings of hunting, shooting, and other country pursuits. The only sounds in the benign atmosphere were the occasional rustle of a newspaper and the murmur of a servant attending the gentlemen in the coffee room. It was the kind of place that would never voluntarily admit Grant. He might have sufficient fortune, but he didn't have the distinguished family name or the country estate, and his hunting was usually confined to catching human prey.

As Grant entered the club, he paused to glance in the famous bow window where gentlemen sat and smoked. He was immediately approached by a butler who seemed none too pleased to see him.

"Sir?" The butler's face had all the expressiveness of a sea bass. "May I ask your business?"

"I was told I could find Lord Lane here. I'm Morgan, from the Bow Street office."

A tiny glint of surprise appeared in the butler's eyes. Clearly it was inconceivable that a patron of Boodle's could be involved in any way with Bow Street affairs. "Is Lord Lane expecting you, Mr. Morgan?"

"No."

"Then you will have to seek him out at some other time, sir. And in some other place." Dismissively the butler reached for the edge of the door, preparing to usher Grant out.

A large, booted foot was planted firmly in the door's path, and Grant smiled insolently at the butler. "Forgive me, I've given you the wrong impression. You seem to think I was asking for permission. The fact is, I'm *going* to see Lord Lane. Tonight. Here. Now . . . will you tell me which room he's in, or shall I search the place myself? Mind you, I'm not always tidy in my searches. Things sometimes get broken."

The butler's face stiffened with panic as he envisioned the havoc one large, irritable Bow Street Runner could wreak in the quiet club. "This is most untoward," he gasped. "You mustn't disturb the patrons. Most appalling. I believe Lord Lane is in the coffee room. If you are capable of exercising the least amount of discretion, I beg you—"

"I'm the most discreet man I know," Grant assured him with a flashing grin. "Settle your feathers—I'll have a chat with Lane and be gone before your patrons have even noticed me."

"I doubt that," the butler said, watching in dismay as the intruder strode into the hallowed terrain.

Clusters of silent gentlemen sat at the round tables, reclining in Hepplewhite chairs upholstered in horsehair. A chandelier with chunky crystal drops was suspended from the white-paneled, vaulted ceiling. A somber painting of a stag hunt loomed over the mantelpiece, lending a solid masculine ambience to the room. Heads turned as Grant entered the coffee room, and a score of judgmental glances passed over his travel-dusty clothes and short, rumpled hair. Refusing to look gracefully abashed by his own appearance, Grant stared speculatively at each table, until he saw one man sitting alone near the fire.

The gentleman was lean and long-limbed, with iron-gray hair and an angular, deeply lined face. Staring down the length of his hawklike nose, he concentrated on a newspaper. A plate set before him contained biscuits, a spoonful of ripe Stilton, and a dab of red preserves.

Grant approached his table with a measured stride. "Lord Lane," he said quietly. The man did not look up from his paper, though he surely had heard. "I'm Morgan, of the Bow Str—"

"I know who you are," Lane murmured, appearing to finish one last paragraph before deigning to set aside the paper. His voice was cultured but exceptionally dry and brittle, like the sound of old bones rubbing together.

"I want to talk with you."

Lane's oddly colorless eyes surveyed him coldly. "How dare you approach me in my club!"

"We can go somewhere else if you like," Grant offered, in an overly polite manner that was unmistakably mocking.

"What I would like, Morgan, is for you to leave."

"I'm afraid I can't oblige you, my lord. What I have to discuss can't wait. Now . . . shall we talk here in front of your friends, or in one of the private rooms?"

Lane glanced at a nearby servant, who surveyed them anxiously from the side of the room. The servant was clearly at a loss to know how to handle the unexpected intrusion. "I believe I'll have the club management arrange for your removal from the premises," Lane said, snapping his fingers at the servant, who approached them with alacrity.

Grant held up one hand in a restraining gesture and waved the servant back to his place by the wall. He smiled at Lane without warmth. "I'm not in the mood to play games, my lord. In fact, I'm this close"—he indicated a space of a quarter inch between his thumb and forefinger—"to dragging you out of here and taking you to the Bow Street holding room for questioning."

A flush of outrage crested Lord Lane's slanted cheeks. "You wouldn't dare."

"Oh, I would," Grant assured him. "I'm vastly entertained by the notion of arresting a member of Boodle's right in the coffee room—just to show the club patrons that it can be done. But I'll restrain myself, milord, if you make an effort to be accommodating and provide the answers I'm seeking."

Lane's eyes blazed with impotent fury. "You filthy piece of gutter scum—"

"I know, I know." Grant signaled to the servant, who crept forward uneasily. "A carafe of coffee, please. Black." He paused and arched an expectant brow at Lane. "Where shall we talk, my lord?"

"Is room number four vacant?" Lane growled at the servant.

"I believe so, milord."

"Number four it is," Grant said. "I'll take my coffee there."

"Yes, sir."

With the attention of the entire room on them, the two men walked past the tables and crossed the threshold. They went down a hallway to a succession of private rooms.

"You have no idea of the extent of my influence," Lane sneered. "I can have your chief magistrate replaced in a day, if I so desire. I can have you placed in chains for your insolence, you ignorant mongrel!"

"Let's discuss Vivien Duvall," Grant suggested softly.

Lord Lane's color, which was not good to start with, faded to a shade of aged parchment. "What in God's name are you talking about?"

The servant entered the room with a tray of coffee and biscuits, poured a cup of the brew for Grant, and departed speedily. When the door was firmly closed, Grant downed half the coffee in a single swallow and lifted a steady gaze to Lane's watchful face. "Someone attempted to murder her a month ago," he said. "I suspect you may be able to shed some light on the matter."

The name caused the elderly man to grit his teeth angrily. "I refuse to say anything in connection with that malicious slut."

"She's not on my list of favorites, either," Grant replied. "But you have more cause to hate her than most, don't you? You blame her for causing your son's suicide."

"She is responsible for Harry's death," Lane acknowledged. "I've said as much to many others."

"Responsible in what way?"

Though Lord Lane made an effort to conceal his emotions, his voice contained betraying tremors of grief and fury. "My son suffered from melancholy for years. It caused him to turn to all manner of excessive behavior. He was easy prey for gamblers and thieves ... and women such as the Duvall creature. She had an affair with Harry, and when she ended the relationship, my son shot himself."

"That isn't all you have against her," Grant said. "After Harry's death, Vivien then seduced his son Thomas—your only grandson—and schemed to marry him."

There was a long silence, during which Lane struggled to mask his emotions. "I'm aware of no schemes concerning my grandson," he said, his voice cool and dry.

Lane was a fairly good liar, Grant reflected—but the issue was too close to the old man's heart, and his rage was too great to conceal the truth for long.

"You bought Thomas a commission and packed him off on the first ship to India when you found out Vivien was after him," Grant continued. "I suppose you thought he'd be safer braving heathens, wild game, and exotic disease than to be exposed to Vivien's influence. God knows you may have been right. But you should have stopped it there, my lord. Hiring someone to murder Vivien was going a bit too far."

"Nonsense," Lane said curtly. "Had I wanted the harlot dead, I would have done it myself."

"Men in your position never do it themselves. But I am surprised that you apparently hired an idiot to take care of your dirty business. He didn't finish the job. The clumsy ass couldn't manage to kill one small, defenseless woman—something you learned about on the night of the Lichfield ball, when you saw that Vivien was still alive. And you became understandably keen on having the bastard finish what he was paid to do."

The barely suppressed outrage on Lane's face was infused by cunning and smugness. "What proof do you have of any of this?"

"I'll have proof enough when my investigation is concluded and I've caught your hired killer."

And then something strange happened . . . something that had never occurred in Grant's previous years of detective work. The defensive barrier suddenly broke, and Lane stared at him with a gaze of glittering, triumphant malice. And he made a four-word confession.

"You won't catch him."

The admission of guilt was completely unexpected. Had Grant been in Lane's position, he would have prevaricated indefinitely and hid behind a shield of age, respectability, and political influence. There was no reason for Lane to confess anything. However, later Grant would reflect that it was understandable in light of Lane's sense of invulnerability. Lane must have been certain that a man in his position—a peer of the realm—would never have been tried for the death of a whore. And moreover, Lane was so enraged over his son's suicide that deep inside he wanted someone to know that Harry's death had been properly avenged. He was an old man with very few years left, and he had been robbed of his only son.

Motionless, Grant stared at Lane as the old man continued with a quiet certainty that sent chills down his spine. "Vivien Duvall will soon be deep in her grave, her killer will disappear from England—and you can do nothing to stop it."

Inwardly unnerved, Grant had to remind himself that Victoria was safe in his own house, with a Runner to protect her.

"The imbecile you hired won't get anywhere near Vivien," Grant said softly. "So far he's never managed to lay a finger on her. From the beginning of your damnable bargain, he's been pursuing the wrong woman. *The wrong one*, do you understand? The woman he attacked and threw into the

Thames—the same woman I escorted to the Lichfield ball—isn't Vivien Duvall. It's her sister. Vivien's been in hiding all this time, and your hired man has been trying to kill her innocent sister."

"It isn't true!" Lane shot to his feet so quickly that his chair toppled backward. Clearly the suggestion that Vivien Duvall was healthy and out of harm's way was enough to make him insane. Even the ends of his coarse gray hair seemed to crackle with fury. "Lying cur! Only a fool would believe such a cock-and-bull claim—"

"Vivien's sister has been put through hell because of your stupidity," Grant said, his own anger welling in an ungovernable flood. "And the nightmare she's been living is going to end tonight." Before he was quite aware of what he was doing, he felt his hands close around the other man's throat in a threatening vise. "Shall I do to you what was done to her?" he asked thickly. "Let's see how you feel after a good throttling and a nice long swim in the Thames—"

"Take . . . your hands . . . *off* me . . ." the other man wheezed.

"Tell me your man's name, so I can put a stop to this damned nonsense," Grant said grimly. "Tell me, you bastard."

Lord Lane's face purpled, and his eyes bulged with bitter fury. "If it's true," he choked, "if there are two of them . . . I'll have both of them destroyed, just to make certain—"

"Never. It's *finished*, do you understand?" Deliberately he tightened his fingers on Lane's windpipe. "His name," he repeated grimly, staring like an angel of vengeance into the old man's watery eyes.

Lane spat out the name with a force that sprayed flecks of spittle over Grant's face.

Suddenly Grant's hands loosened, and he stared at the gasping, choking man before him. "What did you say?" he demanded, trying to hear above the sudden annoying buzz in his own ears.

Staggering backward, Lord Lane repeated the name as if it were a profanity. "Keyes," he spat. "Neil Henry Keyes . . . one of your damned comrades. A *Runner.*" He laughed harshly. "He had need of the money. He assured me the task would be easy. I should have known one of your ilk would prove to be incompetent for the job. But I'll hire someone else, do you hear me? Vivien Duvall will never be safe!"

Shaking his head, Grant made his way to the door, feeling as if he were wading through quicksand. He was suffocating, fighting to breathe . . .

"My God," he gasped, as horror stole every coherent thought. For the first time in his life, he experienced a panic so great it made him momentarily unable to act. Keyes was the Runner who had been assigned to watch over Victoria this evening. Victoria had been delivered into the hands of her own murderer, with Grant's approval. "If anything happens to her," he whispered hoarsely to Lane, "your life is over."

And so was his. He ran, stumbled, tore his way out of the tomblike atmosphere of the club and into the cold shock of rain outside.

"My life ended when Harry's did," Lane cried,

rushing after Grant, his voice echoing in the astonished silence that had settled over Boodle's. A tremendous pain settled in his chest, squeezing, pressing, but he ignored it in his mounting rage. "The only thing I live for now is to see that slut dead! I will never rest until she dies, do you understand? If I have to crush the last bit of life from her . . . with my own hands . . ."

Lane stopped in the center of the great saloon, while servants and patrons hurried toward him. He was surrounded by a dark blur, and he shouted into the thickening haze, while the crushing pain in his chest increased and spread. Hands were on him now, a myriad of voices tried to calm him, but that infuriated him all the more. His shouts faded to insistent gasps of vengeance, and the floor rose inexorably as he began to fall . . . He felt himself dissolving in the sea of hatred he would never, could never, relinquish.

Fifteen

"The Runner is here, my dear." Mrs. Buttons stood at the library door. "His name is Mr. Keyes, and he's a good, kind gentleman— the most experienced man Sir Cannon could offer. Mr. Morgan esteems him highly. We've been left in good hands, to be sure."

"Give Mr. Keyes my thanks for looking after things during Mr. Morgan's absence," Vivien murmured. She paused before the library window with a book in hand, gazing at the gathering storm outside. A blanket of clouds had made the afternoon as dark as night, while gusts of wind sifted through the trees and garden. A few patters of rain began to fall, the plump, heavy drops heralding worse to come.

"Shall you thank him yourself, miss?" the housekeeper asked. "He is waiting in the entrance hall, and he seems intent on speaking to you right away."

"Of course," Vivien said reluctantly. "Would you show him in here?"

"Yes, miss."

Holding the poetry book against her midriff, Vivien splayed her fingers over the embossed leather cover and heaved a great sigh. She didn't want to make conversation with Mr. Keyes, she wanted Grant to come home right away. Knowing that he was temporarily out of reach made her feel strangely uneasy. She had come to rely on him so completely that she hated the thought of being separated from him, even for a day and night.

But she couldn't allow herself to give in to such feelings. Their relationship, such as it was, would end all too soon, and she must retain some vestige of dignity when they parted. To reveal how she craved his attention, his smiles, his companionship, would only embarrass them both. She faced a lifetime bereft of Grant Morgan, and she had better accustom herself to doing without him.

Making her breathing quiet and deep, Vivien loosened her anxious grip on the book and turned just as Mrs. Buttons brought the Runner into the room. Mr. Keyes was an average-sized man wearing an obviously costly salmon-colored coat. A wide-brimmed gray hat was clasped in one hand. He was attractive and rather dashing, his silver hair fluffy and windswept. Vivien couldn't take her eyes from him. His dandyish appearance contradicted her notions of what a Bow Street Runner should look like. Shaping her mouth in a polite smile, Vivien curtsied as he approached her. Mrs. Buttons began to leave with a small murmur.

Keyes stopped her with a light touch. "Wait, if you please, Mrs. Buttons," he said. "You may as well hear what I have to tell Miss Duvall."

"Yes, sir." Folding her hands together, the housekeeper stood obediently, her brow knitting with a touch of perplexity.

"To begin with, Miss Duvall," the Runner said with old-fashioned courtliness, "I am gratified, to say the least, to be assigned the duty of protecting you."

"Thank you," Vivien said, noting that the rain outside had begun to slow, its heaviness suspended high and full in the sky. "Mrs. Buttons assures me that you are greatly esteemed by my—" She stopped in a sudden shock of confusion, and prickly color inched over her face and neck. "By Mr. Morgan," she managed to choke out. What other betraying words would have slipped out had she not caught herself? *My* . . . She had no right to apply that word to Grant, denoting possessiveness and attachment. He was not hers in any sense. How could she forget herself so easily?

Ignoring the slip, Keyes apparently sought to cover her confusion. His attractive, weathered face creased with a smile. "I will do everything in my power to justify Mr. Morgan's confidence in me."

"Thank you, Mr. Keyes."

"In that vein," he continued carefully, "I must inform you of a slight change in plans. Do not be distressed—you are in no danger—but just before coming here I received word from Sir Ross that I am to bring you to Bow Street at once."

"I would prefer to stay here," Vivien said in surprise, her hand creeping to her throat.

Keyes shook his head. "I understand, Miss Duvall. However, Sir Ross has received new information in Morgan's absence, which has led him to request your presence at his office."

"What kind of information might that be, sir?" Mrs. Buttons asked, coming forward to stand at Vivien's side.

"I'm not allowed to say," Keyes replied, smiling slightly at the two distressed women. "But I assure you, Mr. Morgan would want you to comply. And certainly there is no safer place in London than number four Bow Street."

"How long must I stay there?" Vivien asked. "Until Mr. Morgan returns?"

"Possibly." Suddenly a twitch of impatience pulled at his mouth. "Come, Miss Duvall, we're wasting time. Sir Ross requested me to escort you to him immediately."

"All right." Vivien was perturbed by the unexpected change of plans. An unpleasant feeling crept over her. Mr. Keyes appeared to be a nice man, but there was something about him that she did not like, something difficult to identify. It seemed that his genial facade concealed something reptilian and cold. She instinctively wanted to avoid him. Her heart had picked up its pace, beating in an anxious, uneven staccato. It was rather amazing, the reaction of her body, when her mind could discern no reasonable cause for it.

The desire to escape him rose strongly in her,

making it difficult to keep from bolting into an outright run. "Mr. Keyes," she managed to say, "may
I take one of the maids with me? I would like some
female companionship."

"Mary will go with you," Mrs. Buttons said,
clearly approving of the idea.

Keyes shook his head at once. "There's no need
of that. This is hardly a social call, Miss Duvall, but
official business. I would prefer to leave right
away, if you don't mind. Before the storm wors-
ens."

Vivien exchanged a long, questioning glance
with the housekeeper. *Is he trustworthy?* her own
gaze asked, while Mrs. Buttons silently responded,
I believe so.

Mrs. Buttons was clearly worried, but her graying head tilted in a posture of helpless acquies-
cence. "Miss Duvall," she murmured, "if Mr.
Keyes says you must go, I don't think there's much
to be said about it." A troubled frown pulled at her
forehead. "And he's right—there is no safer place
for you than Bow Street."

Vivien glanced at the darkening sky visible
through the window. "Very well," she said calmly.
"If you'll excuse me, Mr. Keyes, I should like to
change my shoes and put on a hooded pelisse."

"Of course, Miss Duvall."

Vivien backed away a step, staring at him intently. A memory seethed and writhed in her
brain, pushing urgently at the wall of forgetfulness.
"Sir . . . we've met before, haven't we?"

"I don't believe so, miss." His gaze held a coiled
enmity that caused a sudden fearful pang in her

stomach. He did not like her, she realized. He must have heard the terrible rumors about her—or the real Vivien, as it were—and believed every one of them.

A rumble of thunder scored through the silence, and Keyes turned his head to glance at the gathering darkness. Something about his profile, the small hump at the bridge of his nose, the outline of his hair, the way the little jut of his chin met the soft folds of his throat, made her nerves screech in alarm.

Keyes looked back at her, catching the flare of tension in her face. "We don't have long, Miss Duvall."

She turned and left the room, forcing herself to walk normally even though panic had begun to leak and spread inside her. Breathing in deepening pants, she cast a quick glance over her shoulder. Keyes stood at the foot of the staircase, watching her intently. He looked like a malevolent demon planning to drag her into the bowels of hell.

All she wanted was the safety of her room, to close and lock the door and hide. The stairs loomed like a mountainside before her, and she stumbled a little as she lunged and climbed upward. After an eternity passed, she found herself before the door of her room. Clumsily she closed herself inside and stood there shuddering. She was lost in the sensation of drowning, straining to breathe, her limbs stiffening against the stabbing coldness that surrounded her. *"Grant."* She tried to say his name in a desperate plea for help, but she had lost the ability to even whisper. *"Grant—"*

And she sank to her knees as memory came rushing over her. The night of her attack . . . the silver-haired man with the merciless face . . . wiry hands locked around her throat, thumbs digging into her throat until her windpipe was crushed shut . . . She lost the struggle to breathe as the darkness consumed her . . . and then the punishing coldness of the river, the black water pulling her beneath the surface.

Mr. Keyes had done this to her. She knew it down to the bottom of her soul. He had tried to kill her, and failing once, he would try again.

A momentary sense of betrayal cut through her terror.

Grant . . . how could you send him here? How could you leave me here with him?

But it was not his fault, her heart insisted stubbornly. He would never have done this to her intentionally.

She was in danger, in the place that had been such a haven until this moment. Quaking, gasping, she crawled to the chamber pot concealed in the bedside cabinet and fumbled with the concealing door in front. But in a moment the rolling wave of nausea subsided, and she filled her lungs with huge gulps of air.

Closing her eyes, she leaned against the smooth side of the mahogany cabinet, savoring the coolness of the wood against her hot, damp face. For the first time in weeks, she knew her own name. "Victoria Devane," she said aloud. "I'm Victoria." Her lips moved in countless repetitions of the sounds . . . her name, her *real* name. It was like a key that unlocked all the sealed places in her mind. Images of her past paraded before her . . . the country cottage where she spent her days occupied with books and visiting schoolchildren. Her friends from the village . . . a long-ago trip to the seashore . . . her father's funeral.

Closing her eyes tightly, she pictured the patient, kind face of her father. He had been a scholarly man, a philosopher, preferring his books to the harsh reality of the world outside. Victoria had adored him, and had spent hours and days reading alongside him.

She had never loved any man in the romantic sense, had never wanted to. Since her mother had left Forest Crest, Victoria had cared only for her father and seldom-seen sister . . . There had been no room for anyone else. Love was too dangerous; it was much better to stay alone and safe. In the quiet haven of the village, she had few responsibilities except to look after herself. She would never have ventured away had her irresponsible sister not landed herself in more trouble than she could manage.

The relief of rediscovering herself, her memories, her identity, was overwhelming. However, the man downstairs would not be convinced that she was anyone other than her sister.

"Oh, Vivien," she whispered shakily. "If I live through this, you have a great deal to answer for."

She wiped at a trickle of sweat that traveled down her cheek to the edge of her chin. She felt like a mouse trapped in a barrel with a cat. Her first impulse was to crawl into bed and pull the covers over her head, and hope that Keyes would leave her alone. But he would not, of course. He would insist on dragging her out of here, and the servants would do nothing to stop him. They would believe him over her . . . they would assume that her amnesia had made her unbalanced. Any claim she made that the respected Bow Street Runner was a vicious killer would never be accepted.

Wherever it was that Keyes wanted to take her, it certainly wasn't Bow Street. Desperately she tried to decide what to do. With Grant away, the only man she trusted to protect her was Sir Ross. She had to reach him right away. A shuddering sigh escaped her lips, and she blotted her moist forehead with her sleeve. She didn't know precisely where the Bow Street office was, only that it was located somewhere on the other side of Covent Garden. But it was such a well known place, surely it could not be that difficult to find.

She sprang into action before second thoughts occurred. Hurrying to the armoire, she found a dark green long-sleeved pelisse with a capuchin "monk's" hood that draped in concealing folds over her hair and face. After donning the garment and changing her shoes to ankle-high walking boots, she opened the bedroom door and glanced along the empty hallway.

She clenched the edge of the doorframe with shaking fingers. It was difficult to proceed with caution when every instinct screamed for her to dart forward like a terrified rabbit. Her veins pulsed with barely contained alarm. She took one cautious step into the hallway, then another, and broke into a rapid walk toward the stairs—not the main staircase, but the small, winding one the servants used at the back of the house. Gray light from the small-paned windows provided the barest excuse for illumination as she began a hasty descent along the narrow spiral of stairs. Her hand gripped the iron balustrade at frequent intervals, steadying her balance as her feet flew down the steps.

A shadowy shape materialized at the first-floor landing, and Victoria stopped with a scream climbing in her throat. *Keyes*, was her first thought ... but immediately she realized that the form was that of a small woman. It was Mary, the housemaid, carrying a basket of folded linens.

The maid stopped and regarded her with surprise and confusion. "Miss Duvall?" she asked hesitantly. "What are you doing here, on the servants' stairs? Is there something I can fetch for you? What can I do—"

"Don't tell anyone you've seen me," Victoria said in a low, urgent voice. "Please, *please*, Mary. I want everyone to think I'm still in my room."

The housemaid's gaze seemed to question her sanity. "But where could you be going, with such a fearful storm collecting outside?"

"Promise me you won't tell anyone."

"When will you come back?" the housemaid asked worriedly. "Miss, if anything happens to you, and I didn't tell anyone that I saw you leave, I could lose my position. I could find myself on the streets! Oh, please, miss, don't go anywhere—"

"Mary," Victoria said desperately, "I don't have time to stand here. I'll return when Mr. Morgan has come home. But in the meantime, don't mention this to anyone. Or if you must, then at least wait a few minutes. It's life and death to me."

Victoria brushed by the maid and continued speedily to the basement. After reaching the final landing, she passed the door to the coal vault, and after that, the kitchen quarters. Mercifully she encountered no other servants as she went to the door that led outside and pushed it open.

The air was heavy and electric with the promise of rain. Inhaling deeply, Victoria crossed a small service road and hurried along the gravel path that led to the enclosed garden. Thick poplar hedges protruded over the top of the ivy-covered brick walls. She passed beneath a pedimented arch and ran the length of the fifty-foot-long garden, skirting around a stone table surrounded by windsor chairs and stone pots of flowering nectarine trees.

Her heart began to thump with exertion, but her pace did not lessen as she exited the door at the back of the garden. With each step she took away from the main house, a feeling of hope and relief surged inside. She edged around the stables and coach house, and strode swiftly through the mews that bordered the back row King Street town houses.

There was no doubt in her mind that leaving the house was the right thing to do. Let Keyes stay there and assume he had cornered her. She would be long gone by the time he realized she had disappeared. Victoria imagined his frustration upon discovering that she had already left, and a nervous, almost giddy laugh broke from her lips. She quickened her step, heading toward the welcome bustle and mayhem of Covent Garden.

The large, smooth stones of the carriageway became rough and pebbled as it led to the Garden piazza. Victoria kept to the paved walkway, pulling her hood low over her face. She brushed by mop trundlers washing soil from the walkways of elegant houses, lamplighters climbing to the suspended globes of oil lamps hung from iron brackets, and itinerant musicians playing fiddles and tambourines. The street rumbled with wagons, drays, carriages, and animals, a mass of sound that assaulted her ears.

A few more drops of rain fell, promising relief from the odors of smoke and manure that wafted through the hazy air. The storm was holding back, however, as if waiting for a cue to begin. Ladies with metal patten rings on their feet made clinking sounds on the pavement, while gentlemen kept their umbrellas tucked tightly beneath their arms and cast furtive glances at the blanket of clouds overhead. The premature darkness threw an ominous cast over the scene, and Victoria shivered beneath the folds of her pelisse.

Bow Street was just a short walk away, she told herself. She would cross through Covent Garden, remaining as inconspicuous as possible, and then she would reach the safety of Cannon's office.

At Mr. Keyes's request, Mrs. Buttons brought wine as they waited for Vivien to return downstairs. Holding the stem of the rare Charles I silver wine goblet between his thumb and forefinger,

Keyes examined the piece closely. Its shape was elegantly simple, the rim slightly flared, the bowl smooth and highly polished. "Morgan's done very well for himself," he mused aloud, his tone not altogether admiring. "Wealthier than any Runner I've ever known. Has a knack for making the chinks, doesn't he?"

"Mr. Morgan works very hard, sir," the housekeeper replied, feeling vaguely defensive on her employer's behalf. Morgan was a clever, brave, and celebrated man—it was only right that he had been generously rewarded for his accomplishments.

"No harder than the rest of us," Keyes observed, his mouth shaping into a smile, his eyes remaining cool. "Yet *he* lives like a king, whereas I . . ." His voice faded, and his expression turned blank, as if he had regretted the words.

"Well," Mrs. Buttons said, concealing her own touch of discomfort, "I would like to thank you on behalf of Mr. Morgan's staff for taking care of Miss Duvall. We have confidence that she will be as safe under your protection as she would be with Mr. Morgan himself."

"Yes," he said beneath his breath, "I'll take care of his precious pet."

Mrs. Buttons cocked her head, not certain she had heard correctly. "Sir?"

Before any reply could be made, they were interrupted by a small dark-haired housemaid, whose face was taut and streaked with tears. She was highly agitated, her hands gathered into trembling fists. "Mrs. Buttons, ma'am," she said in a small voice, standing half hidden at the side of the doorway. "Mrs. Buttons, I thought I should come to you right away, even though she asked me not to . . . Oh, I don't know what to do, but I wouldn't hurt her for the world, truly!"

"Mary," the housekeeper said in concern, approaching her immediately, while Keyes straightened in his chair.

"What is it?" he asked sharply. "Whom are you referring to? Is it Miss Duvall?"

The maid gave a jerky nod. "She's gone, sir."

"Gone?" Mrs. Buttons repeated in surprise, while Keyes shot up from his chair.

"What the hell do you mean, gone?" His tone turned ugly, and the women's gazes focused on him in surprise.

The maid replied in an incoherent jumble. "N-not five minutes ago . . . I passed her on the servants' stairs, and she s-said for me not to . . . Oh, I should never have told, except . . . well, she's in *danger* out there, isn't she?" She gazed at the housekeeper in abject misery. "Mrs. Buttons, have I done wrong?"

"No, Mary," the housekeeper soothed, patting the girl's arm. "You did exactly as Mr. Morgan would have wished you to."

"The damned bitch," Keyes exploded, throwing his goblet to the floor, heedless of the wine spilling over the fine hand-knotted carpet. An ugly blood-colored stain sank quickly into the yellow and blue pattern. "She won't get away from me," he vowed, striding from the room and bellowing for his coat and hat.

Mrs. Buttons rubbed her forehead as a small, insistent ache began in the front of her skull. Uneasy speculation carved deep lines into her features. "He is behaving oddly," she said, more to herself than the girl beside her. "It's plain he has no great liking for our Miss Duvall."

"I hope he finds her," Mary remarked in a subdued tone. "Then she'll be safe, won't she?"

The housekeeper did not answer, only wandered to the entrance hall and flinched as the heavy door slammed closed behind the departing Runner.

Though Covent Garden had begun as a pair of aristocratic piazzas containing spacious town mansions and a small church designed by Inigo Jones, it had undergone many incarnations in the passing centuries. In its present condition, it boasted of the most famous theaters in the world, not to mention coffeehouses filled with writers, artists, and musicians. A spectacularly large covered market had extended its tentacles outward from the piazzas into the surrounding streets and alleyways. It was at least an acre wide, attracting noise and bustle that only seemed to grow with each passing year. The nobility had long since evacuated their fine mansions, of course, and now the stately old buildings with majestic staircases were occupied by shops, taverns, and figures of the London underworld.

Cautiously Victoria stepped beneath the arches of the covered arcade, where people milled around shops and stalls. She blended into the crowd at once, letting the current push her past a profusion of flower baskets and old women who made bouquets on request. Dozens of hands skimmed over piles of vegetables, plucking and gathering the choicest ones for purchase. Strings of eels hung over fish stalls, where men deftly cleaned and gutted the freshest catch and wrapped them. A bird dealer held a screeching parrot aloft on his gloved hand, while cages of canaries, larks, and owls raucously advertised their availability for sale.

Victoria passed the doorway of an herb and root shop, where glass containers of leeches were lined along wooden shelves, and a perfumery with a window full of unguents, creams, and heavily fragrant oils encased in colored glass jars.

" 'Ere, luv," came a cackling cry, and Victoria turned with a start as a clawlike hand caught at her sleeve. A diminutive, gaudily dressed old woman wearing bangles, scarves, and red skirts held tightly to her arm. "Let me tell yer fortune, dearie . . . a shilling to learn the secrets of tomorrow! Only a shilling, mind ye . . . an' wiv a face like yers, what a fine future it may be!"

"Thank you, but I have no money," Victoria said in a low tone, jerking her arm free and walking away.

The fortune-teller persisted, however, following with a spry step and catching once more at her wrist. "I'll tell it fer nothing, luv!" Her voice rose to an inviting screech not unlike the parrots at the bird dealer's. "Come one an' all . . . Who wants to 'ear the lovely lass's fortune?"

Realizing the woman intended to use her as some kind of advertisement, Victoria pulled hard against the restraining clutch of her hand. "No," she said sharply. "Let me go."

The minor scuffle attracted a few gazes, and Victoria glanced warily over the crowd as she broke free from the fortune-teller. Suddenly she caught sight of a gentleman's pale gray hat, and her chest contracted painfully with alarm. It looked exactly like the one Mr. Keyes wore. But he couldn't have followed her so quickly, could he?

She searched for another glimpse of the hat, but it was gone. Perhaps she had imagined it, she thought anxiously, and hurried eastward toward the massive pillared portico of the opera house. The towering height of the four fluted columns that fronted the building made the swarming public look like a colony of ants. Some sort of protest was being staged, a mob in front shouting at the closed doors. Gentlemen and beggars alike contributed to the tumult, all of them barking and braying about a recent increase in admittance prices.

"Old prices!" many of the disgruntled patrons were calling. "We want old prices!"

"Too high, too high!" others screamed.

Plunging into the noisy throng, Victoria pushed her way deep into the crowd until she came to the lee of one of the Doric columns. Leaning back against the cold stone, she stood very still, pulse thrumming, while the crowd surged and booed and moved around her. She stared fixedly at the reliefs set in the panel before her, a carved figure of Shakespeare, the Muses, and above it, a statue of Comedy set in a niche.

Keyes was following her; she could *feel* it.

Keyes thought she was Vivien, and he was going to kill her either out of vengeance or because he had been hired to do so. If he knew she had left the house, he would guess that her first thought of sanctuary was number 4 Bow Street. He would do everything in his power to stop her from reaching Sir Ross.

Suddenly Victoria experienced a flare of anger at the unjust situation. She was in danger through no fault of her own. She had come to London out of worry for her sister, and then one bizzare event after another had led to this.

It seemed the sky opened up, torrents of water suddenly breaking through the air, causing the mob to disperse rapidly and search for shelter. The heavy splashing rain saturated the scene, sluicing over umbrellas and hats, soaking through clothes and shoes.

Taking a deep breath, Victoria looked around the column again and glanced over the crowd. She caught sight of the gray hat again, and terror shot through her as she recognized Keyes. He was standing perhaps fifty yards away as he questioned someone, his face set and cold, his posture betraying extreme tension. "Oh, God," she whispered.

As if he sensed her gaze, Keyes turned and looked directly at her. His expressionless face suddenly contorted angrily. He shoved the man he was questioning out of the way and started for Victoria with murder in his eyes. Victoria bolted at once, pushing her way through the scattering throng and running alongside the opera house. She saw the corner of Russell Street and tripped on the cobbled carriageway. She fought to regain her balance, aware that Keyes was closing the distance between them. *You won't stop me*, she thought with grim determination. She *would* reach Bow Street, damn him . . . She had come too far to fail now.

Grant hurtled through his own front door, his face white as a skull as he beheld the unusual gathering of servants in the entrance hall, footmen and housemaids clustered around Mrs. Buttons.

"Mr. Morgan!" the housekeeper exclaimed, rushing forward without her usual calm dignity. She seemed anxious, perplexed, a few skeins of her graying hair escaping the usually immaculate coil atop her head. Grant had never seen her in such disarray.

"Where is she?" he asked savagely, though his insides were already screaming in denial at the obvious answer.

"Thank the Lord you're back," Mrs. Buttons chattered nervously. "I was about to take it upon myself to send a note to Bow Street, as we didn't know when you might return, and I thought it important to verify Sir Ross's request—"

"What the devil are you talking about?" He glanced at the assembled servants with their funereal expressions. "Where is Victoria?" he snapped.

The question caused all the faces in the entrance hall to pucker in confusion. "Victoria?" the housekeeper repeated bemusedly.

Grant shook his head impatiently. "Vivien. Miss Duvall. The woman who has been living here for the past few weeks, dammit. Where is she? Where is Keyes?"

A moment of heavy silence ensued, charging his nerves with immediate alarm and fury. No one wanted to answer him, he realized, and in his consternation he barked out a question at a volume that made all of them jump.

"Someone tell me what's happened, damn you!"

Mary stepped forward, her shoulders slumped and her head slightly ducked, as if she suspected he might be tempted to strike her. "It was my fault, sir," she said in a small voice. "I saw Miss Duvall leave the house. On the servants' stairs, heading to the outside door by the kitchen. She asked me not to tell anyone. She said it was life and death to her. But I thought 'twould be best to go to Mrs. Buttons, and so I did."

Grant's blood pumped brutally hard, causing a drumming noise in his ears. "Life and death," he repeated thickly. Victoria had somehow realized the danger she was in, and bolted.

Mrs. Buttons smoothed her hands repeatedly on her apron front, as if she couldn't seem to blot her palms thoroughly enough. "You see, sir, Mr. Keyes said immediately upon his arrival that Sir Ross had asked him to bring Miss Duvall to Bow Street. His manner was rather odd and cold. In the years that I've been acquainted with him, I've never seen him quite like this. It was clear Miss Duvall did not want to go away with him, but she asked leave to change into her walking shoes. And while we waited for her in the library, she slipped out of the house. I suppose any woman in her position would be a bit fearful of strangers."

"I watched her from the window as she left,"

Mary interceded. "She was heading to the market, it looked like. With Mr. Keyes going right after her."

"She's going to Bow Street," Grant muttered. As far as Victoria knew, it was the only place of safety other than this house. He snapped out a command for one of the footmen to take a horse and ride hell-for-leather to Bow Street. "Tell Cannon to call out every man available. Tell him to cover every inch of Covent Garden and the surrounding streets with constables, Runners, and watchmen until Miss Duvall and Keyes are both found. Now, *hurry*—I want your arse in Cannon's office in less than five minutes."

"Yes, sir." The footman headed for the back of the house in an outright run, taking the shortest possible route to the stables.

Grant charged outside, barely aware of the rain that soaked his hair and clothes. A strange feeling had taken hold of him, a fear he had never experienced before. He had never given a thought to his own safety, had known that he possessed sufficient wits and physical strength to muddle through whatever danger he found himself in. But this fear for someone else, this blend of love and terror and fury, was the worst kind of agony.

He ran toward Covent Garden at a breakneck pace, while animals and carriages sloshed through the wet, dirty streets and pedestrians scattered for cover from the storm. If anything happened to Victoria . . . The thought caused a hellish pain in his chest, making his lungs feel as if they were filled with fire rather than air.

He passed the churchyard of St. Paul's, the sacred ground layered with two centuries worth of human remains. The charnel scent of accumulated bones greeted him as he cornered the eastern portico of the church. Covent Garden spread before him, a massive intermingling of traffic and squalor. Pickpockets, procurers, thieves, bloods, and bullies wandered freely about the place . . . and all of them would take a great interest in an unaccompanied woman with a pretty face and red hair. Panic welled inside him as he debated whether Victoria might have skirted around the Garden and traveled through the dark alleys filled with vagrants and criminals, or possibly gone straight through the market square. He had to find her before Keyes did.

"Victoria, where are you?" he said beneath his breath, his frustration doubling with each minute that passed. It took all his self-control to keep from bellowing the question aloud.

Blinking hard against the deluge, using both hands to wipe the streaming water from her face, Victoria blundered down a side street that branched from Russell, and realized in despair that she was heading in the wrong direction. She should have reached Bow Street by now. If only she knew the way. If only a few more minutes had passed before Keyes had learned of her absence.

The hem of her rain-soaked skirts tangled around her ankles as she ran farther into an accretion of dilapidated buildings. As everywhere else in London, there was a jumble of whorehouses, thieves' kitchens, and slum cottages tucked behind the clean, well-fronted high streets. Without pausing to glance over her shoulder, Victoria darted into the nearest place of refuge. She hurried down the basement steps of a two-story building, with signs outside identifying it as a betting shop.

Struggling to catch her breath, she opened a wooden door and plunged into the shadowy, lamplit basement room. It was filled with at least a dozen men, all of them too engrossed in the proceedings to immediately notice her presence. Gentleman and louts alike huddled at a counter lined with tobacco jars and cigar bundles, studying lists of odds on the back wall. A bookmaker wearing heavy leather pouches at each hip swaggered behind the counter and conducted transactions at a rapid pace. "... got an 'eavy bag against all comers ..." he was proclaiming, stroking the ends of his curly sideburns with thumb and forefinger, then jotting down bets with a stubby pencil.

There was a rank masculine smell in the air, a mixture of sweat, tobacco, and rain-dampened wool and broadcloth. Shrinking into a corner, Victoria yanked her hood down low over her face and waited with her arms wrapped tightly around herself. She prayed silently that Keyes would pass the betting shop and continue searching for her elsewhere. However, she feared the hope was futile. This area of London was well known to Keyes, as all the Runners were routinely assigned to comb through the rookeries in search of criminals. This was what the Runners excelled at—hunting and catching their prey.

"Well, now." A gentleman's cultured voice interrupted her thoughts, and a pair of black Hessian boots approached her. "It seems a pretty little bird has found a dry place to perch during the storm."

The betting was temporarily interrupted as Victoria's presence became noticed. Biting her lower lip, she steeled herself not to flinch as the man pulled away her concealing hood. She heard his breath catch, and a meaty hand reached for a damp lock of her glowing red hair. "A lovely bit of goods," he said thickly, and laughed while his gaze roved over her. "What business are you about, little bird? Searching for an evening's companion? You've found your man, then. I've got a nice big coin in my pocket for you."

"That's not all 'e's got in 'is pocket, I'll wager," someone said, and a rumble of masculine laughter ensued.

Miserably aware that she was becoming the focus of all attention, Victoria stared steadily into the man's face. He had the appearance of a gentleman, perhaps even a member of the lower nobility, his round face clean-shaven, his stocky form clad in coffee-brown breeches, a high-collared broadcloth coat, and a fancifully tied cravat.

"Someone was bothering me in the marketplace," she said in a low voice. "I though to avoid him by hiding here for a few minutes."

He clucked his tongue in false sympathy and slid an arm around her back in an insultingly familiar manner. "Poor dove. I'll give you all the protection you desire." He reached for the bodice of her pelisse and began to pluck at the fastenings, ignoring

her outraged gasp. "No need to protest—I just
want to have a look at the goods."

Now the full attention of the room was on them.
Even the bookmaker had taken pause to watch the
goings-on, joining in the shouts of encouragement
as the men clamored to see what was concealed
beneath the pelisse.

"I came here to avoid being molested by one
man," Victoria said, pushing his hands away and
retreating farther into the corner. "I'm not looking
for another."

The oaf merely grinned at the comment, clearly
thinking she was playing a game with him. "I'm
offering you a night with a randy stallion, and a
generous reward for your services," he said. "What
more could any woman want?"

"I'll give *you* a reward if you help me to Bow
Street," she countered. "Surely you've heard of Mr.
Grant Morgan, the Runner. I know he would consider it a personal favor if you would take me there
safely."

Some of the lust seemed to fade from his expression, and he looked at her with new interest.
"Yes, I've heard of Morgan. What connection do
you have with him?"

A tendril of relief broke through her agitation.
Grant's name had definitely captured his attention.
If this man could somehow be persuaded to take
her to Bow Street, she would be safe from Keyes.
In her eagerness to convince him to help her, she
caught at his sleeve and held it tightly. Before she
could say a word, however, someone entered the
betting shop.

After one glimpse of the man's gray hat, Victoria gave a muffled exclamation of fright. "It's him," she said shakily.

"The man who was bothering you?" her self-styled protector asked.

Victoria nodded, her throat closing as she stared at Keyes. He was breathing rapidly from exertion, his face set and furious. As soon as he saw her, his eyes gleamed with mean-spirited triumph.

"I'm a Bow Street Runner in pursuit of a suspect," he said in a cold, clear voice. "Give the woman to me."

The announcement of a Runner on the premises caused a hubbub of consternation throughout the small crowd. The bookmaker came out from behind the counter and began an angry rant. "I'm running a straight business, I am! What will it take to keep you pigs out o' my lister?" It was well known that bookmakers and Runners despised each other, as the authorities were often wont to sift through the betting shops in search of criminals. Runners considered the bookies to be one small step above actual criminals, and usually treated them as such.

"I'm about the Crown's business," Keyes said sharply, coming toward Victoria. "I'll thank you to hand over the wench, as she is wanted for questioning."

"He's lying," Victoria cried, throwing herself at the gentleman beside her, grabbing at whatever meager protection she could find. "I've done nothing wrong!"

"What crime is she accused of?" the man asked, one arm closing around Victoria.

"I haven't time to enumerate the offenses," Keyes replied. "Now, release the woman and go about your business."

"Do as 'e says," the bookmaker commanded tersely. "Let 'im 'ave the goods and take 'is leave. 'Tis bad for business to 'ave a Runner about the place."

The man sighed and gently began to urge Victoria forward. "Well, you have a wish to go to Bow Street, dove. It seems you have your escort."

"He won't take me there," she cried, clutching at him. "He's going to kill me. Don't let me go!"

"Kill you?" the man repeated, chortling at what he clearly perceived as a wild exaggeration. "Come, dove, whatever you've done, it can't be all that bad. When you go to the bench, just give the magistrate your prettiest smile, and I've no doubt he'll let you off easy."

"Please," she said desperately, "help me to reach Sir Ross Cannon. Or Mr. Morgan. I . . . I'm begging for my life."

Uncertainty skittered across the man's face as he stared down at her. It seemed that whatever he read in her eyes convinced him. The arm around her strengthened. "All right," he said. "No doubt I could do worse than rescue a damsel in distress this soggy evening." He looked up at Keyes with an affable, condescending smile. "Surely it would do no harm if I accompany the girl to Bow Street," he said. "That's where you want her taken, yes?

What difference does it make if I bring her there on your behalf?"

Victoria tensed as Keyes approached them, his eyes dark and lethal in his calm face. He appeared to be considering a response, in the manner of a man carrying on a reasonable conversation. "I'll show you what difference it makes," he said quietly. At the same time he spoke, he withdrew an object from inside his coat and raised it in a swift, high arc. In a flashing instant, Victoria saw that it was a neddy, a small weighted cudgel the Runners used to subdue unruly criminals. She let out a sharp cry and turned away just as Keyes struck the man about the head and shoulders, three times in rapid succession. She felt the shock of the blows resound through the man's heavy frame, and he collapsed in a moaning heap on the ground, his arm dropping away from her.

Keyes snatched her, seizing one arm and twisting it behind her until a shaft of pain seared through her back and shoulder. Victoria grunted through her clenched teeth and bent forward to ease the piercing ache. A burst of angry cries echoed throughout the room, and Keyes's voice cut through the cacophony. "If anyone else wishes to tangle with me, I'll have you charged with interfering with an officer's execution of his duty. Care for an evening's stay at Newgate?" He laughed contemptuously at the suddenly subdued crowd. "I thought not," he sneered. "Carry on, gentlemen, and put this little piece of mutton out of your minds."

"Get yer arse out o' my lister!" the bookmaker

snapped, and joined the small gathering around the injured man on the floor.

"Gladly," Keyes said, tugging and pushing Victoria up the steps, back into the downpour.

"You can't kill me now," she cried, blinking against the sheet of rain that struck her in the face. "There are witnesses ... they'll all say you were the one who took me away. You'll be tried ... hanged ..."

"I'll be long gone before an investigation has even begun," Keyes sneered, continuing to twist her arm as he ushered her along the street, around a flooding cess-trench dug in the middle.

Victoria glanced frantically about the street in the hope of finding someone to help her. Hopeless gazes stared out from the depths of crammed cellar homes. The stench of an underground slaughterhouse surrounded them as they passed the doorway, where the pelting rain was doing little to wash away layers of dried blood and fat. She felt her eyes aching and stinging, her leaking tears mingling with the rivulets of rain that coursed down her cheeks.

"Why are you doing this to me?" she cried.

Surprisingly, Keyes heard her through the tumult of the storm. "I'm too bloody old to be a Runner, and I've only a few pounds to retire on. I'll be damned if I live like a dog for the rest of my days."

"Wh-who paid you to kill me—" She broke off with a pained cry as he pushed her arm another inch upward.

"Enough yapping," he said. They turned a cor-ner and ventured deep into a rookery. Rapidly they strode toward a deserted factory. The walls of the building appeared so decayed and unstable that no one dared occupy it, not even the poor who were tightly packed in nearby slums like rabbits in a warren. Victoria screamed and dug in her heels as Keyes tried to force her past the doorway.

A sharp pain exploded on the side of her head, and she realized dimly that he had just hit her, hard enough to subdue her resistance. Sagging against him, her mind buzzing, she fought to collect her wits. He gagged her efficiently, using his own cravat, and she recoiled at the taste of starch and sweat. Drawing her hands behind her back, Keyes snapped the cold metal rings of handcuffs around her wrists.

Helplessly Victoria stumbled forward as the Runner shoved her toward a set of broken stairs. The remnants of the steps groaned and splintered as they ascended. It would have been pitch-black in the building, except that a good part of the roof had rotted away, and there were holes and gaping fissures in the walls. The air was foul and still, every visible surface covered with oily dust that barely stirred when gusts of rain-filled wind blew inside.

No one would find her now, Victoria thought dully, gasping for breath as Keyes pushed her into a second-story factory. The floor was pebbled with rodent droppings, and the fractured walls were coated with grime and webs and bird nests. There were squeaking, flapping noises as the current occupants of the factory fled their perches. Rain leaked from the broken roof and puddled in the center of the floor. Dragging her to a corner, Keyes thrust her down until she fell back in a heap, the hem of her skirts sliding to her knees.

Then he was still, staring at her wet stockings. His face tautened in a way that made her ill. "I was planning to finish you off quickly," he said. "Now I want something extra for my pains, you troublesome bitch. I wouldn't mind a cut of what Morgan had."

Suddenly nothing seemed real. Victoria thought dazedly that she must be having a nightmare, that very soon she would awaken and Grant would be there, telling her that everything was all right. Her mind turned inward, and she concentrated desperately on the idea that it was all a horrible dream. She didn't even cringe as Keyes crouched over her and began to jerk at the fastenings of his breeches. "You'll be no loss to the world," he muttered. "I've seen thousands of your kind. I'll give you one thing—you're a hardy little bitch. No woman should have lived through what you did." His tone was suddenly scored with jealousy. "Only the best for Morgan . . . Aye, you're a choice piece of mutton." Continuing to mutter angrily, he pulled up handfuls of her skirts, while Victoria began to wish she were already dead.

Sixteen

*a*s Grant had demanded, Covent Garden and its environs were soon swarming with foot patrols, captains, Runners, and watchmen. Horse patrols comprised of retired calvary soldiers divided the area into sections and covered them with military precision. Cannon, of course, remained at Bow Street with the command that all developments be reported to him immediately.

Grant knew that Cannon's desire for Victoria and Keyes to be found went beyond personal concern. A suspicious public was ever on the lookout for signs of corruption among the Bow Street force. If there had been wrongdoing on Keyes's part, it would be used against Cannon—against all of them—to hinder Cannon's planned reorganization and expansion of the policing system. It was likely that this concern weighed on all the Runners' minds, spurring them to search even harder.

"Morgan," Flagstad said worriedly, angling the brim of his hat against a cascade of raindrops, "for the life of me, I can't come up with a sound reason for Miss Duvall to run from Keyes like that. She must have simply lost her head, panicked . . . but why? We all know for certain that Keyes is a good man."

Grant shook his head, walking toward the opera house. He found it difficult to force a reply through his clenched teeth. "I don't know anything for certain," he said roughly.

"But of course you do," Flagstad persisted, hurrying to match his ground-covering strides. "Keyes has done nothing out of order—he's merely looking for Miss Duvall as we are, to bring her back to safety!"

Flagstad's testimony on behalf of his longtime friend should have touched Grant. The man's weathered face was fraught with distress over the inexplicable events of the evening. Flagstad had known Keyes for years, and would be sorely troubled over any implications that Keyes had done something wrong.

Grant knew he should have reacted with understanding, perhaps said a word or two to ease Flagstad's obvious worry. Instead, he found himself stopping to seize the other man by his coat front. "Then where the hell is he?" His temper, tightly repressed until this moment, exploded in a bonfire of frustration. "Don't tell me what kind of man Keyes is—just help me find the bastard!"

"Yes . . . yes . . ." Flagstad's hands came over his,

prying them loose from his coat. He stared at Grant with bewildered dismay. "Calm yourself, Morgan. My God, I've never seen you so . . . Well, you've always kept a cool head, even during a riot!"

Grant released him with a grunt of muted fury. Yes, he had always been cool during riots, mobs, battles, and skirmishes of every kind. This was different. Time was running out for Victoria. She was in mortal danger, and not being able to reach her was causing something inhuman to disperse inside him and rise to the surface. He realized suddenly that he had to keep control of himself or he could quite possibly kill someone. Machinelike, he forced himself to continue to the opera house, where a captain of the foot patrol had gathered two men.

"You don't think they've run away together, do you?" Flagstad mused aloud. "I mean, the ladies do seem to like Keyes, and Miss Duvall has a definite reputation in that regard—"

"Get away from me." Grant's voice was low and deadly. "Before I slaughter you."

Flagstad seemed to understand it was not an idle threat. Paling, he stopped and edged away hastily. "I think I'll get a report from Captain Brogdon on the progress of his foot patrol."

"Morgan! Morgan!" A breathless shout caused Grant to look about alertly. A constable was running neck-or-nothing alongside the opera house, coming from the streets north of the marketplace. "Mr. Morgan . . . they sent me to tell you . . ."

Grant reached him in three strides, nearly knocking the young man over. "What is it?"

"The betting shop on the alleyway off Russell . . .

something you'll want to hear about . . ." Gasping frantically, the constable paused and hung his head in the struggle for more air.

"Tell me, dammit!" Grant snapped. "You can breathe later."

"Yes, sir." The constable nodded jerkily and forced himself to continue. "The list-maker and some of his customers claim"—he paused for another gulp of air—"a girl came into the shop tonight, asking for someone to help her to Bow Street. They say a Runner came in and forced her to come away with him."

"Praise God," Flagstad exclaimed, having lingered to hear the report. His face was transformed with relief. "It's Keyes and Miss Duvall, obviously. He found her! Everything is all right now."

Grant ignored the Runner's excitement and questioned the constable grimly. "How long ago did it happen?"

"It appears to be less than ten minutes, sir."

Flagstad interrupted eagerly. "I'll go directly to Bow Street and await them. No doubt Keyes will have her there momentarily."

"You do that," Grant said, and took off at a dead run toward Russell.

The betting shop was easy to locate. A cluster of constables had gathered outside the basement steps, while a squatty, imperious figure stood beneath the questionable shelter of a tattered umbrella and uttered loud complaints to all and sundry. The bookmaker wore heavy leather pouches that made him instantly identifiable.

The constables straightened and backed away a

step en masse as Grant reached them. They looked at him strangely—no doubt he presented an odd appearance with his hair plastered over his skull, his face stiff and bloodless beneath the falling rain, and his lips drawn back from his teeth in a sort of frozen snarl he couldn't erase.

The bookmaker squinted at him speculatively. "Bloody big bastard, you are," he commented. "You must be Morgan. She was asking for ye, the wench that came in my place an' started the 'ole bloody rucktion."

"Tell Mr. Morgan what happened," one of the constables urged.

"The Runner came in my shop for 'er, an' she wouldn't go wiv 'im. The addlepate said 'e was going to kill 'er."

"And then there was a fight," the constable prompted.

"Aye," the bookmaker said sourly. "One ow my customers tried to claim the wench, an' the Runner knocked the piss out ow my customer, 'e did." He spat in contempt at the thought of the departed runner. "Bloody Robin Redbreast, trying to ruin a man's honest business!"

Grant experienced an excruciating mingling of panic and pain that rose higher and higher until he felt hot pressure in the center of his head.

"What direction did they go in?" he heard himself ask hoarsely.

The question produced a sudden sly smile that stretched from one curling sideburn to the other. "I may know," the bookmaker said diffidently, "or I may not."

One of the constables seized him impatiently, giving him a brief shake that elicited an angry squawk. "Rough me again," the bookmaker threatened, "an' I won't tell ye where they went! 'Ow'd ye like to put the wench to bed wiv a shovel?"

"What the hell do you want?" Grant asked softly, staring at the bookmaker with a savage intensity that seemed to rattle him.

The bookmaker blinked uneasily. "I want ye stinkin' Redbreasts to keep yer arses out o' my lister from now on!"

"Done."

"But, Mr. Morgan . . ." the constable said, protesting the hastily struck bargain. His voice trailed away meekly as Grant's murderous gaze swerved to him for one chilling instant.

The bookmaker regarded Grant suspiciously. " 'Ow do I know ye'll keep yer word?"

"You don't," Grant replied, his voice rising to a thunderous pitch that rivaled that of the storm outside. "But you know for certain that I'll kill you in the next ten seconds if you don't tell me *where the hell they went!*"

"Awright," the bookmaker said, and began to call for someone named Willie. Instantly a small, skinny lad of eleven or twelve appeared, dressed in ragged clothes that were far too big for him, and a cap that nearly engulfed his small, stubby head. "Me bookie's runner," the bookmaker said with pride. "I sent 'im to follow the bastard when 'e took the wench."

"They went to an' old building not far from here," the boy said breathlessly. "I'll show ye, Mr.

Morgan, sir." He began to scamper along the street at once, looking over one shoulder to see if Grant would follow. Grant was at his heels at once. "I know 'xactly where 'tis, sir," the boy cried, and quickened his pace to a run.

The building, or rather the remains of one, stood like a ragged sentinel on the corner, its walls perforated with yawning holes and jagged slivers of glass. "There," Willie cried, stopping well short of the entrance, staring at it mistrustfully. "That's where they went. But I wouldn't go inside, sir . . . 'Tisn't a sound stick o' wood in the 'ole place."

Grant barely heard him as he stepped across the threshold. The factory groaned and creaked around him, as if the entire structure would collapse any second. Rain trickled from the gaps in the walls and roof, its clean scent doing little to freshen the rank atmosphere. There were no sounds of voices, no signs of a struggle, and it seemed impossible that Victoria was here. For a moment Grant wondered if the boy had been mistaken in bringing him here, or if he had been directed by the bookmaker to play a trick on him. If this was the wrong place, it was a waste of precious time. However, a pattern of scuffs and arcs on the floor drew his attention, and his gaze shot to the stairs. There was freshly splintered wood on the third and fourth steps, and more higher up. Someone had just been here.

The sight was a visceral shock. All at once Grant found himself hurtling up the stairs, ignoring the wood cracking beneath his weight, scrambling upward with hands and feet. He had never known real desperation until now, had never felt it racing like hot oil through his veins until every inch of his skin seemed to burn. He had to reach Victoria before it was too late . . . and if it was . . . he knew that he could not live in a world without her.

Half running, half crawling up the fragmenting stairs, he reached the second floor. Through a red blur of rampant fury, he saw two figures directly across the factory space . . . Keyes, crouching over Victoria's prostrate form, fumbling at her skirts while a crack of lightning threw a harsh, brilliant glare through the broken roof. The only color in the room was Victoria's hair, rich as rubies, pooling brightly beneath her head. She was gagged. Eyes closed, motionless, she lay flattened beneath the Runner without a hint of movement.

An unholy noise came from Grant's throat, a devil cry that erupted from the bottom of his soul. No longer aware of his own actions, he sprang at Keyes, his entire being occupied with the need to attack and kill. The other man had only a split second to look up before Grant was on him. A curse exploded from Keyes as he was thrown halfway across the room. He rolled, fumbled for his brace of pistols, but just as he grasped the butt of a weapon, Grant seized his arm and slammed it against the floor with a force that broke bones. Screaming with pain, Keyes struck out with his other fist, ramming it into Grant's jaw. Grant barely felt the blow, so intent was he on murder.

"She's *nothing*, you bloody animal!" Keyes screamed, glaring into Grant's savage, pitiless face. "You wouldn't kill me over a whore!"

Grant didn't reply, only hammered brutally until

no more words came from the Runner's mouth. Gradually Keyes stopped fighting and brought up his arms to defend his face and head. When the Runner was subdued to a groaning heap, Grant reached into his boot and extracted his knife, relishing the feel of it in his hand. He would be satisfied only with death, and nothing would stop him now. All the things he believed in, the strictures of law, fairness, justice, had disappeared like dust in the wind. Nearly demented with bloodlust, he raised the knife in the air.

But a muffled sound made him pause. Panting in harsh, irregular bursts, he looked in the direction of the sound. Victoria was on her side, watching him, her throat working silently, her eyes wide and staring above the gag in her mouth. Grant tensed until he shook from repressed force. He couldn't take his gaze from her face. Victoria's blue eyes seemed to imprison him, preventing him from moving. A thread of sanity penetrated through the first few layers of warlike rage, but he resisted fiercely.

"Turn your face away," he said in a voice that didn't seem to belong to him.

Victoria shook her head immediately, understanding that he could not bring himself to kill a man while she was watching.

"Damn you, look away," Grant growled.

She did not. Their gazes held, his demonic, hers insistent, until finally she defeated him. He acceded with a low groan and slid the knife back into his boot. Delivering one last blow to Keyes, he knocked the man unconscious and searched his pockets rapidly. He found the key to the handcuffs that tethered Victoria's arms and brought it to her, dropping to his knees by her side. She quivered as the key turned in the handcuffs and the manacles dropped away from her bruised wrists.

As soon as the gag was removed from Victoria's tear-ravaged face, Grant dragged her into his lap and crushed her against his body. The feel of her, soft and small and alive, caused him to groan with tortured relief. His hands raked over her, his mouth dragging hungrily over her hair, skin, clothes, as if he would devour her whole.

"Grant," she gasped, flinching from the force of his kisses.

He gave an animal growl of pleasure and need, crushing his lips hard over hers.

He felt her arm slide around his neck, and her breath puffed against his ear as she spoke. "I thought I would die here. I thought . . . his face would be the last thing I saw in this lifetime."

"*My* face is the last one you'll see in this lifetime," he said gruffly.

"I remembered everything . . . that man, Keyes . . . he tried to kill me before."

Grant knew he was holding her too tightly, but he couldn't seem to loosen his arms. "I'm sorry," he finally managed. "I'm so sorry. It's my fault—"

"No, no. Please don't say that." Her hands clasped the hard nape of his neck. "How did you find me? How did you know?"

"I found out about Keyes from Lord Lane. For the last half hour I've been insane, thinking I wouldn't reach you in time." He buried his face against her bodice with a groan. "Oh, God."

He felt her fingers slide gently through his wet hair, and she murmured something soft and indistinguishable.

"I'll never let you out of my sight again," he said, his voice muffled against her breast, and she let out an unsteady gasp of laughter.

"F-fine. That's just fine with me."

As the storm continued to rage and blow outside, the factory creaked and shuddered. The sounds galvanized Grant into action. Reluctantly he set Victoria out of his lap and pulled her up with him. "I have to get you out of here," he muttered.

"Yes." She cast a glance of loathing about the wretched place, her gaze lingering on Keyes's prostrate form. "What about him?"

"We'll leave him to the others," Grant said, not caring if the entire building collapsed around the bastard . . . as long as they were safely out of it first. He slid a supportive arm around her back. "Can you walk, Victoria?"

She nodded, and to his amazement, a smile tugged at her chapped lips. "What is it?" he asked, wondering if the terror of the last few minutes had caused her to become temporarily unbalanced.

"You said my name," she said, her voice scratchy and strained, the smile remaining on her lips. "How did you—"

"I'll explain later." Unable to help himself, he bent and possessed her mouth in a hard, impassioned kiss. "Let's go."

Carefully they made their way down the broken stairs, Grant leading the way. He tested each step and landing before allowing Victoria to proceed. She was surprised by the weakness of her own legs. Although she knew she was safe, she could not stop trembling. Shivers and chills passed over her skin, and she stiffened in reaction.

"Are you hurt?" Grant asked at one point, and although his voice was calm, she heard the under-tones of anguished concern.

"No," she said, clamping her teeth together to stop a spate of chattering. "He didn't . . . that is, you reached me before he . . ." She fell silent as Grant lifted her gently over a broken step. "I'm perfectly fine," she said, strengthening her voice in an effort to reassure him. However, he seemed far from convinced. She winced as she saw the hard-ness of his profile, knowing that he was silently berating himself for what had happened.

It seemed an eternity passed before they finally reached the ground floor and stepped outside. As soon as they reached solid ground, Grant lifted her in his arms, holding her high against his chest. Vic-toria pushed at his shoulder as she realized that they were in the midst of a crowd of constables and Runners and curious onlookers. "I can walk," she murmured as rumbles of praise and relief went through the assemblage.

Ignoring the words, Grant continued to hold her. One of the horse patrol captains approached, dis-mounting and nodding to Grant respectfully. "Sir," he said, "I'm glad to see that Miss Duvall is safely recovered." He paused and glanced at the crum-bling factory. "Is Mr. Keyes still in there? That is, what should we—"

"He's alive," Grant replied, sounding none too pleased about the fact. "But he'll need assistance coming down from the second floor."

The captain frowned with dismay. "The place is a death trap, sir. I couldn't guarantee the safety of any man who might venture in there."

"Then knock the place over and dig Keyes out of the rubble," Grant said flatly. "I don't give a damn how you get him."

The captain blinked uneasily at Grant's callousness toward a former comrade. "Sir, may I offer the use of my own mount?" He signaled a member of the horse patrol, who led a large chestnut to them.

Grant lifted Victoria into the saddle, immediately swinging up behind her. He flicked a cold glance toward the dilapidated building. "When Mr. Keyes is brought to the ground floor," he said to the captain, "arrest him and have him sent to the Bow Street holding room. I have unfinished business with the bastard . . . and after Cannon is through with him, he's mine."

"Yes, Mr. Morgan," the captain said, regarding him with a mixture of awe and trepidation. Clearly Grant was not a man he would risk displeasing.

Too exhausted to bother with modesty, Victoria sat astride the chestnut, her skirts riding to her knees. She leaned back against Grant while his steady arm came around her front. His long fingers curved around the cage of her ribs, and he pressed her against him as he signaled the horse to an immediate canter. She was jostled a bit, her body too stiff and tired to move naturally with the horse. But she welcomed the cold, pattering rain on her face, and the soreness of her limbs, all physical reminders that she was still alive.

Grant had come for her, she thought in wonder. He had stopped Keyes from killing her. It was a miracle almost too great to comprehend. She was filled with gratitude, and more than that, there was a sense of intimacy that went beyond all her previous feelings for him. She knew now that he would risk anything, do anything, for her, that he cared for her more than anyone ever had. She knew also that he would have killed Keyes, but instead had left him alive because she had willed it. The thought caused a thrill of pleasure inside her. Grant was a magnificent man, and very much his own master . . . but she had the power to influence him. Because he loved her.

Savoring the feeling, Victoria leaned back harder against him, not minding the cold and discomfort of the ride. The rain-pierced darkness was barely illuminated by the light of a streetlamp as they reached number 4 Bow Street. Dismounting first, Grant reached up for Victoria and lowered her carefully to the ground. He kept his hands at her waist, steadying her. She smiled up at him, sensing the worry lurking behind his expressionless face.

"I'm all right," she said.

His jaw hardened. "I keep thinking of you lying on that factory floor. And Keyes over you—"

"But you stopped him." She reached up and caressed his cheek, his stubbled skin startlingly warm to her chilled fingers. A tremor of fierce emotion went through him, and she felt the vibration against her palm.

"What if I had been too late?" he asked hoarsely, his eyes so dark they appeared black instead of green.

Victoria stared at him compassionately, realizing that he needed comfort as much as she did, perhaps even more. Since the death of his brother, Grant had never faced the possibility of losing someone he cared about. He had not allowed himself to truly love someone, because he had not wanted to risk feeling such pain again.

"It wouldn't have been your fault," she said carefully. "Some things are beyond your control."

But that wasn't what he wanted to hear, she saw with a sudden flash of amusement. He wasn't the kind of man who would admit that anything was beyond his control.

"That's damned cold comfort," he muttered, one dark brow lifting in a sardonic arch. "Can't you do better than that?"

She managed a smile as she saw that he was gradually returning to his old self. "Well, you weren't late," she said. "You arrived in time to save me. Why worry about what might have happened?"

"Because I . . ." Grant stopped and scowled. "Because it's not every day that a man discovers that one small, fragile, accident-prone woman is the center of his very existence."

"Accident-prone?" she repeated with a touch of feigned indignation, while her heart gave a joyful lurch at the rest of his words.

Sir Ross's errand boy, Ernest, emerged from the building to take the horse and lead him to the stable in back. To Victoria's surprise, Grant did not take her to the office entrance in the tiny south-facing yard, but directly into the house. The main building was connected to offices in back, which in turn led to the court where inquiries were conducted and cases were heard.

"Who are all these people?" Victoria asked, instinctively pressing closer to Grant as she stared at the multitude crammed into every conceivable corner of the building.

"Informants, criminals, potential jurors, lawyers . . . Take your pick."

"Is it always this busy?"

"This is nothing. I've seen the place when the walls are straining at the seams." Looking over the crowd, Grant nodded to a plump silver-haired housekeeper who was attempting to direct the flow of human traffic to the appropriate rooms. Catching his gaze, she hurried over to him. She stopped short, her mouth forming a round O of dismay. "Dear, me," she murmured, her gaze traveling from his wet, filthy, disheveled form to Victoria's. "The two of you are a sight, Mr. Morgan."

Grant's mouth curved in a faint smile, but it was clear he was in no mood for conversation. "I need to see Cannon now," he said curtly. "We only have a few minutes. Miss Duvall . . . that is, Miss Devane . . . has been through an ordeal and requires rest."

"Yes, of course." The housekeeper regarded Victoria with kindly concern. "Come this way at once, please." She urged them through the bustling crowd and brought them to Sir Ross's office, a small room with rectangular windows facing the street. The office was furnished with oak pieces, ponderous bookshelves, and a library terrestrial globe.

Sir Ross, who was talking with two men who appeared to be clerks or assistants of some kind, stopped in midsentence as Grant brought Victoria into the room. "Morgan," he said, his gray eyes flashing as he stared at the two of them. "Where is Keyes?"

"He'll be brought here soon," Grant said flatly.

Somehow, Cannon seemed to understand exactly what had happened just by reading Grant's face. He closed his eyes, and his shoulders slumped a bit. He rubbed his temples with a thumb and fore-finger, as if a tremendous headache had suddenly descended. "Mrs. Dobson," he said to the house-keeper, "bring hot drinks and blankets."

"Yes, sir." She disappeared at once.

Efficiently Cannon ushered the other two men out of the room and closed the door firmly. The noise and commotion outside the office was muted but still audible. Turning to Grant and Victoria, Cannon gestured for them to have a seat.

Victoria shivered slightly, grateful for the protec-tive arm Grant slid behind her back as she huddled in the oak chair. Her clothes were wet and clammy, and she was uncomfortably aware of the filth that clung to her pelisse and hair. She had never wanted a bath as badly as she did right now. She longed to be clean and dry and to find a warm bed to sleep in.

"This won't take long," Grant murmured, seeing her weariness.

Cannon heard the quiet comment. "No indeed," he said, drawing up a chair in front of Victoria's. He startled her by taking her hand in his large, cool one and staring at her intently. Her wide gaze flew to his serious gray eyes. "Miss . . ." he began, and paused.

"Devane," she supplied with a tremulous smile.

"Devane," he repeated softly. "You must feel like you've gone to sea in a sieve."

Despite her exhaustion, Victoria laughed suddenly at the description. "Something like that."

"That fact that this ordeal was caused by one of my Runners grieves me more than I can say. I can offer no sufficient redress for what you've suffered . . . but I give you my word that if I can ever be of service to you, I will use every means at my disposal. You have only to ask."

"Thank you," Victoria replied softly, finding it a bit unnerving to have one of London's most powerful men offer her an apology.

Seeming satisfied, Cannon released her hand and waited until Mrs. Dobson had brought the blankets. When Victoria was snugly wrapped in a layer of wool and there was a steaming mug of tea clasped in her icy fingers, the magistrate's implacable gaze returned to her. "Miss Devane . . . please tell me as best you can what happened this evening."

Occasionally fumbling for words, Victoria described the events that had passed since Grant had left her earlier in the day. Now and then Grant interceded, filling in the necessary explanations. The only interruption came when the office door reverberated from a curious scraping motion. Victoria paused and looked around questioningly at the odd noise.

Rolling his eyes, Cannon rose and opened the door. Immediately a large striped cat with no tail sauntered inside the office and surveyed the visitors with a speculative gaze. "Chopper," Cannon said in a warning tone that would have caused any other creature to slink into the nearest corner.

Instead, Chopper flicked him a rebellious glance and jumped straight into Victoria's lap. Automatically Victoria handed her half-filled mug to Grant as the cat settled into a massive furry heap over her thighs.

Muttering an apology, Cannon began to remove the creature, but Victoria shook her head with a smile. "It's all right," she said. "I like animals."

Cannon's eyes glimmered with an answering smile. "Well, now you've met the real head of Bow Street," he remarked, indicating the smug feline, and returned to his chair.

With the cat purring quietly in her lap, Victoria finished the description of all that had happened, and blinked tiredly. The office was warm, and the realization that she was finally safe had made her feel peaceful for the first time in weeks. She felt Grant's hand settle on the back of her neck, beneath her wet, dirty hair, and his gentle touch soothed her.

A long reflective silence followed as Cannon stared absently at the landscape on his wall. The painting depicted a small, bright stream rushing over crags and rocks, against a backdrop of forest-covered hills. Victoria suspected that at times like this, the magistrate must wish to be in a place as serene as the one in the landscape.

"Keyes," the magistrate said softly, as if he were sorting through memories in his mind. Small, cold lights burned in his gray eyes, conveying fury and a hint of grief. It was a personal tragedy for Cannon, as well as a professional one.

"I'm sorry for what has happened," Victoria said sincerely, her concerned gaze turning to Grant. "Will this make things more difficult for you and the other Runners?"

Grant's green eyes were caressing as he regarded her with a slight smile. "No need to worry, sweet pea. Bow Street has weathered worse than this before." Deftly he pushed the cat from her lap, ignoring Chopper's protesting yowl, and urged her to stand. "It's time for Miss Devane to go home," he said to Cannon. "We'll deal with the official business tomorrow."

"My carriage will convey you to King Street." Cannon opened the door, summoned his errand boy, and murmured instructions to him. At the same time the housekeeper appeared, asking if there was something else she could bring for Victoria.

"We're finished for now," Cannon said. "Thank you, Miss Devane. I hope you will suffer no lasting effects from this disastrous day."

"I'll be quite well after a good rest," she assured him.

Cannon's comment caused Grant to frown in worry. "I should send for Linley," he said. "He should have a look at you, after what you've been through."

"Again?" Victoria shook her head instantly. "I certainly don't need to see a doctor twice in one day. *You* can go see Dr. Linley if you're so desirous of his company. I want to go home."

"Home it is," he said softly, guiding her from the office.

Mrs. Dobson stepped into the hallway to observe the pair's departure. When she glanced back at Ross, the housekeeper wore a pleased, slightly bemused expression. "Well," she remarked, "it seems our Mr. Morgan has finally fallen in love."

"And fallen hard," Ross added wryly. "Poor bastard."

An affectionate smile brightened Mrs. Dobson's plump face. "Someday, sir, a little slip of a thing may yet reduce you to the state our poor Mr. Morgan is in."

"I'll slit my own throat first," he replied calmly. "In the meanwhile, I want a jug of coffee."

The housekeeper looked outraged at the suggestion. "At this hour? I won't hear of it. What you need is rest, and plenty of it, not some brew that will shred your nerves to ribbons . . ."

Sighing, Cannon returned to his desk and endured the lecture that ensued.

Seventeen

*U*pon returning to King Street, Victoria was greeted by a worried Mrs. Buttons and a tearful Mary, both of whom were astonished by the news that Keyes had intended to do her harm.

"You should have told me, miss!" the housekeeper exclaimed. "If you had, I should have done whatever was necessary to help you."

"I'm sorry," Victoria replied with a wan smile. "With the sudden shock of my memory returning, and my fear of Mr. Keyes, I'm afraid I lost my head." She did not want to hurt anyone's feelings by admitting that she hadn't been certain of whether she could trust the servants to take her side against a Bow Street Runner. "And in any case," she added, "everything has turned out well, thanks to Mr. Morgan."

"I suppose we'll get another ha'penny novel out

of this," Mrs. Buttons said. "More exciting adventures of the Bow Street legend, Mr. Morgan."

"The Bow Street lummox, more like," Grant muttered. "The entire situation was my fault. I had originally wanted Flagstad to guard Victoria—I should never have agreed to let Keyes do it."

"You couldn't have known," Victoria protested. "No one suspected him—not even Sir Ross."

Grant scowled in reply, obviously not accepting her defense of him. Gently he lifted a hand to her forehead and brushed back a straggling tendril of hair. "Mrs. Buttons," he said, still staring at Victoria, "I believe Miss Devane requires a bath. And perhaps some warm milk with brandy."

"Oh, yes," Victoria said, shivering in pleasure at the thought of soaking in hot soapy water.

"We'll take excellent care of her, Mr. Morgan," the housekeeper assured him, and gestured to the housemaid standing nearby. "Mary, you and the girls fill a bath for Miss Devane, and then fill a separate one in the guest room for Mr. Morgan."

"Yes, ma'am," Mary said eagerly, disappearing on swift feet.

Grant's tone was soft as he spoke to Victoria. "Shall I carry you upstairs?"

Smiling, Victoria shook her head. She was so enmeshed in the tender warmth of his gaze that she was barely aware of the housekeeper leaving them. "Will you come to me after your bath?" she asked.

His face was expressionless, but his mouth was soft as he leaned closer and pressed a kiss to her temple. "No," he murmured so quietly that she could barely hear him.

Surprised, she drew back a few inches. "You won't?"

"You've endured enough for one day—you don't need a great rutting brute in your bed to-night."

Unable to restrain herself, Victoria reached out and hugged herself against his hard chest. "What if I want him there?"

"You need to sleep," he said firmly.

"Sleep is a waste of time."

A reluctant laugh rumbled in his throat, and slowly his arms came around her. She felt him breathe into the locks of hair above her ear. "That proves how exhausted you are. You don't know what you're saying."

"I do," Victoria insisted, not allowing him to push her away.

"Sweet pea..." Grant's voice was slightly strained. "It's been a hell of a trying day for me as well. I'm afraid if I visit you tonight..." He paused to search for the appropriate words. "I don't think I would have any..."

"Strength?" she supplied.

"Self-control."

"Oh." Victoria swallowed hard as she stared at his unfathomable face. "But if you—"

"Go," he muttered, easily prying her loose and turning her to face the stairs. He gave her a strong nudge. "I've been through too much, Victoria. I don't trust myself with you tonight. Get some rest. I'll see you in the morning."

Frowning, Victoria ascended the stairs, occasionally pausing to glance back at him. Grant waited until she had reached the top before he turned and went to the library in search of a much-needed brandy.

With the servants' help, Victoria washed and rinsed her hair twice, sighing in bliss as the hot water whisked away all traces of grime. The bath soaked away the soreness of her strained muscles, and warmed the deep-set chill from her bones. That and a cup of brandy-laced milk combined to relax her deeply. She dressed in a clean muslin night rail and pelisse that fastened up the front with a row of tiny peal buttons. Drowsily she sat before the fire as the servants carefully combed her damp hair and allowed the heat from the hearth to dry the crimson locks. "More milk?" Mrs. Buttons asked. "Or something to eat? A plate of toast, or a bowl of soup . . . an egg, perhaps—"

"Thank you, no." Victoria rubbed her eyes and yawned.

Understanding her weariness and her need for privacy, the housekeeper nodded to Mary, and they prepared to leave the room. "Ring for me if there is anything you need, Miss Devane," Mrs. Buttons said softly.

Eyes half closed, Victoria extended her bare feet toward the fire and watched the yellow light play upon her toes. She wondered if Grant had finished bathing, if perhaps he was already asleep in the guest room. She knew he would keep to his vow not to visit her tonight, having decided it was best for her to sleep. Undoubtedly he was right. But she needed to be with him, to be held and comforted, and to comfort him in return.

She had come close to dying this evening, barely a month after the first attempt on her life, and the realization made her desperate to savor every moment for the rest of her days. Sleep was indeed a waste of time . . . especially when the man she loved was only a room away.

Before Victoria had consciously made the decision, she was at the door of the guest suite. With fingers that trembled just a little, she turned the knob and entered the small antechamber that led to the bedroom. As in the master suite, a small fire on the grate spread ruddy flickering light over the room and made shadows dance in the corner.

And on the bed . . . What she beheld caused her to stop in her tracks, flustered, her heart pounding hard and heavy in her chest. Grant was stretched out on the guest bed, one foot dangling over the edge, one knee propped up slightly. He held a book in his hand, reading with a slight frown on his forehead and a moody set to his mouth. There was not a stitch of clothing anywhere in sight.

The firelight turned his skin a light shade of amber and scattered gold flecks throughout his shiny black hair. Every detail of his long, muscled body was visible, from the triangular hollow at the base of his throat, to the dusting of dark wiry hair on his legs. Amid a riot of excitement and confusion, Victoria wondered why it was that he seemed so much larger with his clothes off than on. She had never seen such a startling expanse of naked skin.

Victoria knew she must have made some small sound, for his narrowed gaze switched to her, and automatically he covered his lap with the open book. The defensive gesture struck her as amusing, and his forbidding scowl only heightened the comic effect. Clamping her lips together, she repressed a sudden laugh and ventured farther into the room. "You shouldn't read in such bad light," she said, her voice cracking just a little. She was more nervous than she had realized. "You'll strain your eyes."

His frown deepened. "That's not the only thing I'll strain if you don't go back to your room."

Ignoring the command, she closed the door and approached the bed in cautious steps. "I'm not sleepy."

Grant sat up and swung his legs over the side of the bed, the muscles of his stomach rippling as he kept the book over his loins. "You would lose consciousness in less than a minute if you went to bed and closed your eyes." But his gaze swept over her white muslin pelisse, lingering on the row of tiny buttons that fastened it, and she heard the change in his breathing. Encouraged, she stepped closer to him. "I mean it, Victoria," he warned. "Not tonight."

"Don't you want to be with me?"

"I want what's best for you."

"*You're* what's best for me." Staring into his intent green eyes, she reached for the top button of her pelisse and fumbled with it. Her nervousness made her clumsy, and it was difficult to pull the pearl button through the tiny silk loop. Grant was silent, continuing to watch her without blinking. Blushing in sudden embarrassment, she wrenched the fastening, and the tiny button popped free, bouncing to the carpet. In rising frustration, Vic-

toria realized there were more than a dozen buttons remaining. At this rate it would take all night
just to remove her pelisse. Abandoning the hopeless task, she looked at Grant and made a wry face.
"I'm not a very accomplished seductress, am I?"

All at once the book went sailing halfway across
the room, landing on the floor with a muffled thud.
Victoria gasped as she was abruptly lifted in the
air and deposited on the bed. Grant leaned over
her, his broad shoulders blocking the fire from her
vision. "Considering the fact that I'm as hard as an
iron pike," he said huskily, "I'd say you're doing
something right."

She was clasped against more than six feet of
solid, aroused male, his sex protruding against her
abdomen, one of his muscular thighs pressing between hers. Tentatively she slid her arms around
his midriff, her hands coming to rest on his hard
back. She was startled by the heat of his body,
burning with almost feverish intensity. "Your skin
is so hot," she whispered, her cool fingers wandering across the flexing plane of his back.

His breath filtered through his teeth as if he were
in pain, and she froze in uncertainty. "Did I do
something wrong?"

"No, no . . ." Grant buried his face in the loose
locks of her hair, rubbing his cheek against the
scarlet silk. "When you touch me, I'm not sure if
I'm in heaven or hell."

"Is that good?"

"That's good," he said, his voice muffled in her
hair.

She smiled against his ear and locked her arms

around his back, holding on with all her strength. Grant murmured love words against her throat, her cheeks, pressing unhurried kisses over her skin as his fingers worked at the buttons of her pelisse. He unfastened them without any haste, taking his time as he freed each pearl from its confining loop.

"Kiss me," Victoria said breathlessly, wanting something more than the light, tantalizing brushes of his mouth. His lips hovered over hers, teasing her with his restraint, and she slid her arms around his neck to tug his head closer. She couldn't repress a moan as he gave the openmouthed kiss she wanted, his tongue exploring her with luscious, softly gauging strokes.

Realizing that her pelisse was spread open, Victoria struggled to rid herself of the garment. He soothed her with more kisses and fitted his solid arm beneath her neck, helping to tug the pelisse away from her body. Now all that separated their skin was the gossamer layer of her night rail. He fondled her through the thin muslin, finding the shape of her breast and cupping it in his warm hand, squeezing gently until her nipple tightened against his palm.

Trembling with excitement, Victoria touched him with growing boldness, her fingertips dipping into the valley of his spine, the hard inward curve ridged with thick muscle on both sides. And lower, to the dense flesh of his buttocks, her hands delighting in the solid masculine curvature. His body moved as she touched him there, his hips pushing urgently at hers, the sturdy shape of his arousal nudging into the pocket of muslin that draped between her thighs. She started at his involuntary thrust, remembering when he had taken her the first time, the intimate sundering of her body and the pain it had caused.

Clearly sensing her uneasiness, Grant went still over her, resting his weight on his elbows to keep from crushing her. "Don't be afraid," he said hoarsely.

"I'm not," she lied, forcing her fists to unclench. She spread her hands on the backs of his shoulders. "You said it wouldn't hurt if I was prepared for it."

"That's right." He kissed her, his mouth indescribably delicious as it ground gently over hers. She opened completely to his kiss, her body pliant and trusting beneath his. She did not tense again, even when he paused to strip away her night rail completely. He shaped and lifted her breasts in both hands, kissing one rosy peak and then the other. His lips parted over a sensitive nipple, and she felt the sliding caress of his tongue. The softly tickling touch caused her to arch higher against his mouth. His hand clasped her knee and wandered upward, not stopping until he reached the thatch of hair that protected her tender feminine flesh. His fingertips played lightly among the spicy red curls, sliding and teasing until she groaned and pushed the small mound directly into his hand.

Grant shuddered from the effort not to take her then. He knew she was ready for him, he felt the moisture seeping through the cinnamon silk . . . but not yet. Not until she begged him for it. Whispering his love to her, he caressed her intimately, his fingertip stroking through her softness until he found the entrance to her body. He relished the catch of her breath, her sudden quiver as he slid his finger forward, stroking the hot inner sleekness. She held his shoulders as if she couldn't decide whether to pull him closer or push him away. He watched her face as he pushed his finger as deep as it would go, and her eyes closed, the fine russet brows knitting together. Bending over her chest, he caught one pink nipple in his mouth and tugged rhythmically.

"Please," she finally gasped, unconsciously drawing her knees up and spreading her thighs. "Please . . . it's too much, I . . ."

"Do you want me now?" he asked.

"Please," she entreated again, her face flushed and damp.

His heart thundered with desire as he mounted her, positioned himself, and exerted steady pressure against her vulnerable opening. Suddenly her eyes flew open, and she brought her hands between them. Her palms pushed against the taut muscles of his chest, and she writhed and struggled to accommodate him. "Oh, I can't—" she said unsteadily.

"You'll take it for me," he whispered. "You'll take it, Victoria. Let me inside you." He increased the pressure and felt her body ease, turning slick and welcoming as he began to enter. Groaning with relief, he penetrated her in a slow thrust, not pausing until he was buried deep in the succulent warmth of her body. She whimpered and wrapped her arms around him, enclosing him in a secure embrace. Sensation and emotion swirled together inside him, flooding him with bliss.

Part of his brain went dark and quiet, all thought extinguished as physical awareness ruled supreme.

He moved in deep nudging strokes, angling himself to press against the peak of her sex. Awkwardly she pushed upward into the thrusts, struggling to get closer to him. He grunted with satisfaction, and his huge hands slid beneath her buttocks, guiding her rhythm so that it corresponded with his.

Victoria wrapped her arms around his back, while her hips surged upward with a force that nearly lifted his heavy weight. It seemed her entire existence had been distilled to this writhing quest for pleasure. She stared at the dark face above hers, his features hard and sweat-misted, and then everything blurred as she felt an exquisite contraction in her loins. Grant gasped and drove harder, sinking his teeth into the delicate place where her neck joined her shoulder. Arching, cresting, Victoria felt rings of ecstasy spread outward until her entire body was inundated with sensation.

Somewhere amid the cataclysm she felt Grant climax as well, his rhythm breaking with a few final thrusts, his throat filled with a violent groan. He remained inside her for a minute or two, then relieved her of his weight and relaxed beside her. She nestled in the crook of his arm, hot and exhausted and satiated, and felt his mouth touch her temple and the rim of her ear.

"I love you," she whispered, and heard him say it at exactly the same time. Smiling sleepily, she let the flood of weariness overtake her and fell into a dreamless sleep while the scent and feel of him surrounded her.

Eighteen

*V*ictoria awakened as she felt Grant leaving the bed, and she protested with a sleepy sound. She heard his quiet laugh, and he returned to her arms for just a moment, kissing her throat gently. The early morning bristle of his jaw brushed against her skin, making her shiver pleasantly.

"Go back to sleep," came his low murmur. "I have to leave for Bow Street."

She curled her arms around his neck. "Is it morning already?"

"I'm afraid so." He nuzzled the wild cascade of her hair.

Victoria stroked his powerfully muscled back. The feel of him was deliciously masculine, the weight of his body, the scrape of his unshaven cheek . . . and the insinuation of one long, hairy leg between hers. "Stay with me," she entreated, wriggling in pleasure as his warm hand cupped her breast.

Grant responded with a laughing groan, finding it difficult to resist temptation. "I can't, sweet love. Cannon is waiting for me, and there is much to be done today. But I'll return soon enough." He kissed the soft white skin of her breast. "I plan never to spend more than a few hours away from your arms."

Victoria stroked his short black hair and stared into his face with undisguised longing. "I wish that could be true."

His green eyes surveyed her intently, and his hand moved over her front in a slow caress that caused her to shiver. "Why can't it, my love?"

"I suppose because . . ." She found it difficult to think clearly as his hand came to rest low on her abdomen, his thumb brushing the tiny rim of her navel. "Well, there are dreams," she managed to say, "and then there is reality."

"I've had enough reality for ten lifetimes so far," Grant informed her. "I'd like to try a dream or two."

"Such as?"

"Marrying you, to start with."

The straightforward statement dazed Victoria. Of all things she had expected upon waking this morning, receiving a proposal of marriage had not been one of them. Making an effort to gather her wits, she replied hesitantly. "I . . . I know that any woman in the world would be honored by such an offer."

"And you?" he asked softly.

"I'm afraid that you—" Victoria stopped and regarded him uncertainly, and eased herself away from his warm body. Gathering the bedclothes around herself, she regarded Grant with a mute plea that made him frown.

"Victoria," he said, reaching out to gather her hair into a glowing red river that streamed over her shoulder. He touched her with great care, his fingertips barely grazing her fragile skin. "I shouldn't have started this conversation now. You're still exhausted, and I'm pressed for time. But there is no way in hell I'm leaving until you tell me what you're afraid of."

Victoria kept her gaze on the gleaming blue silk counterpane as she replied. "I think you might desire me only because I'm an imitation of my sister." There was no sound from Grant, and after pausing a few seconds, she forced herself to continue stiffly. "Vivien is the one you first wanted . . . and I could never blame you for that. She's sophisticated and exciting, and all the men desire her. I could never match her in that regard. And I wouldn't be able to bear seeing the eventual disappointment in your eyes when you awaken next to me one morning."

Stunned, Grant wondered where this unexpected well of insecurity had come from. How was it that Victoria could feel so lost in her sister's shadow? Good Lord, the few bedroom tricks that Vivien knew could never give her a fraction of the appeal Victoria held for him. For any man. Victoria was warm, intelligent, giving . . . and ideal companion in bed and out.

"You sweet . . . beautiful . . . *lunatic*," he heard himself mutter. "How in the hell can you think I would prefer her to you? How could you doubt my feelings? Believe me, I understand the differences

between you, and I'm more than capable of deciding what I want."

Annoyed by her doubts of her own worth, he
jerked the bedclothes away from her, ignoring her
startled exclamation. Easily he caught her wrist and
brought her hand down between his thighs. At the
feel of her cool little hand pressed against him, he
felt an instant throb of desire, and his flesh swiftly
burgeoned and rose to full readiness. "Feel this,"
he said hoarsely, levering himself above her, staring hard into her face as her cheeks pinkened. "Feel
me, and look into my eyes, and tell me if you see
disappointment."

"You're only proposing to me because I was a
virgin," she said, "and you're trying to be a gentleman and do the right thing—"

Grant covered her mouth with his in an ardent
kiss, stopping only when he heard a moan of desire
caught in her throat. "*That* much of a gentleman,
I'm not," he said huskily.

Victoria's doubtful gaze locked with his. "You
once told me you weren't the marrying kind."

"I am when it comes to you."

"You don't have to," she said earnestly, pulling
her hand away and clenching it by her side. "I
want you to understand . . . you're under no obligation because of what happened. We can part as
friends, very dear ones—"

"I don't want a friend. I want *you.* Every day and
night. Every minute for the rest of my life." Grant
held her tightly and stared into her small, flushed
face. What he saw there gave him cause to ask
huskily, "Isn't that what you want?"

Her cheeks burned even brighter, and she managed a bobbing nod and a soundless *yes*.

"Thank God," he said, smoothing her hair back from her face. "Because I couldn't live without you. Now, is there anything else standing in our way?"

"Your work . . ." Her voice cracked with painful honesty. "It would be difficult for me to know that you were in danger so much of the time . . . that each morning you left me, you might not come back. Perhaps if I loved you less, I could bear it . . . but I don't think I could live like that."

His arms tightened around her. "I've already decided to leave the Bow Street force," he said. "I've spent too many years of my life on the streets. There are other choices open for me now . . . I'll find something else to occupy myself with."

"Is that what you want to do?" she asked gravely.

He nodded and pressed his mouth to her forehead. "Be my wife, Victoria."

Victoria could not reply as she stared into his steady green eyes. She loved him more than she had ever suspected it was possible to love. But there was something inside her, some uneasiness that must be addressed. She tried to uproot the feeling, lay it before her and examine it to find the answers she needed. However, she couldn't do that now. She needed privacy and time to think.

"Let me have a few days," she begged. "I can't make such a decision quickly. I want to go home, to see my sister, and . . . to find myself again."

Grant frowned and shook his head slightly. "Find yourself? You said you had completely recovered your memory."

"Yes, but I don't feel as if I'm back to my ordinary self just yet. And I'm not ready to start making changes in my life before I've spent a few days
of peace and privacy in my own home."

"It's a simple question, Victoria," he said tersely.
"Do you love me or not?"

"Yes, I love you." She touched the side of his
face gently, her eyes suddenly misting with emotion. "I do love you," she said again, her voice low
and fervent.

"Then accept my proposal."

"Not yet," she said, matching his stubbornness
with her own.

A frustrated laugh broke from him, and he
looked as though he longed to shake her. "Dammit,
why won't you just say yes? You're postponing the
inevitable."

"I'll give you my answer when I'm able," she
said. "But it's too soon. If you'll just be patient . . ."

"I can't be patient. I want you too badly."
Grant's mouth covered hers, and he kissed her in
a way that blotted out everything but pure sensation. His tongue played and stroked inside her
mouth, and the allure of that small penetration
caused her to strain against him hungrily. There
was still a bit of linen sheeting caught between
them . . . She struggled to push it away, suddenly
needing to feel all his skin against hers. He obliged
at once, matching her small body against the
greater length of his, rubbing her against a hard
plane of muscle and sinew, his sex pulsing and insistent between her thighs. She opened to him, a

keening, welcoming sound coming from her throat, and he smiled at her eagerness.

"Victoria," Grant muttered, reaching down between their bodies to the crest of red curls, his clever fingers circling and teasing. "You know you belong to me, don't you?" He spread a touch of moisture across the swollen softness, preparing her for his possession. His mouth pressed against her throat, and he paused to inhale the faint remnant of vanilla fragrance she had applied after her bath the previous evening. The hot silken head of his arousal fitted against her, and she felt him thrust inside her with maddening gentleness.

"More," she said with a gasp, wanting him to press deeper, harder, but he was exquisitely controlled, moving at a leisurely pace that made her writhe desperately.

Grant whispered for her to be patient, to relax beneath him, but she was too much a novice to govern her own responses. Trembling, sweating, she arched upward repeatedly, pulling and clutching at him until he finally relented with a breathless laugh. Obeying her silent demand, he fused their hips together in a tight, deeply satisfying grinding motion that shot pleasure through her like a bolt of lightning. She folded herself around him and purred as sweet release streaked and spread through her, until every inch of her glowed with delight.

"Well," Grant said a few minutes later, his voice muffled between her soft breasts, "that should give you something to think about."

Unable to repress a smile, Victoria circled her arms around his head and pressed a kiss amid the thick black locks. "Hurry," she murmured. "You're going to be late to work . . . and I should hate for you to have to explain why."

"They won't have to ask," he returned, not moving. "I have the most beautiful woman in England in my bed . . . Something would be wrong if I *weren't* late."

As it happened, Grant arrived at Cannon's office only a few minutes later than usual. He took care to conceal the signs of his good mood as he saw the surly gleam in Cannon's gray eyes. As always, the magistrate's expression was composed, but Grant sensed the welter of thoughts and worries that seethed beneath his facade. No doubt Bow Street was under siege from the press, the public, and the government.

Grant knew that he himself would look nearly as careworn as Cannon had it not been for the night of pleasure in Victoria's arms. It was on the tip of his tongue to suggest that the magistrate find a woman for himself. However, Grant wasn't about to stick his nose in someone else's business . . . especially of a man who was notoriously protective of his privacy.

After asking after Victoria's welfare, Cannon informed Grant that Keyes was in custody at the strong room, and had given a full confession in the presence of Cannon and a clerk. Grant was not surprised by the news, knowing that Cannon could wring a confession from a hearthstone. Keyes would be charged and tried, and all that Cannon would require of Victoria Devane was that she appear in his chambers before the second session that day and have a clerk take down her deposition. The matter was going to be handled as efficiently and quietly as possible, in an attempt not to excite the public any further.

"Victoria won't have to face Keyes in court, then," Grant said, having arrived this morning with an argument already prepared. He would go to hell and back before allowing Victoria to be in the same room with Keyes.

"No, there is no need to put Miss Devane through yet another ordeal," Cannon replied. "Her testimony in chambers, as well as Keyes's own confession, will be sufficient to have him indicted and bound for trial before the King's Bench."

"What of Lord Lane?" Grant asked. "Is he to be arrested this morning? If so, I'll gladly volunteer for the task."

The magistrate paused in the act of lifting a coffee mug to his lips and stared at him with a flicker of surprise. "You haven't heard, then. Lord Lane is dead."

Grant shook his head slightly, not certain he had heard correctly. "What did you say?"

"It seems he suffered an attack of apoplexy last evening, just after your departure from Boodle's."

Grant stroked his shaven chin for a moment, struggling with a mixture of emotions. On one hand, he was glad that the old bastard had finally gone to meet his Maker. On the other hand, he was distinctly sorry that Lord Lane had managed to escape the discomfort and humiliation of being indicted, tried, and punished. "Good," he finally said grimly. "I only wish I'd been able to stay at Boodles long enough to enjoy the show."

The magistrate frowned at the callous comment. "The sentiment is beneath you, Morgan, though I understand its source."

Grant did not respond to the quiet rebuke. He was not sorry in the least for what he had said. In his opinion, Lord Lane's death had been far too merciful, much better than he had deserved. However, something else troubled him, and it would have to be addressed before any plans for his own future could be discussed. "I don't have your dispassionate nature, sir . . . though God knows I wish I did."

"Well, dispassionate or not, I have an offer for you. One I hope you'll consider carefully."

"What kind of offer?"

"Well . . . it pertains to the fact that I've just accepted commissions to serve as justice for Essex, Kent, Herfordshire, and Surrey, in addition to the ones I already hold."

Grant threw him a glance of surprise and let out a low, appreciative whistle. The new appointments would extend Cannon's reach considerably. He had been doing the work of two men so far. Now he would be doing the work of six. So far as Grant knew, no police magistrate had ever been granted such authority.

"The public uproar is only just beginning," Cannon continued dryly. "The general consensus will be that I'm power-mad and reaching far beyond my rightful jurisdiction. And perhaps I am. It's only that I can't see another way to deal with crime, other than to regard it as a war that must be waged inside *and* outside London."

"Then your critics can go hang themselves," Grant commented.

"If only they would," Cannon agreed ruefully.

Smiling, Grant reached out and shook the magistrate's hand. "Congratulations," he said cheerfully. "You've a hell of a job before you. I wouldn't want to be in your shoes, but I've no doubt you'll find some way to manage."

"Thank you," Cannon murmured, expressionless save for a sudden gleam of amusement in his wolfish eyes. "Actually, that leads to the question I have for you. I want to submit you as my choice for assistant police magistrate, to serve alongside me."

Grant stared at him in open amazement. The idea instantly took root inside him. Serving as a police magistrate would allow him to stay close to the work that fascinated him, but at the same time it would remove him from the danger of the streets. He would have to learn a great deal about the law—a welcome challenge—and he would still be required to investigate difficult cases. However, he couldn't help reflecting on what he knew of the magistrate's celibate, orderly, industrious life, and comparing it with his own. A doubtful, self-mocking smile touched his lips.

"The position automatically confers honorary knighthood," Cannon remarked, "if that appeals to you."

"Sir Grant," he said with a short laugh, and shook his head at the odd sound of it. "Hell. I should jump at the chance, but . . . I don't think I'm suitable."

Cannon regarded him intently. "Why not?"

Grant hesitated and glanced down at his hands. The skin of his knuckles and palms was scraped and battered after his experiences of the previous day. "You saw what I did to Keyes," he muttered.

"Yes," Cannon said after a moment. "You did him considerable violence. However, you had provocation."

"I almost killed him. I had my knife out, and . . . I would have killed him, except that Victoria was watching."

"In the heat of battle—"

"No, there was no heat," Grant interrupted swiftly, laying his soul bare. "For a moment my thoughts were cold and damned clear. I became judge, jury, and executioner. I gave myself the power to end his life, and I would have done it happily. Except that I didn't want *her* to see me do it, and always carry that memory in the back of her mind." He threw a grim smile in Cannon's direction. "Now do you still want me to serve as a magistrate, knowing that I'm capable of such a lapse?"

The magistrate regarded him thoughtfully, considering his reply. "See here, Morgan . . . I'm not dispassionate by nature, no matter what appearances may lead you to believe. Had I seen the woman I loved being attacked in such a manner, I may have done the same thing, or worse. We all have regrettable lapses. As I told you, I'm not a perfect man. And I would hardly expect more of you than I would of myself."

Grant grinned suddenly, relieved that the magistrate did not consider his actions to be unforgivable. "All right, then. I accept the position. I could use a bit of respectability. I'm getting damned tired of spending my days pursuing thieves and cutthroats on foot. Besides, with any luck, I'll soon have a wife and family to think about."

"Ah. You wish to marry Miss Devane, then."

Picturing Victoria waiting at home for him, Grant felt a smile . . . a warm, uncynical smile . . . tugging at the corner of his mouth. "All these years I thought of marriage as a noose around my neck," he said. "I swore it would never happen to me. And now it doesn't sound half bad." The flippant words concealed a sudden ache of longing inside. He needed Victoria . . . His life would not be complete without her. He experienced a sudden urgency to return to her and set about persuading her to accept his proposal.

He could have sworn that Cannon almost smiled at the comment. "It's not half bad," the magistrate assured him. "And with the right woman, it can be . . ." Cannon paused in search of a word, and then appeared to drift into a sweet, long-forgotten memory. He collected himself after a few seconds of silence. The gray eyes were warmer than Grant had ever seen them. "Good luck, Morgan," he said.

Victoria spent most of the morning in the town house's private garden. It was a cool, humid day, the sky liberally laced with clouds, the air stirring with mild breezes. She sat at the stone table and read for a while, then wandered along graveled paths bordered with boxes of lilac, jessamine, and Russian honeysuckle. The carefully tended garden was bordered by poplar hedges and ivy-covered walls. Well-stocked beds of flowering and fruit-bearing plants lined the walking paths and filled the air with perfume.

In this small, secluded world, it seemed as if the city were a hundred miles away. It was difficult not to be contented in such beautiful surroundings.

But she was aware of a growing need to return to White Rose Cottage. She needed to see her sister and be assured of Vivien's well-being. Moreover, Victoria felt a strong urge to return to familiar surroundings and rediscover herself in the comfort of her own home. Although her memory had returned, she knew that she wouldn't feel settled in her mind and heart until she had spent a few days at White Rose Cottage. Sitting at the stone garden table, she rested her head on her folded arms.

"What are you doing out here?"

A masculine voice penetrated the swirl of her thoughts. Lifting her head, Victoria smiled as she saw Grant standing there. He sat in a nearby chair, facing her, and took her hand in his. With the other hand he caressed the cool skin of her cheek, his thumb lightly brushing one of the shadows beneath her eyes. "You should take a nap," he murmured. "I'm going to take you back to Bow Street for a deposition this afternoon—I want you to be well rested."

Victoria leaned the side of her face into his hand. "I can't sleep. I can't stop thinking."

"About what, my love?"

"I want to see my sister. I want to go to Forest Crest and sleep in my own bed."

Grant removed his coat and placed it over her

shoulders, enfolding her in the thick silk-lined broadcloth. The garment held the warmth and scent of his body, and she held it closely around herself. His voice was like a stroke of velvet as he spoke above her head. "I'll take you there after the deposition. We'll stay for as long as you like."

"Thank you, but . . . it's best that I go alone. I want to think clearly, and I can't do it with you there."

Grant was silent, and she knew he was struggling with a burst of impatience. When he spoke again, his voice was quiet and cool. "What exactly do you plan to think about?"

Victoria shrugged. "Who I am . . . my past . . . my future . . ."

His long fingers slid beneath her chin, and he tilted it upward until she was forced to stare into his expressionless face. "You mean your future with me," he said.

"I just want to go home and reflect on everything that's happened to me. My life has changed so quickly, don't you see?"

His short sigh conveyed a wealth of frustration. Reaching out for her, he lifted her into his lap and slid his hand beneath his coat. The warmth of his palm sank through her gown to the side of her breast. "I understand," he said reluctantly. "But I don't like the idea of you traveling alone and staying in Forest Crest without my protection."

The possessiveness in his voice made her smile. "Grant . . . before I met you, I lived for quite a long time without anyone's protection."

"That's about to change," he grumbled.

"Let me go to Forest Crest alone," she coaxed,

though they both knew she wasn't really asking.

Somehow Grant could not return her smile. All he could focus on was his own fear that if he let her out of his sight, she might decide never to marry him. After all, it was a fact that he could never give her the peaceful country life she had always been accustomed to He was not a gentleman—she had seen evidence of the roughness and violence in him, she had seen his many flaws. He was the kind of man she must have disdained and feared in her former sheltered existence.

"All right," he said with difficulty. "I'll send you to Forest Crest after the deposition. You'll go in my carriage, with my driver and a footman to protect you. And I'm going to come for you in a week."

"A week? But that's hardly sufficient—" Victoria stopped in midsentence as she realized that her protest was falling on deaf ears. Her lips curved with a wry smile. "Very well."

A new thought occurred to Grant, and he scowled. "You're not going to see any former suitors in Forest Crest, are you?"

An impish twinkle appeared in her eyes. "No, Mr. Morgan, I was never courted by any of the village lads."

"Why not? What in God's name is the matter with all of them?"

"I was never receptive to their advances," Victoria said, settling herself more comfortably on his lap. "I was always absorbed in taking care of Father, and reading books, and . . ." Tenderly she laid her head on his shoulder. "I suppose I was waiting for you," she said, and felt his arms tighten until he nearly crushed her.

Nineteen

*H*aving bid the coachman to let her off at the end of the unpaved drive, Victoria walked to White Rose Cottage. The familiar sight of the thatched cottage soothed her, and her gaze hungrily absorbed the peaceful scene. Her small, private world was not as well tended as when she had left it. The ivory and cream rosebushes needed pruning, and the beds of thrift, marigold, and sweet pea were choked with weeds. But it was home. Her step quickened as she approached the small arched doorway, feeling as if she had been gone for a year instead of a month.

There was only one thing to mar her happiness, the image of Grant as she had left him in London. He had refused to kiss her good-bye, and had stood watching with a sullen expression as she waved at him through the carriage window. Amused and

touched and yearning, Victoria had almost signaled the driver to stop and turn back. That she
had still refused to accept Grant's marriage proposal had clearly caused him no end of frustration.

She desperately wanted to marry Grant Morgan,
but was a union between them advisable . . . or
might it eventually end in ruins? She feared he
might tire of her someday and come to regret marrying her . . . and that was something she would
not be able to bear.

She badly wanted to talk to her sister, the only
family she had left in the world. Despite Vivien's
occasional vagaries, she was a worldly, ruthlessly
pragmatic woman who knew a great deal about
men. And Victoria knew that in her own way her
sister loved her enough to listen to her problems
and give her the best advice she could offer.

As Victoria's heart pounded eagerly with a sense
of homecoming, she knocked and entered without
waiting for a response.

"Jane?" came a voice from inside. "I hadn't
thought you would be back from the village so . . ."
The voice trailed away as Vivien appeared in the
main room and stared at the newcomer.

Victoria stared at her sister with a beaming smile.
She was struck as always by the sense that Vivien
was at once familiar and exotic. How was it possible to love someone and yet never understand
her? Vivien belonged to a world so far removed
from her own that it seemed impossible they had
come from the same family, much less that they
were twins.

Vivien was the first to break the silence. "It turns

out you were right to refuse all my invitations to come to town. London is definitely not the place for you, country mouse."

Victoria laughed and approached her with extended arms. "Vivien . . . I can't believe my eyes!" Her twin was very obviously pregnant, her stomach rounded, her fair skin glowing from beneath. Vivien's condition had given her an unexpected touch of vulnerability that made her appear lovelier than ever.

"I'm fat," Vivien said.

"No, you're beautiful. Really." Victoria hugged her sister with great care, and felt Vivien relax and sigh with relief.

"Dear Victoria," she murmured, hugging her back. "I thought you might despise me for the trouble I've cause you. I've been so afraid to face you."

"I could never despise my own sister. You're all I have left." Loosening her arms, Victoria drew back and smiled. "But oh, Vivien . . . how I hated being you!"

Vivien looked defensive and amused by turns, then laughed. "I don't doubt you were ill at ease, posing as a demimondaine. But I promise you, it was far better than being buried alive here in Forest Crest."

"I very nearly *was* buried," Victoria said dryly.

Vivien nodded contritely. "Forgive me, dear. You know I would never have intentionally caused any harm to come to you. If only you had stayed here instead of coming to London—"

"I was worried for you."

"In the future, keep in mind that I'm far better

at taking care of myself than you apparently are."
Vivien put a hand at the small of her own back and
made her way to the worn velvet settee. "I must
sit down—my feet ache."

"What can I do?" Victoria asked with instant
concern.

Vivien patted the space beside her. "Sit here and
talk. I gather your presence here means that everything is over?"

"Yes. The man who tried to kill me is being held
at the Bow Street jail. It turns out that Lord Lane
hired one of the Bow Street Runners to kill me . . .
or you, so he thought."

"Good God. Which Runner was it?"

The story came tumbling out, causing a few quiet
exclamations from Vivien at infrequent intervals.
To Victoria's relief, her sister had the grace not to
appear pleased by the news of Lord Lane's death.

"I suppose he's with his son, Harry, now," Vivien commented, smoothing the skirts of her gown
with undue care. "May they rest in peace." She
looked up with a troubled expression. "They were
both remarkably unhappy men, Harry being the
worst. That's why I had the affair with him . . . I
thought a few days of pleasure were just what he
needed. But he refused to accept that I could not
stay with him forever. Perhaps Lord Lane was
right . . . If I hadn't slept with Harry, he might still
be alive."

"But then again, he might not," Victoria replied,
surprised and even a little glad that Vivien was
having an attack of conscience. It was a welcome
discovery that her sister was still capable of re-

morse. "Don't fret over 'might have beens,' Vivien. Just promise me that you won't ever pursue Harry's son again—the poor boy has suffered a great deal."

"I won't," Vivien said automatically. "If I did, I suspect that Lord Lane would haunt me from the grave. However, I do care for the boy, Victoria. He is so sweet and earnest and endearing. I doubt any man that honorable has ever loved me before. I know now that it was foolish and wrong of me to even consider his proposal. But I couldn't help being swept away by him for a little while."

Victoria reached out and squeezed her sister's hand. "What will you do now? I hope you will stay with me and let me care for you until the baby is born."

Vivien responded with a decisive shake of her head. "I'll go to Italy, I think. I have many friends there, and I have need of some amusement after the past month. Besides, there is a particular gentleman . . . a count, actually . . . who has pursued me for years. And he's rich as Croesus." She smiled with pleasurable anticipation, all trace of wistfulness vanishing. "I think it may be time to let him catch me."

"But you can't continue to live that way," Victoria murmured, stricken. "Not after the baby comes."

"Of course I can. Don't worry, I shan't allow the baby to suffer in any way. He or she will have the best of everything; you can rest assured of that. As soon as it's born and I regain my figure, I'll find a new protector and figure out some arrangement for the child. Lord knows I'll have servants aplenty to help me care for it."

Victoria was aware of a sensation of heavy disappointment at her sister's words. "But aren't you tired of living as some man's mistress? I'll do whatever I can, and so will Mr. Morgan, to help you find a new situation."

"I don't want a new situation," Vivien said matter-of-factly. "I like being a courtesan. It's pleasant, easy, and profitable. Why shouldn't I continue in a profession at which I happen to excel? And please spare me the remarks about decency and honor . . . I think there's a certain kind of honor in doing something to the best of one's ability."

Victoria shook her head sorrowfully. "Oh, Vivien . . ."

"Enough," her sister said in a brisk voice. "I don't care to discuss it further. I'm going to Italy, and that's that."

"You must promise me something," Victoria persisted. "If you eventually decide you don't want the child, don't give it to servants or strangers to raise. Please. I can't stand the thought that a member of our family might . . . well, just send it to me."

Vivien stared at her with a skeptical frown. "How odd. Why would you want anything to do with Lord Gerard's bastard?"

"Because it's your child too . . . and my niece. Or nephew. Give me your promise, Vivien." As her sister continued to hesitate, Victoria added, "You owe it to me."

"Oh, all right . . . I promise." Stretching out her slippered feet, Vivien motioned for her to bring a cushioned stool covered in petit point flowers. As Victoria removed her sister's shoes and arranged her feet on the stool, she was aware of Vivien's speculative stare. "You haven't mentioned a word about your relationship with Mr. Morgan," Vivien remarked with deceptive idleness.

Victoria glanced up at her twin's keen blue eyes. "What did he tell you when he came here?"

Vivien laughed and coiled a stray lock of glinting cinnamon hair around her finger. "What little he didn't tell me, I was able to guess. Now, fess up, Victoria . . . Has he come up to scratch yet?"

Blushing, Victoria gave a slight nod. "He has proposed to me, yes."

"And have you accepted?"

Victoria shook her head reluctantly. "I have a few doubts about the suitability of the match."

"Oh, good God," Vivien murmured, looking at her with a touch of loving exasperation. "You've been thinking too much again. Well, let me hear your worries."

It was a pleasure for Victoria to unburden herself to the only person in the world who truly understood the way her life had been until now. "I don't know if this is what Father would have wanted for me," she said. "I don't know if a woman like me is meant for such a life. Oh, Vivien, Mr. Morgan is such a remarkable man—I can't help fearing that he'll need more than I can provide. We're not similar in character, background, or temperament . . . I don't think anyone would consider us a suitable match—"

"Then why didn't you refuse him?"

"Because I love him. It's just that I'm afraid we're not truly right for one another."

Vivien made a scoffing sound. "Let's dispense with the nonsense, Victoria. This isn't a question of suitability, yours or his. You're perfectly capable of accustoming yourself to new circumstances . . . and marrying a man of good fortune, though untitled, is not exactly a hardship." Vivien rolled her eyes and sighed. "It is so like you to analyze a situation until you've made it ten times more complicated that it really is! Just as Father used to do."

"Father was a wonderful man," Victoria said, stiffening.

"Yes . . . a wonderful, virtuous, lonely martyr. After Mama left him, Father retreated into his shell and hid from the world. And you stayed with him and tried to atone for everything that had happened by becoming exactly like him. You've been living in this same damned cottage, poring over the same bloody books. It's morbid, I tell you."

"You don't understand—" Victoria began hotly.

"Don't I?" Vivien interrupted. "I understand your fears better than you do. It's always been safer for you to hide here alone than take the chance of loving someone and have him leave you. *That's* what your real worry is. Mama abandoned you, and now you expect the same of anyone else you might love."

The ring of truth in the words stunned Victoria. She stared at her sister while her eyes prickled with tears. "I suppose . . ." she began, the sudden tightness of her throat making it difficult to speak. Vivien was right—she had never been the same after her mother had left her. The ability to be comfort-able with love, to trust someone with her heart, had been stripped away from her, forcing her to build layers of self-protection that no one could reach through. Until Grant.

But he deserved her trust. He deserved to be loved without reservation or fear, without anything being held back. All she had to do was find the strength within herself.

"It was so much easier when Father was still alive," Victoria said. "I convinced myself that he was all I needed. We kept each other from feeling lonely. But now that he's gone . . ." She stopped, biting her lip as the tears overflowed.

Vivien sighed and stood with difficulty, reaching into the tiny drawer of a side table to procure a handkerchief. She dropped the linen square into Victoria's lap. "That was two years ago," she commented. "It's about time to carry on with the rest of your life."

Mopping her face with the soft linen, Victoria nodded vigorously. "Yes, I know," she said in a muffled voice. "I'm tired of mourning. I'm tired of being alone. And I love Grant Morgan so much that I can't bear the thought of losing him."

"Thank God," her twin said in a heartfelt tone. "I daresay even Father would say you've done penance for long enough. And while we're on the subject, I'm going to tell you something I've always wanted to say . . . Loving a man doesn't make you a 'bad woman,' as you always believed Mama and I were."

"No, I never thought—"

"Yes, you did. I have a fairly good idea of the things Father said about me and Mama behind our backs. And some of them were probably well deserved." Her voice turned self-mocking. "I admit, I may be rather too free with my favors. But I know one thing for certain—giving yourself to a man when you love him, as you have with Morgan, is not wrong. Moldering here in Forest Crest, on the other hand, is a crime. Therefore, I'm leaving this godforsaken village as soon as I can arrange it, and I'd advise you to do the same. By all means, marry Grant Morgan—I daresay you could do much worse."

"Somehow," Victoria said wryly, "I had the impression you and he did not like each other. What has happened to change that?"

"Oh, I still don't like him," Vivien assured her with a quick laugh. "Not really. Except . . . well, it's obvious that he loves you, otherwise he wouldn't have made that ridiculous apology you had required of him."

"He did?" Victoria asked in wondering delight. "He truly brought himself to tell you he was sorry?"

"Yes, he confessed everything and asked for my forgiveness." A catlike smile appeared on Vivien's face. "I'll admit, there was something rather sweet about watching him gag on that apology, simply because you asked it of him. So if I were you, I would marry the man, if you desire to keep from breaking his heart. Or . . ." She paused as another idea seemed to inspire her. "Or you could come with me! We could go to Venice or Paris . . . Do you realize the kind of attention that two sisters with our looks would attract? I'll teach you everything I know about men, and . . . Good Lord, we would make a king's ransom!"

Victoria looked up at her sister's animated face and shook her head decisively. *"Ick."*

"It's a good idea," Vivien said defensively. "Pity you haven't got just a bit more imagination and fewer scruples."

A stew of potatoes, kidney beans, and chopped greens and onions simmered atop the small cast-iron range. The appetizing scent filled the cottage and drifted out the open windows. Remembering the many times she had made the dish for her father, Victoria smiled wistfully. Her father had never been a great lover of food, regarding it solely as a necessity for the body rather than something to be enjoyed. On the rare occasions when Victoria had made plum pudding, or brought currant buns from the bakery, he had nibbled at the treats and quickly lost interest. The only times she had ever seen him eat heartily, and with obvious enjoyment, was when she had made vegetable stew.

"Father," she murmured fondly, pausing in the task of folding clothes and packing them in an ancient leather truck, "I hope you won't mind that I want to marry a man so unlike you." Grant was a physical man with a strong appetite for life. He would never choose to hide away from the world as she and her father had done. Instead, he wrestled with dangerous, complex, often sordid problems. He saw the worst of humanity, whereas the

Devanes had preferred to contemplate only the best of it. And yet . . . she thought her father might have liked Grant after all, if only to admire his utter fearlessness when it came to dealing with the realities of life.

Humming tunelessly, Victoria went to stir the stew and add a pinch of salt to the pot. Returning to her packing, she began to fold an old knitted shawl when she heard a demanding knock at the door. The entire cottage seemed to vibrate from the force of the blows.

Perplexed, a bit uneasy, she went to answer the door. She stepped back with a slight gasp as she saw Grant standing there. He was breathtakingly handsome, dressed in a striking black coat, black stock, silver-gray waistcoat, and charcoal breeches. The clothes were simple but perfectly tailored to fit his broad shoulders and lean torso. The vibrant force of his personality struck her anew . . . He looked large, dangerous, and even a bit irate. However, as Victoria stared into his smoldering green eyes, she felt no fear, only an instinctive desire to kiss his hard mouth and make it soften against her own.

"Hello," she said, self-consciously smoothing her hair, which hung in a disheveled braid down her back. His resplendent appearance made her conscious that she was wearing an old, worn gown, a faded flower-print muslin that was suitable only for chores in the house and garden. She smiled into his dark face, prolonging the delicious moment before she threw herself into his arms. "What are you doing here?"

"You took too long," he muttered with a scowl.

The statement brought a surprised laugh from her. "We agreed I would stay here a week."

"It's been a week."

"It's been precisely two and a half days," she informed him.

"It seemed like a bloody year."

Victoria shivered in pleasure as she felt him reach for her waist and pull her body against his. "I missed you, too," she confessed with a smile. His hand lifted to the side of her face, gently cradling her cheek, his palm hot on her skin.

"Where is Vivien?" he asked.

"She has already left for London. She's had enough of country life. And so have I." Victoria gestured toward the half-filled trunk and the pile of folded clothes beside it. "I was coming back early," she admitted. "I found I didn't have as much to sort through as I thought."

"And our engagement?" he asked with a set face. "Do you have an answer for me?"

"Yes," she said, her voice suddenly catching with emotion. "Yes, I'll marry you . . . if you still want me."

"Only for a lifetime," Grant said thickly, staring into her small, radiant face.

Her eyes closed as he lowered his mouth to hers, not with the urgency she had expected, but with a slow, searing tenderness that pulled a pleasured respiration from her chest. His lips caressed hers so lightly, playfully, imparting intimate heat and moisture until she pushed herself up at him in a search for something deeper. And he gave it to her, sealing his mouth over hers and using his tongue to reach inside her. She moaned and responded eagerly, unable to get close enough to his hard masculine body, unable to hold him tightly enough.

Suddenly Grant pulled his mouth away and laughed breathlessly, his green eyes filled with tender warmth. "I'll have to teach you patience someday," he murmured, his warm hands sliding up and down her sides.

"Why?"

For some reason the question made him laugh again. "It's much better when you don't go charging into it at full tilt."

"But I like it that way," she said in a provocative tone.

Smiling, Grant kissed her again, her mouth and chin and throat, and murmured his love to her as his hands worked on the fastenings at the back of her threadbare muslin gown. One elbow-length sleeve drooped away from her shoulder, and then the other, and his mouth traveled to the freshly exposed skin.

"If I had know you were coming," Victoria said, "I would have worn a pretty gown and ribbons in my hair—"

"I prefer you to wear nothing at all."

Which was soon to be the case, she realized, as he pushed the gown over her hips and let it fall to the floor. Her chemise followed as he eased the straps down her arms and tugged it downward until it, too, was discarded. She stood before him in only her drawers, stockings, and shoes, her bare breasts trembling as she shivered in the slight breeze that came in through the window. The heat of his hands was startling as they gently cupped the pale mounds, her nipples contracting tightly in his palms. Her breath quickened, and she leaned back against the cool plaster wall behind her. He kissed her mouth, her parted lips, with deep, stroking kisses that somehow soothed and excited her at the same time. She whimpered as she felt him take the peaks of her breasts in his fingertips, pulling, softly pinching. Sliding his fingers beneath her breasts, he lifted the warm, silken weights and opened his lips over one aching nipple. He drew her deep inside his mouth, suckling the taut peak, tickling with his tongue, and she writhed as a delicious throbbing began low in her body.

"Touch me," she begged, gasping as he turned his attention to her other breast, and her hips jerked forward involuntarily.

"Where?" he asked softly, and as she felt him smile against her breast, she knew he was teasing. Impatiently she fumbled with the tapes to her drawers, longing to be rid of the garment. To her frustration, she discovered the tapes had somehow become knotted, and her efforts to free them only made the tangle worse.

Grant pushed her hands away from the tightening knots and kissed her bare midriff. "Don't move," he murmured.

"Why? What are you—" She broke off and squeaked in alarm as she saw the flash of a long spearpoint knife. Before she could move, the blade had sliced through the knotted tapes and the legs of the drawers, and the thin linen fell in shreds at her feet.

"Grant," she said, her voice slightly higher-pitched than usual, "that th-thing makes me nervous."

He grinned as he slid the knife back into his boot. "It's proven to be useful on a number of occasions."

"Yes, but I don't—"

"Here, lift your foot." Sinking to his knees before her, he removed one shoe, then the other, and began to reach for the tops of her stockings. He paused, however, his hands sliding to the sides of her hips. "I think we'll leave these on," he murmured. "I like the way they frame your—"

"Grant," Victoria protested, blushing all over as he continued to stare at her. She had never felt so vulnerable, standing before him virtually naked, whereas he was still fully dressed.

The pads of his thumbs passed gently over the tender, almost transparent skin at the tops of her thighs, where a faint lavender tracery of veins was visible. "I'm going to buy you stockings of silk and lace," he said softly. "Black ones. And jeweled garters with ribbons."

Victoria could barely speak. "Let's go into the bedroom," she said faintly.

"Not yet." His fingertips combed gently through the tangle of spicy hair, separating the glinting curls. "How lovely you are."

Victoria quivered, grateful for the support of the wall behind her back as she stood between Grant's spread knees. He leaned forward, kissing her stomach, exploring the delicate edge of her navel with the tip of his tongue. His own breath was coming fast and hard, fanning over her skin in steamy pulses. She must have made some small sound, for he glanced up into her face with hot green eyes.

"Do you want me to kiss you, Victoria?"

She nodded, her wild blush deepening.

Though his face was taut with passion, she saw the barest hint of a smile touch his lips. "Where?"

I can't, she thought in mortified excitement, clenching her hands into fists at her sides. Grant was still, staring at her with a provoking mixture of amusement and desire, clearly waiting for her to make the next move. The tension increased until the very air seemed to spark with heat, and Victoria burned with scarlet color. Unable to stop herself, she reached out with shaking hands and slid her fingers beneath the thick dark locks of his hair, and guided his head to the place she most wanted it. She felt the blazing heat of his mouth cover her, his tongue searching the tender flesh, arrowing to the sensitive bud where her desire centered. Her knees weakened, and she would have collapsed had his hands not cupped beneath her buttocks, gripping and steadying her. Moaning, she strained against the sliding, tormenting delight of his tongue, until she began to stiffen at the imminent approach of climax.

With a suddenness that shocked her, he withdrew his mouth and stood to face her, his burning gaze sweeping over her flushed body.

"Please, Grant . . ."

He responded with a quiet murmur, fumbling at

the fastenings of his trousers. To her astonishment, he did not bear her to the floor, but lifted her in his arms instead, so that her legs wrapped around his waist. He held her weight easily, bracing her against the wall for balance, one arm protecting her from the roughness of the plaster. Her eyes widened as she felt the hard, blunt shape of his sex nudging, probing, sliding easily inside her. She was filled, impaled, her body open and helpless against the heavy intrusion. Gasping in pleasure, she clutched at the backs of his shoulders, her fingers digging into the soft wool of his coat. It felt strangely erotic to be clasped against his fully clothed body, her bare skin tingling from the abrasion of fabric. Hungering for a taste of his skin, she tugged at his black stock and buried her mouth against the damp side of his neck.

"Do you love me?" he muttered, deliberately allowing her weight to press downward, forcing her even harder onto his stiff erection.

"Yes . . . oh, Grant . . ." She arched and cried out as pleasure crested inside her, spreading through her in deep, rolling waves.

"Tell me," he said harshly, moving in deeper, slower thrusts that drove straight into the core of her body. She writhed, her legs flexing as she felt the ebbing sensation build again.

"I love you," she gasped. "Love you . . . love you . . ."

The words sent him over the dizzying edge of rapture, and he drove inside her with a groan, all his senses dissolving in blissful release. His legs locked, and he stood there holding her tightly, reluctant to release the bounty of silken female flesh from his arms. "Victoria," he breathed, pressing a fervent kiss to her lips, while she struggled to catch her breath.

"Now we'll take *your* clothes off," she said, busily unwinding the black cravat from his throat.

Grant laughed and loosened his arms, allowing her feet to touch the floor. "And then?"

Victoria dropped the cravat to the floor and ducked her face against his throat, breathing in his salty masculine scent. "And then I'll show you again how much I love you." Drawing back, she looked up at him with a hopeful smile. "If you're able."

He grinned and crushed a warm kiss on her lips. "I'm not a man to back down from a challenge."

"Yes, I know." And she laughed exultantly as he lifted her in his arms and carried her to the bedroom.

Epilogue

*A*lthough Victoria had thought she knew her husband well, she made many discoveries about him in the first six months of marriage. Agreeing with the general opinion that Grant was not the kind of man to take easily to domesticity, she had vowed to give him as much freedom as he required. She had decided never to render an opinion about his companionship. If he chose to stay out all hours of the night socializing, drinking, and cavorting, so be it. And if he allowed himself to be drawn into dangerous situations, she would try to restrain her criticism. After all, he had been a remarkably independent man until he had met her, and he would resent her efforts to rein him in. And Victoria had no desire to eventually be regarded as a millstone around his neck.

To her amazement, and that of everyone else

who knew Grant, he took to married life as if he never known any other kind of existence. He inhabited the role of husband with ease and enjoyment, displaying the kind of devotion that most wives only dreamed of. Instead of carousing at the London taverns with friends, Grant preferred to spend his nights at home with Victoria sharing books and bottles of wine, drinking and debating and making love well into the night.

Grant took her everywhere, to balls, dinners, and musical evenings, as well as prizefights, races, and even gambling hells. He protected but did not shelter her, allowing her to see the seaminess of London as well as its beauty. He treated Victoria as a partner, a beloved companion, a lover, and because of him her life was infused with a vigor and vividness that she had never dreamed of in Forest Crest.

On the evenings they stayed at home, Victoria helped Grant to study and analyze mountains of books on law and theory, loaned to them by Sir Ross. Grant had found that the work of a police magistrate was demanding but fascinating, and offered more of a challenge than serving merely as a Runner. He relished his increased power in settling legal disputes and conducting inquiries, and had begun to accumulate a measure of political influence. That and his honorary knighthood had given him a social stature that far exceeded his previous celebrity.

Victoria, for her part, did her best to find her own place in London society, carefully selecting and accepting invitations from the piles that arrived each week. She consulted with architects and

designers concerning the mansion Grant was planning to build in Mayfair, and solicited advice from
newfound friends she had made in London. Before
long she had also joined ladies' committees in support of charities benefiting reformed prostitutes
and disadvantaged children, though it seemed that
the efforts of these committees were puny in comparison to the size of the problems they sought to
address.

"The numbers of women and children who need
help are so overwhelming," Victoria told Grant one
evening, feeling discouraged rather than hopeful
about a planned charity event. "Even if the com-
mittee's efforts are successful, we'll have benefited
only a fraction of those who need it. It makes me
wonder why we should even try."

Holding her in his arms, Grant stroked back a
stray lock of her hair and kissed her forehead. "It's
always better to try," he murmured, smiling into
her worried face. "I've felt the same way in the
past, wondering why I risked my neck to catch one
thieving bastard when there were thousands more
remaining out there."

"Then why did you keep at it?"

He shrugged slightly. "I thought that by taking
one criminal off the streets, I might be saving someone in the future. And saving even one person is
worth all the effort, isn't it?"

Victoria smiled and hugged him, feeling a great
rush of love. "I knew it," she said, her voice muffled against his shoulder. "At heart you're an ide-
alist."

She felt him grin against her ear. "I'll teach you

to call me names, milady." Drawing his head back, he kissed her until she had no breath left.

Absorbed in pages of notes on an inquiry he was conducting, Grant barely noticed the knock on the door of his office at Bow Street. "Yes," he said gruffly, resenting the disruption to his concentration.

The door opened a crack, revealing Mrs. Dobson's face. "Sir Grant, you have a visitor."

He scowled in response. "I told you I won't receive visitors until sessions are concluded this afternoon—"

"Yes, sir, but . . . it's Lady Morgan."

Immediately the scowl left his face. Victoria seldom ventured to the Bow Street office, which was a good thing, considering that it was frequently populated by scoundrels and criminals. However, any chance to see her in the middle of the day was greatly welcome. "For God's sake, don't keep her waiting," he said. "Bring her in at once."

The housekeeper smiled and opened the door wider, and Victoria entered. She was a lovely sight, especially against the drab backdrop of the office, her trim figure clad in a gown of pale pink muslin, its high collar and long sleeves trimmed with rose ribbons. The bodice of the gown was plaited and laced with silk cords that tied snugly over the tantalizing curves of her breasts. Rising from his chair, Grant waited until Mrs. Dobson had closed the door, and then he swept his wife in his arms and captured her smiling mouth in an ardent kiss.

"Just what I needed," he murmured when their

lips parted. "A pretty wench to relieve my tedium."

"I hope I haven't interrupted some important work," she said apologetically.

"No work is as important as you." He toyed with the ribbon that trimmed her collar, and nuzzled the soft, perfumed space behind her earlobe. "Tell me what brings you to Bow Street, milady. Do you have a complaint to lodge or a crime to report?"

She laughed breathlessly. "Not exactly."

"Some testimony or information to offer?"

"In a way."

He sat in his chair and drew her down to his lap, his green eyes gleaming roguishly. "I want a full confession, milady."

"Grant, no," she scolded with a discomfited laugh, wriggling on his knee and glancing uneasily at the door. "Someone might come in—what would they think?"

His hand slid beneath her skirts and wandered boldly up her knee. "That I'm a newly married man with an itch for his wife."

"Grant," she pleaded, her cheeks turning red, and he laughed, taking pity on her.

"Just when I thought I had rid you of all modesty," he said, squeezing her knee. "All right, then . . . I'll try to restrain myself. Tell me why you're here."

Victoria linked her arms around his neck, her expression turning serious. "I wouldn't have disturbed you, but . . . I sent for Dr. Linley today."

"Linley," Grant repeated warily.

Victoria nodded. "You see, I haven't been feeling

quite myself lately, and rather than worry you un-
necessarily, I kept it to myself until—" She broke
off with a wince as his hand gripped her leg with
unconscious force. "Grant!" she exclaimed, staring
at him with bewildered dismay.

His heart pounded with sudden painful jerks. He
found it difficult to speak through a flood of instinctive dread. "Victoria," he said scratchily, "are
you ill?"

"Oh, dear, no . . . no, I'm only . . ." Victoria
paused, hurriedly searching for a proper euphe-
mism, but in her own anxiety, she couldn't think
of a single one. "I'm pregnant," she said, her
gloved hands rubbing his chest as if to soothe him.
"There's nothing to worry about. We're going to
have a baby."

Relief began to penetrate the sudden whirl of
panic. He pulled her close, burying his face in the
soft mounds of her breasts, and tried to slow his
breathing. "God, Victoria," he said. He heard her
laugh shakily, and she clasped his head.

"How do you feel about enlarging our family?"
she asked.

"Just that it's a miracle." Grant turned to press
his ear against her heart, listening to the fast steady
beat, thinking that everything in the world that
mattered was right here in his arms.

"A rather commonplace miracle," she pointed
out with a smile in her voice. "It happens to fam-
ilies every day."

"Not to mine, it doesn't." Easing her backward,
Grant stared at her slim body, imagining her belly

swollen with his child. "How do you feel?" he asked in concern.

Victoria caressed his face. "Impatient," she replied. "I can hardly wait for the day when I hold a baby in my arms."

As it turned out, a baby was delivered to the Morgan household far sooner than expected. Almost a month after the revelation of Victoria's pregnancy, she and Grant were enjoying a private supper at home when Mrs. Buttons interrupted them. The housekeeper wore a strange, almost comical expression, as if something had startled her and she still hadn't recovered from the shock.

"Lady Morgan," the housekeeper said uncomfortably, "a . . . a parcel has arrived for you . . . from Italy."

"At this time of the evening?" Victoria exchanged a perplexed frown with her husband. "It might be a gift from my sister," she said. "How wonderful. It's been months since I've received word from her. Is there a letter attached, Mrs. Buttons?"

"Yes, but—"

"Please bring the letter to me now, and have the parcel placed in the family parlor. We'll open it after supper."

Before the housekeeper could reply, a strange sound caused Victoria to freeze. It was a high, mewling wail, similar to that of a cat . . . or a crying baby.

Grant stood from the table, wiping his mouth with a napkin. "I don't think this particular parcel wants to be left in the parlor," he muttered, brushing by the housekeeper as he strode from the room.

"A baby?" Victoria said, dazed, her gaze meeting Mrs. Buttons's.

The housekeeper nodded in confirmation. "Yes, milady. Sent from Italy with a wet nurse who doesn't speak a word of English."

"Oh, Lord." Victoria hurried after her husband, following the sound to the entrance hall.

Several servants had gathered in the hall to stare in amazement at the anxious, dark-haired young woman dressed in peasant clothes overlaid with a rough gray apron. The wet nurse clutched a wailing bundle in her arms, and seemed ready to burst into tears herself. "Signora," she said as soon as Victoria appeared, and a chattering stream of foreign syllables erupted.

Victoria placed a calming hand on the young woman's shoulder. "It's all right," she said, hoping the girl would understand her tone if not the actual words. "Thank you for bringing the baby here safely. You must be tired, and hungry." She glanced at Mrs. Buttons, who instantly directed one of the housemaids to have a room prepared for the girl. Victoria gestured toward the screaming baby and gave the girl a gentle smile. "May I?" she asked.

The girl handed her the bundle at once, seeming relieved. Receiving the baby awkwardly, Victoria stared into the infant's tiny, purple face surmounted with a tuft of orange-red hair tied with a bow. No one could mistake it for anyone else's child but Vivien's. "Oh, darling creature," she murmured, torn between joyous laughter and tears. "Precious, sweet girl—"

"Here, give it to me," Grant said brusquely, standing right behind her. "The head's dangling."

Surrendering the child, Victoria took the letter the wet nurse handed to her. It was addressed to her, and the handwriting was unmistakably Vivien's. Frowning, Victoria broke the seal and read the letter aloud. "Dearest Victoria, as I promised, I have sent the baby to you, as I am too busy to look after her at present. If you wish, arrange for someone to take care of Isabella and I will reimburse you for the expenses whenever I return to England. My love as always . . . Vivien."

Turning toward her husband, Victoria realized that the baby had quieted and was staring up into Grant's dark face with round, unblinking eyes. A miniature hand was clasped around his finger, the tiny fingers turning white at the tips from the pressure she exerted. The baby looked impossibly small against Grant's broad chest, seeming to enjoy the security of his firm clasp.

"I didn't know you had experience with babies," Victoria remarked, watching the pair with a wondering smile.

Bouncing the child in a soothing, even rhythm, Grant spoke quietly. "I don't. I just have a way with redheaded females."

"I'll vouch for that." Smiling slightly, a frown still pulling at her forehead, Victoria stroked the tuft of fiery hair atop the infant's head. "Poor little Isabella," she murmured.

"Will Vivien come for the child someday?"

Grant asked without taking his gaze from the baby.

"It's impossible to say for certain, but..." Victoria paused and stared at her husband, finding it impossible to color the truth. "No," she said quietly. "She won't want a child around to remind her of the passing years ... and she's never desired to be a mother. I don't believe she'll come for the baby, ever."

"Then what's to be done with her?"

"Would you have objections to enlarging our family a bit early?" Victoria asked hesitantly.

For a moment Grant found it difficult to believe he was considering becoming the de facto father of Vivien Duvall's bastard. He had no liking for Vivien, and never would. But as he stared at the small face cradled against his shoulder, he somehow didn't see any of Vivien in her. He saw only the vulnerability and innocence of a child, and he felt an elemental instinct to protect her. "I suppose no one else would take care of her as we would," he murmured, more to himself than to Victoria.

His wife moved closer to him, sliding one arm around his waist. "I suppose not," she agreed with a smile. "Oh, Grant ... I knew you wouldn't refuse." She stood on her toes to kiss him. "You never disappoint me, you know."

More than a few sardonic comments came to mind, but as he looked into his wife's sparkling blue eyes, he was too suffused with love to voice any of them.

"Never," Victoria repeated, holding his gaze. "I wouldn't change a single thing about you."

"Well, milady," he replied softly, "that's why I married you."